A DESCRIPTION OF

MILLENIUM HALL

A DESCRIPTION OF

MILLENIUM HALL

Sarah Scott

edited by Gary Kelly

broadview literary texts

Canadian Cataloguing in Publication Data

Scott, Sarah, 1723-1795
    A description of Millenium Hall

(Broadview literary texts)
Includes bibliographical references.
ISBN 1-55111-015-6

I. Kelly, Gary. II. Title. III. Series.

PR3671.S33M55 1994 823'.6 C94-930557-X

Broadview Press
Post Office Box 1243, Peterborough, Ontario, Canada K9J 7H5

in the United States of America:
3576 California Road, Orchard Park, NY 14127

in the United Kingdom:
B.R.A.D. Book Representation & Distribution Ltd.,
244A, London Road, Hadleigh, Essex. SS7 2DE

Broadview Press gratefully acknowledges the support of the Canada
Council, the Ontario Arts Council, and the Ministry of Canadian Heritage.

PRINTED IN CANADA

For Mitzi Myers

Contents

Preface

This edition of Sarah Scott's *Millenium Hall* is designed for students as well as specialists. The introduction aims to establish the importance of this feminist utopian novel as a contribution to political economy, politics, social and cultural criticism, and experimental literary form in mid-eighteenth-century England. The note on the text addresses some issues in the historical gendering of language. The notes explain words, objects, and practices that may now be obscure for most students, and also trace the main changes in the text over its four editions.

In carrying out this work I have been much indebted to the assistance of Lynda Schultz, Rhonda Batchelor, and Eleana Yun. I am grateful to Albert Levine and Ted Ruml for suggested additions. I received indispensable help from John Charles and the staff of the Bruce Peel Special Collections of the University of Alberta Library, Canada. The University of Alberta Library also supplied the copy text for this edition and texts of Sarah Scott's other works. My understanding of Sarah Scott and her work was greatly enriched by being able to read her letters in the Montagu papers at the Henry E. Huntington Library, California. Throughout the work on this edition I have benefitted greatly from the support of the Social Sciences and Humanities Research Council of Canada and the Central Research Fund of the University of Alberta. The edition would not have been undertaken, however, were it not for the encouragement and enthusiasm of Don LePan.

The dedication is a small acknowledgement of the value to me of a long and sympathetic professional friendship.

Gary Kelly
Keele, England

Introduction: Sarah Scott, Bluestocking Feminism, and Millenium Hall

1. Bluestocking Feminism

Sarah Scott's novel *A Description of Millenium Hall* (1762) was the fullest literary expression of the first wave of 'bluestocking' feminism. This was a feminizing and feminist movement among upper- and middle-class women that emerged in the mid-eighteenth century and was developed by later generations of middle-class women. It was created from several different social, cultural, and political traditions, including Renaissance humanism, the legacy of seventeenth- and eighteenth-century intellectual women, classical republicanism, and resistance to dominant court culture. In narrow terms, the 'bluestocking clubs' or 'bluestocking ladies,' as they were called, formed a movement for the moral and cultural reform of salon society in the middle decades of the eighteenth century (Myers). More broadly, bluestocking feminism developed from the convergence of class and gender issues and interests within a particular coalition of the progressive gentry and the professional middle class. Bluestocking feminism addressed gender issues and women's oppression from the viewpoint of that coalition, but it did so as a feminization of gentry capitalism that also addressed the interests of men of those classes.

Bluestocking feminism was formulated in a situation of expanding gentry capitalism. This was the application of capitalist practices of entrepreneurship, investment, and modernization to the agrarian economy of the landed estate (Mingay, Stone, Malcolmson, Porter). The resulting rise in prosperity of the landed class, or gentry, then produced an increase in the number and variety of professional people, or those who served the increasingly complex legal, administrative, political, ideological, cultural, material, and physical needs of the gentry (Holmes). Often these professionals were drawn from the gentry themselves. They would be second or third sons and daughters of a class that relied on male primogeniture, arranged marriages, and certain legal instruments to maintain the integrity and continuity of the family property – the foundation of the family's prosperity, status, and power. For others, however, the professions were a step up in a family's rise from the commercial and manufacturing middle classes to gentry estate and status.

Increasing numbers of such gentry and professionals, however, felt frustrated by what they saw as institutional, social, and cultural obstacles to their own advance in prosperity, prestige, and power. One obstacle was the patronage system, or network of mutual self-interest, power, favouritism, and monopoly, thought to derive from and to sustain the court system of government and culture, and to be manipulated by a small group of landed magnates and financiers for their own benefit. A different obstacle was the traditional culture of the labouring classes. This was seen as a debased version of court culture, typified by 'superstition,' fecklessness, and improvidence arising from the lower classes' irrational emulation of their 'betters.' Such a culture was seen as an obstacle to 'reason,' 'improvement,' and 'progress' – which in fact meant the calculated application of capital to increase production in agriculture and manufacturing, whatever the cost to the labouring classes. Finally, many in the middle classes, too, were accused of excessive emulation of the courtly classes, through the 'fashion system,' or commercialized consumption in imitation of the tastes and social practices of the courtly upper classes. By the mid-eighteenth century, then, many in the gentry and professional middle class were voicing a comprehensive critique of these obstacles to advancement of their own interests.

The social, cultural, political, and economic roles of women were major themes in this critique because of women's central place in the family and property structure of the dominant social class. This structure was a complex of property, status, and social, political, and economic interests affirmed through relationships of blood and patronage. The dominant upper-class property system and the culture it sustained required that women be subordinated for three reasons: to transmit property and status from one man to another through marriage; to sustain the status of the landed family by representing and presiding over certain cultural and social practices; and to ensure the perpetuation of the family as a social and property institution through the generations.

In order to secure women for this class interest they were constructed as instruments, not agents. Thus they were denied the education, vocations, and social experience afforded to men, and trained to internalize their class's ideology. Women were also seen as the element in the family or class that was most vulnerable to ideological or sexual seduction by more powerful social superiors. If a woman were independent of her husband's control, or worse still controlled him, her indulgence in the fashion system of social emulation might erode the family's capital base. Yet women were expected to supervise the early moral and cultural formation of the inheriting generation. This contradiction stimulated a vigorous debate on women's education and socialization. The debate was carried on in a variety of books that inform *Millenium Hall*. These range from 'conduct books,' or guides to female education, self-discipline, and social comportment, to novels of manners that fictionalize the arguments of the conduct books. In addition, upper- and middle-class women were often portrayed as custodians of lower-class welfare at a time when traditional and customary economic relations were being replaced by capitalist ones. Thus upper- and middle-class women were supposed to feminize, or mask and moderate, the effects of gentry capitalism on the labouring class.

As a result of these expectations, women were made representative of an emergent ideology of domesticity (Armstrong). The family as primarily an institution of property and patronage was being replaced by (or concealed behind) the family as primarily a network of subjective relationships — what historians now call the egalitarian and companionate family (Trumbach). Women were expected to preside over and foster this network of relationships, and thus were implicated in a growing opposition between the private and public spheres. For the individual identity required by capitalist enterprise was based not on inherited or ascribed rank and wealth but on autonomous, self-directed subjectivity, or inward merit. In cultural forms of expression, including literature, the courtly system of interlocked paternalism, patronage, and patriarchy was typically represented as a domineering male figure. Accordingly, the new, oppositional subjectivity of economic individualism and merit required by capitalism could be represented as a female, or at least a feminized figure such as the 'man of feeling.' This representation implicitly dignified and elevated the role of women, while using femininity to conceal the actual aggressive and exploitative character of capitalism — represented in social and cultural terms as 'masculine.' In effect, a certain figure of woman was made to represent the resistance to court government and culture by a coalition of the gentry and the professional middle class.

At the same time, this coalition was constructing a distinctive culture of its own, based on a more thorough application of capital, be it material capital (mainly in the hands of the gentry) or intellectual capital (mainly in the hands of the professionals), or more usually a combination of both. In this culture, however, women remained subordinate and oppressed in order to prevent them from betraying the coalition's interests and aims. For there was a deeply rooted assumption that women were the 'weak' element in any class identity because they were subordinated and oppressed in all classes and therefore had less to lose in joining – in being seduced or appropriated – by the men of another class.

Some women, especially a group on the margin between upper and professional middle classes, attempted to intervene in the new construction of woman. They did so in order to improve their own lot and to play a greater role within their classes' project of achieving social and cultural leadership and economic and political change. Many of these women came together in the bluestocking movement of the mid-eighteenth century. They drew in part on a certain tradition of female education and interest in intellectual life otherwise denied to women. This tradition went back to Renaissance humanism, in which some upper-class and middle-class women had managed to participate (Hobby). This tradition of intellectual women was kept alive among certain politically liberal social circles in the seventeenth and early eighteenth century, partly in resistance to the courtization or trivialization of women that was associated with the authoritarian political and social regimes of court monarchy.

Among the women active in this area, for example, was Bathsua Makin (born 1600), who had helped educate Sarah Scott's grandmother. In *An Essay to Revive the Ancient Education of Gentlewomen* (1673), Makin argues that better education of females would make them better wives and also inspire boys to surpass them in intellectual accomplishment. Mary Astell (1666-1731) followed a similar line in *A Serious Proposal to the Ladies* (1694-7). In general the women writers advocated a broader education and more fully intellectual training for women, though in order to fit them better for the domestic sphere rather than to enter the public sphere. Female conduct books written by men, such as Fénelon's *Traité de l'éducation des filles* (1687; English translation 1707) and the Marquis of Halifax's *The Lady's New Year's Gift; or, Advice to a Daughter* (1688), tended to take a more restricted view of these matters, concerned that female intellectualism would frighten prospective suitors, make women discontented with domestic life and duties, or worse still inspire them to meddle in matters beyond their sphere, such as politics. Paradoxically, intellectual women came to be associated with the presumption and ungovernability attributed to courtly women. In the early and mid-eighteenth century these different arguments became commonplace. By mid-century a diverse tradition of feminist writing and arguments had developed, diffused in writings of various kinds by women and men, including conduct books, periodical essays, novels, and plays (Rogers, Browne). Sarah Scott would have known this literature. She would, too, have known such pro-feminist works as George Ballard's *British Ladies* (1752), a biographical dictionary of women intellectuals dedicated to Catherine Talbot, a leader of the bluestocking circles. In effect, Scott's *Millenium Hall* synthesizes the arguments of writers such as Makin and Astell, the female experience of oppression represented in early eighteenth-century literature, and the lives of intellectual women collected by Ballard.

Certainly there was a political dimension to the debate on women's education and roles. More liberal and proto-feminist views tended to predominate in 'Whig' circles. These were social and family networks of those who stood for a limited monarchy and a progressive social order led by enlightened upper and upper middle classes. Some of them drew on the traditions of the 'commonwealthmen,' or supporters of the Commonwealth under Oliver Cromwell, and classical republicanism, or reverence for the republics of classical antiquity. They were active propagandists in many different print media and literary genres, since they recognized and depended on the power of print to form a social coalition capable of sustaining their own power in the face of encroachment by the crown. They also relied on social contact through coteries and salons, or informal social gatherings and networks of correspondents that promoted mutual interests and relationships and a common culture. Coterie and salon culture gave women more importance and influence than they could obtain otherwise, and it had a direct influence on the formation of the bluestocking circles.

The very origin of the name 'bluestocking' indicates the movement's character within a class-based project. Around 1750 a number of society women in London, led by Elizabeth Montagu, Elizabeth Vesey, and Ann Ord, set about reforming upper-class assemblies in town houses (Scott). They did so by doing away with card-games and the formal, courtly manner of socializing, and emphasizing conversation – less courtly wit and repartee and more 'candid' and serious conversation centred around literary and cultural topics and guests who were men of literature and culture. The name 'bluestocking clubs' was applied to these informal gatherings because one of the regulars, Benjamin Stillingfleet, acknowledged the informal, uncourtly nature of the gatherings by wearing the blue worsted stockings of informal, domestic dress rather than the black silk stockings of formal or courtly social occasions.

Politics as such were excluded from discussion, but in attempting to combine upper-class social life with intellectual culture led by professional men, the bluestockings were transmuting political discourse into cultural and social discourse. The 'bluestocking clubs' met in informal and domestic situations, in contrast to the formal, courtly, semi-public character of much upper-class social life. The bluestocking clubs were organized and led by women and enabled women to exercise a certain degree of patronage, thereby feminizing otherwise male-dominated social culture. Thus the bluestocking clubs were a form of feminist culture and practice for their time, but within a class-based project of social and cultural reform.

This double character is hardly surprising considering the social background and experience of many bluestocking ladies – indeed the title 'lady,' like that of 'gentleman,' indicated membership in the upper or upper middle class. Most bluestocking ladies were daughters of professional middle-class families, though the leaders came from the gentry or even aristocracy. For example, Elizabeth Montagu, called the 'queen of the bluestockings,' came from a gentry family and married a man with large estates. Her sister Sarah Scott married a professional man, though one with clear claim to the status of gentleman. Many bluestocking ladies received an education unusual for women at that time, including training in classical languages, scholarship, and theory normally reserved for men, especially those intended for the elite 'learned' professions. Most bluestocking ladies were unmarried, widowed, separated from their husbands, or living independently while married. Several had been married for reasons of family property interest. Many had close and long-lasting friendships with women of similar background and experience. Some lived much of their lives together in all-female households. Some, especially the founders of the 'bluestocking clubs,' were well-known society hostesses. Others, such as Elizabeth Carter and Sarah Scott, led retired lives, participating in bluestocking culture mainly through correspondence – though the bluestocking circles were mainly sustained by epistolary networks. Many practised various kinds of social charity and literary patronage, in accordance with their means. Many had a religious turn, since religion provided solace, as with other oppressed groups, for lack of control over one's own life. Religion also gave a feminine character to the bluestockings' version of humanist and Enlightenment intellectual culture, which was otherwise dominated by men who were often anticlerical if not anti-religious in their views.

Despite the bluestockings' strong interest in literary and intellectual culture as a distinguishing attribute, and their extensive networks of correspondence, few published, and those who did so published little. Elizabeth Montagu published three anonymous pieces in Lord Lyttelton's moral and pious *Dialogues of the Dead* (1762), as well as an *Essay on Shakespear* (1769) defending the 'national bard' against certain critics, especially Voltaire. Catherine Talbot (1721-70) published a few pieces in *Athenian Letters* (1741) and Samuel Johnson's essay-periodicals *The Rambler* and *The Adventurer*. Much of her work circulated in manuscript and was published only after her death, including *Reflections on the Seven Days of the Week* (1770), *Essays on Various Subjects* (1771), and *Works* (1771). Elizabeth Carter (1717-1806) was relatively prolific, publishing occasional pieces in the *Gentleman's Magazine* and Johnson's *Rambler*, *Poems on Particular Occasions* (1738); *Poems* (1762); a rare female intrusion into controversial theology entitled *Remarks on the Athanasian Creed* (1758); and translations of a French critique on Alexander Pope, of an Italian work on optical theory for the use of women, and of the Greek stoic writer Epictetus (1758). Hester Chapone (1727-

1801) published pieces in *The Rambler* and *The Adventurer*, occasional poems, *Letters on the Improvement of the Mind* (1773), *Miscellanies in Prose and Verse* (1775), and *A Letter to a New-Married Lady* (1777).

The second and third generations of bluestocking writers published more, and included Hannah More, Frances Burney, Hester Thrale Piozzi, and Ellis Cornelia Knight. Nevertheless, a woman who published, even in the minor discourses and genres conventionally permitted to women, risked forfeiting her 'naturally' private, domestic character. By publishing, or making her work public, she also risked becoming a 'public' or commodified woman, other varieties of which were the prostitute and the actress (often considered little better than a prostitute). Only after their deaths were the bulk of the bluestockings' writings published, as selections from the enormous correspondence that mainly constructed and disseminated their ideology and culture. Among these posthumous works were letters of Mary Delany, Elizabeth Montagu, Elizabeth Carter, and Catherine Talbot.

This publication took place, significantly, during the Romantic period, or aftermath of the Revolution debate in Britain. By that time the feminisms produced by the culture of sensibility of the 1770s and 1780s and the Revolution debate of the 1790s had become widely discredited through association with Revolutionary insubordination and violence. Bluestocking letters could be seen as manifestations of a less threatening feminism because they had been produced in an earlier era, had circulated in higher social ranks, did not go as far, and were not as overtly political as the work of the later feminists. Thus bluestocking letters could be used to sustain a kind of feminism less threatening than those that had followed, and could constitute a reassuring connection to an apparently less conflicted past.

2. Sarah Robinson Scott and Her Work

Sarah Robinson Scott (1723-95) was the most published yet one of the least known of the first-generation bluestocking writers in their time. This was partly due to the fact that she did not participate directly in the bluestocking assemblies and was connected only indirectly to the other bluestockings through her sister Elizabeth Montagu. In addition, she published anonymously, her work attracted little public comment in its time, and unlike her sister she was not associated with some more famous male writer, such as Samuel Johnson. Nevertheless, Scott produced the clearest and most comprehensive literary embodiment of bluestocking principles.

She was well placed by education, social rank, experience, and interests to do so (Climenson, Blunt). She experienced directly and personally the trivialization and courtization of women that were commonplace in gentry culture of the early eighteenth century. She was raised largely on one of the Robinson family estates, at Mount Morris in Kent. Her father, Matthew Robinson, seems to have acquired something of the antifeminist, libertine values of seventeenth-century court and gentry culture. He seems to have taken little interest or pride in his daughters, in contrast to his attitude to his sons. There is an impression, too, that he did not particularly value his wife's good education and good sense. He was capable of a crude joke at his daughter Elizabeth's expense, even after she was married and a notable society figure. After his wife's death he seems to have taken his housekeeper as a mistress. He seems to have been niggardly in providing for his daughters, affording them merely an education in the decorative 'accomplishments' to fit them for the marriage market, and allowing them dowries just large enough to lure a husband. Their brothers, by contrast, were educated for public careers and public affairs, and went into professions including diplomacy, law, the clergy, and the merchant navy, as well as estate ownership and parliamentary politics.

This was common enough in the Robinsons' social class, and the gender relations characteristic of court culture in the landed gentry. The Robinson sisters may, however, have acquired from their mother expectations somewhat different from those of most women of their class. An heiress, she had been educated by the feminist Bathsua Makin and may have passed on to her daughters the possibility of a woman having an intellectual life. Another important factor may have been the sisters' visits to their well educated and intellectual maternal grandmother, who had remarried to become the second wife of Conyers Middleton, the Cambridge scholar and leading voice of classical republicanism (Robbins 291-3). The sisters were also great readers in French and English fiction, history, and *belles-lettres*. In such books they would have found enough to enable them to question the predominantly courtly character of their domestic milieu, education, and social culture.

Sarah Robinson was known in the family as 'Sally,' and she and her sister Elizabeth were said to be as alike as two peas in a pod, though she seems to have considered herself inferior to her sister in looks and ability. Her earlier letters show her to be interested and involved in the predominantly courtly culture and social life of her class, but also critical of them. She expresses an independent attitude toward courtly conventions of femininity, and a self-deprecating view of herself in relation to those conventions. She could be cruel about both the vain society lady and the arrogant man of fashion. She could be *galante*, insisting that women naturally liked a man more for being handsome and good-natured, yet she could also be sarcastic about the language of idealized love and courtship, and mildly risqué in joking about sex. She enjoyed going to places of amusement in London and Bath, and relished flirting with men. Somewhat lonely in the family after her sister's marriage, she read widely, took long strenuous walks, and made detailed drawings of flowers. She also spent time at Bath, for her health and for the social life. Around 1748 she befriended Lady Barbara Montagu, known as 'Lady Bab,' who was to be her companion until the latter's death in 1765.

Sarah Robinson published her first novel, *The History of Cornelia* (1750), in the same year that the bluestocking assemblies were supposedly started by her sister and others. Since she did not yet need to write for money, the book was probably a product of her interest in literature. The work is modelled on a widely-read sub-genre of prose fiction derived from the seventeenth-century French *nouvelle galante*, or moralistic short novel of sentimental courtly love in high society. With its reliance on formal social interchange, stylized dialogue, and hackneyed language of feeling, *Cornelia* was a conventional work. It ignores Samuel Richardson's recent innovations in his novels *Pamela* (1740) and *Clarissa* (1747-8), with their intense and detailed representation of subjectivity or inward emotional life. Although Sarah Robinson read Richardson's work and would write five more novels, she never did join the 'Richardsonian revolution,' but continued to work in the line of earlier eighteenth-century fiction she had read when younger (Richetti, Williams, McKeon).

In 1751 she was married, apparently from mutual inclination and respect more than family interest, to George Lewis Scott (1708-80). He had known her since the mid-1740s and seems to have been recognized as a suitor from about the time that she had befriended Lady Barbara Montagu. He was highly respected as a mathematician and musician, was considered witty, well-mannered, and agreeable in company, and was well known in society. He was also well connected at court, having been made sub-preceptor to the young Prince George (later George III) in 1750, a position that may have given him the income required to maintain a family. This appointment soon led to trouble, however, since he had been nominated for the post by Lord Bolingbroke. Bolingbroke was the ideological voice of the Tory political faction associated with loyalty to the deposed Stuart line, whereas the court was dominated by Whigs, who supported the Hanoverian line. These political differences had recently come to the fore in the 1745 military expedition of 'Bonny Prince Charlie' to retake the throne for the Stuarts. Sarah Robinson herself was known to have an intense interest in politics of the day. Thus the marriage seemed highly suitable from several points of view, and the couple went to live in a house in the neighbourhood of Leicester Fields (now Leicester Square) in London.

The marriage soon failed, however, for reasons never fully divulged. The affair aroused a certain public notoriety, and Sarah Scott maintained a strong and long-lasting contempt for her husband. Her family do not seem to have doubted the rightness of her leaving him. These facts suggest different reasons for her doing so – perhaps brutal behaviour or the disclosure of some illicit amorous connection on his part. In any case, under the laws of the time it would have been very difficult and expensive for the couple to have obtained a divorce. Throughout Sarah's courtship and marriage she had maintained her close friendship with Lady Barbara, who was never implicated in any way in the marriage breakdown. Sarah's father refused to release to her the financial settlement that was to have gone with her in the marriage, lest her husband claim it from him at some future date. This argument was regarded by his daughters as an excuse to keep Sarah's dowry for himself. Her brothers persuaded her husband to provide a decent allowance, though this gave him power over her and made her continuously anxious as to whether or not he would keep up payments.

She soon settled down with Lady Barbara to a life of cultured domesticity and private charities in Bath. She continued to write books, now to subsidize their household expenses and philanthropic projects. Translating from modern languages, especially works of fiction, was an acceptably feminine line of literary work, and in 1754 she published *Agreeable Ugliness; or, The Triumph of the Graces*, from a French novel entitled *Le Laideur aimable* (1752) by Pierre Antoine, Marquis de La Place. The lively and sentimental first-person narrative tells the story of an ugly but intelligent, intellectual, and good-natured woman, who endures the contempt of her mother and the machinations of her beautiful sister to marry well and then, when widowed, to marry for love. The novel attacks the corrupting influence of court culture and emulation in the upper classes, and advances an ideology of merit. These themes were increasingly favoured by middle- and upper-class readers as expressing their own aspirations in face of the dominant system of court government and patronage.

In the same year Scott published an original novel entitled *A Journey through Every Stage of Life*. This work seems more characteristic of its author in being witty and satirical, though it too argues for the superiority of moral and intellectual merit over mere social status. It is a frame narrative in which the servant Sabrina tells a series of stories in order to amuse her mistress, the princess Carinthia, who has been confined by her brother lest she supplant him on the throne. Thus the oppression of woman generates narrative as a relief and as illustration of the vicissitudes of women's lives under patriarchy. The commentary by Carinthia and dialogue between her and Sabrina add elements of explicit feminist protest. In these two ways *A Journey* anticipates Scott's *Millenium Hall*, and in fact one chapter contains, in the description of the domestic and philanthropic economy of Mrs Traverse, a brief version of the bluestocking economy described in more detail in *Millenium Hall*.

Scott's next two books enabled her to publish, in the oblique form of historiography, her views on affairs of state and the public sphere – matters otherwise conventionally barred to women. Scott had a longstanding and intense interest in politics, and followed closely the careers of leading public figures such as William Pitt. The Preface of her

History of Gustavus Ericson, King of Sweden (1761) promotes the usefulness of historical biography as more likely to arouse and educate the reader's moral sensibility than general history that deals only with public affairs and events. Gustavus is presented as a Christian hero and reformer, dedicated to the moral, cultural, and material improvement of his people, unlike his rivals for power and heroes of merely military cast. Thus the book again attacks the court culture of intrigue and self-interest and advances an alternative vision of civil society created and sustained by the leadership of persons of subjective merit. In her advocacy of social civility and peace as the basis for a well-ordered and prosperous society Scott was intervening in the public, political sphere in a way often adopted by women writers, with their supposedly 'natural' tendency to conciliation, mediation, and pacification of otherwise dangerously conflictual masculine tendencies.

The History of Gustavus Ericson is also characteristic of historiography written by eighteenth-century commonwealthmen and classical republicans like Conyers Middleton. It can be read as an oblique commentary on contemporary affairs, two in particular. One was the accession to the throne in 1760 of the young George III, from whom much was expected in leading the way to the kind of society and nation that Scott's *History* claims was constructed by Gustavus. The other issue was the career of William Pitt, considered by many to be the great national leader whom Britain needed during the military and imperial struggle with France known as the Seven Years War. His career reached a crisis late in 1761 with his resignation from government over the terms of the treaty of Paris (1763), ending the Seven Years' War. For many like Scott and her sister, who had known Pitt since before his rise to political power, he was a warmonger, maintaining his own power by keeping the nation at war. The contemporary political orientation of Scott's *History of Gustavus* would have been recognized. Had it come from a male writer it would have been the basis for his claim to political and other forms of patronage. Being written by a woman, with no access to a public career, it remained a distanced though apparently respected intervention in affairs of state.

Scott followed this up with another history directed at current events. *The History of Mecklenburgh*, published the same year as *Millenium Hall*, was clearly designed to cash in on interest in the bride of

George III and new Queen of England, Charlotte of Mecklenburgh. The book's frontispiece is a portrait of the Queen, the book is dedicated to her by the publisher, and the author's preface draws the connection between her and the book's subject. The preface also makes an implicit claim for a kind of history written from a feminine or feminized perspective. The author asserts that the character of a king's consort is of the greatest importance in influencing his character and actions toward pacific and civilizing policies. Moreover, the preface claims, 'the peaceful virtues' are too seldom celebrated in historiography, as seen in the existing historical record concerning Mecklenburgh. Thus Scott's project is to integrate the history of the Germans, notoriously crowded with wars, conquests, and struggles for independence, into a prospect of Britain's future as a pacific, cultivated, and prosperous nation. Scott's history is also feminine, if not feminist, in pointing out the various roles of women in the history of Mecklenburgh and the German states, and in praising princes who avoided conflict and war. Implicitly, then, *The History of Mecklenburgh* is also directed at public opinion during the critical debate over the Peace of Paris and its consequences for British domestic politics.

Scott's most important work was *A Description of Millenium Hall and the Country Adjacent, Together with the Characters of the Inhabitants and such Historical Anecdotes and Reflections as May Excite in the Reader Proper Sentiments of Humanity, and Lead the Mind to the Love of Virtue* (1762). It is considered more fully below. It too promotes the feminization of society and thereby addresses the political conditions of the early 1760s. It describes the feminized economy of Millenium Hall estate as a metonymy for the reformed economy of the state itself. This description is also related to the various ways in which women are exploited in courtly patriarchal society, as seen in the inset life-stories of the female proprietors and managers of Millenium Hall. Thus critique of court politics, culture, and society is related particularly to the emancipation of women for a larger, beneficent, and feminizing social role.

After Lady Barbara's death in 1765, Scott published three more books. The first, *The History of Sir George Ellison* (1766), develops the project of *Millenium Hall* by showing a man carrying out a feminization of estate economy and social relations. Ellison makes his fortune as a successful yet humane planter in Jamaica, managing his estate and his slaves for the benefit and improvement of all. On returning to England to set up as a landed gentleman, he bases his plan of estate management on that of Millenium Hall, outlined for him by Mrs Maynard, a central character in Scott's earlier novel. The new novel contains a description of Ellison's practice, thus reinforcing the lesson of *Millenium Hall* by showing the women's program carried out by a man, and thereby disseminating the economy of Millenium Hall to other places and the other sex, in an implied colonization of the whole of Britain by the values and practices of bluestocking feminism. (I have included two excerpts from *The History of Sir George Ellison* in an Appendix.)

In her next work Scott returned to historiography. *The Life of Theodore Agrippa d'Aubigné* (1772) is an approving biography of the leader of French Protestants during the civil wars of the seventeenth century. These wars were often used in eighteenth-century politicized historiography as an analogy for religious-political struggles in Britain and as an illustration of the evils of court politics, with their intertwined sexual and political intrigues, involvement with powerful ecclesiastical interests and foreign powers, and dangerous appeals to plebeian support. Here Scott singles out for attack the notorious court intriguer, Cathérine de Médicis, and her imitators, who are resisted by the consistently principled, disinterested, and ethical counsels of d'Aubigné. As readers would know, however, d'Aubigné failed to stem the forces of court politics, church self-interest, and consequent general social corruption. The implication is that Britain, which had escaped this fate in the seventeenth century, could yet experience a similar decline and fall. More particularly, Scott is again commenting obliquely, through history, but in the manner of eighteenth-century classical republicans and 'commonwealthmen,' on current events around the factional conflicts and renewed political career of William Pitt (now Lord Chatham).

Scott turned to the novel once more with *The Test of Filial Duty* (1772), a novel in letters more in the style of contemporary fiction than her earlier novels were. As the title indicates, the theme is one of those broached in Richardson's *Clarissa*, though here treated in a lighter manner, with a happy ending. The correspondence between Emilia and Charlotte also contains much satire and comment on courtly emulation in the upper and middle classes, as Scott appropriates elements of the novel of manners, sentiment, and emulation, soon to be made more familiar and popular through Frances Burney's novels, beginning with *Evelina* (1778). Such novels paralleled the popular sentimental comedies of the contemporary theatre. Both were designed to represent (through characters) and plot (through romantic courtship) the conflict and reconciliation of gentry and professional middle-class values, culture, and practice. This progressive social coalition, which would dominate late eighteenth-century culture, was built on the work of bluestocking feminism, among other movements of the mid-century.

This was Scott's last work, however. In the remaining two decades of her life she stayed at various places, including the fashionable spa towns of Bath and Tunbridge, and eventually settled at Catton, a village near Norwich, where she lived the kind of retired life she always preferred. She continued to take a lively interest in politics, literature of the day, and the various affairs of her sister and brothers. *Millenium Hall* continued to hold a place with the reading public, with a fourth and last edition in 1778. She remained close to her sister, who had been widowed in 1775, but who became if anything even more active in bluestocking philanthropic and cultural projects and more prominent in literary circles.

3. *Millenium Hall*

Millenium Hall creates a utopian vision of gentry capitalism reformed according to bluestocking feminism. It does so by particular thematic and formal means. It outlines a program to reform economic, social, and cultural relations at a time of major political change in Britain, centred on the domestic effects of the Seven Years War with France, the coronation of the young monarch George III, and attendant changes at the centre of power and patronage. This reform program includes relations between the classes and sexes, education as social and cultural reproduction, the commercialization of consumption or 'fashion system,' and new ideas of 'political economy.' The program is validated by reference to the transcendent authority of Providence or divine will. Finally, the program is set forth through use of characters, description, dialogue, allusion, and plot designed to imply a reformative relationship between Millenium Hall and the world outside.

Millenium Hall opens when the narrator, who is a gentleman on his travels, and his companion, the young and worldly Lamont, have an accident while travelling. Seeking help, they come upon a paradisal estate and country house that the narrator names Millenium Hall. The name refers to the Biblical myth, set forth in the book of Revelation, that general evil will soon be overcome, initiating a millennium, or thousand-year reign of peace, by the righteous together with Christ. Then a final struggle with and victory over evil would be followed by the end of time and the last judgment, with the ascent of the righteous into heaven. In seventeenth-century England, Puritan republicans saw the millennium as a 'fifth monarchy,' following the four unrighteous monarchies in the Bible, and many equated it with the Commonwealth or English republic (1652-60). Later on, republicans and commonwealthmen were sometimes called 'fifth monarchy men.' Thus 'Millenium Hall' suggests both a Christian tradition and a political one, except that this 'fifth monarchy' is ruled by women.

The narrator describes Millenium Hall, its environs, its wards (the poor, the abandoned, and the deformed), its female inhabitants, its proprietors, its cultural life, the history of its formation, and its material economy. Interspersed in this description are passages of dialogue between the proprietors of the Hall, some of its wards, and the narrator and his friend Lamont. Also interspersed, and more prominent, are the 'histories' of the proprietors – Miss Mancel, Mrs Morgan, Lady Mary Jones, Miss Selvyn, and Miss Trentham. These stories are told by Mrs Maynard, the other proprietor, who turns out to be a distant cousin of the narrator. By the end of the novel the narrator has decided to disseminate Millenium Hall in several ways. He will imitate Millenium Hall himself, though on a smaller scale, on his own estate. He will also communicate his 'description of Millenium Hall' to others: the text is in the form of a letter to a male friend of the narrator. Millenium Hall has also and already had another effect: the narrator's young companion, the courtly, gallant, free-thinking Lamont, has been so moved by what he has seen that he has begun reading the Bible and reconsidering his values, including his attitude to women.

Thus the structure of *Millenium Hall* has three dominant elements: description, inset narratives, and plot. The passages of description, by the narrator with inset testimonies from the poor, deformed, or disabled wards of the estate, build up a picture of the social and material economy of the place, down to annual accounts of expenditure, as seen by the male visitors and explained by the female proprietors and those they protect. As in most utopian writing, these descriptive elements not only represent an idealized society but criticize the social and economic values and power relations in the 'real world' outside utopia. Then there are the 'histories' or inset narratives of the proprietors' lives, recounted by Mrs Maynard, the Hall's historian. These show how, through various experiences of social injustice to women, these women came to be inhabitants of Millenium Hall. Their narratives are more strongly critical of social and economic values and power relations in the 'real world,' as these affect the condition of women in the upper and middle classes. The descriptions and the 'histories' alternate throughout the text, and together they link the oppression of women to oppression of other powerless social groups under the unjust system of intertwined paternalism, patronage, and patriarchy.

Millenium Hall shows how representatives of one set of the oppressed – women – have reformed this system to provide properly for the dispossessed and powerless of several kinds, including women. Janet Todd sees the economy of Millenium Hall as 'conservative' and 'communal' rather than 'individualistic' and capitalist (202). Yet the reform that makes this economy possible seems more like a feminization of gentry capitalism. Since the landed estate was widely seen as a metonymy and metaphor for the larger estate of the nation, the feminist implications of this reform are clear. Women (or at least women of education and virtue) are not only capable of managing the 'estate' – a task usually restricted to men – but can improve the 'estate' precisely by applying attributes conventionally assigned to women, in domains conventionally left to them. These attributes include nurturing, healing, and conciliating, and these domains include domestic management, the arts, and local charity.

The reform of gentry capitalism by bluestocking feminism is formalized in the particular composition or structure of *Millenium Hall*. In the first place, the descriptive part is linked to the narrative parts in an argumentative structure. Taken together, the inset narratives of female oppression and the description of Millenium Hall show how oppression may be cured by one group of the oppressed, in a process or plot of feminization. This argument by structure may seem undermined, however, by the fact that the master narrator of *Millenium Hall* is a man. His discourse frames the stories by Mrs Maynard and is descriptive and 'factual' – a kind of discourse conventionally associated with men's domains of learning and knowledge. Mrs Maynard's discourse is mainly narrative, comprising the life-stories of individual women, and this kind of domestic narrative, whether fictional or factual, was conventionally associated with women's literary culture. Mrs Maynard's narratives have many of the characteristics of a dominant fictional genre of the early eighteenth century – the courtly novella featuring an upper-class heroine's often unfortunate experience of the systemic sexism of a society dominated by court values and culture (Spencer ch. 4). Thus the male narrator's discourse would seem both to 'contain' and to dominate Mrs Maynard's.

In fact, the narrator's description is prompted by Millenium Hall, which is the work of Mrs Maynard and the other proprietors of the place, and it is explained by Mrs Maynard's discourse. The narrator merely describes and reports; Mrs Maynard reflects and explains – more important tasks in terms of what *Millenium Hall* signifies. Furthermore, according to the conventions of utopian writing, the narrator describes in a straightforward and naive manner, like a child in an unfamiliar place. But according to another convention of utopian writing there is an all-wise insider who explains utopia to the visitor. In *Millenium Hall* this role is fulfilled by Mrs Maynard, who explains in maternal, educative fashion the significance and origins of what the narrator can only see and admire. Mrs Maynard is thus the master of the discourses in utopia.

This relationship is reinforced by the novel's complex of plots, including imbedded plots, implied plot, main plot, and subplot. The imbedded plots of the inset narratives tell how the proprietors of Millenium Hall were oppressed and excluded by patriarchal and courtly gentry culture in the world outside utopia. The implied plot takes up these plots to suggest that their protagonists were driven to build the utopian world of Millenium Hall as a refuge for themselves and other women like themselves, extended to other social groups marginalized by the same unjust economic and social practices of the dominant culture. The main plot shows the narrator's enlightenment, or growing understanding of the significance, or 'millennial' character, of the place he then names Millenium Hall. The subplot shows the gradual change effected in the narrator's young companion, Lamont, who goes from having a courtly, gallant, condescending, witty, sceptical, masculinist, and generally incredulous view of Millenium Hall and its proprietors to acceptance of their competence, their feminization of estate economy, and the religious inspiration of their work.

Thus the enlightenment of the narrator and the conversion of Lamont represent a reformation of relations between men and women, especially since the narrator and Lamont are not feminized in order to become marital partners for any of the ladies of Millenium Hall. Though that is a possible convergence and closure of the plots of *Millenium Hall*, it is rejected. The rationale for this rejection is found in the imbedded plots of the stories related by Mrs Maynard. These plots show how the oppression and exploitation of women in the world outside Millenium Hall paradoxically produced its feminized and feminist utopia, by forcing its proprietors out of that society to seek refuge and build a better world for themselves and all their dependents. From the perspective of Millenium Hall the oppression of women is seen as but one aspect of the social injustice that results from the dominant upper-class system of courtly culture and agrarian capitalism.

The inset narratives of *Millenium Hall* together present a comprehensive picture of the oppression and exploitation of women that results from this system. The system forces women to subordinate themselves to men as mistresses or wives (Miss Mancel or Mrs Morgan), or to use courtly coquetry to gain power over men (the second Lady Melvyn, the young Lady Mary Jones, or Miss Melman). The heroines of the inset 'histories' are superior to almost all of the men around them (fathers, brothers, suitors, would-be seducers) in every respect except fortune and control of their own destiny. Most men are shown to be courtly gallants. Even when men have honourable intentions toward women, as with Lord Peyton or Sir Robert St George, they remain gallants at heart. The few men who are not rakes, such as Mr Alworth, are all too susceptible to coquetry. Furthermore, women are often or usually the enemies of women, men usually try to exploit women, and the rare true friendship between a man and woman – as with Harriot Trentham and Mr Alworth – falls victim to a coquette. There are no significant examples of the egalitarian and companionate marriage that was supposedly becoming the pattern for the upper and middle classes. This vicious and unjust treatment of women is sustained and reproduced by the cultural and economic practices of the gentry. Money is clearly shown to be power, and most women lack money of their own. Even women with money, such as Lady Lambton in the 'History of Miss Mancel and Mrs Morgan,' use this power only to defend their own rank and interests. Similarly, women who gain power over men through coquetry and intrigue, such as the second Lady Melvyn or Miss Melman, use their power for mere self-interest, to pursue fashion and social advancement, and to eliminate female rivals. Finally, the 'histories' show that the education of most women only internalizes court culture in their subjective consciousness, making their subordination seem 'natural' rather than artificial (or man-made) and produced by their education and socialization to serve the needs and desires of men.

The internalization of courtly ideology, or courtization of women, leaves them only the alternative of coquetry, or manipulating the erotic desires of men, if they wish to gain some degree of power themselves. By doing this, women manipulate the system of court culture and patriarchy for merely personal ends, in competition with other women. Thus coquetry only reinforces courtliness and patriarchy. Yet Mrs Maynard's narratives show some women preferring virtuous poverty to courtly seduction, independence to subjection in marriage, and female friendship to competition with other women in the game of coquetry. These alternatives of true female friendship and financial independence, albeit for exceptional women, are seen to culminate in the female community and feminized economy of Millenium Hall, described by the narrator.

If Millenium Hall is an alternative, however, it is a problematic one. The Hall is given its nickname by the male narrator and not by its female proprietors or lower-class dependents. To name is to define and valorize, and the name suggests a utopian vision rather than a reality. Furthermore, as the 'histories' of the proprietors show, the Hall is a refuge from the world. There is also a contradiction in the creation of Millenium Hall. The proprietors have gained their utopia through exceptional moral and intellectual qualities and the conventionally feminine virtue of fortitude – the ability to withstand the oppression of courtly patriarchy, and thus to transcend it. On the other hand, they also gain their utopia by providential means – an unexpected inheritance, a lucky discovery, a fortunate friendship. Then, too, the proprietors of Millenium Hall are virtuous more by nature than by education.

Thus their agency, their power to reform courtly patriarchy, has limits. Utopia is created as much by good fortune or divine gift as by human agency. Moral and intellectual excellence are personal attributes over which one has control, even if the power of these qualities in the world outside Millenium Hall seems to be limited. This power comes from the kind of self-discipline, self-culture, and independence promoted by the possessive individualism, economic rationalism, and investment mentality of capitalism. Reliance on good fortune and Providence, however, are characteristic of the lottery mentality and customary economy of those who have no control over their own lives, like the social groups gathered together at Millenium Hall. Gentry capitalism and Enlightenment rationalism aimed to supersede this economy and this mentality in the process historians call modernization.

Millenium Hall attempts to reconcile these conflicting ideologies through a particular form of religious piety, associated here specifically with the Hall's proprietors, and absorbed from them by their dependents. This religious outlook involves resignation to Providence and is emphasized at key points in the book. For example, Mrs Maynard relates how Louisa Mancel was fortuitously enabled to marry her beloved Sir Edward after years of denying him on grounds that the match would harm his prospects in life. She soon learns, however, that he had died of a wound received in battle, and she is overcome by grief and remorse. Her mother and Mr d'Avora

> endeavoured to convince her, she was no way to blame, that what she had done was laudable, and she ought not to judge of an action by its consequences, which must always remain in the hands of the Almighty, to whom we are accountable for our motives, but who best knows when they ought to be crowned with success. When they had prevailed with her to exculpate

herself, her piety and patience made it the more easy to persuade her calmly to submit to the decrees of providence. She soon saw, that to suffer was her duty, and though she might grieve, she must not repine. The good advice of her two friends was some support to her mind, but her chief strength arose from her frequent petitions to him who tried her in sufferings, to grant her patience to bear them with due resignation. Such addresses, fervently and sincerely made, can never be unavailing, and she found the consolation she asked for. (154)

This kind of resignation is a religious form of the lottery mentality, and both are ideologies of the oppressed, or those who lack agency and power. In the first place, resignation to Providence removes responsibility for suffering from the plane of the human and social to that of the divine and absolute—an agent against whom one cannot or should not protest. Secondly, it places individual suffering in a universal and transhistorical context, generalizing it and disarming it as a motive for individual or collective protest and reform. It also confers special significance on personal suffering, within the plot of the individual life, but only by extending that life-plot beyond the here and now, in which the individual has no power, to the hereafter, when personal agency will no longer be an issue. Meanwhile, resignation to Providence gives divine and transcendental validation to individual suffering. Thus resignation to Providence offers consolation for lack of agency and power at the cost of forestalling individual or collective action for change. Such an abandonment of agency for women hardly seems consistent with a feminist position.

Yet *Millenium Hall* not only advances a feminist critique of courtly patriarchy but also sketches a utopia created by female agency. This utopia is a providential reward of virtue in this life for its proprietors as well as its tenants, inhabitants, and clients; but it is also a model of gentry capitalism—reformed according to conventionally 'feminine' values and practices. This model economy replaced the one that had prevailed on the estate before it was taken over by the ladies and that had ruined both part of the estate and its owners. The estate was owned by a reclusive and unmarried miser, and on his death it passed to his nephew, who 'till then [had] been exposed to all the evils of poverty, [and] was almost distracted with joy at the sudden acquisition of a large fortune' (221). Not surprisingly he soon squandered it in extravagance and gambling – familiar figures for misuse of capital and property. The ladies restored the estate and its Hall, its traditional social structure and culture, and its capitalist economy. They did so, however, according to values of charity. These values are coded here as both feminine and Christian. Female agency, operating at the local level but in domains conventionally reserved for men, is validated by an authority above society, culture, material economy, and time.

In part, then, the novel's critique of courtly patriarchy is based on the values and practices of gentry capitalism, since patriarchy is seen to interfere with capitalism. Gentry capitalism itself is also criticized, however. As capitalist practices of estate management spread they were accompanied by enclosures of common land; investment in projects such as mines, canals, and manufactures; replacement of freeholders by tenant farmers; displacement of the customary economic and social relations by a wage economy supplemented by poor relief; and increasing class alienation (Malcolmson, Berg, Bushaway). These developments enriched the gentry and their professional dependents but depressed the rural middle and labouring classes.

Scott's sister knew this well, since her husband owned estates and mines in the north of England and she herself helped to make them much more profitable precisely by taking a more aggressively capitalist and less traditionally genteel approach to managing them. Partly to compensate, Elizabeth Montagu also developed programs to ameliorate the condition of the labourers on her husband's properties, that of the miners and their families in particular. These programs were also designed, however, to pacify the labourers and head off any revolt against abandonment of customary relations for the new capitalist methods. This double-edged program created the framework of the self-interested philanthropy that would be promoted and practised by following generations of bluestockings, along with many others in the upper and middle classes.

The feminized, Christian economy of Millenium Hall is designed to promote similar ends, and to redress the wrongs of women. The economy of Millenium Hall corrects both the gender bias and class injustice portrayed as consequent on the intertwined systems of court culture, patriarchy, and gentry capitalism. The Hall's proprietors achieve their aims by detaching gentry capitalism from courtliness and patriarchy—male-dominated cultures—and re-attaching it to femininity and Christianity. This reform is divinely sanctioned by the providential events that brought the 'society' of 'ladies' to the Hall and enabled them to transform it.

That sanction is reinforced by representation of the Hall in particular utopian terms, associated with paradisal, mythological, and classical literary traditions. Millenium Hall is clearly a utopia—though an unusual one—designed by and for women. The utopian tradition of writing that represents ideal worlds in the past or future goes back to classical literature and beyond into myth (Manuel). Part of the task of such literature was to critique the actual world of its writers and readers. Thus each age had its own utopian writing in Western culture, from classical Greece (Plato) through the Middle Ages (Augustine and Dante) and the Renaissance (Thomas More, Francis Bacon, Tommaso Campanella) to the Enlightenment of Scott's own time (James Harrington, Jonathan Swift, Denis Diderot). Many of these utopias were in effect critiques of court government, culture, and society, and the eighteenth-century commonwealthmen and classical republicans were especially interested in this kind of writing, represented by James Harrington's *Oceana* (1656). In the period of the French Revolution many thought utopia was achievable and imminent (Tom Paine, William Godwin), while in the postrevolutionary Romantic and Victorian periods utopian projects took specifically economic and political forms (Robert Owen, William Morris). Meanwhile, as W.H.G. Armytage has shown, there were numerous attempts to create utopia in reality.

Women often had an important or even equal place in these experiments, but most utopian writing was produced by and for men and largely dealt with their cultural, social, intellectual, and political interests (Davis). Only in the early twentieth century was there a significant female and feminist engagement in utopian writing, represented by Charlotte Perkins Gilman's *Herland* (1915). In the later twentieth century there has been a great increase in both utopian and anti-utopian writing, ranging from Doris Lessing and George Orwell to Angela Carter and Margaret Atwood (Kumar), and this includes a number of feminist utopias (Bammer). *Millenium Hall* is, however, a rare early female utopia as well as a feminist attempt to appropriate a largely male and masculine literary tradition to a project with broad social, economic, and political implications (Schnorrenberg). Scott aims to disguise the innovativeness of her utopia by appealing to what could be seen as the feminine interests and feminist potential of a long and well-established tradition in Western literature and culture. This is the tradition of an original idealized society that may yet be regained in the future.

When the narrator first approaches the Hall a shepherd's music reminds him of the pastorals of Theocritus, thus associating the place with Arcadia, or the idealized and egalitarian rural world of classical myth. Soon after, the narrator describes the fields and meadows outside the Hall as 'this earthly paradise.' He refers to the inhabitants of the house as the 'Primum Mobile,' or first movers of this paradise, thus suggesting that they are god-like directors and motivators of the world they have designed and set in motion. In other words, the female proprietors of Millenium Hall are agents in a powerfully original and originating way, by having returned to an 'original' and pre-lapsarian state of society. The scene inside the Hall, with women and girls practising various arts, then makes the narrator think he is 'in the Attic school' of the golden age of historic classical culture in Athens. This culture, too, was conventionally viewed as a predominantly male domain, with women allowed at best to play the role of muse. Near the end of the novel, as Mrs Maynard closes her last inset narrative, she describes the Hall as 'this heavenly society' (200). These allusions bring together and feminize three different but related cultural traditions – humanist classicism, aristocratic pastoral idealism, and Christianity.

Humanist classicism provided a common culture and ideology for the sons though rarely the daughters of the gentry and upwardly mobile middle classes from the Renaissance to the nineteenth century. An anti-monarchist, anti-court branch of this culture was developed by seventeenth- and eighteenth-century 'commonwealthmen' or 'classical republicans' such as James Harrington and Conyers Middleton. These commonwealthmen looked back to the Commonwealth period in English history, as to the republican period of ancient Rome, as the closest that human society had come to a truly virtuous state. The commonwealth and classical republican traditions could appeal to upper- and middle-class women, however, since the women of republican Rome were presented as a contrast to courtly women of imperial Rome, as virtuous state-builders from the commonwealth of domesticity, and as nurturers, educators, and inspirers of republican men. In this light, *Millenium Hall* could be read as a feminized and feminist version of the commonwealth and classical republican tradition that was otherwise sustained by and for men in eighteenth-century England.

The arcadian pastoral tradition was part of classical literature; during the Renaissance it circulated mainly in upper-class culture, for several reasons. By aestheticizing, sentimentalizing, and idealizing rural life it masked the exploitative nature of economic and social relations in an agrarian economy controlled by the landed gentry. For the same reason the arcadian pastoral could serve as an idealized and imaginary alternative to political reality for the landed classes – the dangers and conflicts of participating, as most of the aristocracy and gentry felt they had to, in court government, society, and culture. Arcadian pastoral could, then, be read as a form of utopian literature and thus serve as a critique of court power and culture. In this way it could also work with classical republicanism. Arcadian pastoral mainly addressed the concerns of men, but because the pastoral world often centred on women and courtship, or often represented an apparently egalitarian society, in terms of both gender and class, it could be read as a feminized tradition. The tradition of arcadian pastoral could be extended to include Renaissance and seventeenth-century verse and prose romance, which is often pastoral in setting, characters, and themes, and much of which was written by or addressed to women. Thus again the tradition could be read as a feminized one. *Millenium Hall* is clearly such an arcadian pastoral.

More complex is the way *Millenium Hall* uses the biblical, Christian tradition of paradise lost and regained. In the biblical narrative of the fall, Eve succumbs to temptation and then tempts Adam to sin, resulting in their expulsion from paradise to a world of time, mortality, and work. Women are condemned to the additional pain of childbearing. For centuries this myth was used in Western European culture to justify antifeminism, or literature critical of women in general, and even misogyny. In the Christian theology of the Church of England, to which Sarah Scott adhered, the implication of the myth is that while humanity has to endure mortal life it can choose good over evil by exercising good works as well as true faith, and thus win eternal salvation, and regain paradise. This theology seems to place women at a disadvantage, however, since their inferior education and narrow sphere of action give them less opportunity than men to acquire true faith and perform good deeds. Millenium Hall is clearly represented as a paradise not only regained by women through true faith and good deeds, but is itself a good deed and one that opens greater opportunity for good deeds by women. Thus *Millenium Hall* both fulfils and 'corrects,' in terms of women's experience and abilities, the creed of the established Church of England, itself a pillar of the state.

The one 'classic' English text that brings these three traditions together is Milton's *Paradise Lost*, together with its sequel, *Paradise Regained*. Milton's poem is quoted once in *Millenium Hall* and is not otherwise mentioned or discussed there. Nevertheless, the novel seems to conduct a dialogue with the poem. Milton was not an Anglican, or a member of the Church of England, but his poem does embody the theology of free will, or salvation by true faith and good works, and as such it became a religious classic in eighteenth-century Anglican culture. It was well known that the poet himself was a republican and a commonwealthman, having served Oliver Cromwell's government. His writings, especially in prose, were included in the libraries of eighteenth-century commonwealthmen and classical republicans. His poem was at least in part intended to counter courtly and aristocratic forms of romance and pastoral by returning to what was, for him, the original and ultimate arcadia – Eden. Here Sarah Scott would seem to side with Milton, for her arcadian pastoral is more like his than the kind his poem counters, especially in criticizing the aristocratic culture of courtly love, which is often central to aristocratic pastoral. On the other hand, *Millenium Hall* is unwilling to accept the antifeminism that many readers have found in *Paradise Lost*, in the role played by Eve. If women, represented by Eve, lost paradise, then the woman author of *Millenium Hall* and the women represented there show how it may be regained, on earth.

This is accomplished by an appropriately earthly means – gentry capitalism. Here again, Scott undertakes to treat major issues in contemporary society – indeed, in the Western social and cultural tradition

– for the pursuit of profit had long existed in a state of tension with Christian ethics and theology. The conflict between 'the world' and eternity was a central theme in Christian moral writing. During the mid-eighteenth century there was increasing attention to the relation between customary and capitalist economics, as theorists tried to detach capitalist economics from traditional religious ethical arguments. Scott's sister, Elizabeth Montagu, seems to have been aware of these issues through the interests and activities of her brothers and husband. Certainly there was a gendered dimension to this issue, since women were conventionally characterized as both more material and less intellectual, more worldly and less spiritual than men. Yet women were also represented as social mediators and nurturers, palliating the effects of poverty and misery, be they divinely ordained or the 'inevitable' consequences of capitalism. It is a revisionist move for Scott, then, to show women effectively practising capitalism, yet under Christian guidance, thereby adapting worldly means to spiritual ends.

This achievement is clearly a form of feminization. For example, when Miss Trentham joins 'the society' of Millenium Hall her fortune is used to establish 'in the parish a manufacture of carpets and ruggs, which has succeeded so well, as to enrich all the country round about' (243). This capitalist enterprise is paternalist but humanized, or rather feminized, for 'the ladies' act not solely for profit but according to benevolent social policy:

> ... as they feared an enterprising undertaker might ruin their plan, they themselves undertook to be stewards; they stood the first expence, allowed a considerable profit to the directors, but kept the distribution of the money entirely in their own hands: thus they prevent the poor from being oppressed by their superiors, for they allow them great wages, and by their very diligent inspection hinder any frauds.... As the ladies have the direction of the whole, they give more to the children and the aged, in proportion to the work they do, than to those who are more capable, as a proper encouragement, and reward for industry in those seasons of life in which it is so uncommon. (243-44)

This feminized capitalism is then placed under a divine aegis, and described as a 'duty.' Miss Mancel assures the sceptical Lamont,

'... we are told by him who cannot err, that our time, our money, and our understandings, are entrusted with us as so many talents, for the use of which we must give a strict account. How we ought to use them he has likewise told us; as to our fortunes in the most express terms, when he commands us to feed the hungry, to cloath the naked, to relieve the prisoner, and to take care of the sick.' (244)

The capitalism of Millenium Hall may be subsumed under charity and the biblical story of the talents, but it is capitalism nevertheless, and a thorough plan of social control. It participates in a growing capitalist appropriation of charitableness and alleviation of the social inequality and distress caused – at least in part – by capitalism. This fact is made clear by the precautions taken by the proprietors of Millenium Hall against outside 'undertakers' ('entrepreneurs' in modern usage). Such a divinely sanctioned and feminized capitalism would have considerable appeal through the eighteenth century and beyond, and was a major legacy of first-generation bluestocking feminism.

Members of this generation themselves practised, insofar as means permitted, the plan of Millenium Hall. For example, Sarah Scott and Lady Barbara Montagu together organized work-for-welfare programs for indigent women. One such scheme involved preparing material for a dozen poor girls to make bed-linen and clothes that were then distributed to the local poor. The girls' education was also paid for, with Scott instructing the more capable ones in writing and arithmetic. On Sunday mornings Scott instructed the girls in their catechism and sent them to the parish church, together with twelve boys, whose education was also paid for (letter of 16 Oct. 1755 from Elizabeth Montagu to Gilbert West, in Climenson, vol. 2, p. 78-9). Scott and Lady Barbara also participated in a scheme that involved selling the needlework and ornamental objects produced by their dependents. In the same letter Elizabeth Montagu describes her sister and Lady Barbara's household as 'their convent, for by its regularity it resembles one.' With her greater resources, Elizabeth Montagu could organize charitable and educational schemes for a wide variety of the labouring classes, from the coal miners on her husband's estates in Northumberland to the chimney-sweeps of London to the labourers on her estate in Berkshire. Both she and her sister tried to help individual working-class men and women who got into difficulties. Occasionally they undertook to protect individuals from the sexual exploitation and victimization common to lower-class women.

These projects and those outlined in *Millenium Hall* were paralleled or imitated by others, and by increasing numbers of middle-class women in particular, as the bluestocking reform impulse spread down the social scale. Hannah More (1745-1833), a former school proprietor and second-generation bluestocking, was one of the most active imitators. In her part of Somerset she and her sisters organized a number of programs designed both to ameliorate the condition of the poor and to impose a version of upper middle-class ideology and culture on them. Several of these programs follow those found in *Millenium Hall* and range from Sunday schools promoting literacy to rewards for young women who preserved a reputation for chastity until their wedding. Sarah (Kirby) Trimmer (1741-1810), daughter of an engraver and herself a prolific writer for children, produced a plan for middle-class women to act as local social reformers, published as *The Œconomy of Charity* (1787, substantially revised 1801). In Mary Wollstonecraft's (1759-97) autobiographical novel of social and feminist criticism, *Mary: A Fiction* (1788), the heroine carries out a plan on her estate similar to that of the proprietors of Millenium Hall.

The political debates of the 1790s, stimulated by the French Revolution, divided bluestocking feminism as it divided other reform movements. Some women intellectuals and social critics, such as Mary Wollstonecraft, took elements of bluestocking feminism into a more explicit, thorough, and middle-class form of feminism addressing the egalitarianism and civic idealism that was being advanced by many Revolutionaries, though seldom extended to women (Landes). First- and second-generation bluestockings such as Sarah Scott and Hannah More, however, rejected the Revolution and its British sympathizers. They were shocked by the kinds of direct political activism and explicit feminism promoted by Wollstonecraft and others. In the aftermath of the Revolution debate, from the mid and late 1790s on, any kind of female intellectual, social critic, or social reformer, however 'radical' or 'conservative,' was liable to be equated with revolutionary transgression, excess, and violence, and to be condemned as a danger to social and political stability. It was in this period that the term 'bluestocking' acquired definitively negative associations, especially within the emergent and male-dominated post-Revolutionary movement later called Romanticism. One aspect of Romanticism was the reclaiming of social, cultural, and political themes feminized by earlier movements ranging from bluestocking feminism to Revolutionary feminism.

In the Revolutionary aftermath many women writers did try to sustain the concerns of these movements. They had to mask the fact that they were doing so, to disguise the feminist implications of what they were doing, or to attach their concerns to some larger ideological and cultural theme. For example, Hannah More's *Strictures on the Modern System of Female Education* (1799), calls on the upper-class and upper middle-class women of Britain to lead the struggle for national and imperial survival against Napoleonic France from the bastion of domesticity and local life dominated and purified by virtuous, rational, and well-educated women. Other women followed this line with a host of tracts, novels, plays, poems, essays, and histories (Kelly, Mellor). Middle-class women in increasing numbers engaged in local and even national campaigns and organizations devoted to social improvement and control (Prochaska).

These disguised and oblique forms of feminization in turn informed early Victorian 'women's mission' feminism, down to feminist, suffragist, and women's education movements of the later nineteenth and early twentieth century (Levine). Then the term 'bluestocking' acquired further associations, mainly with a certain kind of female intellectualism and independence, such as that promoted by the new women's colleges at Oxford and Cambridge, or by writers such as Virginia Woolf and the Bloomsbury group. Meanwhile, from the early nineteenth century, feminist aims and feminization of the public sphere were established among the aims of socialist movements, leaving both earlier and more recent bluestockings to be associated with gentrified upper middle-class culture (Taylor).

By then *Millenium Hall* was almost forgotten, and retained a small place in literary history as an expression of upper-class feminine culture distantly associated with certain prominent male literary figures, such as

Samuel Johnson. In fact, *Millenium Hall* is quite a bit more than that. It is the manifesto of bluestocking feminism, itself a major attempt to redefine class and gender relations at a critical point in the transformation of English society and culture. It is an important document in a major social and cultural achievement of women writers before the modern age – synthesizing and popularizing social and economic thought, political economy, and Christian ethics. Not least, it turns aside from the more influential innovations of Samuel Richardson and his followers to merge long-standing literary and cultural traditions in an important experiment in literary form and social criticism. This in itself was an important and exemplary instance of the beneficent female agency that *Millenium Hall* envisions and celebrates.

References

Armstrong, Nancy. 'The Rise of Domestic Woman.' *The Ideology of Conduct: Essays in Literature and the History of Sexuality*. Ed. Nancy Armstrong and Leonard Tennenhouse. New York and London: Methuen, 1987.

Armytage, W.H.G. *Heavens Below: Utopian Experiments in England 1560-1960*. London: Routledge and Kegan Paul, 1961.

Bammer, Angelika. *Partial Visions: Feminism and Utopianism in the 1970s*. London: Routledge, 1991.

Berg, Maxine. *The Age of Manufactures: Industry, Innovation and Work in Britain 1700-1820*. London: Fontana, 1985.

Blunt, Reginald. *Mrs. Montagu, 'Queen of the Blues': Her Letters and Friendships from 1762 to 1800*. 2 vols. London: Constable and Company, 1923.

Browne, Alice. *The Eighteenth Century Feminist Mind*. Detroit: Wayne State University Press, 1987.

Bushaway, Bob. *By Rite: Custom, Ceremony and Community in England 1700-1880*. London: Junction Books, 1982.

Climenson, Emily J., *Elizabeth Montagu, The Queen of the Blue-stockings: Her Correspondence from 1720 to 1761*. 2 vols. New York: E.P. Dutton and Company, 1906.

Davis, J. C. *Utopia and the Ideal Society: A Study of English Utopian Writing 1516-1700*. Cambridge: Cambridge University Press, 1981.

Hobby, Elaine. *Virtue of Necessity: English Women's Writing 1649-88*. London: Virago, 1988.

Holmes, Geoffrey. *Augustan England: Professions, State and Society, 1680-1730*. London: Allen and Unwin, 1982.

Kelly, Gary. *Women, Writing, and Revolution 1790-1827*. Oxford: Clarendon Press, 1993.

Kumar, Krishnan. *Utopianism*. Milton Keynes: Open University Press, 1991.

Landes, Joan B. *Women and the Public Sphere in the Age of the French Revolution*. Ithaca, N.Y., and London: Cornell University Press, 1988.

Levine, Philippa. *Victorian Feminism: 1850-1900*. London: Hutchinson, 1987.

Malcolmson, Robert W. *Life and Labour in England 1700-1800*. London: Hutchinson, 1981.

Manuel, Frank E., and Fritzie P. Manuel. *Utopian Thought in the Western World*. Oxford: Basil Blackwell, 1979.

McKeon, Michael. *The Origins of the English Novel 1600-1740*. Baltimore: The Johns Hopkins University Press, 1987.

Mellor, Anne K. *Romanticism and Gender*. New York and London: Routledge, 1993.

Mingay, G. E. *English Landed Society in the Eighteenth Century*. London: Routledge and Kegan Paul, 1965.

Myers, Sylvia Harcstark. *The Bluestocking Circle: Women, Friendship, and the Life of the Mind in Eighteenth-Century England*. Oxford: Clarendon Press, 1990.

Porter, Roy. *English Society in the Eighteenth Century*. Harmondsworth: Penguin Books, 1982.

Prochaska, Frank. *Women and Philanthropy in Nineteenth-Century England*. Oxford: Clarendon Press, 1980.

Richetti, John J. *Popular Fiction before Richardson: Narrative Patterns 1700-1739*. Oxford: Clarendon Press, 1969.

Robbins, Caroline. *The Eighteenth Century Commonwealthman: Studies in the Transmission, Development and Circumstance of English Liberal Thought from the Restoration of Charles II until the War with the Thirteen Colonies*. New York: Athenaeum, 1968.

Rogers, Katherine M. *Feminism in Eighteenth-Century England*. Brighton: Harvester Press, 1982.

Schnorrenberg, Barbara Brandon. 'A Paradise Like Eve's: Three Eighteenth Century English Female Utopias.' *Women's Studies*, vol. 9 (1982), pp. 263-73.

Scott, Walter S. *The Bluestocking Ladies*. London: John Green and Co., 1947.

Spencer, Jane. *The Rise of the Woman Novelist: From Aphra Behn to Jane Austen*. Oxford and New York: Basil Blackwell, 1986.

Stone, Lawrence, and Jeanne C. Fawtier Stone. *An Open Elite? England 1540-1880*. Abridged edn. Oxford and New York: Oxford University Press, 1986.

Taylor, Barbara. *Eve and the New Jerusalem: Socialism and Feminism in the Nineteenth Century*. London: Virago, 1983.

Todd, Janet. *The Sign of Angellica: Women, Writing, and Fiction 1660-1800*. London: Virago, 1989.

Trumbach, Randolph. *The Rise of the Egalitarian Family: Aristocratic Kinship and Domestic Relations in Eighteenth Century England*. New York: Academic Press, 1978.

Williams, Ioan. *The Idea of the Novel in Europe 1600-1800*. New York: New York University Press, 1979.

Sarah Scott's Works

1. *The History of Cornelia*. London: A. Millar, 1750.
2. *Agreeable Ugliness; or, The Triumph of the Graces; Exemplified in the Real Life and Fortunes of a Young Lady of Some Distinction*. London: R. and J. Dodsley, 1754. Translation of Pierre Antoine, Marquis de La Place, *Le Laideur aimable*, 2 vols, 1752.
3. *A Journey through Every Stage of Life, Described in a Variety of Interesting Scenes, Drawn from Real Characters. By a Person of Quality*. 2 vols. London: A. Millar, 1754.
4. *The History of Gustavus Ericson, King of Sweden; With an Introductory History of Sweden, from the Middle of the Twelfth Century*. 'By Henry Augustus Raymond, Esq.' London: A. Millar, 1761.
5. *The History of Mecklenburgh, from the First Settlement of the Vandals in that Country, to the Present Time; including a Period of about Three Thousand Years*. London: J. Newbery, 1762.
6. *A Description of Millenium Hall and the Country Adjacent, Together with the Characters of the Inhabitants and such Historical Anecdotes and Reflections as May Excite in the Reader Proper Sentiments of Humanity, and Lead the Mind to the Love of Virtue*. London: J. Newbery, 1762. Second "corrected" edition 1764; third edition 1767, fourth edition 1778.
7. *The History of Sir George Ellison*. 2 vols. London: A. Millar, 1766.
8. *The Life of Theodore Agrippa d'Aubigné, Containing a Succinct Account of the Most Remarkable Occurrences during the Civil Wars of France in the Reigns of Charles IX., Henry III., Henry IV., and in the Minority of Lewis XIII*. London: Edward and Charles Dilly, 1772.
9. *The Test of Filial Duty; In a Series of Letters between Miss Emilia Leonard, and Miss Charlotte Arlington: A Novel*. 2 vols. London: T. Carnan, 1772.

Note on the Text

I have followed the text of the first edition, as being probably closer to what Sarah Scott wrote than are the later editions of 1764, 1767, and 1778. It seems unlikely that she had anything to do with the other three editions published in her lifetime, though they make some corrections to obvious errors. I have followed these corrections, noting where I have done so. In other respects I have preferred to follow what was probably her own way of spelling, and composing and punctuating sentences, except in a few cases where the later editions alter readings that might confuse the modern reader; again, I have noted these changes. Sarah Scott's usage was more or less acceptable for women and also men in the middle decades of the eighteenth century. Many of the spellings and forms used by Scott, which were altered in the second to fourth editions, and which now look irregular if not incorrect, were in fact, as my notes point out, common usages at mid-century.

Collation produces about 1200 variants between the first and second to fourth editions, the vast majority having to do with spelling and punctuation. For example, use of double consonants became more regular with standardization in the decades after the novel was published, so that Scott can write *postilion, linnen, sollicitude, shuned, dazle, ruggs,* and *carressed.* The later editions alter these to modern forms, but hers were not unacceptable in the 1760s. Use of vowel combinations was also more flexible then, so that Scott can write *croud, aukward, cloathes, chuse* (but also *choose*), *murmours, agreable, chearfulness,* and *langour,* as well as *meerly* (for *merely*), without erring in relation to usage at the time the novel was written. Similarly, use of *en-* or *in-* had not yet become fixed, so that Scott can write *encrease* and *inclosures* without offending against usage of her time.

In sentence construction and punctuation Scott's practice of long sentences with phrases and clauses loosely joined by commas, semicolons, colons, and dashes is consistent with informal writing of her day. The text of *Millenium Hall* will seem over-punctuated and inconsistently punctuated by modern standards. Yet her practice also gives her discourse a rhythm of conversational and narrative speech that could be seen as the appropriate form of the language for the dialogue enacted in the novel and in the bluestocking circles themselves. At the risk of occasionally and momentarily confusing the modern reader, I have decided, unlike other modern editors, not to modernize Scott's punctuation, so that the rhythm of her bluestocking discourse may be retained.

Linguists have largely abandoned a 'whig' or teleological history of English – the idea that the language was trying for hundreds of years to get to the usage of Samuel Johnson or Queen Victoria or Margaret Thatcher. The history of the language is now seen as part of a wider history of social differences, conflict, and change. Inevitably, these differences included and include differences of gender. *Millenium Hall* was first published when the cultural gatekeepers, ranging from schoolteachers to printers, the great majority of whom were men, were becoming more prescriptive and less flexible and less permissive about spelling, syntax, and punctuation. The rigidification of written English usage was being carried out mainly to serve the practices and interests of professional middle-class men. The later editions of *Millenium Hall* are increasingly marked by that process, which was completed, in the form of 'standard' written English much as we still know it, just after the fourth edition was published. In that process, women's usage in written English was increasingly stigmatized as substandard – a sign of their intellectual inferiority and thus a justification for subordinating them.

Thus the apparently greater 'correctness' of the second to fourth editions of *Millenium Hall*, as compared to the first, reflects in large part, though not entirely, the social politics of language during the particular period when those editions were published. (In fact, the fourth edition in particular introduces many new errors into the text.) These politics of language were politics of gender and class, politics that *Millenium Hall* challenges. It seemed appropriate in preparing this edition to retrieve Sarah Scott's usage as well as, or as part of, her broader feminist project. Again, this may make the text seem stranger to the modern student than it should, but any editor knows that this kind of work inevitably involves losses and gains, compromise and mediation. Above all, then, I have aimed to produce a text that is useful while remaining as true as possible to what is likely to have been Sarah Scott's own language and way of writing.

A DESCRIPTION of

MILLENIUM HALL,

AND THE

COUNTRY ADJACENT:

Together with the

CHARACTERS of the INHABITANTS,

And such Hiſtorical

ANECDOTES and REFLECTIONS,

A S

May excite in the READER proper Sentiments of
Humanity, and lead the Mind to the Love of
VIRTUE.

B Y

A GENTLEMAN on his Travels.

LONDON:

Printed for J. NEWBERY, at the Bible and Sun,
in St. Paul's Church-yard.

MDCCLXII.

ADVERTISEMENT.

THE Publisher of this Volume is under some Difficulties; not from any Apprehensions of losing by the Book; for great part of the Impression is bespoke; his Anxiety arises from the Author's addressing the Volume to him, and making him a Compliment in the Beginning; which, as he is conscious he does not deserve, he hopes the Reader will impute to its proper Cause, namely, to the Warmth of Friendship, which is too apt to exalt the Object it esteems. The Gentleman who wrote this Volume, is of too much Consequence to be obstinately contradicted; and as the Bookseller could not prevail on him to leave out the Compliment above-mentioned, he hopes his publishing of it will not be imputed to any other Motive, but that of his Readiness to obey.

Truth - claims?

❖❖❖

A Description of

MILLENIUM HALL.

DEAR SIR,

THOUGH, when I left London, I promised to write to you as soon as I had reached my northern retreat, yet, I believe, you little expected instead of a letter to receive a volume; but I should not stand excused to myself, were I to fail communicating to you the pleasure I received in my road hither, from the sight of a society, whose acquaintance I owe to one of those fortunate, though in appearance trifling, accidents, from which sometimes arise the most pleasing circumstances of our lives; for as such I must ever esteem the acquaintance of that amiable family, who have fixed their abode at a place which I shall nominate Millenium Hall,[1] as the best adapted to the lives of the inhabitants, and to avoid giving the real name, fearing to offend that modesty which has induced them to conceal their virtues in retirement.

In giving you a very circumstantial account of this society, I confess I have a view beyond the pleasure, which a mind like yours must receive from the contemplation of so much virtue. Your constant endeavours have been to inculcate the best principles into youthful minds, the only probable means of mending mankind; for the foundation of most of our virtues, or our vices, are laid in that season of life when we are most susceptible of impression, and when on our minds, as on a sheet of white

---

1   Millenium Hall] "millenium" suggests a utopian theme, based on the assertion in the Bible, book of Revelation, that with the return of Christ there would commence a millennium, or thousand-year reign of peace, after which there would be a final struggle with evil, the end of time, a last judgment, and entry of the righteous and deserving into paradise; in the seventeenth century the millennium was seen as a "fifth monarchy," which republicans associated with the Commonwealth; thus "millennium" also has political associations; "hall" refers to the manor house of a landed estate, the basis of economic, social, and political power in the eighteenth century; thus "millenium hall" suggests a paradisal or utopian version of the gentry-dominated economy, society, and culture based on the landed estate

paper,[1] any characters may be engraven; these laudable endeavours, by which we may reasonably expect the rising generation will be greatly improved, render particularly due to you, any examples which may teach those virtues that are not easily learnt by precept, and shew the facility of what, in meer speculation, might appear surrounded with a discouraging impracticability: you are the best judge, whether, by being made public, they may be conducive to your great end of benefiting the world. I therefore submit the future fate of the following sheets entirely to you, and shall not think any prefatory apology for the publication at all requisite; for though a man who supposes his own life and actions deserve universal notice, or can be of general use, may be liable to the imputation of vanity, yet, as I have no other share than that of a spectator, and auditor, in what I purpose to relate, I presume no apology can be required; for my vanity must rather be mortified than flattered in the description of such virtues as will continually accuse me of my own deficiencies, and lead me to make an humiliating comparison between these excellent ladies and myself.

You may remember, Sir, that when I took leave of you with a design of retiring to my native county, there to enjoy the plenty and leisure for which a few years labour had furnished me with the necessary requisites, I was advised by an eminent physician to make a very extensive tour through the western part of this kingdom, in order, by frequent change of air, and continued exercise, to cure the ill effects of my long abode in the hot and unwholsome climate of Jamaica,[2] where, while I increased my fortune, I gradually impaired my constitution; and though one, who like me, has dedicated all his application to mercantile gain, will not allow that he has given up the substance for the shadow,[3] yet perhaps it

---

1   minds ... sheet of white paper] the idea, broadly associated with the philosopher John Locke (1632-1704), that when one first comes into the world one's mind is a blank, or tabula rasa, on which sensory experience, processed by reflection, imprints or inscribes one's knowledge and thus one's character

2   Jamaica] colony of Britain since 1670, developed as a sugar-producing economy organized in plantations owned by white Europeans and worked by black African slaves and their descendants; attained independence in 1962

3   substance for the shadow] Shakespeare, *Titus Andronicus*, III, ii, line 80: "He takes false shadows for true substances"; but the same idea is found in several other plays, and was proverbial

would be difficult to deny, that I thus sacrificed the greater good in pursuit of the less.

The eagerness with which I longed to fix in my wished for retirement, made me imagine, that when I had once reached it, even the pursuit of health would be an insufficient inducement to determine me to leave my retreat, I therefore chose to make the advised tour before I went into the north. As the pleasure arising from a variety of beautiful objects is but half enjoyed, when we have no one to share it with us, I accepted the offer Mr. Lamont (the son of my old friend) made of accompanying me in my journey. As this young gentleman has not the good fortune to be known to you, it may not be amiss, as will appear in the sequel, to let you into his character.

Mr. Lamont is a young man of about twenty-five years of age, of an agreeable person, and lively understanding; both perhaps have concurred to render him a coxcomb. The vivacity of his parts soon gained him such a degree of encouragement as excited his vanity, and raised in him an high opinion of himself. A very generous father enabled him to partake of every fashionable amusement, and the natural bent of his mind soon led him into all the dissipation which the gay world affords. Useful and improving studies were laid aside for such desultory reading, as he found most proper to furnish him with topics for conversation, in the idle societies he frequented. Thus that vivacity, which, properly qualified, might have become true wit,[1] degenerated into pertness and impertinence. A consciousness of an understanding, which he never exerted, rendered him conceited; those talents which nature kindly bestowed upon him, by being perverted, gave rise to his greatest faults. His reasoning faculty, by a partial and superficial use, led him to infidelity, and the desire of being thought superiorly distinguishing, established him an infidel.[2] Fashion, not reason, has been the guide of all his thoughts and actions. But with these faults he is good-natured, and not unentertaining, especially in a tête à tête,[3] where he does not desire to shine, and therefore his vanity lies dormant, and suffers the best qualifications of his mind

---

1   wit] in the eighteenth century the usual sense was cleverness, including superior intellectual capacity, rather than just verbal or mental sprightliness
2   infidel] a disbeliever in religion of any kind
3   tête-à-tête] a private conversation between two people, from a French phrase

to break forth. This induced me to accept of him as a fellow traveller.

We proceeded on our journey as far as Cornwall, without meeting with any other than the usual incidents of the road, till one afternoon, when our chaise[1] broke down. The worst circumstance attending this accident was our being several miles from a town, and so ignorant of the country, that we knew not whether there was any village within a moderate distance. We sent the postilion on my man's horse to the next town to fetch a smith, and leaving my servant to guard the chaise, Mr. Lamont and I walked towards an avenue of oaks, which we observed at a small distance. The thick shade they afforded us, the fragrance wafted from the woodbines with which they were encircled, was so delightful, and the beauty of the grounds so very attracting, that we strolled on, desirous of approaching the house to which this avenue led. It is a mile and a half in length, but the eye is so charmed with the remarkable verdure and neatness of the fields, with the beauty of the flowers which are planted all round them, and seem to mix with the quickset hedges, that time steals away insensibly.

When we had walked about half a mile in a scene truly pastoral, we began to think ourselves in the days of Theocritus,[2] so sweetly did the sound of a flute come wafted through the air. Never did pastoral swain make sweeter melody on his oaten reed. Our ears now afforded us fresh attraction, and with quicker steps we proceeded, till we came within sight of the musician that had charmed us. Our pleasure was not a little heightened, to see, as the scene promised, in reality a shepherd, watching a large flock of sheep. We continued motionless, listening to his music, till a lamb straying from its fold demanded his care, and he laid aside his instrument, to guide home the little wanderer.

Curiosity now prompted us to walk on; the nearer we came to the house, the greater we found the profusion of flowers which ornamented every field. Some had no other defence than hedges of rose trees and sweet-briars, so artfully planted, that they made a very thick hedge, while at the lower part, pinks, jonquills, hyacinths, and various

---

1   chaise] from the French for "chair," in English designating a variety of travelling carriages, usually light in construction, as distinct from the more heavily built coaches

2   Theocritus] Greek native of Sicily who wrote pastoral poetry in the third century B.C.

other flowers, seemed to grow under their protection. Primroses, violets, lillies of the valley, and polyanthuses enriched such shady spots, as, for want of sun, were not well calculated for the production of other flowers. The mixture of perfumes which exhaled from this profusion composed the highest fragrance, and sometimes the different scents regaled the senses alternately, and filled us with reflections on the infinite variety of nature.

When we were within about a quarter of a mile of the house, the scene became still more animated. On one side was the greatest variety of cattle, the most beautiful of their kinds, grazing in fields whose verdure equalled that of the finest turf, nor were they destitute of their ornaments, only the woodbines and jessamine, and such flowers, as might have tempted the inhabitants of these pastures to crop them, were defended with roses and sweet-briars, whose thorns preserved them from all attacks.

Though Lamont had hitherto been little accustomed to admire nature, yet was he much captivated with this scene, and with his usual levity cried out, 'If Nebuchadnezzar[1] had such pastures as these to range in, his seven years expulsion from human society might not be the least agreeable part of his life.' My attention was too much engaged to criticize the light turn of Lamont's mind, nor did his thoughts continue long on the same subject, for our observation was soon called off, by a company of hay-makers in the fields on the other side of the avenue. The cleanliness and neatness of the young women thus employed, rendered them a more pleasing subject for Lamont's contemplation than any thing we had yet seen; in them we beheld rural simplicity, without any of those marks of poverty and boorish rusticity, which would have spoilt the pastoral air of the scene around us; but not even the happy amiable innocence, which their figures and countenances expressed, gave me so much satisfaction as the sight of the number of children, who were all exerting the utmost of their strength, with an air of delighted emulation between themselves, to contribute their share to the general undertaking. Their eyes sparkled with that spirit which health and activity can only give, and

---

1   Nebuchadnezzar] King of Babylon in the Bible, book of Daniel, who mistreated the captive Jews and was punished by God by being reduced to behave like a wild beast

their rosy cheeks shewed the benefits of youthful labour.

Curiosity is one of those insatiable passions that grow by gratification; it still prompted us to proceed, not unsatisfied with what we had seen, but desirous to see still more of this earthly paradise. We approached the house, wherein, as it was the only human habitation in view, we imagined must reside the Primum Mobile[1] of all we had yet beheld. We were admiring the magnificence of the ancient structure, and inclined to believe it the abode of the genius which presided over this fairy land, when we were surprized by a storm, which had been for some time gathering over our heads, though our thoughts had been too agreeably engaged to pay much attention to it. We took shelter under the thick shade of a large oak, but the violence of the thunder and lightening made our situation rather uncomfortable. All those whom we had a little before seen so busy, left their work on hearing the first clap of thunder, and ran with the utmost speed to Millenium Hall, so I shall call the noble mansion of which I am speaking, as to an assured asylum against every evil.

Some of these persons, I imagine, perceived us; for immediately after they entered, came out a woman, who, by her air and manner of address, we guessed to be the house-keeper, and desired us to walk into the house till the storm was over. We made some difficulties about taking that liberty, but she still persisting in her invitation, had my curiosity to see the inhabitants of this hospitable mansion been less, I could not have refused to comply, as by prolonging these ceremonious altercations I was detaining her in the storm, we therefore agreed to follow her.

If we had been inclined before to fancy ourselves on enchanted ground,[2] when after being led through a large hall, we were introduced to the ladies, who knew nothing of what had passed, I could scarcely forbear believing myself in the Attick school.[3]

---

1   Primum Mobile] original cause or mover

2   enchanted ground] from the Prologue to John Dryden's heroic drama *Aureng-Zebe* (1675), line 10

3   Attick school] the Attic school or group of philosophers at Athens, led by Plato and Aristotle, revered by the Renaissance Humanists, and celebrated by the painter Raphael in "The School of Athens" (1508-11), a fresco in the Vatican commissioned by Pope Julius II to suggest the continuity between ancient Platonic philosophy and the Christian church

the scene of learning

The room where they sat was about forty-five feet long, of a proportionable breadth, with three windows on one side, which looked into a garden, and a large bow at the upper end. Over against the windows were three large book-cases, upon the top of the middle one stood an orrery,[1] and a globe on each of the others. In the bow sat two ladies reading, with pen, ink, and paper on a table before them, at which was a young girl translating out of French. At the lower end of the room was a lady painting, with exquisite art indeed, a beautiful Madona; near her another, drawing a landscape out of her own imagination; a third, carving a picture-frame in wood, in the finest manner; a fourth, engraving; and a young girl reading aloud to them; the distance from the ladies in the bow-window being such, that they could receive no disturbance from her. At the next window were placed a group of girls, from the age of ten years old to fourteen. Of these, one was drawing figures, another a landscape, a third a perspective view, a fourth engraving, a fifth carving, a sixth turning in wood, a seventh writing, an eighth cutting out linnen, another making a gown, and by them an empty chair and a tent, with embroidery, finely fancied, before it, which we afterwards found had been left by a young girl who was gone to practise on the harpsichord.

As soon as we entered they all rose up, and the house-keeper introduced us, by saying, she saw us standing under a tree to avoid the storm, and so had desired us to walk in. The ladies received us with the greatest politeness, and expressed concern, that when their house was so near, we should have recourse to so insufficient a shelter. Our surprize at the sight of so uncommon a society, occasioned our making but an awkward return to their obligating reception; nor when we observed how many arts we had interrupted, could we avoid being ashamed that we had then intruded upon them.

But before I proceed farther, I shall endeavour to give you some idea of the persons of the ladies, whose minds I shall afterwards best describe by their actions. The two who sat in the bow window were *the ladies* called Mrs. Maynard and Mrs. Selvyn. Mrs. Maynard is between forty and fifty years of age, a little woman, well made, with a lively and gen-

1   orrery] a mechanical model of the planetary system
2   tent] a frame on which embroidery or tapestry is kept while being worked on

teel air, her hair black, and her eyes of the same colour, bright and piercing, her features good, and complexion agreeable, though brown. Her countenance expresses all the vivacity of youth, tempered with a serenity which becomes her age.

Mrs. Selvyn can scarcely be called tall, though she approaches that standard. Her features are too irregular to be handsome, but there is a sensibility and delicacy in her countenance which render her extremely engaging; and her person is elegant.

Mrs. Mancel, whom we had disturbed from her painting, is tall and finely formed, has great elegance of figure, and is graceful in every motion. Her hair is of a fine brown, her eyes blue, with all that sensible sweetness which is peculiar to that colour. In short, she excels in every beauty but the bloom, which is so soon faded, and so impossible to be imitated by the utmost efforts of art, nor has she suffered any farther by years than the loss of that radiance, which renders beauty rather more resplendant than more pleasing.

Mrs. Trentham, who was carving by her, was the tallest of the company, and in dignity of air particularly excels, but her features and complexion have been so injured by the small pox, that one can but just guess they were once uncommonly fine; a sweetness of countenance, and a very sensible look, indeed, still remain, and have baffled all the most cruel ravages of that distemper.

Lady Mary Jones, whom we found engraving, seems to have been rather pleasing than beautiful. She is thin and pale, but a pair of the finest black eyes I ever saw, animate, to a great degree, a countenance, which sickness has done its utmost to render languid, but has, perhaps, only made more delicate and amiable. Her person is exquisitely genteel, and her voice, in common speech, enchantingly melodious.

Mrs. Morgan, the lady who was drawing, appears to be upwards of fifty, tall, rather plump, and extremely majestic, an air of dignity distinguishes her person, and every virtue is engraven in indelible characters on her countenance. There is a benignity in every look, which renders the decline of life, if possible, more amiable than[1] the bloom of youth. One would almost think nature had formed her for a common parent,

---

1   than] that in first edition

such universal and tender benevolence beams from every glance she casts around her.

The dress of the ladies was thus far uniform, the same neatness, the same simplicity and cleanliness appeared in each, and they were all in lutestring night-gowns, though of different colours, nor was there any thing unfashionable in their appearance, except that they were free from any trumpery ornaments. The girls were all clothed in camblet[1] coats, but not uniform in colour, their linnen extremely white and clean though coarse.[2]

Some of them were pretty, and none had any defect in person, to take off from that general pleasingness which attends youth and innocence.

They had been taught such an habit of attention, that they seemed not at all disturbed by our conversation, which was of that general kind, as might naturally be expected on such an occasion, though supported by the ladies with more sensible vivacity and politeness, than is usual, where part of the company are such total strangers to the rest; till by chance one of the ladies called Mrs. Maynard by her name.

From the moment I saw her, I thought her face not unknown to me, but could not recollect where, or when I had been acquainted with her, but her name brought to my recollection, that she was not only an old acquaintance, but a near relation. I observed, that she had looked on me with particular attention, and I begged her to give me leave to ask her, of what family of Maynards she was? her answer confirmed my supposition, and as she told me, that she believed she had some remembrance of my face, I soon made her recollect our affinity and former intimacy, though my twenty years abode in Jamaica, the alteration the climate had wrought in me, and time had made in us both, had almost effaced us from each other's memory.

There is great pleasure in renewing the acquaintance of our youth; a thousand pleasing ideas accompany it; many mirthful scenes and juvenile amusements return to the remembrance, and make us, as it were,

---

1   camblet] or camlet, a fabric, originally from Asia, made of silk and wool, and much used for
     women's apparel
2   coarse] course in first edition

live over again what is generally the most pleasing part of life. Mrs. Maynard seemed no less sensible of the satisfaction arising from this train of thoughts than myself, and the rest of the company were so indulgently good-natured, as in appearance, to share them with us. The tea table by no means interrupted our conversation, and I believe I should have forgot that our journey was not at an end, if a servant had not brought in word, that my man, who had observed our motions, was come to inform us, that our chaise could not be repaired that night.

The ladies immediately declared, that though their equipage was in order, they would not suffer it to put an end to a pleasure they owed to the accident which had happened to ours, and insisted we should give them our company till the smith had made all necessary reparations, adding, that I could not be obstinately bent on depriving Mrs. Maynard so soon of the satisfaction she received, from having recovered so long lost a relation. I was little inclined to reject this invitation: pleasure was the chief design of my journey, and I saw not how I could receive more, than by remaining in a family so extraordinary, and so perfectly agreeable. When both parties are well agreed, the necessary ceremonies previous to a compliance are soon over, and it was settled that we should not think of departing before the next day at soonest.

The continuance of the rain rendered it impossible to stir out of the house; my cousin, who seemed to think variety necessary to amuse, asked if we loved music? which being answered in the affirmative, she begged the other ladies to entertain us with one of their family concerts, and we joining in the petition, proper orders were given, and we adjourned into another room, which was well furnished with musical instruments. Over the door was a beautiful saint Cecilia,[1] painted in crayons by Mrs. Mancel, and a fine piece of carved work over the chimney, done by Mrs. Trentham, which was a very artificial representation of every sort of musical instruments.

While we were admiring these performances, the company took

---

1   Saint Cecilia] a Roman Christian forced to marry against her will, whereupon she converted her husband and both were martyred for their religious faith in 230 A.D.; she became the patron saint of music and several important English poems commemorated her as such, including Dryden's *Alexander's Feast* (see p. 96)

their respective places. Mrs. Mancel seated herself at the harpsichord, Lady Mary Jones played on the arch lute,[1] Mrs. Morgan on the organ, Mrs. Selvyn and Mrs. Trentham each on the six-stringed bass; the shepherd who had charmed us in the field was there with his German flute[2]; a venerable looking man, who is their steward, played on the violincello, a lame youth on the French horn, another, who seemed very near blind, on the bassoon, and two on the fiddle. My cousin had no share in the performance except singing agreeably, wherein she was joined by some of the ladies, and where the music could bear it, by ten of the young girls, with two or three others whom we had not seen, and whose voices and manner were equally pleasing. They performed several of the finest pieces of the Messiah and Judas Maccabeus,[3] with exquisite taste, and the most exact time. There was a sufficient number of performers to give the choruses all their pomp and fullness, and the songs were sung in a manner so touching and pathetic, as could be equalled by none, whose hearts were not as much affected by the words, as their senses were by the music. The sight of so many little innocents joining in the most sublime harmony, made me almost think myself already amongst the heavenly choir, and it was a great mortification to me to be brought back to this sensual world, by so gross an attraction as a call to supper, which put an end to our concert, and carried us to another room, where we found a repast more elegant than expensive.

The evening certainly is the most social part of the day, without any of those excesses which so often turn it into senseless revelry. The conversation after supper was particularly animated, and left us still more charmed with the society into which chance had introduced us; the sprightliness of their wit, the justness of their reflexions, the dignity

---

1   arch lute] the English term for the theorbo, or double-necked lute with two sets of tuning pegs; lute-playing was going out of fashion in England by the mid-eighteenth century

2   German flute] what is today the normal transverse or side-blown flute; around the mid-eighteenth century this replaced the earlier end-blown flute in popularity

3   Messiah; Judas Maccabeus] popular oratorios by George Frederick Handel (1685-1759); *The Messiah* (first performed 1742) was and remains one of the most popular choral works of the time; *Judas Maccabæus* (first performed 1747) was inspired by the British victory over the Scottish rebel army led by Bonnie Prince Charlie (1746), and was also very popular through the eighteenth century

which accompanied their vivacity, plainly evinced with how much greater strength the mind can exert itself in a regular and rational way of life, than in a course of dissipation. At this house every change came too soon, time seemed to wear a double portion of wings, eleven o'clock struck, and the ladies ordered a servant to shew us our rooms, themselves retiring to theirs.

It was impossible for Lamont and I to part till we had spent an hour in talking over this amiable family, with whom he could not help being much delighted, though he observed, 'they were very deficient in the bon ton,[1] there was too much solidity in all they said, they would trifle with trifles indeed, but had not the art of treating more weighty subjects with the same lightness, which gave them an air of rusticity; and he did not doubt, but on a more intimate acquaintance we should find their manners much rusticated, and their heads filled with antiquated notions, by having lived so long out of the great world.'[2]

I rose the next morning very early, desirous to make the day, which I purposed for the last of my abode in this mansion, as long as I could. I went directly into the garden, which, by what I saw from the house, was extremely pretty. As I passed by the windows of the saloon,[3] I perceived the ladies and their little pupils were earlier risers than myself, for they were all at their various employments. I first went into the gayest flower garden I ever beheld. The rainbow exhibits not half the variety of tints, and they are so artfully mingled, and ranged to make such a harmony of colours, as taught me how much the most beautiful objects may be improved by a judicious disposition of them. Beyond these beds of flowers rises a shrubbery, where every thing sweet and pleasing is collected. As these ladies have no taste but what is directed by good sense, nothing found a place here from being only uncommon, for they think few things are very rare but because they are little desirable; and indeed it is plain they are free from that littleness of mind, which makes people value a thing the more for its being possessed by no one but themselves. Behind the shrubbery is a little wood,

---

1   bon ton] polite or fashionable society, a French phrase only recently introduced into English at the time *Millenium Hall* was published
2   great world] fashionable upper-class society
3   saloon] large room or hall

which affords a gloom, rendered more agreable[1] by its contrast with the dazzling beauty of that part of the garden that leads to it. In the high pale which encloses this wood I observed a little door; curiosity induced me to pass through it; I found it opened on a row of the neatest cottages I ever saw, which the wood had concealed from my view. They were new and uniform, and therefore I imagined all dedicated to the same purpose. Seeing a very old woman spinning at one of the doors, I accosted her, by admiring the neatness of her habitation.

'Ay, indeed, said she, it is a most comfortable place, God bless the good ladies! I and my neighbours are as happy as princesses, we have every thing we want and wish, and who can say more?' 'Very few so much, answered I, but pray what share have the ladies in procuring the happiness you seem so sensible of.'

'Why Sir, continued the old woman, it is all owing to them. I was almost starved when they put me into this house, and no shame of mine, for so were my neighbours too; perhaps we were not so painstaking as we might have been; but that was not our faults, you know, as we had not things to work with, nor any body to set us to work, poor folks cannot know every thing as these good ladies do; we were half dead for want of victuals, and then people have not courage to set about any thing. Nay, all the parish were so when they came into it, young and old, there was not much to chuse, few of us had rags to cover us, or a morsel of bread to eat, except the two Squires;[2] they indeed grew rich, because they had our work, and paid us not enough to keep life and soul together; they live above a mile off, so perhaps they did not know how poor we were, I must say that for them; the ladies tell me I ought not to speak against them, for every one has faults, only we see other peoples, and are blind to our own; and certainly it is true enough, for they are very wise ladies as well as good, and must know such things.'

As my new acquaintance seemed as loquacious as her age promised, I hoped for full satisfaction, and asked her, 'How she and her neighbours employed themselves?' 'Not all alike, replied the good woman, I

---

1   agreable] as elsewhere in the text, altered to agreeable in later editions
2   Squires] principal gentry or landowners of the area

will tell you, all about it. There are twelve of us that live here. We have every one a house of two rooms, as you may see, beside other conveniences, and each a little garden, but though we are separate, we agree as well, perhaps better, than if we lived together, and all help one another. Now, there is neighbour Susan, and neighbour Rachel; Susan is lame, so she spins cloaths for Rachel; and Rachel cleans Susan's house, and does such things for her as she cannot do for herself. The ladies settled all these matters at first, and told us, that as they, to please God, assisted us, we must in order to please him serve others; and that to make us happy they would put us in a way, poor as we are, to do good to many. Thus neighbour Jane, who poor woman is almost stone deaf, they thought would have a melancholy life if she was to be always spinning and knitting, seeing other people around her talking, and not be able to hear a word they said, so the ladies busy her in making broths and caudles, and such things, for all the sick poor in this and the next parish, and two of us are fixed upon to carry what she has[1] made to those that want them; to visit them often, and spend more or less time with them every day according as they have, or have not relations to take care of them; for though the ladies always hire nurses for those who are very ill, yet they will not trust quite to them, but make us overlook them, so that in a sickly time we shall be all day going from one to another.'

'But, said I, there are I perceive many children amongst you, how happens that? your ages shew they are not your own.'

'Oh! as for that, replied my intelligencer, I will tell you how that is. You must know these good ladies, heaven preserve them! take every child after the fifth of every poor person, as soon as it can walk, till when they pay the mother for nursing it; these children they send to us to keep out of harm, and as soon as they can hold a knitting-needle to teach them to knit, and to spin, as much as they can be taught before they are four or five years old, when they are removed into one of the schools. They are pretty company for us, and make us mothers again, as it were, in our old age; then the childrens relations are all so fond of us for our care of them, that it makes us a power of[2] friends, which you

---

1   she has] they have in first edition

know is very pleasant, though we want nothing from them but their good wills.'

Here I interrupted her by observing, that it must take up a great deal of time, and stop their work, consequently lessen their profits.

'There is nothing in that, continued the good woman, the ladies steward sends us in all we want in the way of meat, drink, and firing; and our spinning we carry to the ladies; they employ a poor old weaver, who before they came broke[1] for want of work, to weave it for us, and when there is not enough they put more to it, so we are sure to have our cloathing; if we are not idle that is all they desire, except that we should be cleanly too. There never passes a day that one or other of the ladies does not come and look all over our houses, which they tell us, and certainly with truth, for it is a great deal of trouble to them, is all for our good, for that we cannot be healthy if we are not clean and neat. Then every saint's day,[2] and every Sunday after church, we all go down to the hall, and the ladies read prayers, and a sermon to us, and their own family; nor do they ever come here without giving us some good advice. We used to quarrel, to be sure, sometimes when we first came to these houses, but the ladies condescended to make it up amongst us, and shewed us so kindly how much it was our duty to agree together, and to forgive every body their faults, or else we could not hope to be forgiven by God, against whom we so often sinned, that now we love one another like sisters, or indeed better, for I often see such quarrel. Beside, they have taught us that we are generally in fault ourselves; and we find now that we take care not to be perverse, our neighbours are seldom in the wrong, and when they are, we bear with it in hopes they will bear with us when we are as much to blame, which we may be sure enough will happen, let us try ever so much to the contrary. Then the ladies seem so pleased when we do any kindness to one another, as to be sure is a great encouragement; and if any of us are sick they are so careful and so good, that it would be a shame if we did not do all we can for one another, who have been always neighbours and acquaintance, when such

---

4   power of] many
1   broke] went bankrupt
2   saint's day] day on which a particular Saint is venerated

great ladies, who never knew us, as I may say, but to make us happy, and have no reason to take care of us but that we are poor, are so kind and condescending to us.'

I was so pleased with the good effect which the charity of her benefactors had on the mind, as well as the situation of this old woman, whose neighbours by her own account were equally benefitted by the blessings they received, that I should have stayed longer with her, if a bell had not rang at Millenium Hall, which she informed me was a summons to breakfast. I obeyed its call, and after thanking her for her conversation, returned with a heart warmed and enlarged, to the amiable society. My mind was so filled with exalted reflections on their virtues, that I was less attentive to the charms of inanimate nature than when I first passed through the gardens.

After breakfast the ladies proposed a walk, and as they had seen the course I took when I first went out, they led us a contrary way, lest, they said, I should be tired with the repetition of the same scene. I told them with great truth, that 'what I had beheld could never weary, for virtue is a subject we must ever contemplate with fresh delight, and as such examples could not fail of improving every witness of them, the pleasure of reflection would encrease, as one daily grew more capable of enjoying it, by cultivating kindred sensations.' By some more explicit hints they found out to what I alluded, and thereby knew where I had been, but turning the conversation to present objects, they conducted us to a very fine wood, which is laid out with so much taste, that Lamont observed the artist's hand was never more distinguishable, and perceived in various spots the direction of the person at present most famous for that sort of improvement.

The ladies smiled, and one of them answered, 'He did their wood great honour, in thinking art had lent her assistance to nature, but that there was little in that place for which they were not solely obliged to the latter.' Mrs. Trentham interrupted her who was speaking, and told us, that, 'As she had no share in the improvements which had been made, she might with the better grace assure Mr. Lamont, that lady Mary Jones, Mrs. Mancel, and Mrs. Morgan, were the only persons who had laid out that wood, and the commonest labourers in the country had executed their orders.' Lamont was much surprized at this piece of information, and though he would have thought it still more exquisitely beautiful had it been the design of the person he imagined, yet truth is so powerful, that he could not suppress his admiration and surprize. Every cut[1] in it is terminated by some noble object. In several places are seats formed with such rustic simplicity, as have more real grandeur in them, than can be found in the most expensive buildings. On an eminence, 'bosomed high in tufted trees,'[2] is a temple dedicated to solitude. The structure is an exquisite piece of architecture, the prospect from it noble and extensive, and the windows so placed, that one sees no house but at so considerable a distance, as not to take off from that solitary air, which is perfectly agreable to a temple declaredly dedicated to solitude. The most beautiful object in the view is a very large river, in reality an arm of the sea, little more than a quarter of a mile distant from the building; about three miles beyond it lies the sea, on which the sun then shone, and made it dazzlingly bright. In the temple is a picture of Contemplation, another of Silence, two of various birds and animals, and a couple of moon-light pieces, the workmanship of the ladies.

Close by the temple runs a gentle murmuring rivulet, which flows in meanders through the rest of the wood, sometimes concealed from view, and then appearing at the next turning of the walk. The wood is well peopled with pheasants, wild turkies, squirrels and hares, who live so unmolested, that they seem to have forgot all fear, and rather to welcome than fly those who come amongst them. Man never appears there as a merciless destroyer; but the preserver, instead of the tyrant of the inferior part of the creation. While they continue in that wood, none but natural evil can approach them, and from that they are defended as much as possible. We there 'walked joint tenant of the shade,'[3] with the animal race; and a perfect equality in nature's bounty seems enjoyed by the whole creation. One could scarcely forbear thinking those happy times were come, when 'The wolf shall dwell with the lamb, and the leopard shall lye down with the kid; and the

---

1 cut] a long narrow opening in the woods or shrubbery of an extensive garden

2 'bosomed high in tufted trees'] John Milton, "L'Allegro," line 78: "Bosomd high in tufted Trees"; with its companion piece, "Il Penseroso," and some additions by another writer, "L'Allegro" was set to music by Handel in 1740

3 'walked joint tenant of the shade'] Alexander Pope, Essay on Man, Epistle III, line 152: "Man walk'd with beast, joint tenant of the shade"

Paradise –
regained!

and
a grotto.

calf, and the young lion, and the fatling together, and a young child shall lead them. The wilderness and the solitary place shall be glad for them, and the desart shall rejoice, and blossom as the rose.'[1]

At the verge of this wood, which extends to the river I have mentioned, without perceiving we were entering a building, so well is the outside of it concealed by trees, we found ourselves in a most beautiful grotto, made of fossils, spars, coral, and such shells, as are at once both fine and rustic; all of the glaring, tawdry kind are excluded, and by the gloom and simplicity preserved, one would imagine it the habitation of some devout anchoret. Ivy and moss in some places cover, while they seem to unite, the several materials of the variegated walls. The rivulet which runs through the wood, falls down one side of the grotto with great rapidity, broken into various streams by the spar[2] and coral, and passing through, forms a fine cascade just at the foot of the grotto,[3] from whence it flows into the river. Great care is taken to prevent the place from growing damp, so that we sat some time in it with safety, admiring the smooth surface of the river, to which it lies very open.

As the ladies had some daily business on their hands which they never neglect, we were obliged to leave this lovely scene, where I think I could have passed my life with pleasure, and to return towards the house, though by a different way from that we came, traversing the other side of the wood. In one spot where we went near the verge, I observed a pale, which, upon examination, I found was continued for some acres, though it was remarkable only in one place. It is painted green, and on the inside a hedge of yews, laurel, and other thick evergreens, rises[4] to about seven or eight feet high. I could not forbear asking what was thus so carefully enclosed? the ladies smiled on each other, but evaded answering my question, which only encreased my curiosity. Lamont, not less curious, and more importunate, observed, that 'the inclosure bore some resemblance to one of Lord Lamore's,

---

1   'The wolf shall dwell ... blossom as the rose'] joining two Biblical quotations: Isaiah, ch. 11, verse 6, and Isaiah, ch. 35, verse 1.
2   spar] lustrous crystalline minerals, often used for decorative purposes
3   grotto] an architectural feature designed to imitate a rocky cave, much favoured in eighteenth-century garden design
4   rises] rise in first edition

where he kept lions, tygers, leopards, and such foreign animals,[1] and he would be[2] hanged, if the ladies had not made some such collection, intreating that he might be admitted to see them; for nothing gave him greater entertainment than to behold those beautiful wild beasts, brought out of their native woods, where they had reigned as kings, and here tamed and subjected by the superior art of man. It was a triumph of human reason, which could not fail to afford great pleasure.'

'Not to us, I assure you, Sir, replied Mrs. Mancel, when reason appears only in the exertion of cruelty and tyrannical oppression, it is surely not a gift to be boasted of. When a man forces the furious steed to endure the bit, or breaks oxen to the yoke, the great benefits he receives from, and communicates to the animals, excuses the forcible methods by which it is accomplished. But to see a man, from a vain desire to have in his possession the native of another climate and another country, reduce a fine and noble creature to misery, and confine him within narrow inclosures whose happiness consisted in unbounded liberty, shocks my nature. There is I confess something so amiable in gentleness, that I could be pleased with seeing a tyger caress its keeper, if the cruel means by which the fiercest of beasts is taught all the servility of a fawning spaniel, did not recur every instant to my mind; and it is not much less abhorrent to my nature, to see a venerable lion jumping over a stick, than it would be to behold an hoary philosopher forced by some cruel tyrant to spend his days in whipping a top, or playing with a rattle. Every thing to me looses its charm when it is put out of that station wherein nature, or to speak more properly, the all-wise Creator has placed it. I imagine man has a right to use the animal race for his own preservation, perhaps for his convenience, but certainly not to treat them with wanton cruelty, and as it is not in his power to give them any thing so valuable as their liberty, it is, in my opinion, criminal to enslave them, in order to procure ourselves a vain amusement, if we have so little feeling as to find any while others suffer.'

---

1   lions ... and such foreign animals] it had been customary since ancient times for monarchs and nobles to keep collections of exotic animals, or menageries; in modern times, after the French Revolution, these tended to be kept by the state for the use of the public, as zoos

2   be] first edition has he

'I believe madam, replied Lamont, it is most adviseable for me not to attempt to defend what I have said; should I have reason on my side, while you have humanity on yours, I should make but a bad figure in the argument. What advantage could I expect from applying to the understanding, while your amiable disposition would captivate even reason itself? but still I am puzzled; what we behold is certainly an inclosure, how can that be without a confinement to those that are within it?'

'After having spoken so much against tyranny, said Mrs. Mancel smiling, I do not know whether I should be excusable, if I left you to be tyrannized by curiosity, which I believe can inflict very severe pains, at least, if I may be allowed to judge by the means people often take to satisfy it. I will therefore gratify you with the knowledge of what is within this inclosure, which makes so extraordinary an impression upon you. It is, then, an asylum for those poor creatures who are rendered miserable from some natural deficiency or redundancy.[1]

Here they find refuge from the tyranny of those wretches, who seem to think that being two or three feet taller gives them a right to make them a property, and expose their unhappy forms to the contemptuous curiosity of the unthinking multitude. Procrustes has been branded through all ages with the name of tyrant; and principally, as it appears, from fitting the body of every stranger to a bed which he kept as the necessary standard, cutting off the legs of those whose height exceeded the length of it, and stretching on the rack such as fell short of that measure, till they attained the requisite proportion. But is not almost every man a Procrustes? we have not the power of shewing our cruelty exactly in the same method, but actuated by the like spirit, we abridge of their liberty, and torment by scorn, all who either fall short, or exceed the usual standard, if they happen to have the additional misfortune of poverty. Perhaps we are in no part more susceptible than in our vanity, how much then must those poor wretches suffer, whose deformity would lead them to wish to be secluded from human view, in being exposed to the public, whose observations are no better than expressions of scorn, and who are surprized to find that any thing less than themselves can speak, or appear like intelligent beings. But this is only part of what they have to endure.

---

1   natural deficiency or redundancy] congenital malformation

i.e., they BOUGHT them?

As if their deficiency in height deprived them of the natural right to air and sunshine, they are kept confined in small rooms, and because they fill less space than common, are stuffed into chairs so little, that they are squeezed as close as a pair of gloves in a walnut-shell.

'This miserable treatment of persons, to whom compassion should secure more than common indulgence, determined us to purchase these worst sort of slaves, and in this place we have five who owed their wretchedness to being only three foot high, one grey-headed toothless old man of sixteen years of age, a woman of about seven foot in height, and a man who would be still taller, if the extreme weakness of his body, and the wretched life he for some time led, in the hands of one of these monster-mongers, did not make him bend almost double, and oblige him to walk on crutches; with which infirmities he is well pleased, as they reduce him nearer the common standard.'

We were very desirous of seeing this enfranchised[1] company; but Mrs. Morgan told us it was what they seldom granted, for fear of inflicting some of the pains from which they had endeavoured to rescue those poor creatures, but she would step in, and ask if they had no objection to our admission, and if that appeared really the case she would gratify us.

This tenderness to persons who were under such high obligations, charmed me. She soon returned with the permission we wished, but intreated us to pay all our attention to the house and garden, and to take no more than a civil notice of its inhabitants. We promised obedience, and followed her. Her advice was almost unnecessary, for the place could not have failed of attracting our particular observation. It was a quadrangle of about six acres, and the inward part was divided by nets into eight parts, four of which alternatively were filled with poultry of all sorts, which were fed here for the use of the hall, and kept with the most exact cleanliness. The other four parts were filled with shrubs and flowers, which were cultivated with great delight by these once unfortunate, but now happy beings. A little stream ran across the quadrangle, which served for drink to the poultry, and facilitated the watering of the flowers. I have already said, that at the inward edge of the pale was a row of ever-greens; at their feet were beds of flowers, and a little gravel walk went round the whole. At each corner was an arbour made with woodbines and jessamine, in one or two of which there was always an agreeable shade.

At one side of the quadrangle was a very neat habitation, into which

---

1   enfranchised] here, set free, rather than endowed with the right to vote

a dwarf invited us to enter, to rest ourselves after our walk; they were all passing backwards and forwards, and thus gave us a full view of them, which would have been a shocking sight, but for the reflexions we could not avoid making on their happy condition, and the very extraordinary humanity of the ladies to whom they owed it; so that instead of feeling the pain one might naturally receive from seeing the human form so disgraced, we were filled with admiration of the human mind, when so nobly exalted by virtue, as it is in the patronesses of these poor creatures, who wore an air of chearfulness, which shewed they thought the churlishness wherewith they had been treated by nature sufficiently compensated. The tender inquiries the ladies made after their healths, and the kind notice they took of each of them, could not be exceeded by anything but the affection, I might almost say adoration, with which these people beheld their benefactresses.

This scene had made too deep an impression on our minds, not to be the subject of our discourse all the way home, and in the course of conversation, I learnt, that when these people were first rescued out of their misery, their healths were much impaired, and their tempers more so: to restore the first, all medicinal care was taken, and air and exercise assisted greatly in their recovery; but to cure the malady of the mind, and conquer that internal source of unhappiness, was a work of longer time. Even these poor wretches had their vanity, and would contend for superior merit, of which, the argument was the money their keepers had gained in exhibiting them. To put an end to this contention, the ladies made them understand, that what they thought a subject for boasting, was only a proof of their being so much farther from the usual standard of the human form, and therefore a more extraordinary spectacle. But it was long before one of them could be persuaded to lay aside her pretensions to superiority, which she claimed on account of an extraordinary honour she had received from a great princess, who had made her a present of a sedan chair.

At length, however, much reasoning and persuasion, a conviction of principles, of which they had before no knowledge, the happiness of their situation, and the improvement of their healths, concurred to sweeten their tempers, and they now live in great harmony. They are entirely mistresses of their house, have two maids to wait on them, over whom they have sole command, and a person to do such little

things in their garden as they cannot themselves perform; but the culti-
vation of it is one of their great pleasures; and by their extraordinary
care, they have the satisfaction of presenting the finest flowers of the
spring to their benefactresses, before they are blown in any other place.

When they first came, the ladies told us, that the horror they had
conceived of being exhibited as public spectacles, had fixed in them
such a fear of being seen by any stranger, that the sound of a voice,
with which they were not acquainted at the outside of the pailing,[1] or
the trampling of feet, would set them all a running behind the bushes
to hide themselves, like so many timorous partridges in a mew, hurry-
ing behind sheaves of corn[2] for shelter; they even found a convenience
in their size, which, though it rendered them unwilling to be seen, enabled them so easily to find places for concealment.

By degrees the ladies brought them to consent to see their head servants, and some of the best people in the parish; desiring, that to render
it more agreeable to their visitors, they would entertain them with fruit
and wine; advising them to assist their neighbours in plain work; thus
to endear themselves to them, and procure more frequent visits, which
as they chose to confine themselves within so narrow a compass, and
enjoyed but precarious health, their benefactresses thought a necessary
amusement. These recommendations, and the incidents wherewith
their former lives had furnished them to amuse their company, and
which they now could relate with pleasure, from the happy sense that
all mortifications were past, rendered their conversation much courted
among that rank of people.

It occurred to me, that their dislike to being seen by numbers, must
prevent their attendance on public worship, but my cousin informed
me that was thus avoided. There was in the church an old gallery,
which from disuse was grown out of repair; this the ladies caused to be
mended, and the front of it so hightened,[3] that these little folks when in
it could not be seen; the tall ones contrived by stooping when they
were there, not to appear of any extraordinary height: To this they

---

1   pailing] i.e., paling, or fence
2   corn] grain or seed of cereal plants
3   hightened] heightened in later editions

were conveyed in the ladies coach, and set down close to covered stairs, which led up to the gallery.

This subject employed our conversation till we approached the hall; the ladies then, after insisting that we should not think of going from thence that day, all left us except Mrs. Maynard. It may seem strange that I was not sorry for their departure; but, in truth, I was so filled with astonishment, at characters so new, and so curious to know by what steps women thus qualified both by nature and fortune to have the world almost at command, were brought thus to seclude themselves from it, and make as it were a new one for themselves, constituted on such very different principles from that I had hitherto lived in, that I longed to be alone with my cousin, in hopes I might from her receive some account of this wonder. I soon made my curiosity known, and beseeched her to gratify it.

'I see no good reason, said she, why I should not comply with your request, as my friends are above wishing to conceal any part of their lives, though themselves are never the subject of their own conversation. If they have had any follies they do not desire to hide them; they have not pride enough to be hurt with candid criticisms, and have too much innocence to fear any very severe censures. But as we did not all reach this paradise at the same time, I shall begin with the first inhabitants of, and indeed the founders of this society, Mrs. Mancel and Mrs. Morgan, who from their childhood have been so connected, that I could not, if I would, disunite them in my relation; and it would be almost a sin to endeavour to separate them even in idea.'

We sat down in an arbour, whose shade invited us to seek there a defence against the sun, which was then in its meridian, and shone with uncommon heat. The woodbines, the roses, the jessamines, the pinks, and above all, the minionette[1] with which it was surrounded, made the air one general perfume; every breeze came loaded with fragrance, stealing and giving odour. A rivulet ran bubbling by the side of the arbour, whose gentle murmurs soothed the mind into compo-

---

1   minionette] mignonette, a trailing plant prized for the fragrance of its greenish white flowers, cultivated in England from about the mid-eighteenth century; also known as bastard-rocket and reseda

sure, and seemed to hush us to attention, when Mrs. Maynard thus began, to shew her readiness to comply with my request.

intro to the STORIES of the ladies!

THE HISTORY of
Miss MANCEL, and Mrs. MORGAN.

Y o u may perhaps think I am presuming on your patience, when I lead
you into a nursery, or a boarding-school; but the life of Louisa Mancel,
was so early chequered with that various fate, which gives this world the
motley appearance of joy and sorrow, pain and pleasure, that it is not in
my power to pass over the events of her infancy. I shall, however, spare
you all that is possible, and recommend her to your notice only when
she attracted the observation of Mr. Hintman. This gentleman hearing
that a person who rented some land of him was come to London, and
lodged at one of those public houses which by the landlord is called an
inn, at the out-skirts of London, on the Surry-side; and having some occasion to speak to him, he went thither. The people of the house called
the man Mr. Hintman enquired for, who immediately came down
stairs, wiping tears from his eyes; the continuance of which he could
hardly restrain. Mr. Hintman asking the reason of those appearances of
sorrow, the good-natured old man told him, his visit had called him
from a scene which had shocked him excessively. 'The first day I came
here, said he, I was induced by the frequent groans which issued from
the next chamber, to enquire who lodged there; I learnt, it was a gentlewoman, who arrived the day before, and was immediately taken so
ill that they apprehended her life in danger; and, about two hours ago,
the maid of the house ran into my room, begging me to come to her
assistance, for the gentlewoman was in such strong fits, she was not able
to hold her. I obeyed the summons, and found the poor woman in fits
indeed; but what appeared to me the last agonies of a life, which near
exhausted, lavishes away its small remains in strong convulsions.

'By her bed-side stood the most beautiful child I ever beheld, in appearance about ten years of age, crying as if its little heart would break;
not with the rage of an infant, but with the settled grief of a person mature both in years and affliction. I asked her if the poor dying woman
was her mother; she told me, no, – she was only her aunt; but to her
the same as a mother; and she did not know any one else that would
take care of her.

'After a time the poor woman's convulsions left her; – she just recovered sense enough to embrace the lovely girl, and cried out, Oh!
my dear child, what will become of you! a friendless, helpless infant;
and seeing me at her bed-side, she lifted up her hands in a suppliant
posture; and with eyes that petitioned in stronger terms than words
could express, Oh! Sir, said she, though you are a stranger to me, yet I
see you are not so to humanity; – take pity on this forlorn child; – her
amiable disposition will repay you in this world, – and the great Father
of us all will reward you in the next, for your compassion on a
wretched friendless girl! – but why do I call her friendless! – her innocence has the best of friends in heaven; – the Almighty is a parent she is
not left to seek for; he is never absent; – Oh! blessed Lord! – cried she,
with a degree of extacy and confidence, which most sensibly affected
us all, – to thy care I resign her; – thy tender mercies are over all thy
works, – and thou, who carest for the smallest part of thy creation, will
not deny her thy protection. Oh! Lord defend her innocence! – let her
obtain a place in thy kingdom after death; and, – for all the rest – I submit to thy providence; nor presumptuously pretend, to dictate to supreme wisdom. Thou art a gracious father; – and the afflictions thou
sendest are – Here her voice failed her; – but, by her gestures, we could
perceive she continued praying; and, having before taken the child in
her arms; – the little angel continued there for fear of disturbing her. –
By looks sometimes turned towards the poor infant, and sometimes
with her hand on her own heart, and then her eyes lifted up as it were
to heaven, we saw she mixed prayers for the little mourner, with inter-
cessions for herself, till sense and motion seemed to fail her; she then
fell into a convulsion, and expired.

'The little girl perceived she was dead; and became, almost as senseless, as the lump of clay which had so lately been her only friend. We
had but just taken her from the body sir, when you came; and this was
the occasion of the emotions you observed in me.

'The cause was indeed sufficient, replied Mr. Hintman, but I am
glad your sorrow proceeded from nothing more immediately concerning yourself: – Misery will strike its arrows into a humane heart; but
the wounds it makes are not so lasting, as those which are impressed by
passions that are more relative to ourselves. – Oh sir, – said the old
man, – you cannot form an adequate idea of the effect this scene must

have on every spectator, except you had seen the child! surely nature never formed so lovely a little creature!' He continued his praises of Louisa, till at length he excited Mr. Hintman's curiosity; who expressing a desire of seeing this miracle, he was carried up into the good man's room, to which they had removed her. She, who had cried most bitterly before the fatal stroke arrived, was now so oppressed, as not to be able to shed a tear. They had put her on the bed, where she lay sighing with a heart ready to break; her eyes fixed on one point, she neither saw nor heard.

Though her countenance expressed unutterable woe, yet she looked so extremely beautiful, that Mr. Hintman, highly as his expectation had been raised, was struck with surprize. He allowed he never saw any thing so lovely; and the charms of which her melancholy might deprive her, were more than compensated in his imagination by so strong a proof of extreme sensibility, at an age when few children perceive half the dreadful consequences of such a misfortune.

He advised that she should be blooded,[1] to prevent any ill effects from so severe a shock; for as she felt it as strongly as one of a more mature age, the same precautions should be used. In this he was obeyed; and it gave her such relief that she burst into a flood of tears a change which appeared so salutary, that Mr. Hintman would not immediately interrupt her. But his curiosity did not suffer him long to forbear asking her name, and many other particulars; several of which she could not answer; – all the account she was able to give of herself was, that 'her name was Mancel; that the person for whom she grieved was her aunt; but had had the sole care of her from her earliest remembrance. This aunt, she said, had often told her she had a father and mother living; but when she enquired why she never saw or heard from them; she could get no satisfactory answer, but was put off with being told they were not in England; – and that she should know when she grew older.

'This person had bred her up with the utmost tenderness, and employed the most assiduous care in her education; which was the princi-

---

1   blooded] having some blood let from a vein, either by incision or by the application of leeches; a widely practised medical procedure in the eighteenth century, designed to assist in recovery from fainting or illness by letting of a supposed surfeit of blood

pal object of her attention. They had lived in a neat cottage in the most retired part of Surry from Miss Mancel's earliest remembrance, till her aunt, after having been some time in a bad state of health, fell into a galloping consumption. As soon as she apprehended the danger with which her life was threatned, she prepared every thing for her removal to London; but as she did not expect ever to return, this took more time than the quickness of her decay could well allow. The hasty approach of her dissolution affected her extremely on the account of her little niece, and she often expressed her concern in terms intelligible to her who was the occasion of it, who gathered from the expressions which fell from her aunt, that the motive for the journey was to find out some of Miss Mancel's relations, to whom she might deliver her before death had put a period to her own life; – and where she might safely remain till the return of her parents into England.

'In this resolution she discharged the only servant she kept, delivered up her house to her landlord, and, after having settled all her pecuniary affairs, she set out on her journey with her little charge; but grew so ill on the road, that she desired to be set down at the first inn; and her illness encreased so fast she had no thought of removing; nor was she able to make any very exact enquiries after the persons of whom she came in search.'

This account was interrupted with many tears, which served to render it more affecting, and Mr. Hintman – as much touched as the good old man, who was the occasion of his having heard it, – agreed with him, that it would be proper to examine into the effects of which the deceased was then possessed; and to see if they could find any paper which would in a degree clear up the mysterious part of this affair.

This was accordingly performed; but as to the latter intention without any success; for after all the examination they could make, they remained as much in the dark as ever.

They found in her trunk rather more money than was requisite to bury her in a manner becoming her rank; to defray the expences of her sickness; and to reward those that had attended her.

The old man expressed a willingness to take the child; – he said, 'it was a legacy left him by one who had conceived some confidence in his humanity, and he could not in conscience disappoint an opinion which did him honour; though, having children of his own, he did not pretend to breed her up in the genteel manner to which she seemed by birth entitled.'

Mr. Hintman replied, that, 'he should have great reason to reproach himself, if with the ample fortune he enjoyed, and having no children, or family to partake of it, he should suffer another to take that charge, to whom it could not be so convenient; he therefore would immediately receive her as his child; and see her educated in all accomplishments proper for a young person of fashion and fortune; as he should be able to supply all deficiency, if necessary, in the latter particular.'

The old man was very glad to have the child better established than with him; though he had for some hours looked with so much pleasure on her as his adopted daughter, that no consideration, but the prospect of her greater advantage, could have reconciled him to parting with her.

In pursuance of the resolution Mr. Hintman had taken, he carried Miss Mancel to a French boarding school, which he had heard commended; very prudently judging, that his house was not a proper place for education, having there no one fit to take care of a young person.

Louisa was so oppressed by the forlornness of her situation, that she felt none of that reluctance to going amongst strangers, so usual with children of her age. All the world was equally unknown to her, therefore she was indifferent where she was carried, only she rather wished not to have been taken from the good old man, whose venerable aspect, and compassionate behaviour, had in some degree attached her to him; – but she felt the generosity of Mr. Hintman's declared intentions; and, young as she was, had too much delicacy to appear ungrateful, by shewing an unwillingness to accompany him. Mademoiselle d'Avaux, the mistress of the school, was pleased with the appearance of her young scholar, whose tears had ceased for some time; and her face bore no disfiguring signs of sorrow; the dejection which overspread it, giving charms equal to those of which it robbed it.

Mr. Hintman desired Mademoiselle d'Avaux to take the trouble of providing Miss Mancel with all things requisite, and to put her in proper mourning; those minute feminine details being things of which he was too ignorant to acquit himself well; and gave strict charge that her mind should be cultivated with the greatest care, and no accomplishment omitted which she was capable of acquiring.

What contributed much towards gratifying this wish of Mr. Hintman's, was Mademoiselle d'Avaux's house being so full, that there was no room for Louisa, but a share of the apartment which Miss Melvyn had hitherto enjoyed alone, and of which she could not willingly have admitted any one to partake but the lovely child who was presented to her for this purpose. Her beautiful form prejudiced every one in her favour; but the distress and sorrow which were impressed on her countenance, at an age generally too volatile and thoughtless to be deeply affected, could not fail of exciting a tender sensibility in the heart of a person of Miss Melvyn's disposition.

This young lady was of a very peculiar turn of Mind. She had been the darling daughter of Sir Charles and Lady Melvyn, whose attachment to her had appeared equal; but, in the former, it was rather the result of habit, and compliance with Lady Melvyn's behaviour, than a deep-rooted affection, of which his heart was not very susceptible; while Lady Melvyn's arose from that entire fondness which maternal love, and the most distinguishing reason could excite in the warmest and tenderest of hearts.

Sir Charles was an easy tempered weak man, who gave no proof of good sense, but the secret deference he had to his wife's judgment, whose very superior understanding was on nothing so assiduously employed, as in giving consequence to the man with whom she was united, by the desire of her parents, contrary to her inclination. Their authority had been necessary to reduce her to compliance, not from any particular dislike to Sir Charles, who had deservedly the reputation of sobriety, and great good nature, and whose person was remarkably fine; but Lady Melvyn perceived the weakness of his understanding, and ignorant of the strength of her own, was unwilling to enter into life without a guide, whose judgment was equal to the desire he might naturally be supposed to have to direct her right, through all the various paths in which she might be obliged to walk; an assistance she had always expected from an husband; and thought, even a necessary part of that character. She was besides sensible of the difficulty of performing a promise so solemnly made, as that of honour and obedience to one who, though she knew not half her own excellence, she must be sensible was her inferior.

These reasons had deterred Lady Melvyn from marrying Sir Charles, but when she could no longer avoid it without violating her duty *lady Mrs wise handling of her simple husband —*

to her parents, she resolved to supply the apparent deficiencies in her husband's understanding, by a most respectful deference to his opinions, thus conferring distinction on him, whom she wished every one to esteem and honour; for as there was no affectation in this part of her conduct, any more than in the rest of her behaviour, all were convinced, that the man who was respected by a woman of an understanding so superior to most of her own sex, and the greatest part of the other, must have great merit, though they could not perceive wherein it consisted.

In company Lady Melvyn always endeavoured to turn the conversation on such subjects as she knew were best suited to Sir Charles's capacity, more desirous that he should appear to advantage, than to display her own talents. She contrived to make all her actions appear the result of his choice, and whatever he did by her instigation, seemed even to himself to have been his own thought. As their way of life was in every circumstance consonant to reason, religion, and every virtue which could render them useful and respectable to others, Sir Charles acquired a character in the neighbourhood, which Lady Melvyn thought a sufficient reward for the endeavours she used to secure it to him; – and, for that purpose, fixed her abode entirely in the country, where his conduct might give him the respect, which would not be so easily obtained in a gayer scene, where talents are in higher estimation than virtue.

Sir Charles and Lady Melvyn had no other child than the daughter I have mentioned, whose education was her mother's great care; and she had the pleasure of seeing in her an uncommon capacity, with every virtue the fondest parent could wish; and which indeed she had by inheritance; but her mother's humility, made them appear to her, as a peculiar gift of providence to her daughter.

Lady Melvyn soon began to instil all the principles of true religion into her daughter's infant mind; and, by her judicious instructions, gave her knowledge far superior to her years; which was indeed the most delightful task of this fond parent; for her daughter's uncommon docility and quick parts, continually stimulated by her tenderness for the best of mothers,[1] made her improve even beyond Lady Melvyn's expectation.

---

[1]   mothers] mother's in first to third editions

In this happy situation Miss Melvyn continued till near the end of her fourteenth year, when she had the misfortune to lose this excellent parent, nor was she the only sufferer by Lady Melvyn's death; every poor person within her knowledge lost a benefactress; – all who knew her, an excellent example; – and, some, the best of friends; but her extraordinary merit was but imperfectly known till after her decease; for she had made Sir Charles appear so much the principal person, and director of all their affairs; that till the change in his conduct proved how great her influence had been, she had only shared the approbation, which, afterwards, became all her own.

Human nature cannot feel a deeper affliction than now overwhelmed Miss Melvyn; wherein Sir Charles bore as great a share, as the easiness of his nature was capable of; – but his heart was not susceptible, either of strong, or lasting impressions. He walked in the path Lady Melvyn had traced out for him; and suffered his daughter to imitate her mother in benevolent duties; and she had profitted too much by the excellent pattern, whereby she had endeavoured to regulate her actions, not to acquit herself far beyond what could have been expected at her years.

Miss Melvyn was not long indulged in the only consolation her grief could receive, – that of being permitted to aim at an imitation of her mother, – for Sir Charles had not been a widower quite a year, when he married a young lady in the neighbourhood, who had designed him this honour from the hour of Lady Melvyn's death; and to procure better opportunity for affecting her purpose, had pretended a most affectionate compassion for Miss Melvyn's deep affliction; she visited her continually; and appeared so tenderly attached to her, that Miss Melvyn, – who had neither experience, nor any guile in her own heart to inspire her with suspicions of an attempt to deceive her, made that return of affection which she thought gratitude required; nor was she at all disturbed when she found she was soon to look on this lady in another light, than that in which she had hitherto seen her; it was easy for her to respect one whom she before loved; and she had been taught so true a veneration for her father, that she felt no averseness to obey whomsoever he thought proper to give a title to her duty.

Miss Melvyn had but very little time to congratulate herself on having acquired for a mother, a friend in whose conversation she hoped to enjoy

Sir Charles remarried very badly–

bad
Stepmother

great satisfaction, and to feel the tenderness of an intimate changed into the fondness of a parent. She behaved to her with the same perfect respect, and all the humility of obedience, as if nature had placed her in that parental relation; fearing, if she gave way to the familiarity which had subsisted between them when they were on an equality, it might appear like a failure in the reverence due to her new situation.

But this behaviour, amiable as it was, could not make the now Lady Melvyn change the plan she had formed for her future conduct. She had not been married above a month, before she began to intimate to Sir Charles, 'that Miss Melvyn's education had been very imperfect; – that a young lady of her rank ought to be highly accomplished;[1] but that after she had been so long indulged by her parents, if a mother-in-law were to pretend to direct her, it might not only exasperate Miss Melvyn, but prejudice the world against herself; as people are too apt to determine against persons in that relation, without examining the merits of the cause; and though, she said, she was little concerned about the opinion of the world, in comparison with her tender regard for any one that belonged to him; yet she was much influenced by the other reason she had alledged, for not appearing to dictate to Miss Melvyn, being very desirous of keeping on affectionate terms with her; and she was already much mortified, at perceiving that young lady had imbibed too many of the vulgar prejudices against a mother-in-law; though, for her part, she had endeavoured to behave with submission to her daughter, instead of pretending to assume any authority.' The consequence and conclusion of all these insinuations was, that 'it would be adviseable to send Miss Melvyn to a boarding school.'

Sir Charles was soon prevailed with to comply with his lady's request; and his daughter was acquainted with the determination; which Lady Melvyn assured her, 'was very contrary to her inclination, who should find a great loss of so agreeable a friend, but that Sir Charles had declared his intention in so peremptory a manner, that she dared not contend.'

---

1   accomplished] having what were called "accomplishments," or certain skills such as dancing, the ability to sing and play music or draw and paint, and knowledge of modern languages, especially French and Italian; these skills were supposed to make a woman more attractive on the marriage market

Miss Melvyn had before observed, that marriage had made a great alteration in Lady Melvyn's behaviour; but this was a stroke she did not expect, and a very mortifying one to her, who had long laid aside all childish amusements; had been taught to employ herself as rationally as if she had arrived at a maturer age, and been indulged in the exercise of a most benevolent disposition, having given such good proofs of the propriety with which she employed both her time and money, that she had been dispensed from all restraints; and now to commence a new infancy, and be confined to the society of children, was a very afflicting change; but it came from a hand she too much respected to make any resistance, though she easily perceived that it was entirely at her mother's instigation; and knew her father too well, to believe he could be peremptory on any occasion. *[boarding school]*

A very short time intervened between the declaration and execution of this design, and Miss Melvyn was introduced to mademoiselle d'Avaux by her kind mother-in-law, who with some tears, and many assurances of regret, left her there. Miss Melvyn had been at this school three months when Louisa Mancel was brought thither, and though a separation from a father she sincerely loved, and the fear of the arts Lady Melvyn might use to alienate his affections from her, after having thus removed her from his presence, greatly affected her spirits, and she found no companions fit to amuse her rational mind, yet she endeavoured to support her mortifications with all the chearfulness she could assume; and received some satisfaction from the conversation of Mademoiselle d'Avaux, a woman of tolerable understanding, and who was much pleased with Miss Melvyn's behaviour.

Miss Mancel's dejected air prejudiced Miss Melvyn much in her favour; the usual consequence of a similitude of mind or manners; and when by a farther knowledge of her, she perceived her uncommon share of understanding; her desire to learn; the strength of her application; the quickness of her apprehension;[1] and her great sweetness of temper, she grew extremely fond of her; and as Miss Mancel's melancholy rendered her little inclined to play with those of her own age, she was almost always with Miss Melvyn, who found great pleasure in *[a perfect friendship]*

---

1   apprehension] the power of grasping with the intellect or understanding

endeavouring to instruct her; and grew to feel for her the tenderness of a mother, while Miss Mancel began to receive consolation from experiencing an affection quite maternal.

At the beginning of the winter, Lady Melvyn, who had less ambition to imitate the real merit of her predecessor, than to exhibit her own imaginary perfections, brought Sir Charles to London, there to fix their residence for the ensuing half year. This made little alteration in Miss Melvyn's way of life. Sir Charles and his lady would sometimes call upon her, the latter not choosing to trust Sir Charles alone with his daughter, lest she should represent to him, how unworthily she was treated; but as he was not devoid of affection for her, he would sometimes visit her privately; concealing it from his lady, who endeavoured to prevent this, by telling him, that 'school-mistresses were apt to take amiss a parent's visiting his children too often, construing it as a distrust of their care; and therefore if he offended in that way, Mademoiselle d'Avaux's disgust might affect her behaviour to Miss Melvyn, and render her residence there very disagreeable, which Lady Melvyn's *great tenderness* made her ardently wish to avoid, as she was desirous every thing should be agreeable to her dear daughter.' Sir Charles could not be entirely restrained by these *kind* admonitions, from indulging himself with the sight of Miss Melvyn.

His lady had little reason to be afraid of these interviews, for her daughter-in-law had too strong a sense of filial obedience, and too delicate a regard for her father's happiness, to suffer the least intimation of a fault in his wife to escape her lips, as a good opinion of her was so necessary to his ease; but as she soon found out these visits were made by stealth, they gave her great pleasure, as a plain proof of his affection. Lady Melvyn thought her daughter's coming abroad would be as *hurtful* as her being visited at home, and therefore very seldom sent for her to her house; and when she did, took care to have her carried home before the hour that she expected company, on pretence of preserving the regularity of hours, which she knew would be agreeable to Mademoiselle d'Avaux.

The true reason of this great caution, was an unwillingness to be seen with one whose person, all her vanity could not prevent her from being sensible,[1] was more attractive than her own. Miss Melvyn was

---

1   sensible] endowed with good sense, judicious

very pretty, had an engaging sweetness in her countenance, and all the bloom which belongs to youth, though it does not always accompany it. Her person was elegant, and perfectly genteel.

Lady Melvyn was void of delicacy;[1] she had a regular set of features, but they wanted to be softened into effeminacy, before they could have any just pretence to beauty. Her eyes were black, and not void of vivacity, but they neither expressed penetration nor gentleness. Her person was well proportioned, but she was formed on too large a scale, and destitute of grace. She was not ill bred, but had none of that softness of manners which gives rise to all the sweet civilities of life. In short, Lady Melvyn was one, who, by herself, and many others, would be esteemed a fine woman, and by many more, ranked only under the denomination of a shewey woman; like Mr. Bayes's hero,[2] she was unamiable, but she was great; she excited the admiration of some, but pleased none.

As soon as she appeared in the world as Lady Melvyn, she began to exercise what she thought only lively coquetry; but her entire want of grace and delicacy, often made that appear like boldness, which she designed for vivacity. As her ambition to charm was as great as if she had been better qualified for success, it is not strange, that she did not choose to give opportunities of comparison between herself and a daughter, who, though not so striking at first sight, was filled with attractions.

The contempt which her ladyship thought she must in justice to her own understanding shew for her husband's, and the supercilious coldness with which she treated Miss Melvyn, made that young lady very glad that she was so seldom sent for to her father's house. But she wished to learn such accomplishments, as whilst she lived in the country were out of her power, and therefore intimated to lady Melvyn her desire of being taught music and drawing, with the better hope of success, as the necessity of compleating her education had been made the

---

1   delicacy] refined sense of what is becoming, modest, or proper, together with sensitivity to the feelings of others

2   Mr. Bayes's hero] Bayes is the bad dramatist (supposed to be based on the poet and playwright John Dryden) burlesqued in *The Rehearsal* (1671), a play by George Villiers, Duke of Buckingham; Bayes's hero is Drawcansir, a burlesque of Dryden's swashbuckling martial hero Almanzor in his *The Conquest of Granada*

excuse for sending her to a boarding school; but this request was denied her on frivolous pretences, the real cause, when she perceived the very extravagant turn of her mother-in-law, she soon understood was to avoid expence.

She had flattered herself she might obtain permission to have her books sent to her; but upon enquiry, found that Lady Melvyn had removed them to her dressing-room, and intermixed them with china, in so ornamental a manner, so truly expressive of the turn of her mind, where a pretended love of reading was blended with a real fondness for trifles, that she had no chance for this indulgence.

While Miss Melvyn was suffering all these mortifications from a parent, Miss Mancel was receiving every proof of the most tender affection from one bound to her by no paternal ties. Mr. Hintman, as soon as the season of the year brought him to town, visited his little charge, and was charmed with the vivacity which was now restored to her. He called upon her frequently, and seldom without some present, or a proposal of some pleasure. He would continually entreat her to make him some request, that he might have the pleasure of gratifying her. He frequently gave Mademoiselle d'Avaux tickets for the play and the opera, that the young Louisa might have somebody to accompany her; but as Miss Melvyn did not think it proper at her age to go often with only her school-mistress, or, according to the language of schools, her governess, Miss Mancel frequently declined being of the party, rather than leave her amiable friend and instructor.

There was no one who shewed any particular civility to Miss Mancel, but received some return from Mr. Hintman. Miss Melvyn was very deservedly the chief object of his gratitude; but as she declined accepting the presents he offered her, he chose a way more agreeable to himself, as it would make his little Louisa the rewarder of the favours she received. He therefore was lavish of his money to her, and entreated her to lay it out in such manner, as would be most agreeable to herself and Miss Melvyn; at the same time asking her, 'by what means she could most gratify that young lady?'

Miss Mancel said, 'she knew nothing that would be so acceptable to Miss Melvyn as books.' To this Mr. Hintman replied, 'Since that was the case, he could very easily accommodate them, for he had by him a very pretty library left him by his sister about a year before, which he had never unpacked, having most of the same books in his own study.'

This accordingly he sent to Miss Mancel, with proper book-cases to contain them, which they immediately put up in their apartments. This was the most agreeable acquisition imaginable; for Miss Hintman having been a very sensible young lady, the collection was extremely valuable.

Mr. Hintman's great indulgence could not fail of receiving from Miss Mancel the wish'd for return of affection and gratitude; whenever he came she flew to him with delight, caressed him with all the fondness so enchanting at that age, and parted from him with the extremest reluctance. Her great obligations to him were the frequent subjects of her discourse with Miss Melvyn, who had the highest admiration of his generosity.

His allowance to Miss Mancel was sufficient to have defrayed all her expences, but those were to be the care of Mademoiselle d'Avaux, for the money he gave Louisa was for no other purpose than her gratifications; necessity, or even usefulness was out of the question; every thing of that kind being provided for her. Nor was he more sparing in what concerned her education, she learnt dancing, music, and drawing; besides other things generally taught at schools; but her greatest improvement was from reading with Miss Melvyn, who instructed her in geography, and in such parts of philosophy of which her age was capable; but above all, she was most attentive to inculcate into her mind the principles of true religion.

Thus her understanding opened in a surprizing degree, and while the beauty and graces of her person, and her great progress in genteel accomplishments, charmed every eye, the nice discernment, and uncommon strength of reason which appeared in her conversation, astonished every judicious observer; but her most admirable qualities were her humility and modesty; which, notwithstanding her great internal and external excellencies, rendered her diffident, mild, bashful, and tractable; her heart seemed as free from defects, as her understanding was from the follies, which in a degree are incident to almost every other person.

Miss Melvyn and her little companion received a considerable encrease of happiness from the present of books Mr. Hintman had made them; the latter had no wish, but that Miss Melvyn might receive equal indulgence from parents, that she enjoyed from one who bore no relation to her. The first desire that occurred to her on Mr. Hintman's profuse presents of money, was to treat her friend with masters for music and drawing, and such other things as she knew she had an inclination to learn; but as she was not unacquainted with her delicacy on that subject, as soon as Mr. Hintman left her, she ran to Miss Melvyn with some of the impatience in her countenance, though she endeavoured to conceal it, with which her heart was filled, and tried every tender caress, every fond and humble petition, to obtain a promise from that young lady, that she would grant her a request she had to make. She hung round her neck, and endeavoured to prevail by a thousand engaging infantine arts; and when she found they would not succeed, she knelt down before her, and with all the grace and importunity of the most amiable suppliant, tried to win her to compliance. Nothing would avail, for Miss Melvyn was convinced by her earnestness, that her design was to confer some favour; she knew the generosity of her youthful mind too well to believe she so ardently aimed at any thing that was for her own private gratification.

Thus Louisa found herself reduced to explain the use she intended to have made of the promise she wanted to obtain; and having acquainted Miss Melvyn with Mr. Hintman's generous allowance, and of the payment she had received of the first quarter,[1] she in explicit terms told her, 'Mr. Hintman has indeed given me money, but it depends on you to make that money yield me pleasure, by suffering me to apply it to such uses, as will procure me the inexpressible joy of contributing in some degree to the pleasure of one who renders my life so very happy.'

Miss Melvyn was so pleased with the generosity of her little pupil, that she gave her as many caresses as the other had lavished on her, in order to obtain the promise she so much wished for; but she could not be induced to grant her request. Miss Melvyn was void of that pride which often conceals itself under the name of spirit and greatness of soul; and makes people averse to receiving an obligation, because they feel themselves too proud to be grateful, and think that to be obliged, implies an inferiority which their pride cannot support. Had Louisa

---

1   quarter] of a year, or period of three months

been of the same age with herself, she would have felt a kind of property in all she possessed; friendship, the tenure by which she held it; for where hearts are strictly united, she had no notion of any distinction in things of less importance, the adventitious goods of fortune. The boundaries and barriers raised by those two watchful and suspicious enemies, Meum and Tuum,[1] were in her opinion broke down by true friendship; and all property laid in one undistinguished common; but to accept Miss Mancel's money, especially in so great a proportion, appeared to her like taking advantage of her youth; and as she did not think her old enough to be a sufficient judge of the value of it, she did not look upon her as capable of being a party in so perfect a friendship, as was requisite to constitute that unity of property.

Poor Louisa by this disappointment of the first wish of her heart, found what older people often experience, that her riches instead of pleasure procured her only mortification. She could scarcely refrain from tears at a refusal which she thought must arise from want of affection, and told Miss Melvyn, she saw that she loved her but imperfectly; for, added she, 'Could we change places, with how much pleasure should I have accepted it from you! and the satisfaction that learning these things now give me would be turned into delight, by reflecting on the gratification you would receive in having been the means of procuring them for me. I should not envy you the joy of giving, because I as receiver should not have the less share of that satisfaction, since by reflecting on yours I must partake of it, and so encrease my own.'

Miss Melvyn could not forbear blushing at finding a superior degree of delicacy, and a generosity much more exalted, in one so young, than she had felt in herself. She plainly saw, that the greatest proof of a noble mind is to feel a joy in gratitude; for those who know all the pleasures of conferring an obligation, will be sensible, that by accepting it they give the highest delight the human mind can feel, when employed on human objects; and therefore while they receive a benefit, they will taste not only the comforts arising from it to themselves, but share the gratification of a benefactor, from reflecting on the joy they give to

---

1 Meum and Tuum] from Latin, meaning "mine and thine," referring to rights of property

those who have conferred it: thus the receiver of a favour from a truly generous person, 'by owing owes not, and is at once indebted and discharged.'[1]

As Miss Melvyn felt her little friend's reproach, and saw that she had done her injustice in thinking her youth rendered her incapable of that perfection[2] of friendship, which might justify the accepting of her offer; she acknowledged her error, and assured her, 'she would comply if she had no other means of obtaining the instruction she proposed to purchase for her; but that was not the case, for she found she could very well learn from seeing the masters teach her, and practising in their absence.'

Mr. Hintman expressed a desire that Miss Mancel should learn Italian, if she had no objection to it; for he never dictated to her, but offered any advice he had to give, or any inclination which he chose to intimate, with the humility of a dependant, rather than the authority of a benefactor; and indeed it was sufficient; for the slightest hint that any thing would be agreeable to him, met with the most impatient desire in Miss Mancel to perform it: actuated by sincere affection, and the strongest gratitude, nothing made her so happy, as an opportunity to shew him the readiness of her obedience.

But as they were at a loss for a master to teach her that language, Miss Melvyn told them she knew an Italian gentleman, who had been at Sir Charles's house near two months before she had the misfortune of losing the best of mothers. Lady Melvyn had begun to teach her daughter Italian, but desirous that she should speak it with great propriety, she invited this gentleman to her house, who was reduced to great distress of circumstances, and whose person, as well as his many virtues, she had known from her childhood. He had been a friend of her father's, and she was glad of this excuse for making him an handsome present, which otherwise it was not easy to induce him to accept.

Mr. Hintman was not long before he procured this Italian master for Miss Mancel; nor did she delay making use of his instructions; but I

---

1   'by owing owes not, and is at once indebted and discharged'] John Milton, *Paradise Lost*, Book IV, lines 56-7: "By owing owes not, but still pays, at once/Indebted and discharg'd"
2   perfection] perfecton in first edition

Mr d'Avora, the Italian master

shall not describe her progress in the acquisitions of this, any more than her other accomplishments, in all which she excelled to a surprizing degree; nor did Miss Melvyn fall very short of her, though she was at such disadvantage in her method of learning many of them, not having the assistance of a master. Their time was so entirely engrossed by these employments, that they had little leisure, and still less desire to keep company with the rest of the school; but they saved themselves from the dislike which might naturally have arisen in the minds of the other scholars, from being thus neglected, by little presents which Miss Mancel frequently made them.

These two young ladies were very early risers, and the time which was not taken up by Miss Mancel's masters, and that wherein it was requisite to practise what they taught her, they employed in reading, wherein Mr. d'Avora, their Italian master, often accompanied them.

Mr. d'Avora was a man of excellent understanding, and had an incomparable heart. Misfortunes had softened common humanity into a most tender disposition; and had given him a thorough knowlege of mankind, without lessening his benevolence for individuals; though such as learn it by adversity, the surest school for that science, seldom see them in an amiable light.

Mr. d'Avora was not less acquainted with particular nations than with mankind in general; he had travelled through all the countries in Europe, some parts of Asia and Africa, and having traversed them with discernment, and the curiosity of wisdom, not of impertinence, he received such improvement of understanding, as few travellers can boast.

He had an affection for Miss Melvyn, both for her own merits and the obligations he had to her family, and a very short acquaintance with Miss Mancel made him extremely fond of her. He took great pleasure in assisting them in the improvement they so industriously laboured for, and as he was a man of universal knowlege, he was capable of being very useful to them in that respect. For this purpose he often read with them, and by explaining many books on abstruse subjects, rendered several authors intelligible to them, who, without his assistance, would have been too obscure for persons of their age. He had very few scholars, therefore had much leisure, and with great satisfaction dedicated part of it to our young ladies, as he saw he thereby gave them a very sincere pleasure; and he was much gratified with thinking

How does \[he\] to with the misfortune of beauty —

that by his care, and instruction of Miss Melvyn, he made some return for the friendship he had received from her family; and that could her mother be sensible of his attendance on her much-loved and now neglected daughter, it would be highly agreeable to her.

In the manner I have mentioned, these two young ladies past their time, till Miss Mancel reached her fifteenth year, with little alteration, except the encrease of her charms, and her great improvement in every accomplishment. Her appearance began to grow womanly, she was indeed,

'In the bloom of beauty's pride,'[1]

Dazzlingly handsome at first view; but such numerous and various charms appeared on a more intimate acquaintance, that people forgot how much they had been struck by the first sight of her, lost in wonder at her encreasing attractions, to the force of which she was the only person that was insensible. Humble piety rendered her indifferent to circumstances, which she looked upon rather as snares than blessings, and like a person on the brink of a precipice could not enjoy the beauty of the prospect, over-awed by the dangers of her situation.

She had indeed too much of human nature in her not to feel sometimes a *little* flush of vanity on seeing herself admired; but she immediately corrected the foible, by reflecting, that whatever advantages of mind or form had fallen to her share, they were given her by one who expected she should not suffer her thoughts or attention to be withdrawn thereby from him, who was the perfection of all excellence, while she at best could but flatter herself with being less imperfect than many of her fellow creatures.

She considered flattery and admiration as the rocks on which young people, who are at all superior to the multitude, are apt to be wrecked; deprived of quiet happiness in this world, and exalted felicity in the next; and as she was really convinced, that she had only a few obvious

---

1   'In the bloom of beauty's pride'] John Dryden, *Alexander's Feast; or, The Power of Music: An Ode in Honour of St. Cecilia's Day* (1697), line 11] "In Flow'r of Youth and Beauty's Pride"; the poem, with additions, was set to music by Handel and performed in England under his direction from 1736 to 1755

external advantages over others, she opposed to the praises lavished on *[how to preserve her modesty]* her, reflections on her imperfections, which, though not apparent to any one but herself, she verily believed were uncommonly great, as she beheld them with very scrutinizing and rigid eyes, while she looked on those of others with the greatest lenity. But of all the means she used to preserve her humility, she was the most assiduous in praying to him *[piety]* who made her heart, to preserve it humble.

Though the degree of piety I mention, may sound in the ears of many too grave for so young a person, yet it by no means rendered her so; she had great vivacity; a lively imagination; an uncommon share of wit; and a very happy manner of expressing herself. She had all the amiable gaiety of youth, without the least tendency to imprudence; and when she talked most, and, in appearance, let fancy assume the reins, said nothing to repent of. Her heart was all purity, universal benevolence and good nature; and as out of its abundance her mouth spake,[1] she was in little danger of offending with her tongue.

It is not strange that Mr. Hintman's fondness should increase with Miss Mancel's excellencies, but the caresses which suited her earlier *[Hintman + his impropriety]* years were now become improper; and Mr. Hintman, by appearing insensible of the necessary change of behaviour, reduced her to great difficulties; she could not reconcile herself to receiving of them; and yet to inform him of the impropriety, implied a forward consciousness which she was not able to assume. *[+ how she cannot express this]*

She communicated the vexation of her mind to Miss Melvyn, who was still more alarmed, as her superior age and experience rendered her more apprehensive; but she knew not what to advise.

In this dilemma Miss Melvyn had recourse to their good friend, whose knowledge of mankind, his integrity and prudence, rendered him the safest guide. Accordingly one day when Louisa was called from them to Mr. Hintman, who came to make her a visit, Miss Melvyn inform'd Mr. d'Avora, of the reason why her friend obeyed the summons with less joy, than he had observed in her on the like occasion the year before.

---

1   out of its abundance her mouth spake] Bible, Matthew, ch. 12, verse 34: "out of the abundance of the heart the mouth speaketh"

Mr. d'Avora was much disturbed at this information; but not chusing to increase the uneasiness the young ladies seemed to be under till he had more certain foundation for his opinion, he only intimated, that 'customs were hard to break, but he should hope, that when Mr. Hintman reflected on the impropriety of behaving to a young woman as if she was still a child, he would alter it, and if he was not immediately sensible of the difference a small addition of age makes, yet her behaviour would lead him to recollect it.'

Although Mr. d'Avora seemed to pay little regard to what Miss Melvyn said, yet it made great impression on him, and as soon as he left her, he took all proper measures to enquire into the character, and usual conduct of Mr. Hintman.

This scrutiny did not turn out at all to his satisfaction, every account he received was the same; he had not the pleasure of finding what is usually asserted, that 'all men have two characters;' for Mr. Hintman had but one, and that the most alarming that could be for Miss Mancel. Every person told him, 'that Mr. Hintman had a very great fortune, which he spent entirely in the gratification of his favourite vice, the love of women; on whom his profuseness was boundless. That as he was easily captivated, so he was soon tired; and seldom kept a woman long after he had obtained the free possession of her; but generally was more bountiful than is customary with men of his debauched principles at parting with them.'

This, Mr. d'Avora was assured, was Mr. Hintman's only vice; that he was good-natured, and generous on all occasions. From this account he saw too great reason to fear, that all the care which had been taken to improve Miss Mancel, arose only from a sort of epicurism in his predominant vice, but yet this was too doubtful a circumstance to be the ground-work of any plan of action. A man of acknowledged generosity and good-nature, however vicious, might do a noble action without having any criminal design. In this uncertainty of mind he knew not what to advise her, and was unwilling to excite such fears in the breasts of these two young friends, as might be groundless; but yet would entirely destroy their peace; therefore, he only told Miss Melvyn in general terms, that, 'Mr. Hintman's character was such, as rendered it very necessary that Louisa should be much on her guard; but that whether more than prudent caution, and decent reserve were requisite, her own observation must discover, for no one else could determine that point, since he had the reputation of being generous as well as debauched; therefore his actions towards her might be, and he hoped were, the result of his greatest virtue, rather than of his predominant vice.'

Miss Melvyn made a faithful report of what Mr. d'Avora had said to her, which filled both herself and her friend with inexpressible uneasiness.

Louisa was in great difficulty how to act, between gratitude and affection on the one side, and necessary caution and reserve on the other. She was almost as much afraid of appearing ungrateful, as of being imprudent. She found little assistance from the advice of her friends, who declared themselves incapable of directing her, therefore she was obliged to lay aside all dependance on her own care, and to trust in that of heaven, convinced that her innocence would be guarded by that power who knew the integrity and purity of her heart; and that while she preserved it unblemished, even in thought and inclination, her prayers for his protection would not be unavailing.

The remainder of the winter passed like the former part, only that the encrease of her apprehensions, so far lessened her easy vivacity, that Mr. Hintman observed the alteration, and complained of the constraint and awe which damped her conversation.

As the school broke up at Easter, he entreated her to accompany him that short time into the country, from which she would gladly have excused herself, both on account of her fears, and of her unwillingness to leave Miss Melvyn, of whose conversation she was now more particularly tenacious, as lady Melvyn had determined to suffer her to return home in a short time, not knowing how to excuse her remaining longer at school, as she was entered into her one and twentieth year. Miss Melvyn would have been glad that her ladyship had not shewn this token of regard to popular opinion; for since she had enjoyed Miss Mancel's company, and been in possession of so good a collection of books, she was grown perfectly contented with her situation.

Louisa, to make Mr. Hintman desist from the request he urged with so much importunity, tried every means that did not appear like a total disinclination to accompany him, for any thing that bore the air of ingratitude could not be supported by her, whose heart was so void of it, and who thought she could never feel enough for her benefactor, if his designs were not so criminal, as she feared, but scarcely could suffer herself to suspect.

Mr. Hintman was too ardent in his purposes to give up his favourite scheme, and Louisa beheld with inexpressible concern the day approach, when she must either accompany him into the country, or disoblige him for ever, and make herself appear extremely ungrateful in the eyes of a man, whom she loved and honoured like a father. Her addresses to heaven for protection now became more vehement and continual, and the greatest part of her time was spent on her knees in praying to that power in whom she trusted. Miss Melvyn and Mr. d'Avora were scarcely less anxious, or under fewer apprehensions than herself, but could see no resource except in the protection of the Almighty, to whom we seldom apply with entire faith and resignation while we have any hopes in human assistance.

Two days before that fixed on for the purposed journey, when Louisa's anxiety was risen to the utmost height, the school-mistress entered the room, with a countenance so melancholy, as was more suitable to the situation of mind in which the two young friends were then in, than to any reason they apprehended she could have for an air of so much sorrow. She soon began a discourse, which they immediately apprehended was preparatory to the opening of some fatal event, and which, as is usual in such cases, was, if possible, more alarming than any misfortune it could precede. The ladies expressed their fears, and begged to be acquainted with what had befallen them. After considerable efforts to deliver her of the secret with which she was pregnant, they learnt that a gentleman was in the parlour, who came to inform Miss Mancel, that Mr. Hintman died the day before in a fit of an apoplexy.

All Louisa's fears and suspicions vanished at once, and grief alone took possession of her heart. The shock so entirely overcame her, that she was not able to see the fatal messenger of such melancholy tidings as the death of her benefactor, and second father. Miss Melvyn was obliged to undertake this office, and learnt from the gentleman, that Mr. Hintman died without a will, and therefore left the poor Louisa as destitute, except being enriched by various accomplishments, as he found her, and at a much more dangerous time, when her beauty would scarcely suffer compassion to arise unaccompanied with softer

Miss Mancel destitute!

sentiments. This gentleman proceeded to inform Miss Melvyn, that 'his father and another person of equal relation to Mr. Hintman, were heirs at law. He expressed great concern for Miss Mancel, and wished he had his father's power of repairing Mr. Hintman's neglect, but that his influence extended no farther than to obtain a commission to pay the expences of another year at that school, that the young lady might have time to recollect herself after so fatal a change, and determine at leisure on her future course of life.'

Miss Melvyn was so sensibly touched at the prospect of the approaching distress with which her friend was threatened, that she burst into tears, and uttered some exclamations concerning 'the inconsistency of that affection, which could suffer a man to rest a moment without securing a provision in case of death, to a young woman he seemed to love with the greatest excess of tenderness.' 'Believe me, madam, said the young gentleman, Mr. Hintman was capable of no love that was not entirely sensual, and consequently selfish; all who knew him lamented the fate of a young woman, who by every account is so superiorly lovely. Among his friends he made no secret of his designs in all he had done for her, and boasted frequently of the extraordinary charms which were ripening for his possession. It was but two days ago, that he was exulting in the presence of some of them, that the time was now approaching, when he should be rewarded for long expectation, and boundless expence; for he should then, he said, be sure of her person, and had long secured her heart. He knew he had strong prejudices and strange scruples to combat; but was prepared, and should not find them difficult to conquer; at worst, his steward in a parson's habit would lull them all to sleep.'[1]

Pamelesque plot, too! —

'Good heaven! cried Miss Melvyn, could there be such a wretch, and were there men who would keep company with him, who would bear the disgrace of being called his friends?'[2]

'Your notions, madam, replied the gentleman, are too refined for persons who live in the world: should a man insist on strict morals in all his acquaintance, he might enjoy a solitude in the most populous city;

---

1   in a parson's habit ... to sleep] deceive her by pretending to carry out a wedding ceremony
2   first edition has no quotation mark here

though, I confess, nothing but ties of kindred could have made me intimate with one of Mr. Hintman's character, which I should not thus have exposed to you, but as I imagined a better knowledge of the man, might alleviate the affliction you seemed to feel for Miss Mancel's having lost one whom you esteemed so sincere a friend. I should have been glad, continued he, could I have seen the young lady, of whom Mr. Hintman told such wonders; but I will not presume to press it, time may offer me some opportunity for satisfying my curiosity without paining her, I therefore take my leave, with only requesting your permission to remit the money of which I was made the bearer.'

Miss Melvyn was so much affected with her friend's situation, that she took the paper the gentleman offered her, without having power to reflect whether she ought to accept it, or being able to make him any acknowledgment; and he retired directly. She was obliged to stay some time to compose her spirits before she went to her friend, that she might be the better able to comfort her. On examining the paper, she found it a bank-note of an hundred pounds, which was now become all Miss Mancel's fortune.

Lamont could not forbear interrupting Mrs. Maynard in this place, by some very severe reflexions on Mr. Hintman's having neglected to make a provision for Miss Mancel in case of his death, which I believe was the part of his conduct that to Lamont appeared most inexcusable; for though he is too fashionable to think intriguing[1] very criminal, yet he is naturally generous, as far as money is concerned. 'I cannot think, replied my cousin, that Mr. Hintman's behaviour in that particular can be much wondered at. Death to such a man must be so dreadful an event, that he will naturally endeavour to banish it from his mind, whenever it attempts to intrude, and when a person takes so little care to make provision for his own happiness after death, is it strange he should be unmindful of what shall befall another after that fatal period? When a man neglects his own soul, and deprives himself of all hope of everlasting felicity, can we expect he should take any trouble to provide for the temporal convenience of another person?

'Besides, could he, who aimed at reducing an innocent and amiable

---

1   intriguing] carrying on a secret sexual liaison

young woman to guilt and infamy in this world, and eternal perdition in the next, be under any concern lest she should fall into the lesser miseries of poverty? it would have been an inconsistency in such a character.'

'You see gallantry[1] in a very serious light, madam, said Lamont.'

'I do indeed, sir, answered Mrs. Maynard, I look on it as the most dangerous of vices, it destroys truth, honour, humanity, it is directly contrary to the laws of God, is the destruction of society, and almost as inconsistent with morality as with religion.'

'I beg pardon, madam, interrupted Lamont, (who felt himself a little touched with what she said) for breaking into your narrative, and must beg you will continue it.'

Miss Melvyn, resumed Mrs. Maynard, was too well acquainted with the strength of Louisa's mind, to think it necessary to conceal from her *story resumes* any part of what had passed between herself and Mr. Hintman's relation.

Louisa, much affected by Mr. Hintman's dying, with a heart so unfit to appear at the tribunal before which he was so suddenly summoned, thought not immediately of herself; but when she reflected on the dangers she had escaped, she blessed her poverty, since it was the consequence of an event which delivered her from so much greater evils, and sent up many sincere and ardent thanksgivings to heaven, for so signal a preservation. These thoughts possessed our young friends for the first three or four days after Mr. Hintman's death; but then they began to think it requisite to consult with Mr. d'Avora, on what course of life it was most advisable for Miss Mancel to enter. This was a difficult point to determine; though her understanding and attainments were far superior to her years, yet they were sensible her youth would be a great impediment to her in any undertaking. Mr. d'Avora therefore advised, that she should continue a little longer at the school, and then fix in the most private manner imaginable for three or four years, by which time he hoped to be able to establish her in some widow's family as governess to her children; for he told her she must not expect, while her person continued such as it then was, that a married woman would receive her in any capacity that fixed her in the same house with her husband.

Miss Mancel's prospects

beauty a liability

1   gallantry] courtly behaviour towards women, implying insincerity or lack of true love

the help
of Mr. d'Avora!

As Miss Mancel had many jewels and trinkets of value, she had no doubt but that with œconomy, she might support herself for the term Mr. d'Avora mentioned, and even longer if requisite, as she could add to her little fund by the produce of her industry. As Miss Melvyn's return home drew near, it was agreed, that she should seek out some place in Sir Charles's neighbourhood, where Louisa might lodge cheaply and reputably; and in the mean time Mr. d'Avora should dispose of whatever she had of value, except her books and her harpsichord; these she resolved not to part with till the produce of her other things, and the money she had by her, was spent, as they would not only amuse her in the country, but afford her the power of improving herself in those accomplishments which were to be her future provision.

This plan softened the pangs of separation when the time of Miss Melvyn's departure arrived. It was not long before she found out an apartment at a reputable farmers, where Miss Mancel might lodge conveniently. Had it been a less tolerable place, its vicinity to Sir Charles's house, from which it was but a quarter of a mile distant, would have made it a very delightful abode to her, and she soon repaired thither.

Great was the joy of the two friends at meeting. Miss Melvyn's situation at home was rendered as irksome as possible, by Lady Melvyn's behaviour both to her and Sir Charles, who, notwithstanding her ill treatment, was extremely fond of, and totally guided by her. His mind *the Melvyns* was so entirely enslaved, that he beheld nothing but in the light wherein she pleased to represent it, and was so easy a dupe, that she could scarcely feel the joys of self triumph in her superior art, which was on no subject so constantly exerted, as in keeping up a coldness in Sir Charles towards his daughter; this she had with tolerable facility effected in her absence, and was assiduously careful to preserve now she was present. To those who know not the power an artful woman can obtain over a weak man, it would appear incredible, that any father could be prejudiced against a daughter, whose whole attention was to please him. She had so perfect a command over her temper, that she never appeared to take offence at any thing Lady Melvyn said or did, though that lady endeavoured by every provocation to throw her off her guard. This behaviour only encreased her hatred, which was not in the least abated by Miss Melvyn's taking every opportunity of being serviceable to her brothers and sisters-in-law. Lady Melvyn persuaded *true friendship a refuge*

Sir Charles, that his daughter's calmness was only assumed in his presence, and continually complained of her insolence, when he was not by. If he ever appeared to doubt the truth of her report, she would burst into tears, complain of his want of love, and little confidence in her; and sometimes thought proper to shew her grief at such treatment, by a pretended hysteric fit, always ready at call to come to her assistance, though really so unnecessarily lavished on one easily duped without those laborious means, that it appeared a wantonness of cunning, which was thus exerted only for its own indulgence. She soon perceived that Miss Melvyn rather chose to submit to any aspersions, than to render her father unhappy, by undeceiving him; and taking advantage of this generosity, would sometimes, to establish his opinion of her veracity, accuse Miss Melvyn to her face of offences which she had never committed, and things she had never said.

In such a situation the arrival of a friend, into whose sympathetic bosom she could pour all her griefs, and in whose delightful society she could forget them, was the highest blessing. But Lady Melvyn contrived to make her feel mortifications even in this tenderest particular, for though she was in her heart glad to have her out of the house, that she might not be witness of much improper behaviour, yet she would sometimes mortify herself in order to teaze Miss Melvyn, by preventing her from going to her beloved friend; and continually alledged, her spending so much time with Louisa, as a proof of that aversion she had made Sir Charles believe Miss Melvyn had to her.

Louisa felt deeply her friend's uneasiness, but when they were together they could not be unhappy. They seldom passed a day without seeing each other, but as Lady Melvyn had taken no notice of Louisa, she could not go to her house, therefore their meetings were at her lodgings, where they often read together, and at other times would apply to music to drive away melancholy reflexions. As Louisa wished to remain near her friend as long as possible, she endeavoured, by taking in plain-work,[1] to provide for some part of her current expences, the less to diminish the little fund she had by her. She likewise employed part of her time in painting, having reason to hope, that if she could

---

1   plain-work] simple needlework or sewing, as distinct from fancy work or embroidery

find a means of offering her pictures to sale, she might from them raise a very convenient sum. While she was thus contriving to enable herself to enjoy for many years the conversation of her friend, Lady Melvyn was as industriously laying schemes that, if successful, must disappoint all the young ladies hopes.

Towards the end of the autumn, Mr. Morgan, a man of fortune, who had spent above half a year in a fruitless pursuit after health, made a visit to a gentleman in the neighbourhood. Unfortunately Miss Melvyn's charms made a conquest of this gentleman, in whom age had not gained a victory over passion. Miss Melvyn's humility occasioned her being the last person who perceived the impression she had made on his heart, and his age would scarcely suffer her to believe her senses when the symptoms became most apparent. A girl may find some amusement in a young lover, though she feels no disposition in herself to return his passion, her vanity is flattered by his addresses, and a woman must be very little disposed to be pleased, who receives no pleasure from one who is continually endeavouring to oblige and amuse her; but the most whimsical of the poets never fancied a grey-bearded Cupid, or represented Hymen[1] with a torch in one hand, and a crutch in the other. I allow that,

> Oft the matrimonial Cupid,
> Lash'd on by time grows tir'd and stupid,[2]

And does[3] not always wear that blooming joyous countenance, which the painters give him; but should any capricious artist take the sickle out of the hand of old Time, and in its place put Hymen's torch, the picture might be thought very unnatural, yet would represent a proper hymeneal Cupid to attend Mr. Morgan to the altar.

Such a lover could excite no emotion in his mistress's heart but disgust. Miss Melvyn's principles were too delicate to suffer her to think she had any title to ridicule a man for his partiality to her, however ill-

---

1 Hymen] the god of marriage in Greek and Roman mythology
2 Matthew Prior, *Alma; or, The Progess of the Mind* (1718), canto 2, lines 63-64: 'And now your Matrimonial CUPID/Lash'd on by Time, grows tir'd and stupid'
3 does] dees in first edition

suited to himself; but no consideration could prevent his addresses from being extremely disagreeable: however, she could without any great difficulty have so far commanded herself, as to have treated him with complaisance, till he gave her an opportunity of rejecting his courtship, had she not been apprehensive that this affair would give Lady Melvyn a new subject for persecution. She was pretty certain, that lady would be glad to settle her in another county; and that her averseness to so ill-suited a marriage would only serve as an additional recommendation to her mother. She was indeed determined in justice to Mr. Morgan, and compassion to herself, not to be induced by any sollicitations to marry a man whom she could not hope, that even the strongest attachment to duty could render so well as indifferent to her, but she dreaded the means that might be taken to oblige her to accept Mr. Morgan's proposal.

Little did she guess what those means would be. She expected to be attacked alternately with all the violence of passion, the affected softness of dissimulation, and every art that cunning could devise, to force Sir Charles to concur in her persecution. These indeed were employed as soon as Mr. Morgan made his proposals; but her ladyship had too many resources in her fertile brain to persevere long in a course she found unavailing. The farmer where Miss Mancel lodged had a son, who was in treaty with Lady Melvyn for a farm, which at the end of the year would become vacant. This person she thought fit for her purpose, as Miss Melvyn's going so frequently to Miss Mancel, might give some colour to her invention. She therefore took care to be found by Sir Charles drowned in tears; he pressed to know the occasion of her grief, but she resisted his importunity in such a manner, as could not fail to encrease it, still she declared, that 'she loved him to that excess she could not communicate a secret which she knew must afflict him, even though the suppression and inward preyings of her sorrow should prove fatal to her life.'

Sir Charles now on his knees intreated her 'to acquaint him with the misfortune she endeavoured to conceal, assuring her, that nothing could give him so much concern as seeing her in that condition.' She told him, 'she was sensible, that as his wife it was her duty to obey him; (a duty newly discovered, or at least newly performed by her ladyship) but she feared she had not strength left to give it utterance.' The endeavour threw her into an hysteric fit, which was succeeded by so many others, that Sir Charles was almost frantic with his fears for so tender a wife, who was thus reduced to the last agonies by her affectionate apprehensions of giving him pain.

After rubbing her hands and feet till they were sore, suffocating her with burnt feathers,[1] and half poisoning her with medicines, Sir Charles and her servants so far brought her to life, that after sending her attendants out of the room, she had just power to tell him, 'she had discovered an intrigue between his daughter and Simon the young farmer,' and then immediately sunk into another fit, which however did not last so long; for as she had removed the heavy burden off her mind, she soon began to recover.

Sir Charles was very much shocked at what Lady Melvyn told him, but could not doubt the reality of the fact, when he had seen the very violent effect it had had on his tender wife. He asked her advice how to proceed; and it was soon determined that it was necessary, either to oblige Miss Melvyn to marry Mr. Morgan directly, or to disclaim her for ever, and remove the disgrace of so infamous a conduct as far from themselves as possible. With this resolution she was to be immediately acquainted.

Miss Melvyn was accordingly called in, and bitterly reproached by Sir Charles; to which my Lady added frequent lamentations, that she should so far forget herself, and disgrace so worthy a family, interspersing with them many expressions of the undeserved tenderness she had always had for her, and her great confidence in Miss Melvyn's prudence and virtue, shedding tears for her having so unhappily swerved from them.

As all this passed for some time in general terms, Miss Melvyn was in doubt whether she or her parents had lost their senses; convinced there must be distraction on one side or the other. As soon as she could recover her surprize, she begged to know what crime she had committed? her astonishment was still increased by the answer she received, which was an accusation of this strange intrigue; and her frequent visits to Miss Mancel were brought as proofs of it. The submissive and mild temper

---

1   burnt feathers] producing an acrid smell to help revive someone who has fainted

miss M accused of an intrigue with the farmer's son—visits to Louisa are "proof"

which had hitherto most strongly characterised her, vanished at so injurious a charge, and she denied the fact with that true spirit which innocence inspires. She told Lady Melvyn, that 'though she had hitherto silently submitted to all her ill usage, yet it was her duty to repel an injury like this, and when her reputation was so cruelly aspersed, it would be criminal to suffer the vile inventors to pass unexposed. She insisted on being confronted with her accusers, a privilege allowed to the greatest criminals, and by the severest judges, therefore surely could not be refused by a father to a daughter, on a charge so highly improbable, and for which no lightness in her conduct ever gave the least ground.'

As Mrs. Maynard was in this part of her narrative a bell rang, which informed us that dinner was ready, and we were unwillingly obliged to postpone the continuation of the history of the two young friends, till a more convenient opportunity.

a pause in the story before dinner

In the afternoon before we rose from table, four ladies came to drink tea with this admirable society. No addition was necessary to render the conversation amusing; but the strangers seemed to look on the ladies of the house with such gratitude and veneration, and were treated by them with so much friendly politeness, as gave me pleasure. I found by the various enquiries after different persons, that these visitors likewise lived in a large society. When they rose up to take leave, Mrs. Trentham proposed to walk part of the way home with them. No one objected to it, for the evening was inviting, and they had designed to spend it in the park, through which these Ladies were to pass; for Lady Mary observed, that 'after having shewn us the beauties of the place, they ought to exhibit the riches of it.'

the park

The park is close to one side of the house; it is not quite three miles round; the inequality of the ground much increases its beauty, and the timber is remarkably fine. We could plainly perceive it had been many years in the possession of good œconomists, who unprompted by necessity, did not think the profit that might arise from the sale, a sufficient inducement to deprive it of some fine trees, which are now decaying, but so happily placed, that they are made more venerable, and not less beautiful by their declining age. This park is much ornamented by two or three fine pieces of water; one of them is a very noble canal, so artfully terminated by an elegant bridge, beyond which is a wood, that it there appears like a fine river vanishing from the eye.

Mrs. Morgan stopped us in one spot, saying, 'from hence, as Lady Mary observed, you may behold our riches, that building, (pointing to what we thought a pretty temple) which perhaps you imagine designed only for ornament or pleasure, is a very large pidgeon house, that affords a sufficient supply to our family, and many of our neighbours. That hill on your right-hand is a warren, prodigiously stocked with rabbits; this canal, and these other pieces of water, as well as the river you saw this morning, furnish our table with a great profusion of fish. You will easily believe from the great number of deer you see around us, that we have as much venison as we can use, either in presents to our friends, or our own family. Hares, and all sorts of game likewise abound here; so that with the help of a good dairy, perhaps no situation ever more amply afforded all the necessaries of life. These are indeed our riches; here we have almost every thing we can want, for a very small proportion of that expence which others are at to procure them.'[1]

'Such a situation, said I, would be dangerous to many people, for if, as some have supposed, and, in regard to a great part of the world, I fear with truth, mutual wants are the great bands of society, a person thus placed, would be in danger of feeling himself so independant a being, as might tempt him to disclaim all commerce with mankind, since he could not be benefitted by them. He would look on himself in the light of a rich man gaming[2] with sharpers, with a great probability of losing, and a certainty of never being a gainer.'

'I do not think the danger, replied Lady Mary, so great as you imagine, even though we allow that society arises from the motive you mention. However fortune may have set us above any bodily wants, the mind will still have many which would drive us into society. Reason wishes for communication and improvement; benevolence longs for objects on which to exert itself; the social comforts of friendship are so necessary to our happiness, that it would be impossible not to endeavour to enjoy them. In sickness the langour[3] of our minds makes us wish for the

1 no quotation mark in first edition
2 gaming] gambling
3 langour] altered to languor in later editions

pain + pleasure

amusements of conversation; in health the vivacity of our spirits leads us to desire it. To avoid pain we seek after corporeal conveniencies, to procure pleasure we aim at mental enjoyments; and I believe, if we observe the general course of men's actions, we shall see them at least as strongly actuated by the desire of pleasure, as by the fear of pain; though philosophers, who have formed their judgments more on reason than the knowlege of mankind, may have thought otherwise.'

'I think, said Mrs. Selvyn, somebody has asserted, that he who could live without society must be more than a God, or less than a man; the latter part of this assertion would have held good had he carried it farther, and said lower than a brute, for there is no creature in the universe that is not linked into some society, except we allow the existence of that exploded and unsociable bird the Phœnix.'

society

'I am surprized, interrupted Lamont, to hear Ladies, who seclude themselves from the world in this solitary though beautiful place, so strongly plead for society.'

What

'Do you then, replied Mrs. Mancel, mistake a croud for society? I know not two things more opposite. How little society is there to be found in what you call the world? It might more properly be compared to that state of war, which Hobbes[1] supposes the first condition of mankind. The same vanities, the same passions, the same ambition, reign in almost every breast; a constant desire to supplant, and a continual fear of being supplanted, keep the minds of those who have any views at all in a state of unremitted tumult and envy; and those who have no aim in their actions are too irrational to have a notion of social comforts. The love, as well as the pleasures of society, is founded in reason, and cannot exist in those minds which are filled with irrational pursuits. Such indeed might claim a place in the society of birds and beasts, though few would deserve to be admitted amongst them, but that of reasonable beings must be founded in reason. What I understand by society is a state of mutual confidence, reciprocal services, and correspondent affections; where numbers are thus united, there will be a free communication of sentiments, and we shall then find speech, that peculiar blessing given to man, a valuable gift indeed; but when we see it restrained by suspicion, or contaminated by detraction, we rather wonder that so dangerous a power was trusted with a race of beings, who seldom make a proper use of it.

"the world" vs true society

1   Hobbes] Thomas Hobbes (1588-1679), English philosopher; in *Leviathan* (1651), he asserted
     that, before the formation of society, humans were continually at war with one another

'You will pity us perhaps because we have no cards, no assemblies,[1] no plays, no masquerades, in this solitary place. The first we might have if we chose it, nor are they totally disclaimed by us; but while we can with safety speak our own thoughts, and with pleasure read those of wiser persons, we are not likely to be often reduced to them. We wish not for large assemblies, because we do not desire to drown conversation in noise; the amusing fictions of dramatic writers are not necessary where nature affords us so many real delights; and as we are not afraid of shewing our hearts, we have no occasion to conceal our persons, in order to obtain either liberty of speech or action.'[2]

'What a serious world should we have, madam, replied Lamont, if you were to regulate our conduct!'

'By no means, sir, answered Mrs. Mancel, I wish to make only these alterations, to change noise for real mirth, flutter for settled chearfulness, affected wit for rational conversation; and would but have that degree of dissipation banished, which deprives people of time for reflection[3] on the motives for, and consequences of, their actions, that their pleasures may be real and permament, and followed neither by repentance nor punishment. I would wish them to have leisure to consider by whom they were sent into the world, and for what purpose, and to learn,[4] that their happiness consists in fulfilling the design of their Maker, in providing for their own greatest felicity, and contributing all that is in their power to the convenience of others.'

'You seem, madam, answered Lamont, to choose to make us all slaves to each other?'[5]

'No, sir, replied Mrs. Mancel, I would only make you friends. Those who are really such are continually endeavouring to serve and oblige each other; this reciprocal communication of benefits should be universal, and then we might with reason be fond of this world.'

---

1   assemblies] a gathering for social entertinment, a regular feature of eighteenth-century public life
2   comma after *action* in first edition
3   usually spelt as reflexion in the text
4   semi-colon after learn in first edition
5   no quotation mark here in first edition

'But, said Lamont, this reciprocal communication is impossible; what service can a poor man do me? I may relieve him, but how can he return the obligation?'

beneficence again

'It is he, answered Mrs. Mancel, who first conferred it, in giving you an opportunity of relieving him. The pleasure he has afforded you, is as far superior to the gratification you have procured him; as it is more blessed to give than to receive. You will perhaps say of him, as the apothecary in Romeo and Juliet does of himself, and tell me that,

"His poverty and not his will consents."

So let it be, and do you

"Pay his poverty and not his will."[1]

But certainly the highest satisfaction is on your side, and much obliged you are to that poverty, which enables you to obtain so great a gratification. But do not think the poor can make no adequate return. The greatest pleasure this world can give us is that of being beloved, but how should we expect to obtain love without deserving it? Did you ever see any one that was not fond of a dog that fondled him? Is it then possible to be insensible to the affection of a rational being?'

'If Mr. Lamont, said one of the visitors, has not so high a sense of the pleasure of being gratefully loved and esteemed, we ought not to blame him; he, perhaps, like the greatest part of the world, has not sufficiently tried it, to be a proper judge; Mrs. Mancel is certainly very deep in this knowledge, and her opinion may be received as almost an infallible decision, since it is founded on long experience; and how nobly does she calm the eager wishes of impotent gratitude, in declaring herself to be the most benefitted when she confers obligations.'

This was uttered with so much warmth, and accompanied by looks so expressive of affection and grateful sensibility, that I plainly saw it

---

1 'His poverty and not his will consents'; 'pay his poverty and not his will': Shakespeare, *Romeo and Juliet*, V, i, 75: "My poverty, but not my will, consents"; "I pay thy poverty, and not thy will"

Lamont's reply shows he is learning to speak their language

proceeded from something more than mere speculative approbation. Lamont declared, that 'he was well convinced of the justness of what Mrs. Mancel had said; at first it appeared rather a sentiment uttered in sport, than an opinion which could be proved by argument; but that a little reflexion on ones own sensations, would afford sufficient conviction of the truth of her assertion, and that the general errors in the conduct of mankind plainly evinced they were of the same opinion, though they often mistook the means; for what, continued he, do people ruin themselves by pomp and splendor, hazard their lives in the pursuits of ambition, and, as Shakespear says,

he quotes Shakespeare too —

"Seek the bubble reputation even in the cannon's mouth;"[1]

But to gain popular applause and esteem? For what do others throw away their time in useless civilities, and politely flatter all they meet, but in hopes of pleasing? Even those who make it their business to slander merit, and exaggerate the faults of others, do it from a desire of raising themselves in the opinion of mankind, by lowering those who may be brought into comparison with them.'

During this conversation we had advanced within a field of the house, and the ladies stopped to take their leave, saying, 'as the evening was too far advanced to suffer them to make any stay with their good friends, they would not disturb them by just entering their doors.' But as some parley ensued, several ladies who had seen us from the windows ran out, just to pay their compliments to the worthy inhabitants of Millenium-Hall. The pleasure of this short meeting seemed reciprocal, and both sides appeared unwilling to part, but the setting sun admonished us to return.

The house to which we had so nearly approached was a very large old mansion, and its inhabitants so numerous, that I was curious to know how so many became assembled together. Mrs. Maynard said, that 'if she did not satisfy my inquiries, I was in great danger of remaining ignorant of the nature of that society, as her friends would not be easily prevailed with to break silence on that subject.

---

1   'Seek the bubble reputation even in the cannon's mouth': Shakespeare, *As You Like It*, II, vii, line 152: "Seeking the bubble reputation even in the cannon's mouth"

the home dependent, well-educated middle class women

'These ladies, said she, long beheld with compassion the wretched fate of those women, who from scantiness of fortune, and pride of family, are reduced to become dependant, and to bear all the insolence of wealth, from such as will receive them into their families; these, though in some measure voluntary slaves, yet suffer all the evils of the severest servitude, and are, I believe, the most unhappy part of the creation. Sometimes they are unqualified to gain a maintenance, educated as is called, genteelly, or in other words idly, they are ignorant of every thing that might give them superior abilities to the lower rank of people, and their birth renders them less acceptable servants to many, who have not generosity enough to treat them as they ought, and yet do not choose while they are acting the mistress, perhaps too haughtily, to feel the secret reproaches of their own hearts. Possibly pride may still oftener reduce these indigent gentlewomen into this wretched state of dependance, and therefore the world is less inclined to pity them; but my friends see human weakness in another light.

poor governess + servent)

'They imagine themselves too far from perfection to have any title to expect it in others, and think, that there are none in whom pride is so excusable as in the poor; for if there is the smallest spark of it in their compositions, and who is entirely free from it, the frequent neglects and indignities they meet with must keep it continually alive. If we are despised for casual deficiencies, we naturally seek in ourselves for some merit, to restore us to that dignity in our own eyes, which those humiliating mortifications would otherwise debase. Thus we learn to set too great a value on what we still possess, whether advantages of birth, education, or natural talents; any thing will serve for a resource to mortified pride; and as every thing grows by opposition and persecution, we cannot wonder, if the opinion of ourselves increases by the same means.

'To persons in this way of thinking, the pride which reduces many to be, what is called with too little humanity, toad-eaters,[1] does not render them unworthy of compassion. Therefore for the relief of this race they bought that large mansion.

---

1   toad-eaters] or toadies; flatterers or sycophants, especially female dependents, from the term for a charlatan's attendant who would pretend to eat (poisonous) toads so that his employer could pretend to expell the poison

the rules for the society of indigent gentlewomen

'They drew up several regulations, to secure the peace and good order of the society they designed to form, and sending a copy of it to all their acquaintance, told them, that any gentleman's daughter, whose character was unblemished, might, if she desired it, on those terms be received into that society.'

I begged, if it was not too much trouble, to know what the regulations were.

'The first rule, continued Mrs. Maynard, was, that whoever chose to take the benefit of this asylum, for such I may justly call it, should deposite, in the hands of a person appointed for that purpose, whatever fortune she was mistress of, the security being approved by her and her friends, and remaining in her possession. Whenever she leaves the society, her fortune should be repaid her, the interest in the mean time being appropriated to the use of the community. The great design of this was to preserve an exact equality between them; for it was not expected, that the interest of any of their fortunes should pay the allowance they were to have for their cloaths. If any appeared to have secreted part of her fortune she should be expelled the society.

'Secondly, Each person to have a bed-chamber to herself, but the eating-parlour and drawing-room in common.

'Thirdly, All things for rational amusement shall be provided for the society; musical instruments, of whatever sort they shall chuse, books, tents for work, and in short conveniences for every kind of employment.

'Fourthly, They must conform to very regular hours.

'Fifthly, An house-keeper will be appointed to manage the household affairs, and a sufficient number of servants provided.

'Sixthly, Each person shall alternately, a week at a time, preside at the table, and give what family orders[1] may be requisite.

'Seventhly, Twenty-five pounds[2] a year shall be allowed to each person for her cloaths and pocket expences.

'Eighthly, Their dress shall be quite plain and neat, but not particular[3] nor uniform.

---

1   family orders] directions for carrying out household business
2   Twenty-five pounds] Twenty five-pounds in first edition
3   particular] other than ordinary, attracting notice, peculiar

'Ninthly, The expences of sickness shall be discharged by the patronesses of this society.

'Tenthly, If any one of the ladies behaves with imprudence she shall be dismissed, and her fortune returned; likewise if any should by turbulence or pettishness of temper, disturb the society, it shall be in the power of the rest of them to expel her; a majority of three parts of the community being for the expulsion, and this to be performed by ballotting.

'Eleventhly, A good table and every thing suitable to the convenience of a gentlewoman, shall be provided.

'These were the principal articles; and in less than two months a dozen persons of different ages were established in the house, who seemed thoroughly delighted with their situation. At the request of one of them, who had a friend that wished to be admitted, an order was soon added, by the consent of all, that gave leave for any person who would conform exactly to the rules of the house, to board there for such length of time, as should be agreeable to herself and the society, for the price of an hundred pounds a year, fifty for any child she might have, twenty for a maid-servant, and thirty for a man.

'The number of this society is now increased to thirty, four ladies board there, one of whom has two children, and there are five young ladies, the eldest not above twelve years old, whose mothers being dead, and their families related to some of the society, their kinswomen have undertaken their education; these likewise pay an hundred pounds a year each. It has frequently happened, that widow ladies have come into this society, till their year of deep mourning was expired.

'With these assistances the society now subsists with the utmost plenty and convenience, without any additional expence to my good friends, except a communication of what this park affords; as our steward provides them with every thing, and has the entire direction of the household affairs, which he executes with the most sensible œconomy.'

'I should imagine, said I, it were very difficult to preserve a comfortable harmony among so many persons, and consequently such variety of tempers?'

'Certainly, answered Mrs. Maynard, it is not without its difficulties. For the first year of this establishment my friends dedicated most of their time and attention to this new community, who were every day either at the hall, or these ladies with them, endeavouring to cultivate in this sisterhood that sort of disposition which is most productive of peace. By their example and suggestions, (for it is difficult to give unreserved advice where you may be suspected of a design to dictate) by their examples and suggestions therefore, they led them to industry, and shewed it to be necessary to all stations, as the basis of almost every virtue. An idle mind, like fallow ground, is the soil for every weed to grow in; in it vice strengthens, the seed of every vanity flourishes unmolested and luxuriant; discontent, malignity, ill humour, spread far and wide, and the mind becomes a chaos, which it is beyond human power to call into order and beauty. This therefore my good friends laboured to expel from their infant establishment. They taught them that it was the duty of every person to be of service to others. That those whose hands and minds were by the favours of fortune exempt from the necessity of labouring for their own support, ought to be employed for such as are destitute of these advantages. They got this sisterhood to join with them in working for the poor people, in visiting, in admonishing, in teaching them wherever their situations required these services. Where they found that any of these ladies had a taste for gardening, drawing, music, reading, or any manual or mental art, they cultivated it, assisted them in the pleasantest means, and by various little schemes have kept up these inclinations with all the spirit of pursuit, which is requisite to preserve most minds from that state of languidness and inactivity, whereby life is rendered wearisome to those who have never found it unfortunate.

'By some regulations made as occasions occurred, all burdensome forms[1] are expelled. The whole society indeed must assemble at morning and evening prayers, and at meals, if sickness does not prevent, but every other ceremonious dependance is banished; they form into different parties of amusement as best suit their inclinations, and sometimes when we go to spend the afternoon there, we shall find a party at cards in one room, in another some at work, while one is reading aloud, and in a separate chamber a set joining in a little concert, though

---

1   forms] formalities, ceremonious behaviour, implying lack of real meaning

no oppressive social rules either

none of them are great proficients in music; while two or three shall be retired into their own rooms, some go out to take the air, for it has seldom happened to them to have less than two boarders at a time who each keep an equipage; while others shall be amusing themselves in the garden, or walking in the very pleasant meadows which surround their house.

'As no one is obliged to stay a minute longer in company than she chuses, she naturally retires as soon as it grows displeasing to her, and does not return till she is prompted by inclination, and consequently well disposed to amuse and be amused. They live in the very strict practice of all religious duties; and it is not to be imagined how much good they have done in the neighbourhood; how much by their care the manners of the poorer people are reformed, and their necessities relieved, though without the distribution of much money; I say much, because, small as their incomes are, there are many who impart out of that little to those who have much less.

'Their visits to us are frequent, and we are on such a footing, that they never impede any of our employments. My friends always insisted when they waited on the community, that not one of the sisterhood should discontinue whatever they found her engaged in; this gave them the hint to do the same by us, and it is a rule, that no book is thrown aside, no pen laid down at their entrance. There are always some of us manually employed, who are at leisure to converse, and if the visit is not very short, part of it is generally spent in hearing one of the girls read aloud, who take it by turns through a great part of the day; the only difference made for this addition to the company is a change of books, that they may not hear only part of a subject, and begin by a broken thread. Thus they give no interruption, and therefore neither trouble us, nor are themselves scrupulous about coming, so that few days pass without our seeing some of them, though frequently only time enough to accompany us in our walks, or partake of our music,'

'Have you not, said Lamont, been obliged to expel many from the community? Since you do not allow petulancy of temper, nor any lightness of conduct, I should expect a continual revolution.'

'By no means, answered Mrs. Maynard, since the establishment of the community, there has been but one expelled; and one finding she

Charity — "imitating your Creator"!

the ladies play God!

was in danger of incurring the same sentence, and I believe inwardly disgusted with a country life, retired of her own free choice. Some more have rendered themselves so disagreeable, that the question has been put to the ballot; but the fear of being dismissed made them so diligent to get the majority on their side, before the hour appointed for decision arrived, that it has been determined in their favour, and the earnest desire not to be brought into the same hazard again, has induced them to mend their tempers, and some of these are now the most amiable people in the whole community.

'As for levity of conduct they are pretty well secured from it, by being exposed to few temptations in this retired place.

'Some, as in the course of nature must happen, have died, and most of them bequeathed what little they had towards constituting a fund for the continuation of the community. More of them have married; some to persons who knew them before, others to gentlemen in the neighbourhood, or such as happened to come into it; to whom their admirable conduct recommended them.'

I could not help exclaiming, 'In what a heaven do you live, thus surrounded by people who owe all their happiness to your goodness! This is, indeed, imitating your Creator, and in such proportion as your faculties will admit, partaking of his felicity, since you can no where cast your eyes, without beholding numbers who derive every earthly good from your bounty, and are indebted to your care and example for a reasonable hope of eternal happiness.'

'I will not, said Mrs. Maynard, give up my share of the felicity you so justly imagine these ladies must enjoy, though I have no part in what occasions it. When I reflect on all the blessings they impart, and see how happiness flows, as it were, in an uninterrupted current from their hands and lips, I am overwhelmed with gratitude to the Almighty disposer of my fate, for having so mercifully thrown me into such a scene of felicity, where every hour yields true heart-felt joy, and fills me with thanksgivings to Him, who enables them thus to dispense innumerable blessings, and so greatly rewards them already by the joyful consciousness of having obeyed him.'

The Ladies at this time were at too great a distance to hear our conversation, for not chusing to be present while their actions were the subjects of discourse, they had gradually strayed from us. Upon enquiring of my cousin, whether the persons in the large community we had been talking of brought any fortunes with them, she told me that 'most of them had a trifle, some not more than an hundred pounds. That in general the ladies chose to admit those who had least, as their necessities were greatest, except where some particular circumstances rendered protection more requisite to others. That the house not being large enough to contain more than were already established in it, they have been obliged to refuse admission to many, and especially some young women of near two thousand pounds fortune, the expensive turn of the world now being such, that no gentlewoman can live genteelly on the interest of that sum, and they prefer this Society to a retirement in a country town. Some who wished to board, have likewise been refused. As the expences of the first community, fall so far short of their expectation, and the sums appropriated for that purpose, they determined to hazard another of the same kind, and have just concluded a treaty for a still larger mansion, at about three miles distance, and by the persons now waiting for it, they have reason to believe it will not be less successful than the other, nor more expensive; but should they be mistaken, in that particular, they have laid aside a fund sufficient to discharge it.' Their scheme I find is to have some of the ladies down to Millennium Hall, as soon as they have made the purchase, and there they are to remain, while the necessary repairs and additions are making to the house designed for their habitation, which they imagine will not be compleated in less than half a year. They hope, by having the first admitted part of the community thus in the house with them for so long a time, to compensate, in a good degree, for the disadvantages of being settled so much farther from them. The sisterhood of the other society, likewise, in pity to those who are exposed to the same sufferings from which they have been delivered, have offered to croud themselves for a few months, to leave vacant rooms for some who are destined to the other house, till they can be there accommodated. These also will be fitted for their new way of life, and taught to aim at the happiness enjoyed in this community, by the same means that they have attained to it.

Our subject ended with our walk. Supper was served as soon as we entered the house, and general conversation concluded the evening.

Had I not been led by several facts to repeat already so many con-

[handwritten marginalia: and the community grows—]

versations, I should be induced not to bury all that passed at this time in silence; but though I have taken the liberty, when the relation of facts naturally led to it, to communicate such discourses as were pertinent to the subject, it would be presuming too far on your time, to repeat conversations which did not serve to illustrate any particular actions, however worthy they may be of recollection. I shall therefore only say, that it was not with less reluctance I retired to my chamber, at the hour of bed-time, than the night before.

The next morning proved rainy, which prevented me from making any early excursion. But as it cleared up about eleven o'clock, Lamont and I went into the garden, to enjoy the fragrance which every herb and flower exhales at this time of the year, after the desirable refreshment of gentle showers. I conducted him to the flower garden, which had so much delighted me the morning before; and we had not paid due admiration to all the vegetable beauties there exhibited to our view, when Mrs. Maynard joined us.

I told her, 'It was but a poor compliment to her conversation, to say, I longed for her company, since now my curiosity might occasion that impatience, which I should nevertheless have felt, had I not been left in painful suspense, by the interruption we had received the day before, in the midst of her narrative.'

'It would be unnatural, said she, for a woman to quarrel with curiosity; so far from complaining of yours, I am come merely with a design to gratify it, and only expect you will judge of my desire to oblige you, by my readiness in obeying your commands, were I myself the subject, the motive for my obedience might be equivocal.'

Miss MANCEL and Mrs. MORGAN's History continued.

I THINK, continued Mrs. Maynard, we left Miss Melvyn requiring to be confronted by her accuser, a request which her mother-in-law was not inclined to grant; for though in her dealings with young Simon, she had perceived such a degree of sollicitude for his own interest, and such flagrant proofs of want of integrity, that she did not doubt but that by promising him the farm, on rather better terms than she had yet consented to, he might be prevailed with to join so far in her scheme, as to assert any thing to Sir Charles, yet she dared not venture to produce him face to face to Miss Melvyn, fearing lest his assurance should fail him on so severe a trial.

She replied, therefore, that, 'the proofs were too strong to admit of doubt, but she could not think of exposing Miss Melvyn to the mortification of hearing her depravity witnessed by, perhaps, the last person whom she expected should acknowledge it. Besides, that by such an eclat the disgrace must infallibly become public, and she be deprived of the only means left her of rescuing her reputation from that infamy, to which, in a very short time, it must have been irrecoverably condemned; for it could not be supposed, that Mr. Morgan would accept as his wife a woman with a sullied character.'

Miss Melvyn was almost distracted, at being both so injuriously accused, and denied the liberty of defending herself; she begged, she intreated, on her knees, that Sir Charles would not suffer her to fall a prey to such undeserved malice. She asserted her innocence in the strongest and most persuasive terms, and insisted so warmly on her demand of being confronted with her accusers, that her father grew inclined to grant her just request. Lady Melvyn perceiving he began to comply, repeated her refusal in the most peremptory manner; and declaring to Miss Melvyn, that she had no other choice left her, but either to resolve to marry Mr. Morgan, or to be exposed to shame, in being publicly disclaimed by her parents, who would no longer suffer her to remain in their house, led Sir Charles out of the room; and he, though reluctant, dared not refuse to accompany her.

Miss Melvyn was now left to reflect on this dreadful alternative.

Filled with horror at the shocking conduct of her mother-in-law, terrified with her threats, and sensible there was no villany[1] she was not capable of perpetrating, rather than give up a point she was thus determined to carry, she was incapable of forming any resolution. She ran to her friend, to seek from her that advice and consolation, which her own distracted thoughts could not afford her.

Miss Mancel was so struck with the terror and amazement which were still impressed on Miss Melvyn's countenance, that she had not for some time courage to ask the cause. Trembling with fears of she knew not what, she embraced her distressed friend with an air of such tender, though silent sympathy, as softened the horror of Miss Melvyn's mind, and brought a shower of tears to her relief, which at length enabled her to relate all that had passed between her and her parents. Louisa found it much easier to join in her friend's grief than to administer consolation. She knew not what to advise; two artless, virtuous young women were ill qualified to contend with lady Melvyn, especially in an affair which could not be rendered public without hazarding Miss Melvyn's character; for reputation is so delicate a thing, that the least surmize casts a blemish on it; the woman who is suspected is disgraced; and though lady Melvyn did not stand high in the public opinion, yet it was scarcely possible for any one to believe she could be guilty of such flagrant wickedness.

Miss Melvyn had a very strong dislike to Mr. Morgan, whose disposition appeared as ill suited to her's as his age; to enter into wedlock without any prospect of social happiness, seemed to her one of the greatest misfortunes in life; but what was still of more weight in her estimation, she thought it the highest injustice to marry a man whom she could not love, as well as a very criminal mockery of the most solemn vows. On the other side she considered, that to preserve her reputation was not only necessary to her own happiness, but a duty to society. 'It is true, said she, I am not placed in a very conspicuous sphere of life, but I am far from being of a rank so obscure, that my actions will affect no one but myself; nor indeed do I know any so low, but that they have their equals who may copy after them, if they have no inferiors.

---

1   villany] altered to villainy in later editions

The care of our virtue we owe to ourselves, the preservation of our characters[1] is due to the world, and both are required by Him, who commands us to preserve ourselves pure and unpolluted, and to contribute as far as we are able to the well-being of all his creatures. Example is the means given universally to all whereby to benefit society. I therefore look on it as one of our principal duties, to avoid every imputation of evil; for vice appears more or less hateful, as it becomes more or less familiar. Every vicious person abates the horror which it should naturally excite in a virtuous mind. There is nothing so odious, to which custom will not in some degree reconcile us; can we expect then, that vice, which is not without its allurements, should alone retain all its deformity, when we are familiarized to its appearance. I should never therefore esteem myself innocent, however pure my actions, if I incurred the reputation of being otherwise, when it was in my power to avoid it. With this way of thinking, my Louisa, you may imagine that I might be brought to believe it my duty to sacrifice my ease of mind, to the preservation of my character; but in my case, there is no choice; I must either add to the contamination of a very profligate world, or, in the face of Heaven, enter into the most solemn vows to love a man, whom the most I can do, is not to hate. This is wilful perjury. In such an alternative duty cannot direct me, and misery must follow my decision, let me determine as I will.'

In this irresolution, Miss Melvyn left her friend, but the vent she had given to her grief had greatly calmed her spirits, and restored her to the power of reflexion. At her entrance into the house, she met Lady Melvyn, who with a very stern countenance, ordered her to go and entertain Mr. Morgan, who waited for her in the parlour. She found him alone, and as he began to renew his addresses, which a repulse from her had not discouraged, since he hoped to succeed by the influence her parents had over her, she immediately formed the resolution of endeavouring to make him relinquish his pretensions, in hopes, that if the refusal came from him, he might become the object of her mother's indignation, and her persecution might drop, at least for a time. She therefore frankly told him, that 'Tho' her affections were in-

---

1   characters] reputations

tirely disengaged, yet he was so very repugnant to them, that it was impossible she should ever feel that regard for him, which he had a right to expect from his wife; and therefore intreated him, in consideration of his own happiness, if her's were indifferent to him, not to persist in a pursuit, which, if successful, could not answer his hopes, nor reduce her to render herself wretched by becoming his wife, or to exasperate her parents by refusing him.' She then added all her heart could suggest to flatter him into compliance with this request.

Mr. Morgan's foible was not an excess of delicacy; he told her plainly, 'He admired her eloquence prodigiously, but that there was more rhetoric in her beauty, than any composition of words could contain; which pleading in direct contradiction to all she had said, she must excuse him, if he was influenced by the more powerful oratory of her charms; and her good sense and unexceptionable conduct convinced him, that when it became her duty to love him, she would no longer remain indifferent.

All Miss[1] Melvyn could urge to shew him this was but a very poor dependance, had no sort of weight, and he parted from her only more determined to hasten the conclusion of their marriage.

Lady Melvyn had not been idle all this time; she had prevailed on young Simon to acquiesce in the questions she put to him before Sir Charles, either by giving short answers, or by down cast eyes, which signified assent. With this Sir Charles acquainted Miss Melvyn, and insisted on her not thinking of exposing herself to the indignity of having the whole affair discussed in her presence. All the indignation that undeserved calumny can excite in an innocent mind, could not have enabled Miss Melvyn to bear being charged before so low a creature, with a passion for him, and still less to have heard the suborned wretch pretend to confess it. She therefore found no difficulty in obeying her father in that particular, and rather chose to submit to the imputation, than to undergo the shame which she must have suffered in endeavouring to confute it. She attempted to persuade Sir Charles, 'To permit her to stay in the house under what restrictions he and his lady should think proper, till her conduct should sufficiently convince him of her

---

1   first edition has period after Miss

innocence, and not to force her into a hated marriage, or unjustly expose her to disgrace and infamy.' Her tears and intreaties would soon have softened his heart; and as far as he dared, he shewed an inclination to comply with so reasonable a proposal; but his lady easily obliged him to retract, and to deprive Miss Melvyn of all hopes of any mitigation of the sentence already pronounced against her.

Could she without the loss of reputation have fled to a remote part of the kingdom, and have hid herself in some obscure cottage, though reduced to labour for a subsistence, she would have thought it a state far more eligible than becoming Mr. Morgan's wife; but if she thus turned fugitive and wanderer, in what light could she expect to be seen by the world; especially, as Lady Melvyn would infallibly, to remove any blame from herself, be liberal in her aspersions? Where she should be unknown, whatever disgrace might be affixed to her name, she herself might escape censure; but yet she would not be less guilty of a violation of her duty to society, since she must appear very culpable to those who knew her, and contribute to the depravity of others, as far as was in her power, by an example, which her motives being unknown, would appear a very bad one. *Her decision*

This consideration determined her to sacrifice her peace to her character; for by having told Mr. Morgan the true state of her heart, she had acquitted herself from any charge of attempting, by the gift of her hand, to deceive him into a belief that he was the object of her affections. She still had scruples about entering into the matrimonial state, on motives so different from those which ought to influence every one in an union of that kind: these were not to be removed, but she imagined this might in some measure be excused, as the least culpable part she could act; and since man was herein neither her judge nor accuser, she hoped the integrity of her mind would be received as some alleviation of a fault she was thus forced to commit, since she was determined in the strictest manner to adhere to every duty of her station.

Having formed this resolution, she went to consult her friend upon it, who was a person less perplexed, though scarcely less concerned, as their affections were so strongly united, that one could not suffer without the other's feeling equal pain, might possibly be a calmer judge in so delicate a point. Louisa subscribed to her friend's sentiments on the occasion, only 'desired her to consider well, whether she should be able to bear all the trials she might meet with in the married state, when she was entirely indifferent to her husband.'

'My prospect, said Miss Melvyn, I am sensible is extremely melancholy. All inclination must now be laid aside, and duty must become my sole guide and director. Happiness is beyond my view; I cannot even hope for ease, since I must keep a constant restraint on my very thoughts. Indifference will become criminal; and if I cannot conquer it, to conceal it at least will be a duty. I have learnt to suffer, but was never yet taught disguise and hypocrisy;[1] herein will consist my greatest difficulty; I abhor deceit, and yet must not shew the real sentiments of my heart. Linked in society with a man I cannot love, the world can afford me no pleasure, indeed no comfort, for I am insensible to all joy but what arises from the social affections. The grave, I confess, appears to me far more eligible than this marriage, for I might there hope to be at peace. Mr. Morgan's fortune is large, but his mind is narrow and ungenerous, and his temper plainly not good. If he really loved me, he could not suffer me to be forced into a marriage which he well knows I detest: a knowledge which will not mend my fate, most certainly.

'Could I enjoy the pleasures of self-approbation, it would be impossible to be very wretched, but the most exact performance of my duty will not yield me that gratification, since I cannot be perfectly satisfied that I do right, in marrying a man so very disagreeable to me. I fear the pride of reputation influences[2] me more than I imagine, and though it is as justifiable as any pride, yet still it is certainly no virtue.'

'When I reflect, said she, afterwards, on the step I am going to take, my terrors are inexpressible; how dreadful is it at my age, when nature seems to promise me so many years of life, to doom myself to a state of wretchedness, which death alone can terminate, and wherein I must bury all my sorrows in silence, without even the melancholy relief of pouring them forth in the bosom of my friend, and seeking, from her tender participation, the only consolation I could receive! for after this

---

1   taught disguise and hypocrisy] conduct books for women commonly advised disguising real feelings, opinions, and abilities
2   influences] influencies in first edition

dreaded union is compleated, duty will forbid me to make my distresses known, even to my Louisa; I must not then expose the faults of him whose slightest failings I ought to conceal. One only hope remains, that you, my first and dearest friend, will not abandon me; that whatever cloud of melancholy may hang over my mind, yet you will still bear with me, and remove your abode to a place where I may have the consolation of your company. If it be in my power to make my house a comfortable habitation to my Louisa, I cannot be entirely wretched.'

Duty

Miss Mancel gave her the tenderest assurances of fixing at least in her neighbourhood, since a second paradise could not recompense her for the loss of her society; and that on no terms could she prevail on herself to continue in a house where she must see that wretched Simon, who had been a vile instrument in reducing her friend to that distressful situation. This gleam of comfort was a very seasonable relief to Miss Melvyn's dejected spirits, and gave some respite to her tears.

As soon as she returned home, she acquainted Sir Charles and Lady Melvyn with her resolution, who soon communicated it to Mr. Morgan; and nothing was now thought of but hastening the wedding as much as possible.

'I wonder, interrupted Lamont, how Miss Melvyn could bring herself to let her mother-in-law have such an opportunity of exulting in the success of her detestable arts.'

More audience participation | another lesson for Lamont

'That, replied Mrs. Maynard, was a consideration which had no weight with her, nor should it indeed be any mortification to our pride, that deceit and cunning have triumphed over us. Wickedness serves itself by weapons which we would not use, and if we are wounded with them, we have no more reason to be mortified, than a man would have to think his courage disgraced, because when he lay sleeping in his bed, he was taken prisoner by a body of armed men. To be circumvented by cunning, must ever be the fate, but never the disgrace of the artless.'

As Miss Melvyn's compliance procured her a greater degree of favour at home than she had ever before enjoyed, Miss Mancel was suffered to come to the house, and met with an obliging reception from the whole family. Her continual presence there was a great support to her friend in her very disagreeable situation, and after indulging her sorrow in their private conversation, and mingling their sympathetic[1] tears, she was the better able to endure the restraint which she was obliged to undergo, when any other person was present.

The dreaded day fixed on for this unhappy union soon came, and Miss Melvyn received Mr. Morgan's hand and name with all the fortitude she could assume; but her distress was visible to all, even to Mr. Morgan, who was so little touched with it, that it proved no abatement to his joy; a symptom of such indelicacy of mind, as increased his bride's grief and apprehensions.

The day after their marriage, Mrs. Morgan asked his permission to invite Miss Mancel to his house, to which he answered, 'Madam, my wife must have no other companion or friend but her husband; I shall never be averse to your seeing company, but intimates I forbid;[2] I shall not choose to have my faults discussed between you and your *friend*.' Mrs. Morgan was not much less stunned by this reply, than if she had been struck with lightening. Practised as she had long been in commanding her passions and inclinations, a torrent of tears forced their way.

'I did not want this proof, resumed Mr. Morgan, that I have but a small share of your affections; and were I inclined to grant your request, you could not have found a better means of preventing it; for I will have no person in my house more beloved than myself. When you have no other friend, added he with a malicious smile, I may hope for the honour of that title.'

Mrs. Morgan was so well convinced before of the littleness of his mind, that she was more afflicted than surprized at this instance of it, and wished he would not have rendered it more difficult to esteem him, by so openly professing his ungenerous temper. However she silently acquiesced; but that her friend might not feel the pain of believing herself neglected, she was obliged to tell her what had passed.

The new married couple staid but two days longer at Sir Charles's. Fortunately Mr. Morgan spent the last day abroad in paying visits in

---

1   sympathetic] symphathetic in first edition
2   intimates I forbid] conduct books for women commonly advised against wives having too many or too close female friends, as interference in obligations to one's husband

the neighbourhood, which gave the two unhappy friends leisure to lament their ill fortune in this cruel separation, without giving the cause of it any new offence. They took a melancholy leave that night, fearing that even a correspondence between them might be considerably restrained by this arbitrary husband, who seemed to think his wife's affections were to be won by force, not by gentleness and generous confidence.

This was the severest affliction they had ever yet experienced, or indeed were capable of feeling. United from their childhood, the connection of soul and body did not seem more indissoluble, nor were ever divided with greater pain. They foresaw no end to this cruel separation; for they could not expect that a husband's complaisance to his wife should increase after he ceased to be a bridegroom. Louisa indeed, who wished if possible to reconcile her friend to her fate, pretended to hope that her good conduct might in time enlarge his mind, and cure him of that mean suspicious temper, which then made him fear to have his faults exposed by a wife, whose chief endeavour would be to conceal them.

But such distant views afforded no consolation to Mrs. Morgan's affectionate heart; the present pain engaged her thoughts too much to suffer her to look so far off for comfort. She had flattered herself not only with the hopes of enjoying Miss Mancel's company, but of delivering her from all the difficulties of her situation, in offering her a protection from insult or poverty. To be disappointed of so delightful a prospect was her greatest affliction, and sat much heavier on her mind, than the loss of her beloved society.

The evening was far spent, when Lady Melvyn found them drowned in tears, anticipating the pangs of parting, the employment of that whole day; and as her ladyship's hatred for her daughter-in-law was much subsided, since she no longer feared the observation of her too-virtuous eye, her natural disposition inclined her to prevent the wife's discovering her real sentiments to her husband; she therefore reminded them, that Mr. Morgan must then be on his way home, and advised, that by all means they should part before his return, lest he should be witness of a sorrow which he would take amiss. They were sensible that in this her ladyship judged well, and Louisa's fear of occasioning any additional uneasiness to her friend, gave her resolution and strength to take a last farewel. Mrs. Morgan's maid attended her home, as she was too much affected to be able to perform that little walk without some support. Mrs. Morgan's condition was still more deplorable; more dead than alive, she followed Louisa's steps with eager eyes, till a turning in the road robbed her of the sight of her friend; and then, as if her eyes had no other employment worthy of them left, they were again overwhelmed in tears. Lady Melvyn found her incapable of consolation; but more successfully endeavoured to make her suppress the indulgence of her grief, by alarming her fears with the approach of Mr. Morgan. As soon as she was a little composed, she led her into the garden for air. The night was fine, and the moon shone very resplendent, the beauty of the scene, and the freshness of the air a little revived her; and as Mr. Morgan staid out later than they expected, she had time to acquire a sufficient command over herself to receive him with an air of tolerable chearfulness.

The new married pair set out early the next morning, and arrived at Mr. Morgan's seat the following day. The house was large and old, the furniture not much less ancient, the situation dreary, the roads every where bad, the soil a stiff clay, wet and dirty, except in the midst of summer; the country round it disagreeable, and in short, destitute of every thing that could afford any satisfaction to Mrs. Morgan. Nature no where appears graced with fewer charms. Mrs. Morgan however had vexations so superior, that she paid little regard to external circumstances, and was so fully determined to acquit herself properly in her new sphere, that she appeared pleased with every thing around her. Hypocrisy, as she observed, was now become a virtue, and the only one which she found it difficult to practise. They were received on their arrival by a maiden sister of Mr. Morgan's, who till then had kept his house, and he intended should still remain in it; for as through the partiality of an aunt, who had bred her up, she was possessed of a large fortune, her brother, in whom avarice was the ruling passion, was very desirous of keeping in her favour.

Mrs. Susanna Morgan had lived immaculate to the age of fifty-five. The state of virginity could not be laid to her charge as an offence against society, for it had not been voluntary. In her youth she was rather distinguished for sensibility. Her aunt's known riches gave the niece the reputation of a great fortune, an attraction to which she was indebted for many lovers, who constantly took their leave on finding the old lady would not advance any part of the money which she designed to bequeath her niece. Miss Susanna, extremely susceptible by nature, was favourably disposed to all her admirers, and imagining herself successively in love with each, lived in a course of disappointments. In reality, the impression was made only on her vanity, and her heart continued unengaged; but she felt such a train of mortifications very severely, and perhaps suffered more upon the whole, than if she had been strongly impressed with one passion. In time the parcimony[1] of her old aunt became generally known, and the young lady then was left free from the tender importunity of lovers, of which nothing else could probably have deprived her; for as she never had any natural attractions, she was not subject to a decay of charms; at near fifty-three her aunt departed this life, and left her in possession of twenty-thousand pounds, a fortune which served to swell her pride, without increasing her happiness.

Nature had not originally bestowed upon her much sweetness of temper, and her frequent disappointments, each of which she termed being crossed in love, had completely soured it. Every pretty woman was the object of her envy, I might almost say every married woman. She despised all that were not as rich as herself, and hated every one who was superior or equal to her in fortune. Tormented inwardly with her own ill-nature, she was incapable of any satisfaction but what arose from teazing others; nothing could dispel the frown on her brow, except the satisfaction she felt when she had the good fortune to give pain to any of her dependants; a horrid grin then distorted her features, and her before lifeless eyes glistened with malice and rancorous joy. She had read just enough to make her pedantic, and too little to give her any improving knowledge. Her understanding was naturally small, and her self-conceit great. In her person[2] she was tall and meagre, her hair black, and her complexion of the darkest brown, with an additional sallowness at her temples and round her eyes, which were dark, very large and prominent, and entirely without lustre; they had but one

---

1   parcimony] altered to parsimony in later editions
2   person] body, physical attributes

the awful sister-in-law

look, which was that of gloomy stupid ill-nature, except, as I have already said, when they were enlivened by the supreme satisfaction of having made somebody uneasy, then what before was but disagreeable became horrible. To complete the description of her face, she had a broad flat nose, a wide mouth, furnished with the worst set of teeth I ever saw, and her chin was long and pointed. She had heard primness so often mentioned as the characteristic of an old maid, that to avoid wearing that appearance, she was slatternly and dirty to an excess; besides she had great addition of filthiness, from a load of Spanish snuff, with which her whole dress was covered, as if, by her profusion in that particular, she thought to compensate for her general parsimony.

This lady, Mrs. Morgan found in possession of her house, and was received by her with that air of superiority, to which Mrs. Susanna thought herself intitled by her age and fortune. Mrs. Morgan's charms, though drooping like a blighted flower, excited much envy in Susanna's breast, and she soon congratulated her, on her extraordinary happiness in having captivated a gentleman of so large a fortune, when her own was at present so very small.

At first she commended her, for not being elated with so great an acquisition, but in a little time taxed her with ungrateful insensibility to so prodigious a blessing. She continually criticized her œconomy, accusing her of indolence; representing, how 'she used every morning to rouse the servants from their idleness, by giving each such a scold, as quickened their diligence for the whole day; nor could a family be well managed by any one who omitted this necessary duty.' Mrs. Morgan's desire that her servants should enjoy the comforts of plenty, and when sick, receive the indulgence which that condition requires, brought her continual admonitions against extravagance, wherein Mr. Morgan readily joined; for his avarice was so great, that he repined at the most necessary expences.

His temper was a mixture of passion and pevishness,[1] two things that seldom go together; but he would fret himself into a passion, and then through weariness of spirits cool into fretfulness, till he was sufficiently recovered to rise again into rage. This was the common course

---

1   pevishness] altered to peevishness in later editions

of his temper, which afforded variety, but no relief.

Sensible that his wife married him without affection, he seemed to think it impossible ever to gain her love, and therefore spared himself all fruitless endeavours. He was indeed fond of her person; he admired her beauty, but despised her understanding, which in truth was un-avoidable; for his ideas and conversation were so low and sordid, that he was not qualified to distinguish the charms of her elegant mind. Those who know Mrs. Morgan best, are convinced that she suffered less uneasiness from his ill-humour, brutal as it was, than from his nau-seous fondness. But the account I give of him, I have received from others; Mrs. Morgan never mentions his name, if it can possibly be avoided; and when she does, it is always with respect. In this situation, a victim to the ill-humour both of her husband and his sister; we will leave Mrs. Morgan, and return to that friend whose letters were her only consolation.

Miss Mancel's person was so uncommonly fine, that she could not be long settled in the country without attracting general notice. Though the lower rank of people may be less refined in their ideas, yet her beauty was so very striking, that it did not escape their admiration, and *the handsome lady*, as they called her, became the general subject of discourse. As church was the only place where she was exposed to public view, she had from the first endeavoured to elude observation, by mingling in the croud, and sitting in the most obscure seat; but when fame had awakened the curiosity of those of higher rank, she was easily distinguished, and in a short time many inhabitants of the neigh-bouring parishes came to that church to see her. She more than an-swered every expectation; for such perfection of beauty scarcely ever came out of the hands of nature. Many ladies in the neighbourhood in-troduced themselves to her, and found her behaviour as enchanting as her person. She could not be insensible of the approbation which every eye significantly expressed; but she was abashed, and in some degree more mortified than delighted by it. She well remembered what Mr. d'Avora had said to her on that subject, and saw that in her situation beauty was a disadvantage. He often repeated the same thing to her in letters, (for she and Miss Melvyn keeping up a constant correspondance with him, the latter had acquainted him with the general admiration paid to Louisa) and told her, that he feared the plan they had formed

for her future way of life, was at a still greater distance than they had
hoped, since her beauty was the great obstacle to its being put in execution.

The ladies of the best fashion in the neighbourhood begged leave to
visit her; and though she more than ever wished to have her time uninterrupted, since as she had no prospect of any other means of support,
it was necessary, by such little additions as she could make to her small
fund, to prevent its quick diminution, yet she could not decline the civilities so obligingly offered her, but avoided all intimacy with any of
them as foreign to her plan, and hurtful to her interest. Thus was she
circumstanced in respect to the neighbourhood when Miss Melvyn
married.

As after this event Louisa was determined to change her habitation;
she began to enquire for some family, where she might be accommodated in the same manner, as in that where she was then fixed. Among
the persons who had taken most notice of her was Lady Lambton, a
person of admirable understanding, polite, generous and good-natured; who had no fault, but a considerable share of pride. She piqued
herself upon the opulence of her family, and a distinguished birth, but
her good sense, and many virtues, so qualified this one blemish, that it
did not prevent her being a very amiable woman.

When she found Miss Mancel designed to change her abode, she
told her, that at an honest farmer's near her house, she might be accommodated, but that as some little alterations would be requisite to
make the place fit for her, she, in the most obliging manner, desired
her company till the apartment was ready; which would give her opportunity to see that such things were done to it, as would be most
convenient and agreeable. Lady Lambton insisted so strongly on Miss
Mancel's accepting this invitation, that she could not without incivility
refuse it; and, as after the loss of her friend, all places were alike to her,
she had no reason to decline so obliging an offer.

No great preparations were required for this removal of abode.
Lady Lambton came herself to fetch Miss Mancel home. The old lady
was charmed with her new guest; many of whose accomplishments
were unknown to her till she came under the same roof, and would
not suffer any preparations to be made for another lodging, but insisted
on her continuing much longer with her.

Lady Lambton behaved in so very obliging a manner, and Louisa found so much pleasure and improvement in the conversation of a woman, whose admirable understanding and thorough knowledge of the world are seldom to be parallelled, that she could not be more agreeably placed; as she dared not go even into Mrs. Morgan's neighbourhood, for fear of giving additional uneasiness to one, whose situation she plainly perceived was by no means happy; for though Mrs. Morgan suppressed all complaints, never hinted at the treatment she received, and endeavoured to represent her way of life in the best colours, to save her friend the sympathetic pangs of heart, which she knew she would feel for her sufferings; yet the alteration in her stile, the melancholy turn of mind, which in spight of all her care, was visible in her letters, could not escape the observation of one whose natural discernment was quickened by affection.

The full persuasion of Mrs. Morgan's unhappiness, and that anxious sollicitude which arose from her ignorance as to the degree of her wretchedness, was a source of continual grief to her mind, which Lady Lambton's sincere friendship could scarcely alleviate. But she knew too well, how few people can bear the unhappy, to suffer her uneasiness to appear. She stifled therefore every expression of that kind; for if Lady Lambton had generously sympathized in her affliction, it would have given her pain to know she had occasioned that lady's feeling any; and if she had been insensible to it, complaints would not fail to disgust her.

Lady Lambton was fond of music, and not void of taste for painting; Miss Mancel's excellence in these arts, therefore afforded her the highest entertainment. Her ladyship was likewise a mistress of languages, and was pleased to find Louisa equally acquainted with them. In this house Miss Mancel had passed above a twelve month, when Sir Edward Lambton returned from his travels,[1] in which he had spent four years. As soon as he arrived in the kingdom he came to wait on Lady Lambton, his grandmother; who was likewise his guardian, his father and mother being both dead. She had longed with impatience for his

---

1   travels] at this time young men of well-to-do families were often sent on the "Grand Tour" of Europe to see famous places, so as to complete intellectual and aesthetic education, and to mix in fashionable upper-class European society, so as to polish the manners and social skills

Lady Lambton's Grandson!

Sr. Edward

return, but thought herself well repaid for his absence by the great improvement which was very visible both in his manner and person.

Sir Edward was extremely handsome, his person fine and graceful, his conversation lively and entertaining, politeness adding charms to an excellent understanding. His behaviour, I have been told, was particularly engaging, his temper amiable, though somewhat too warm, and he had all his grandmother's generosity, without any of her pride.

It would have been strange if a man of three and twenty years old (for that was Sir Edward's age) had not been much charmed with so lovely a woman as Miss Mancel. That he was so, soon became visible, but she, as well as his grandmother, for some time imagined the attentions he paid her were only the natural result of the gallantry usual at his age, and improved into a softer address, by a manner acquired in travelling through countries where gallantry is publicly professed. Lady Lambton however, knowing her own discernment, expressed some fears to Louisa, lest her grandson should become seriously in love with her, in order to discover by her countenance, whether there was really any ground for her apprehensions, which she founded on the impossibility of his marrying a woman of small fortune, without reducing himself to the greatest inconvenience, as his estate was extremely incumbered, and he was by an intail[1] deprived of the liberty of selling any part of it to discharge the debt. She was too polite to mention her chief objection to Miss Mancel, which was in reality the obscurity of her birth.

Louisa, who sincerely believed Sir Edward had no real passion for her, answered with a frankness which entirely convinced Lady Lambton that she had received no serious address from him; but Louisa, who saw herself now in the situation which Mr. d'Avora had warned her against, begged permission to leave Lady Lambton's, to prevent her ladyship's being under any uneasiness, and to avoid all danger of Sir Edward's receiving any strong impression in her favour.

Lady Lambton was unwilling to part with her amiable companion; and besides, thought if her grandson was really enamoured, she should

---

1   incumbered] encumbered, or burdened with debts; intail] entail, or settlement of the succession of a landed estate so that it may not be bequeathed at pleasure by any one possessor; in the eighteenth century this legal device was used often to keep an estate in the family

increase the danger rather than lessen it, by not keeping Louisa under her eye; she therefore told her she could not consent to lose her company, and was certain she might depend on her honour. Louisa thanked her for her good opinion, and assured her she would never do any thing to forfeit it.

Sir Edward was more captivated than either of the ladies imagined, and every day increased his passion. Louisa's beauty, her conversation, and accomplishments were irresistible; but as he knew the great occasion he had to marry a woman of fortune, he long endeavoured to combat his inclinations. He might have conceived hopes of obtaining any other woman in her circumstances on easier terms;[1] but there was such dignity and virtue shone forth in her, and he was so truly in love, that such a thought never entered his imagination. He reverenced and respected her like a divinity, but hoped that prudence might enable him to conquer his passion, at the same time that it had not force enough to determine him to fly her presence, the only possible means of lessening the impression which every hour engraved more deeply on his heart, by bringing some new attractions to his view. He little considered, that the man who has not power to fly from temptation, will never be able to resist it by standing his ground.

Louisa was not long before she grew sensible, that what she had offered to Lady Lambton for the ease of her ladyship's mind, was advisable to secure the peace of her own. Sir Edward's merit, his sincere respect for her, which certainly is the most powerful charm to a woman of delicacy, could scarcely fail to make an impression on a heart so tender, so generous as her's. She kept so strict a watch over herself, that she soon perceived her sensibility, and endeavoured to prevail on Lady Lambton to part with her; but the old lady imagining it was only in order to quiet her apprehensions, would not consent; and the difficulty in finding a place where she could be properly received, strongly discouraged her from insisting on it. If she continued in the neighbourhood, her purpose would not be answered; for she could not avoid Sir Edward's visits; her only friend was denied the liberty of protecting her, and to go into a place where she was unknown, would subject a young

---

1   on easier terms] that is, as a mistress rather than a wife

woman of her age and beauty to a thousand dangers.

These difficulties detained her, though unwillingly, at Lady Lambton's for above half a year after Sir Edward's return; who, at length, unable to confine in silence a passion which had long been obvious to every observer, took an opportunity, when alone with Louisa, to declare his attachment in the most affecting manner. She received it not with surprize, but with real sorrow. She had no tincture of coquetry in her composition; but if she had been capable of it, her affections were too deeply engaged to have suffered her to retain it. Her sensibility was never so strongly awakened; all her endeavours to restrain it were no longer of force, her heart returned his passion, and would have conquered every thing but her justice and her honour; these were deeply engaged to Lady Lambton; and she would have detested herself, if she could have entertained a thought of making that lady's goodness to her, the occasion of the greatest vexation she could receive. She therefore never hesitated on the part she should act on this trying occasion; but the victories which honour gains over the tender affections, are not to be obtained without the severest pangs. Thus tormented by the struggles between duty and affection, she was not immediately capable of giving him an answer; but finding that her difficulties were increasing, by his repeated professions, and animated by the necessity of silencing a love, which too successfully sollicited a return of affection, she assumed a sufficient command over herself to conceal her sentiments, and with averted eyes, lest her heart should through them contradict her words, she told him, 'he distressed her to the greatest degree; that the respect she had for him on account of his own merit, and not less for the relation he bore to Lady Lambton, made her extremely concerned that he should have conceived a passion for her, which it was not in her power to return; nor could she listen to it in justice to Lady Lambton, to whom she was bound in all the ties of gratitude; neither should any thing ever prevail with her to do any thing prejudicial to the interests of a family into which she had been so kindly received.'

Sir Edward was too much in love to acquiesce in so nice a point of honour; but Louisa would not wait to hear arguments which it was so painful to her to refute, and retired into her own chamber, to lament in secret her unhappy fate in being obliged to reject the addresses of a man, whose affections, were she at liberty, she would think no sacrifice

(Louisa stands firm)

too great to obtain.

Miss Mancel endeavoured as much as possible to avoid giving Sir Edward any opportunity of renewing his addresses; but his vigilance found the means of seeing her alone more than once, when he warmly urged the partiality of her behaviour, representing 'how much more his happiness was concerned in the success of a passion which possessed his whole soul, than his grandmother's could be in disappointing it. She, he observed, was actuated only by pride, he by the sincerest love that ever took place in a human heart. In accepting his addresses Louisa could only mortify Lady Lambton; in rejecting them, she must render him miserable. Which, he asked, had the best title to her regard, the woman who could ungenerously and injudiciously set a higher value on riches and birth than on her very superior excellencies, or the man who would gladly sacrifice fortune, and every other enjoyment the world could afford, to the possession of her; of her who alone could render life desirable to him?' By these, and many other arguments, and what was more prevalent than all the arguments that could be deduced from reason, by the tenderest intreaties that the most ardent passion could dictate, Sir Edward endeavoured to persuade Louisa to consent to marry him, but all proved unavailing. She sometimes thought what he said was just, but aware of her partiality, she could not believe herself an unprejudiced judge, and feared that she might mistake the sophistry of love, for the voice of reason. She was sure, while honour, truth, and gratitude, pleaded against inclination they must be in the right, though their remonstrances were hushed into a whisper by the louder sollicitations of passion. Convinced that she could not be to blame, while she acted in contradiction to her secret choice, since the sincerity of her intentions were thereby plainly, though painfully evinced, she persisted in refusing to become Sir Edward's wife, and told him, that 'if he did not discontinue his addresses, he would force her to leave the house, and retire to any place that would afford her a quiet refuge from his importunity.'

A hint of this sort was sufficient to drive Sir Edward almost to distraction, and Louisa dared not pursue the subject. When he found she could not be induced to consent to an immediate marriage, he endeavoured to obtain a promise of her hand after Lady Lambton's decease; though to a man of his impatient and strong passions such a delay was

(self-denial?)

worse than death; but Miss Mancel told him, 'by such an engagement she should be guilty of a mean evasion, and that she should think it as great a breach of honour as marrying him directly.'

The despair to which Louisa's conduct reduced Sir Edward, whose love seemed to increase with the abatement of his hopes, was very visible to his grandmother, but her pride was invincible; neither her affection for him, nor her great esteem for Miss Mancel's merit, could conquer her aversion to their union. She saw them both unhappy, but was convinced the pangs they felt would not be of very long continuance, trusting to the usual inconstancy of young persons, while the inconveniencies attending an incumbered fortune, and the disgrace which she imagined must be the consequence of Sir Edward's marrying a woman of obscure birth, would be permanent, and influence the whole course of his life.

Louisa, unable to support so hard a conflict, continually resisting both her lover, and her love, was determined to seek some relief from absence. She wrote Mr. d'Avora a faithful account of all the difficulties of her situation, and intreated him to receive her into his house, till he could find some proper place wherein to fix her abode.

This worthy friend approved her conduct, while he grieved for her distress; his honest heart felt a secret indignation against Lady Lambton, who could, by false pride, be blinded to the honour which he thought such a woman as Miss Mancel must reflect on any family into which she entered. He wrote that young lady word, that 'she might be assured of the best reception his house could afford, and every service that it was in his power to render her; desiring that she would let him know when she proposed setting out, that he might meet her on the road, not thinking it proper she should travel alone.'

This letter gave Miss Mancel much satisfaction; she was now secure of an asylum; but the great difficulty still remained, she knew now how to get away from Lady Lambton's in a proper manner; for to go clandestinely was not suitable to her character, and might bring it into suspicion. In this dilemma she thought it best to apply to that lady, and with her usual frankness told her, (what had not escaped her discernment) the affection Sir Edward had conceived for her, and the return her own heart made to it; only suppressing his solicitations, as her ladyship might be offended with his proceeding so far without her consent.

She represented 'the imprudence of her continuing in the house with Sir Edward, whereby both his passion and her own must be increased; and yet she was at a loss how to depart privately, but was convinced it could not be effected[1] with his knowledge, without such an eclat as must be very disagreeable to them all; nor could she answer for her own resolution, when put to so severe a trial; as she should have more than her full measure of affliction in going from thence, without being witness to its effect on him.'

One should have imagined that the generosity of Miss Mancel's conduct, might have influenced Lady Lambton in her favour; but though it increased her esteem, it did not alter her resolution. With inexcusable insensibility she concerted measures with her, and engaged to procure Sir Edward's absence for a short time. Some very necessary business indeed demanded his presence in a neighbouring county, where the greatest part of his estate lay, but he had not been able to prevail on himself to leave Louisa; too much enamoured to think any pecuniary advantage could compensate for the loss of her company. But as it was natural that an old grandmother should see the matter in another light; her pressing him to go and settle his affairs, gave him no cause to suspect any latent meaning, and was too reasonable to be any longer opposed.

Though Sir Edward was resolved on so quick a dispatch of business, as promised him a speedy return, yet any separation from Miss Mancel, however short, appeared a severe misfortune. The evening before the day of his departure, he contrived to see her alone, and renewed his importunities with redoubled ardour, but with no better success than before. He lamented the necessity he was under of leaving her, though but for a little time, with an agony of mind better suited to an eternal separation. She, who saw it in that light, was overcome with the tender distress which a person must feel at taking a final leave of one who is extremely dear to her. Her own grief was more than she could have concealed; but when she anticipated in her thoughts, what he would suffer when he knew he had lost her for ever, and judged from the pain he felt on the approach of what he thought so short an absence; how

---

1   effected] affected in first edition

very great his distress would be, she was unable to support the scene
with her usual steadiness. Tears insensibly stole down her face, and bestowed on it still greater charms than it had ever yet worn, by giving
her an air of tenderness, which led him to hope that she did not behold
his passion with indifference. This thought afforded him a consolation
which he had never before received; and though it increased his love,
yet it abated his distress, and rendered him more able to leave her, since
he flattered himself she would with pleasure see him return, which he
was now more than ever resolved to do as speedily as possible.

The day of his departure she spent chiefly in her own room, to conceal, as far as she was able, a weakness she was ashamed of, but could
not conquer. She had written the day before to inform Mr. d'Avora,
that she should set out for London four days after her letter. Accordingly at the time appointed, after having agreed with Lady Lambton,
that Sir Edward must be kept ignorant of the place to which she was
gone, she set out with that lady, who carried her in her coach twelve
miles of the way, and then delivered her to Mr. d'Avora, who was
come thither to receive her. Lady Lambton could not part with her
amiable companion without regret, and expressed her true sense of her
merit in such strong terms to Mr. d'Avora, who could not forgive that
pride which occasioned so much pain both to Louisa and Sir Edward,
that he told her in plain terms, how very happy, and how much honoured any man must be, who had her for his wife. Perhaps Lady
Lambton would have subscribed to his opinion, had any one but her
grandson been concerned; but the point was too tender, and it was no
small command over herself, that prevented her giving the good old
man a hint that she thought him impertinent.

Our travellers arrived in town the next day, after a melancholy journey, for even the company of a friend she so much loved and esteemed,
could not restore Miss Mancel's natural vivacity, though in compassion
to the good old man, who sympathised tenderly in her distress, she endeavoured to the utmost of her power, to conceal how very deeply she
was afflicted. It was some little time before her spirits were sufficiently
composed to form any scheme for her future life, nor were they
benefitted by a letter from Lady Lambton, which acquainted her that Sir
Edward, at his return, finding she had left the place, that his grandmother
had consented to her departure, and refused to tell him where she was

gone, was for some days frantic with rage and grief, and had just then left Lady Lampton, with a determination to serve as volunteer in the army in Germany,[1] in hopes, he said, to find there a release from his afflictions, which nothing but the hand of death could bestow.

The old lady was much shocked at this event, but hoped a little time would restore his reason, and enable him to bear his disappointment with patience. 'There was room to believe, she said, that the rest of the campaign would pass over without a battle, and if so the change of scene might abate his passion.'

Louisa's heart was too tenderly engaged to reason so philosophically, she was almost distracted with her fears, and was often inclined to blame her own scruples, that had driven so worthy a man to such extremities. All Mr. d'Avora could urge to reconcile her to herself, and to calm her apprehensions for Sir Edward, were scarcely sufficient to restore her to any ease of mind; but at length he brought her to submit patiently to her fate, and to support her present trial with constancy.

They were still undetermined as to her future establishment, when Mr. d'Avora one day met an old acquaintance and countryman in the street. As this person had many years before returned to his native country, Mr. d'Avora inquired what had again brought him into England? His friend replied, that he was come in quality of factotum to a widow lady of fortune. In the course of their conversation he asked Mr. d'Avora, if he could recommend a waiting woman to his lady, her's having died on the road. The character this man gave of his mistress inclined Mr. d'Avora to mention the place to Miss Mancel, who readily agreed, that he should endeavour to obtain it for her.

Mr. d'Avora had engaged the man to call on him the next day, by telling him he believed he might be able to recommend a most valuable young person to his lady. He was punctual to his appointment, and conducted Mr. d'Avora and Louisa to Mrs. Thornby's, that was the name of the lady in question.

Miss Mancel was dressed with care, but of a very different sort from

---

1   army in Germany] during the War of the Austrian Succession (1740-8) Britain financed armies fighting against the French and on the side of Austria; the war was widely unpopular in Britain

what is usually aimed at; all her endeavours had been to conceal her youth and beauty as much as possible under great gravity of dress, and to give her all the disadvantages consistent with neatness and cleanliness. But such art was too thin a veil to hide her charms. Mrs. Thornby was immediately struck with her beauty, and made some scruple of taking a young person into her service, whom she should look upon as a great charge, and she feared her maid might require more attention from her, than she should think necessary for any servant to pay to herself. Mr. d'Avora represented to her, 'how cruel it was that beauty, which was looked upon as one of the most precious gifts of nature, should disqualify a young woman for obtaining a necessary provision. That this young person's prudence was so irreproachable, as sufficiently secured her from any disadvantages, which might naturally be feared from it. But still he allowed, her person would justly deter a married woman from receiving her, and might make a cautious mother avoid it, since her good conduct would rather add to, than diminish her attractions, therefore it was only with a single lady she could hope to be placed; and he was well convinced, that such an one would have reason to think herself happy, in so accomplished a servant; since her mind was still more amiable than her person.'

Mrs. Thornby allowed what he said to be reasonable,[1] and was so charmed with Louisa's appearance, that she assured him she would receive her with pleasure. She was in haste for a servant, and Miss Mancel had no reason to delay her attendance, therefore it was agreed she should enter into her place the next day.

When Lady Lambton took leave of Louisa, she would have forced her to receive a very handsome present; Louisa had accepted many while she lived with her ladyship, but at this time she said, 'it would look like receiving a compensation for the loss of Sir Edward; and as she chose to sacrifice both her inclinations and happiness to her regard for Lady Lambton, she could not be induced to accept any thing that looked like a reward for an action, which if she had not thought it her duty, nothing could have prevailed with her to perform.' The tenderest affections of her heart were too much concerned in what she had

---

1   reasonable] reasona- in first edition

done, to leave her the power of feeling any apprehensions of poverty; all the evils that attend it then appeared to her so entirely external, that she beheld them with the calm philosophy of a stoic,[1] and not from a very contrary motive; the insensibility of each arose from a ruling passion; the stoic's from pride, her's from love. But though she feared not poverty, she saw it was advisable to fix upon some establishment, as soon as it could be obtained; and therefore received great satisfaction from being assured of Mrs. Thornby's acceptance of her services. Mr. d'Avora was not without hopes, that if Sir Edward continued constant till Lady Lambton's death, Louisa might then, without any breach of honour or gratitude, marry him; though to have engaged herself to do so, would, as she observed, have been scarcely less inexcusable than an immediate consent; therefore he advised her to assume another name, as Sir Edward might not choose, after she was his wife, to have it known that she had been reduced to servitude.

Louisa was accordingly received at Mrs. Thornby's by the name of Menil. Her good sense and assiduity enabled her to acquit herself so well in her new place, as greatly delighted her mistress; and though she concealed the greatest part of her accomplishments, sensible they could be of no assistance, and might on the contrary raise a prejudice against her; yet her behaviour and conversation so plainly indicated a superior education, that before she had been there a week, Mrs. Thornby told her, she was certain she had not been born for the station she was then in, and begged a particular account of her whole life.

Louisa fearing that a compliance would render her less agreeable to her mistress, who already treated her with a respect, which seemed more than was due to her situation, and often appeared uneasy at seeing her perform the necessary duties of her place; intreated to be spared a task, which, she said, was attended with some circumstances so melancholy, as greatly affected her spirits on a particular recollection.

Mrs. Thornby's curiosity was not abated by this insinuation, and she repeated her request in a manner so importunate, and at the same time so kind, that Louisa could no longer, without manifest disrespect, de-

---

1   stoic] someone who tries to be indifferent to pleasure or pain, named after the Greek school
     of philosophers around Zeno of Athens, who lived about 300 B.C.

her mother!! — is Mrs. Thornby!

reunion scene

cline it.

She began then by acquainting her, that she went by a borrowed name; but had proceeded no farther in her narration, than to tell her that her real name was Mancel, and that she had been left to the care of an aunt, in her earliest infancy, by parents who were obliged, for reasons she could never learn, to leave their country, when Mrs. Thornby exclaimed, My child! my child! and sinking on her knees, with eyes and hands lifted up towards heaven, poured forth a most ardent thanksgiving, with an extacy of mind not to be described. Her first sensation was that of gratitude to the Almighty Power, who had reserved so great a blessing for her; maternal tenderness alone gave rise to the succeeding emotions of her heart; she threw her arms round Louisa, who on seeing her fall on her knees, and not comprehending the meaning of her action ran to her; but struck with astonishment and reverence at the awful piety in her countenance and address, bent silent and motionless over her. Mrs. Thornby leaning her head on Louisa's bosom, burst into such a flood of tears, and was so oppressed with joy, that the power of speech totally failed her. Louisa raised her from the ground, crying, 'Dear madam, what can all this mean; What does this extreme agitation of your mind give me room to hope?'

'Every thing, my child! my angel! that a fond parent can bestow, replied Mrs. Thornby. I am that mother, that was obliged to leave thee to another's care; and has Heaven preserved my daughter, and restored her to me so lovely, so amiable! Gracious Providence! Merciful beyond hope! Teach me to thank thee as I ought for this last instance of thy goodness!' And then her whole soul seemed again poured forth in grateful adoration.

Louisa could scarcely believe this event was real; thus unexpectedly to meet with a parent, whom she supposed lost to her for ever, almost stunned her; her thoughts were so engrossed by the raptures of her joyful mother, that she did not feel half her good fortune; and the delight she received in seeing her mother's happiness, robbed her of every other sensation.

It was some hours before Mrs. Thornby's mind was sufficiently composed to enter into any connected conversation. From broken sentences Miss Mancel learnt, that 'her father and mother, by the complicated distress of ruined fortune, and the too fatal success of a duel, in

Her parents'
story

which Mr. Mancel was unwillingly engaged, had been obliged to absent themselves from England. They went to one of the American colonies, in hopes of finding means to improve their circumstances, leaving the young Louisa then in her cradle, with a sister of Mr. Mancel's, who readily undertook the care of her. They were scarcely arrived in America, when Mr. Mancel was seized with a fever, of which he soon died, and with him all their hopes. Mrs. Mancel was left entirely destitute, at a loss how to hazard the tedious passage home, without the protection of a husband, and with hardly a sufficient sum remaining to discharge the expences of it.

'Her melancholy situation engaged some of the inhabitants of the place to offer her all necessary accommodations, till she could find a proper opportunity of returning to England. During this time, Mr. Thornby, a gentleman who had acquired a fortune there, saw her, and was so well pleased with her person and conduct, that he very warmly sollicited her to marry him. Every person spoke in his favour, and urged her to consent; her poverty was no faint adviser, and with general approbation, at the conclusion of the first year of her widowhood, she became his wife.

'His affairs soon called him into a more inland part of the country, to which she attributed her never having heard from her sister, to whom she wrote an account of her husband's death; but by what Miss Mancel told her she imagined her letter had not been received.

'Mr. and Mrs.[1] Thornby continued in the same place, till about two years before her arrival in England; but his health growing extremely bad, he was advised by his physicians to return to Europe. He wished to re-visit his native country, but was persuaded, for the re-establishment of his constitution, to spend some time in Italy. The climate at first seemed to relieve him, but his complaints returning with greater violence, he died in the latter part of the second year of his abode there.

'His estate in the Indies he bequeathed to a nephew, who lived upon the spot; but the money he had sent before him into England, which amounted to about forty thousand pounds, he left to his widow.

---

1   first edition has no period after Mrs

He had desired to be interred at Florence, where he died. As soon as
the funeral was over, and some other necessary affairs settled, Mrs.
Thornby set out for England, where she no sooner arrived than she
employed intelligent persons to find out her sister-in-law and daughter, but had not received any account from them, when her daughter
was restored to her as the free gift of providence.'

Mrs. Thornby was now more desirous than ever, to hear each minute particular that had befallen her Louisa; but Louisa begged that before she obeyed her orders, she might have permission to communicate
the happy event to Mr. d'Avora, whose joy she knew would be nearly
equal to her own. A messenger was dispatched for this purpose, and
then she related circumstantially all the incidents in her short life, except her partial regard to Sir Edward Lambton, which filial awe induced her to suppress.

Mrs. Thornby grew every day more delighted with her daughter, as
her acquired accomplishments, and natural excellencies, became more
conspicuous on longer acquaintance. Her maternal love seemed to
glow with greater warmth for having been so long stifled, and Louisa
found such delight in the tender affection of a mother, that she was
scarcely sensible of the agreeable change in her situation, which was
now in every circumstance the most desirable. All that fortune could
give, she had it in her power to enjoy, and that esteem which money
cannot purchase, her own merit secured her, besides all the gratification a young woman can receive from general admiration. But still
Louisa was not happy, her fears for Sir Edward's life, while in so dangerous a situation, would not suffer her mind to be at peace. She might
hope every thing from her mother's indulgence, but had not courage
to confess her weakness, nor to intimate a wish, which might occasion
her separation from a parent, whose joy in their re-union still rose to
rapture. Chance, that deity, which though blind, is often a powerful
friend, did what she could not prevail on herself to do.

One morning the news paper of the day being brought in, Mrs.
Thornby taking it up, read to her daughter a paragraph, which contained an account of a battle in Germany,[1] wherein many of the Eng-

---

1   battle in Germany] during the War of the Austrian Succession

lish were said to be slain, but few of their names specified. Louisa immediately turned pale, her work dropped out of her hand, and an universal trembling seized her. Mrs. Thornby was too attentive not to observe her daughter's distress, and so kindly inquired the reason, that Louisa ventured to tell her for whom she was so much interested; and gave an exact account of Sir Edward's address to her, her behaviour upon it, and the great regard she had for him.

Mrs. Thornby affectionately chid her for having till then concealed a circumstance whereon so much of her happiness depended, and offered to write to Lady Lambton immediately, and acquaint her, that if want of fortune was her only objection to Miss Mancel, it no longer subsisted, for that she was ready to answer any demands of that sort, which her ladyship should chuse to make, as she thought she should no way so well secure her daughter's happiness, as by uniting her with a gentleman of Sir Edward's amiable character, and whose affection for her had so evidently appeared.

Louisa could not reject an offer which might rescue Sir Edward from the dangers that threatened him, and with pleasure thought of rewarding so generous and so sincere a passion. Perhaps she found some gratification, in shewing that gratitude alone dictated her refusal. The letter was immediately dispatched, and received with great pleasure by lady Lambton, whose esteem for Miss Mancel, would have conquered any thing but her pride. She accepted the proposal in the politest manner, and that Sir Edward might be acquainted with his happiness as soon as possible, dispatched her steward into Germany, ordering him to travel with the utmost expedition, and gave him Mrs. Thornby's letter, with one from herself, containing an account of the great change in Louisa's fortune.

The servant obeyed the directions given him, and performed the journey in as short a time as possible; but as he entered the camp, he met Sir Edward indeed, but not as a future bridegroom. He was borne on mens shoulders, pale and almost breathless, just returned from an attack, where, by[1] his too great rashness, he had received a mortal wound. He followed him with an aching heart to his tent, where Sir

---

1   where, by] whereby in first edition

Sir Edward's death, anyway – Divine judgment?!

Edward recovering his senses, knew him, and asked, 'What brought him there so opportunely, to close his eyes, and pay the last duties, to one of whose infancy he had been so careful?' for this servant lived in the family when Sir Edward was born, and loved him almost with paternal fondness, which occasioned his desire of being himself the messenger of such joyful news.

The poor man was scarcely able to answer a question expressed in such melancholy terms, and was doubtful whether he ought to acquaint him with a circumstance, which might only increase his regret at losing a life, which would have been blessed to his utmost wish, but incapable in that state of mind of inventing any plausible reason, he told him the truth, and gave him the two letters.

The pleasure Sir Edward received at the account of Louisa's good fortune, and the still greater joy he felt at so evident a proof of her regard for him, made him for a time forget his pains, and flattered the good old steward with hopes, that his case was not so desperate as the surgeons represented it; but Sir Edward told him, 'he knew all hope was vain.' 'I must accuse myself, said he, of losing that lovely generous woman; what a treasure would have gladdened my future days, had I not rashly, I fear criminally shortened them, not by my own hand indeed, but how little different! Mad with despair, I have sought all means of obtaining, what I imagined the only cure for my distempered mind. Weary of life, since I could not possess her, in whom all my joys, all the wishes of my soul were centered, I seized every occasion of exposing myself to the enemy's sword. Contrary to my hopes, I escaped many times, when death seemed unavoidable; but grown more desperate by disappointment, I this morning went on an attack, where instead of attempting to conquer, all my endeavour was to be killed, and at last I succeeded, how fatally![1] Oh! my Louisa, continued he, and do I then lose thee by my own impatience! Had I, like thee, submitted to the disposition of providence, had I waited, from its mighty power, that relief which it alone can give, I might now be expecting with rapture the hour that should have united us for ever, instead of preparing for that which shall summon me to the grave, where even thou shalt be

---

[1]   first edition has a quotation mark here

forgotten, and the last traces of thy lovely image effaced from my too faithful remembrance. How just are the decrees of the Almighty! Thy patience, thy resignation, and uncommon virtues are rewarded as they ought; my petulance, my impatience, which, as it were, flew in the face of my Maker, and sought to lose a life which he had intrusted to my keeping, and required me to preserve, is deservedly punished. I am deprived of that existence, which I would now endure whole ages of pain to recal, were it to be done, but it is past, and I submit to thy justice, thou all wise disposer of my fate.'

The agitation of Sir Edward's mind had given him a flow of false spirits, but at length they failed, leaving him only the more exhausted. He kept Mrs. Thornby's letter on his pillar,[1] and read it many times. Frequent were his expressions of regret for his own rashness, and he felt much concern from the fear that Louisa would be shocked with his death. Her mother's proceedings convinced him she was not void of regard for him; he now saw that he had not vainly flattered himself, when he imagined, from many little circumstances, that her heart spoke in his favour; and the force she must have put on her affections, raised his opinion of her almost to adoration. He often told his faithful attendant, that in those moments he felt a joy beyond what he had ever yet experienced, in believing Louisa loved him; but these emotions were soon checked by reflecting, that if she did so, she could not hear of his death without suffering many heart-felt pangs.

He lingered for three days, without the least encouragement to hope for life, and on the last died with great resignation, receiving his death as a punishment justly due to his want of submission in the divine will, and that froward petulance which drove him to desperation, in not succeeding to his wishes, just at the time, that to his impetuous passions, and short-sighted reason, appeared most desirable.

The afflicted steward wrote an account of this melancholy event to Lady Lambton, and staid to attend Sir Edward's body home, that his last remains might be deposited in the family vault.

Lady Lambton received these mournful tidings with excessive grief,

---

1   pillar] probably Sarah Scott's spelling of "pillow" according to the way she pronounced it; altered to pillow in later editions

and communicated them to Mrs. Thornby. Louisa, from the time of the messenger's setting out for Germany, had been pleasing herself with reflecting on the joyful reception he would meet with from Sir Edward, and had frequently anticipated, in imagination, the pleasures she and Sir Edward would receive at seeing each other, after so melancholy a separation. She now every hour expected him, and when Mrs. Thornby began to prepare her against surprize, she imagined he was arrived, and that her kind mother was endeavouring to guard her against too sudden joy. She attempted to break through the delay, which must arise from all this caution, by begging to know if he was in the house, desiring her not to fear any ill effects from his sudden appearance, and rose from her seat, in order to attend her mother to Sir Edward. Mrs. Thornby made her sit down again, and with a countenance which spoke very different things from what she expected, acquainted her with the fatal end of all her hopes.

Louisa was shocked in proportion to the degree to which she was before elated. She sunk lifeless in the arms of her mother, who had clasped her to her breast, and it was a considerable time before their cruel endeavours to bring her to her senses succeeded. Her first sensation was an agony of grief; she accused herself of being the occasion of Sir Edward's death, and from the unfortunate consequences of her actions, arraigned her motives for them. Mrs. Thornby and Mr. d'Avora, whom she had sent for on this occasion, endeavoured to convince her, she was no way to blame, that what she had done was laudable, and she ought not to judge of an action by its consequences, which must always remain in the hands of the Almighty, to whom we are accountable for our motives, but who best knows when they ought to be crowned with success. When they had prevailed with her to exculpate herself, her piety and patience made it the more easy to persuade her calmly to submit to the decrees of providence. She soon saw, that to suffer was her duty, and though she might grieve, she must not repine. The good advice of her two friends was some support to her mind, but her chief strength arose from her frequent petitions to him who tried her in sufferings, to grant her patience to bear them with due resignation. Such addresses, fervently and sincerely made, can never be unavailing, and she found the consolation she asked for. Her affliction was deep, but silent and submissive, and in no part of her life did she ever appear more amiable than on this trying occasion, when her extreme sensibility could never extort one word or thought which was not dictated by humble piety, and the most exemplary resignation. That Sir Edward had had so just a sense of his own error, and so properly repented his impatience was a great consolation, and she hoped to meet him whom she had so soon lost, in a state of happiness, where they should never more be parted.

Mrs. Morgan had borne a tender share in all Louisa's joys and sorrows; for in the frequency of her correspondence, every circumstance that attended the latter was faithfully imparted, though the communication was less free on Mrs. Morgan's side, who, contrary to her natural temper, acted with reserve on this particular; induced by a double motive, a belief that it was her duty to conceal her husband's faults, and a desire to spare her friend the pain of suffering participation in her vexations. She longed to attend Miss Mancel in her affliction, but dared not urge a request with which she knew Mr. Morgan would not comply. He lived intirely in the country, and seemed to be totally insensible to the pleasure of contributing to the happiness of others. All his tenderness was confined within the narrow circle of himself. Mrs. Morgan daily beheld distress and poverty without the power of relieving it, for his parcimony[1] would not let him trust her with the disposal of what money was necessary for her own expences, his sister always bought what they in their wisdoms judged requisite, and Mrs. Morgan was treated in those affairs like a little child.

In matters too trifling to come within Mr. Morgan's notice, Mrs. Susanna, fearing her sister should enjoy a moment's ease, took care to perform her part in teazing, as if their joint business was only to keep that poor woman in a constant state of suffering. To compleat her vexation, Mr. Morgan, who had always drank hard, increased so much in that vice, that few days passed wherein he was not totally intoxicated. Mrs. Morgan saw no means of redress, and therefore thought it best to suffer without complaint; she considered, that, by contention, she could not prevail over their ill temper, but must infallibly sour her own, and destroy that composure of mind, necessary to enable every

---

1   parcimony] altered to parsimony in later editions

one to acquit herself well in all Christian duties. By this patient acquiescence her virtues were refined, though her health suffered, and she found some satisfaction in reflecting, that him whom she most wished to please, would graciously accept her endeavours; however unavailing they might be towards obtaining the favour of those on whom her earthly peace depended.

At this part of Mrs. Maynard's narration we were again interrupted by dinner, but the arrival of some visitors in the afternoon, afforded Lamont and myself an opportunity of begging her to give us the sequel, and for that purpose we chose a retired seat in the garden; when she thus proceeded.

The next six years of Miss Mancel's life passed in a perfect calm; this may appear too cold an expression, since her situation was such, as would by most people have been thought consummate happiness. Mrs. Thornby's ample fortune enabled them to live in great figure, and Miss Mancel's beauty and understanding rendered her the object of general admiration. Had her conduct been less amiable, she could not but have acquired many lovers; it is not strange then, such as she was, that she should be addressed by many men of distinguished rank and fortune. Wherever she appeared, she attracted all eyes, and engrossed the whole attention. Mrs. Thornby, more delighted with the admiration paid her daughter than she herself, carried her frequently into public, and kept a great deal of company. Louisa could not be insensible to the general approbation, but was hurt with the serious attachment of those who more particularly addressed her. As she was determined never to marry, thinking it a sort of infidelity to a man, whose death was owing to his affection for her, she always took the first opportunity of discouraging every pursuit of that kind; and restrained the natural vivacity of her temper, lest it should give rise to any hopes which could end only in disappointment. She endeavoured to make publickly known her fixed determination never to marry; but as those resolutions are seldom thought unalterable, many men flattered themselves, that their rank and fortunes, with their personal merits, might conquer so strange an intention, and therefore would not desist without an express refusal.

In the seventh year after Mrs. Thornby's return into England, she was taken off by a fever, and left Miss Mancel, at twenty four years of age, in possession of forty thousand pounds, a fortune which could not afford her any consolation for the loss of so tender a parent. Having nothing to attach her to any particular part of the kingdom, she more than ever longed to settle in Mrs. Morgan's neighbourhood, but feared to occasion some new uneasiness to her friend, and was sensible, that if, when vicinity favoured them, they should be denied the pleasure of each others company, or very much restrained in it, the mortification would be still greater than when distance would not permit them to meet. She had the satisfaction of hearing from her friend, that Mr. Morgan seemed to esteem her more than for some years after their marriage, and often gave her reason to think he did not despise her understanding, and was well pleased with her conduct. The truth was, this gentleman's eyes were at last opened to the merits of his wife's behaviour, the long trial he had made of her obedience, which was implicit, and performed with apparent chearfulness; if compared with his sister's conduct, could not fail of appearing in an amiable light, when he was no longer beset with the malicious insinuations of Susanna, who had bestowed herself on a young ensign, whose small hopes of preferment in the army, reduced him to accept that lady and her fortune as a melancholy resource, but his only certain provision. This alteration in Mr. Morgan's temper gave Mrs. Morgan and Louisa room to hope that he might not always continue averse to their becoming neighbours.

While they were flattering themselves with this agreeable prospect, Mr. Morgan was seized with a paralytic disorder, which at first attacked his limbs, but in a very short time affected his head so much, as almost to deprive him of his senses. He was totally confined to his bed, and seemed not to know any one but his wife. He would take neither medicine nor nourishment except from her hands; as he was entirely lame, she was obliged to feed him, and he was not easy if she was out of the room. Even in the night he would frequently call to her; if she appeared at his bed-side, he was then contented,[1] being sure she was in the chamber, but would fall into violent passions, which he had not words to express (for he was almost deprived of his speech) if she did not instantly appear.

When Miss Mancel heard of his deplorable situation, she was under

---

1   contented] contended in first edition

the greatest apprehensions for her friend's health, from so close and so fatiguing an attendance, and begged she might come to her, as he was then incapable of taking umbrage at it. The offer was too agreeable to be rejected, and these ladies met after so long an enforced separation, with a joy not to be imagined by any heart less susceptible than theirs, of the tender and delicate sensations of friendship. Louisa was almost as constantly in Mr. Morgan's room in the day time, as his wife, though she kept out of his sight, and thus they had full opportunity of conversing together; for though the sick man often called Mrs. Morgan, yet as soon as he saw she was in the chamber, he sunk again into that state of stupefaction, from which he never recovered. Mrs. Morgan put a bed up in his room,[1] and lay there constantly, but as he was as solicitous[2] to know she was present in the night, as in the day, she could never quite undress herself the whole time of his sickness.

In this condition Mr. Morgan lay for three months, when death released him from this world; and brought a seasonable relief to Mrs. Morgan, whose health was so impaired by long confinement, and want of quiet rest, that she could not much longer have supported it; and vexation had before so far impaired her constitution, that nothing could have enabled her to undergo so long a fatigue, but the infinite joy she received from Miss Mancel's company.

When Mr. Morgan's will was opened, it appeared, that he had left his wife an estate which fell to him about a month before the commencement of his illness, where we now live. The income of it is a thousand pounds a year; the land was thoroughly stocked, and the house in good repair. Mr. Morgan had at his marriage settled a jointure on his wife of four hundred pounds a year rent charge, and in a codicil made just after his sister's wedding, he bequeathed her two thousand pounds in ready money.

After Mrs. Morgan had settled all her affairs, it was judged necessary, that, for the recovery of her health, she should go to Tunbridge,[3]

---

1   put a bed up in his room] at this time upper-class married couples had separate bedrooms
2   solicitous] solicitious in first edition
3   Tunbridge] or Tunbridge Wells, in the eighteenth century a place of fashionable resort ostensibly for the benefits from the spring water available there; Sarah Scott's sister Elizabeth Montagu went there often, and wrote to her sister describing the place's fashionable society

Collecting more like-minded friends

to which place Miss Mancel accompanied her. As Mrs. Morgan's dress *i.e. not stylish enough?* confined her entirely at home, they were not in the way of making many acquaintance; but lady Mary Jones being in the house, and having long been known to Miss Mancel, though no intimacy had subsisted between them, they now became much connected. The two friends had agreed to retire into the country, and though both of an age and fortune to enjoy all the pleasures which most people so eagerly pursue, they were desirous of fixing in a way of life where all their satisfactions might be rational, and as conducive to eternal, as to temporal *lady Mary* happiness. They had laid the plan of many things, which they have since put into execution, and engaged Mr. D'Avora to live with them, both as a valuable friend, and an useful assistant, in the management of their affairs.

Lady Mary was at that time so much in the same disposition, and so charmed with such part of their scheme as they communicated to her, that she begged to live with them for half a year, by which time they would be able to see whether they chose her continuance there, and she should have experienced how far their way of life was agreeable to her. Lady Mary's merit was too apparent not to obtain their ready consent to her proposal, and when they had the satisfaction of seeing Mrs. Morgan much recovered by the waters, and no farther benefit was expected, they came to this house. *Settling in*

They found it sufficiently furnished, and in such good order, that they settled in it without trouble. The condition of the poor soon drew their attention, and they instituted schools for the young, and alms-houses for the old. As they ordered every thing in their own family with great œconomy, and thought themselves entitled only to a part of their fortunes, their large incomes allowed them full power to assist many, whose situations differed very essentially from theirs. The next expence they *early schemes* undertook, after these establishment of schools and alms-houses, was that of furnishing a house for every young couple that married in their neighbourhood, and providing them with some sort of stock, which by industry would prove very conducive towards their living in a comfortable degree of plenty. They have always paid nurses for the sick, sent them every proper refreshment, and allow the same sum weekly which the sick person could have gained, that the rest of the family may not lose any part of their support, by the incapacity of one.

Good management

the composition of the school

When they found their fortunes would still afford a larger communication, they began to receive the daughters of persons in office, or
other life-incomes,[1] who, by their parent's deaths, were left destitute of
provision; and when, among the lower sort, they meet with an uncommon genius, they will admit her among the number. The girls you
see sit in the room with us are all they have at present in that way; they
are educated in such a manner as will render them acceptable, where
accomplished women of an humble rank and behaviour are wanted,
either for the care of a house or children. These girls are never out of
the room with us, except at breakfast and dinner, and after eight
o'clock in the evening, at which times they are under the immediate
care of the house-keeper, with whom they are allowed to walk out for
an hour or two every fine day; lest their being always in our company
should make them think their situation above a menial state; they attend us while we are dressing, and we endeavour that the time they are
thus employed shall not pass without improvement. They are clad
coarse and plain for the same reason, as nothing has a stronger
influence on vanity than dress.

preparing them as servants

Each of us takes our week alternately of more particular inspection
over the performances of these girls, and they all read by turns aloud to
such of us, as are employed about any thing that renders it not incon-
venient to listen to them. By this sort of education my friends hope to
do extensive good, for they will not only serve these poor orphans, but
confer a great benefit on all who shall be committed to their care, or
have occasion for their service; and one can set no bounds to the advantages that may arise from persons of excellent principles, and enlarged understandings, in the situations wherein they are to be placed.
In every thing their view is to be as beneficial to society as possible, and
they are such œconomists even in their charities, as to order them in a
manner, that as large a part of mankind as possible should feel the
happy influence of their bounty.

In this place, and in this way of life, the three ladies already mentioned have lived upwards of twenty years; for Lady Mary Jones joined

---

1   office ... life-incomes] a position with a certain income, ceasing with the office-holder's death
with no provision for his family members

her fortune to those of the two friends, never chusing to quit them, and
is too agreeable not to be very desirable in the society. Miss Mancel has
often declared, that she plainly sees the merciful hand of providence
bringing good out of evil, in an event, which she, at the time it happened, thought her greatest misfortune; for had she married Sir Edward Lambton, her sincere affection for him would have led her to
conform implicitly to all his inclinations, her views would have been
confined to this earth, and too strongly attached to human objects, to
have properly obeyed the giver of the blessings she so much valued,
who is generally less thought of, in proportion as he is more particularly bountiful. Her age, her fortune, and compliant temper, might
have seduced her into dissipation, and have made her lose all the heart-
felt joys she now daily experiences, both when she reflects on the past,
contemplates the present, or anticipates the future.

I think I ought to mention Mrs. Morgan's behaviour to her half sisters. Sir Charles died about five years ago, and through his wife's extravagance, left his estate over-charged with debts, and two daughters
and a son unprovided for. Lady Melvyn's jointure was not great; Sir
George, her eldest son, received but just sufficient out of his estate to
maintain himself genteelly. By the first Lady Melvyn's marriage settlements, six thousand pounds were settled on her children, which, as
Mrs. Morgan was her only child, became her property; this she divided
between her mother-in-law's three younger children, and has besides
conferred several favors on that family, and frequently makes them
valuable presents. The young gentlemen and ladies often pass some
time here; Lady Melvyn made us a visit in the first year of her widowhood, but our way of life is so ill suited to her taste, that, except during
that dull period of confinement, she has never favoured us with her
company.

My cousin, I believe, was going to mention some other of the actions of these ladies, which seemed a favorite topic with her, when the
rest of the[1] company came into the garden, and we thought ourselves
obliged to join them.

The afternoons, in this family, generally concluded with one of

---

1   the] he in first edition

Rustics as entertainment!

the rustic marriage

their delightful concerts; but as soon as the visitors were departed, the ladies said, they would amuse us that evening with an entertainment, which might possibly be more new to us, a rustic ball. The occasion of it was the marriage of a young woman, who had been brought up by them, and had for three years been in service, but having for that whole time been courted by a young farmer of good character, she had been married in the morning, and that evening was dedicated to the celebration of their wedding.

We removed into the servants hall, a neat room, and well lighted, where we found a very numerous assembly; sixteen couple were preparing to dance; the rest were only spectators. The bride was a pretty genteel girl, dressed in a white callico gown, white ribbons, and in every particular neat to an excess. The bridegroom was a well looking young man, as clean and sprucely dressed as his bride, though not with such emblematic purity. This couple, contrary to the custom of finer people on such occasions, were to begin the ball together; but Lamont asked leave to be the bride's partner for two or three dances, a compliment not disagreeable to the ladies, and highly pleasing to the rest of the company, except the bride, whose vanity one might plainly see did not find gratification enough in having so genteel a partner, to recompence her for the loss of her Colin[1]; he, however, seemed well satisfied with the honour conferred on his wife.

That the bridegroom might not be without his share of civility, the ladies gave him leave to dance with the eldest of the young girls more particularly under their care, till his wife was restored to him.

We sat above an hour with this joyous company, whose mirth seemed as pure as it was sincere, and I never saw a ball managed with greater decorum. There is a coquettry and gallantry appropriated to all conditions, and to see the different manner in which it was expressed in this little set, from what one is accustomed to behold in higher life, afforded me great amusement; and the little arts used among these young people to captivate each other, were accompanied with so much innocence, as made it excessively pleasing. We staid about an hour and half in this company, and then went to supper.

---

1   Colin] a stock name for the love-lorn shepherd in pastoral literature

My cousin told me that Mrs. Mancel gave the young brid[e]
tune, and that she might have her share of employment, and co[n]
to the provision for her family, had stocked her dairy, and fu[rnished]
her with poultry. This, Mrs. Maynard added, was what they di[d]
the young women they brought up, if they proved deserving; shewing,
likewise, the same favor to any other girls in the parish, who, during
their single state, behaved with remarkable industry and sobriety.[1] By
this mark of distinction they were incited to a proper behaviour, and
appeared more anxious for this benevolence, on account of the honour
that arose from it, than for the pecuniary advantage.

As the ladies conduct in this particular was uncommon, I could not
forbear telling them, that 'I was surprized to find so great encouragement given to matrimony by persons, whose choice shewed them little
inclined in its favour.'

Does it surprize you, answered Mrs. Melvyn[2] smiling, 'to see people
promote that in others, which they themselves do not chuse to practise? We consider matrimony as absolutely necessary to the good of society; it is a general duty; but as, according to all antient tenures, those
obliged to perform knight's service,[3] might, if they chose to enjoy their
own fire-sides, be excused by sending deputies to supply their places;
so we, using the same privilege substitute many others, and certainly
much more promote wedlock, than we could do by entering into it
ourselves. This may wear the appearance of some devout persons of a
certain religion,[4] who equally indolent and timorous, when they do
not chuse to say so many prayers as they think their duty, pay others for
supplying their deficiencies.'

'In this case, said I, your example is somewhat contradictory, and
should it be intirely followed, it would confine matrimony to the
lower rank of people, among whom it seems going out of fashion, as

---

1   behaved with remarkable industry and sobriety] toward the end of the century Hannah
     More, a bluestocking of the next generation, would employ a similar scheme to influence the
     conduct of lower-class young women
2   Melvyn] Morgan in second to fourth editions
3   ancient tenures; knight's service] the military or other manifestation of loyalty owed by a
     knight to his lord under the feudal system
4   certain religion] Roman Catholicism, still viewed with suspicion by the Protestant English in
     the mid-eighteenth century

well as with their superiors; nor indeed can we wonder at it, for dissipation and extravagance are now become such universal vices, that it requires great courage in any to enter into an indissoluble society. Instead of being surprised at the common disinclination to marriage, I am rather disposed to wonder when I see a man venture to render himself liable to the expences of a woman, who lavishes both her time and money on every fashionable folly, and still more, when one of your sex subjects herself to be reduced to poverty, by a husband's love for gaming, and to neglect by his inconstancy.'

'I am of your opinion, said Mrs. Trentham, to face the enemy's cannon appears to me a less effort of courage, than to put our happiness into the hands of a person, who perhaps will not once reflect on the importance of the trust committed to his or her care. For the case is pretty equal as to both sexes, each can destroy the other's peace. Our's seems to have found out the means of being on an equallity with yours. Few fortunes are sufficient to stand a double expence. The husband must attend the gaming-table and horse-races; the wife must have a profusion of ornaments for her person, and cards for her entertainment. The care of the estate and family are left in the hands of servants, who, in imitation of their masters and mistresses, will have their pleasures, and these must be supplied out of the fortunes of those they serve. Man and wife are often nothing better than assistants in each others ruin; domestic virtues are exploded, and social happiness despised, as dull and insipid.

'The example of the great infects the whole community. The honest tradesman who wishes for a wife to assist him in his business, and to take care of his family, dare not marry, when every women of his own rank, emulating her superiors, runs into such fashions of dress, as require great part of his gains to supply, and the income which would have been thought sufficient some years ago for the wife of a gentleman of large estate, will now scarcely serve to enable a tradesman's wife to appear like her neighbours. They too must have their evening parties, they must attend the places of public diversion, and must be allowed perpetual dissipation without controul. The poor man sighs after the days when his father married; then cleanliness was a woman's chief personal ornament, half the quantity of silk sufficed for her cloaths, variety of trumpery ornaments were not thought of, her husband's business employed her attention, and her children were the objects of her care. When he came home, wearied with the employment of the day, he found her ready to receive him, and was not afraid of being told she was gone to the play or opera, or of finding her engaged in a party at cards, while he was reduced to spend his evening alone. But in a world so changed, a man dare not venture on marriage which promises him no comfort, and may occasion his ruin, nor wishes for children, whose mother's neglect may expose them to destruction.

'It is common to blame the lower sort of people for imitating their superiors; but it is equally the fault of every station, and therefore those of higher rank should consider it is their duty to set no examples that may hurt others. A degree of subordination is always acquiesced in, but while the nobleman lives like a prince, the gentleman will rise to the proper expences of a nobleman, and the tradesman take that vacant rank which the gentleman has quitted; nor will he be ashamed of becoming a bankrupt, when he sees the fortunes of his superiors mouldering away, and knows them to be oppressed with debts. Whatever right people may have to make free with their own happiness, a beneficial example is a duty which they indispensibly owe to society, and the profuse have the extravagance of their inferiors to answer for. The same may be said for those who contribute to the dissipation of others, by being dissipated themselves.'

'But, madam, interrupted Lamont, do you think it incumbent on people of fashion to relinquish their pleasures, lest their example should lead others to neglect their business?'

'I should certainly, replied Mrs. Trentham, answer you in the affirmative, were the case as you put it, but much more so in the light I see it. Every station has its duties, those of the great are more various than those of their inferiors. They are not so confined to œconomical attentions, nor ought they to be totally without them; but their more extensive influence, their greater leisure to serve their Creator with all the powers of their minds, constitute many duties on their part, to which dissipation is as great an enemy, as it can be to those more entirely domestic; therefore on each side there is an equal neglect; and why should we expect that such as we imagine have fewer advantages of education, should be more capable of resisting temptations, and dedicating themselves solely to the performance of their duties, than persons whose minds are more improved?'

cannot deny, answered Lamont, but what you say is just, yet I fear
ave uttered truths that must continue entirely speculative; though
people have a right to turn reformers, you ladies are best quali-
ned, since you begin by reforming yourselves; you practise more than
you preach, and therefore must always be listened to with attention.'

'We do not set up for reformers, said Mrs. Mancel, we wish to
regulate ourselves by the laws laid down to us, and as far as our
influence can extend, endeavour to inforce them; beyond that small
circle all is foreign to us; we have sufficient employment in improving
ourselves; to mend the world requires much abler hands.'

'When you talk of laws, madam, by which you would regulate your
actions, said Lamont, you raise a just alarm; as for matter of opinion,
every one may demand an equal power, but laws seem to require obedience; pray, from whence do you take those which you wish to make
your rule of life?'

'From whence, answered Mrs. Mancel, should a Christian take
them, from the Alcoran, think you, or from the wiser Confucius,[1] or
would you seek in Coke on Littleton,[2] that you may escape the iron
hand of the legislative power? No, surely, the Christian's law is written
in the Bible, there, independent of the political regulations of particular
communities, is to be found the law of the supreme Legislator. There,
indeed, is contained the true and invariable law of nations; and according to our performance of it, we shall be tried by a Judge, whose wisdom and impartiality secure him from error, and whose power is able
to execute his own decrees. This is the law I meant, and whoever
obeys it, can never offend essentially against the private ordinances of
any community. This all to whom it has been declared are bound to
obey, my consent to receive it for the rule of my actions is not material;
for as whoever lives in England must submit to the laws of the country,
though he may be ignorant of many of the particulars of them; so whoever lives in a Christian land is obliged to obey the laws of the Gospel,
or to suffer for infringing them; in both cases, therefore, it is prudent

---

1   Alcoran] the Koran, or holy book of Muslims; Confucius: or K'ung fu-tzu (551-479 B.C.),
     the most widely revered sage of the Chinese
2   Coke on Littleton] a widely-known legal commentary by Sir Edward Coke (1552-1634) on
     Sir Thomas Littleton's (1422-81) treatise on English property law

for every man to acquaint himself thoroughly with these ordinances, which he cannot break with impunity.'

'If such obedience be necessary, said Lamont, what do you imagine will be the fate of most of the inhabitants of Christendom; for you will allow, that they do not regulate their conduct by such severe commands?'

'What will be their fate, replied Mrs. Mancel, I do not pretend even to suppose, my business is to take care of my own. The laws against robbery are not rendered either less just, or less binding, by the numbers that daily steal, or who demand your purse on the high-way. Laws are not abrogated by being infringed, nor does the disobedience of others make the observance of them less my duty. I am required to answer only for myself, and it is not man whom I am ordered to imitate. His failings will not excuse mine. Humility forbids me to censure others, and prudence obliges me to avoid copying them.'

Lamont thought Mrs. Mancel too severe in her doctrine; but there was something so respectable in her severity, that he forbore to contest it, and owned to me afterwards, that, while she spoke, and he contemplated that amiable society, his heart silently acquiesced in the justness of her sentiments.[1]

We parted at our usual hour; and at the same time the company in the lower part of the house broke up, eleven o'clock being the stated hour for them on those occasions to return to their respective homes.

The next morning, as I went down stairs, I met the house-keeper, and entered into conversation with her, for which the preceding night's festivity furnished me with topics. From her I learnt, that since the ladies had been established in that house, they had given fortunes from twenty to an hundred pounds, as merit and occasion directed, to about thirty young women, and that they had seldom celebrated fewer than two marriages in a year, sometimes more. Nor does their bounty cease on the wedding-day, for they are always ready to assist them on any emergency; and watch with so careful an eye over the conduct of these young people, as proves of much greater service to them than the money they bestow. They kindly, but strongly, reprehend the first er-

---

1   there are quotation marks around this paragraph in all editions

an industry that produces wives?

ror, and guard them by the most prudent admonitions against a repetition of their fault. By little presents they shew their approbation of those who behave well, always proportioning their gifts to the merits of the person; which are therefore looked upon as the most honourable testimony of their conduct, and are treasured up as valuable marks of distinction. This encouragement has great influence, and makes them vye with each other in endeavours to excel in sobriety, cleanliness, meekness and industry. She told me also, that the young women bred up at the schools these ladies support, are so much esteemed for many miles round, that it is not uncommon for young farmers, who want sober good wives, to obtain them from thence, and prefer them to girls of much better fortunes, educated in a different manner, as there have been various instances wherein their industry and quickness of understanding, which in a great measure arises from the manner of their education, has proved more profitable to their husbands than a more ample dower.

She added, that she keeps a register of all the boys and girls, which, by her good ladies means, have been established in the world; whereby it appears, that thirty have been apprenticed out to good trades, threescore fixed in excellent places, and thirty married. And it seldom happens, that any one takes an apprentice or servant, till they have first sent to her ladies to know if they have any to recommend.

I expressed a desire to see the schools, which she obligingly offered to shew me, but feared we could not then have time to go thither, as breakfast was just ready. While I was talking with her, I observed, that the fingers of one of her hands were contracted quite close to the palm. I took notice of it to her, Oh! sir, said she, 'it was the luckiest accident that could possibly be; as I was obliged to work for my support, I was very much shocked at my recovery from a fever, to find myself deprived of the use of an hand, but still tried if I could get myself received into service; as I was sensible I could, notwithstanding my infirmity, perform the business of an house-keeper; but no one would take me in this maimed condition. At last I was advised to apply to these ladies, and found what had hitherto been an impediment, was a stronger recommendation than the good character I had from my last place; and I am sure I have reason to value these distorted fingers, more than ever any one did the handsomest hands that ever nature made. But, added she, smiling, few of my

the housekeeper here—

fellow-servants are better qualified; the cook cannot walk without
crutches, the kitchen maid has but one eye, the dairy maid is almost
stone-deaf, and the house maid has but one hand; and yet, perhaps, there
is no family where the business is better done; for gratitude, and a conviction that this is the only house into which we can be received, makes
us exert ourselves to the utmost; and most people fail not from a deficiency of power, but of inclination. Even their musicians, if you observed it, sir, are much in the same condition. The steward,[1] indeed,
must be excepted; he is one whom the good Mr. d'Avora chose for the
sake of his integrity some years before he died, as his successor in the care
of the ladies affairs, and employed him for some time under his own inspection, that he might be sure he was fit for the purpose, though he persuaded the ladies to receive their own rents, and direct all the chief concerns of their estates, which they have done ever since, so that theirs is
rather an houshold than a land steward. But, except this gentleman and
the shepherd, there is not one of their musicians, that is not under some
natural disadvantage; the defects of two of them are so visible, I need not
point them out, but of the other two, one is subject to violent fits of the
stone,[2] and the other to the asthma. Thus disabled from hard labour,
though they find some employment in the manufacture, yet the additional profit which accrues from their playing here, adds much to their
comfort, as their infirmities render greater expences necessary to them
than to others in their station.'
    There was something so whimsically good in the conduct of the la-
dies in these particulars, as at first made me smile; but when I considered it more thoroughly, I perceived herein a refinement of charity,
which, though extremely uncommon, was entirely rational. I found,
that not contented[3] with meerly[4] bestowing on the indigent as large a
part of their fortunes as they can possibly spare, they carry the notion of
their duty to the poor so far as to give continual attention to it, and endeavour so to apply all they spend, as to make almost every shilling

---

1   steward] manager of the estate
2   violent fits of the stone] attacks of pain caused by passing a stone, or hard concretion formed
     in the kidney or bladder
3   contented] contended in first edition
4   meerly] accepted spelling of merely at that time

heh, like it's tax-deductible ...

contribute towards the support of some person in real necessity; by this means every expence bears the merit of a donation, in the sight of him who knows their motives; and their constant application is directed towards the relief of others, while to superficial observers they seem only providing for their own convenience. The fashionable tradesman is sure not to have them in the list of his customers; but should he, through the caprice of the multitude, be left without business, and see his elated hopes blasted, in all probability he will find these ladies his friends. Those whose youth render them disregarded, or whose old age breeds neglect, will here meet with deserved encouragement. This sort of œconomy pleases me much, it is of the highest kind, since it regards those riches which neither moth nor rust can corrupt, nor thieves break through and steal;[1] and is within the reach of every person's imitation, for the poorest may thus turn their necessary expences into virtuous actions. In this they excel others, as much as the bee does the common butterfly; they both feed on the same flowers; but while the butterfly only gains a transient subsistence, and flies and flutters in all its gaudy pride, the bee lays up a precious store for its future well being, and may brave all the rigours of winter. Man, indeed, often encroaches on the labours of the bee, and disappoints it of its reasonable hope; but no one without our own concurrence can despoil us of the treasures laid up in heaven.

As the good house-keeper foretold, the bell soon summoned me to breakfast; which, like every other hour spent in that society, was rendered delightful by their rational chearfulness, and polite freedom. We offered to take our leave, but should have been disappointed had we not been asked to prolong our visit; nor were we so insincere as to make much resistance to this agreeable invitation; we expressed some fears of interrupting their better employments; to which Mrs. Morgan replied, by assuring us, that we did not do so in the least; but added, 'I will tell you plainly, gentlemen, the only alteration we shall wish to make, if you will favour us with your company a few days longer. Our family devotions are regular, as you were strangers we have not sum-

Rational Charitable economy

bees, not butterflies indeed

---

1   neither moth nor rust can corrupt] Bible, Luke, ch. 12, verse 33: "where neither moth nor rust corrupt"

moned you to them, but for the rest of your visit we must beg leave to alter that method; for we do not think it a proper example to our servants, to suffer any one in this house to be excluded from them; though as your coming was sudden, and has been prolonged only, as it were, from hour to hour, we at first did not think it necessary to require your presence.'

You may imagine we expressed ourselves obliged by this frankness; and, for my own part, I was glad of what appeared to me like being received into a community of saints; but was forced to wait for it till night, the devotion of the morning having been paid before breakfast, as was usual in that family.

Mrs. Maynard accompanied us that morning into the park, and having placed ourselves on a green bank under an elm, by the side of the canal, I called on her to perform her promise, and increase my acquaintance with the rest of the ladies, by giving some account of them.

'I shall not the less readily comply, she answered, for being able to bring what I have to say of them into less compass, than I did my history of Mrs. Morgan and Miss Mancel, of whom, when I begin to speak, I always find it difficult to leave off, and am led by my fondness for the subject into a detail, perhaps too circumstantial. Lady Mary Jones, by what I have already said, you may have perceived must come next in order.'

THE HISTORY OF
Lady MARY JONES.

[handwritten marginalia: Lady Mary ... of Brumpton ... a victim ... unkowng as well]

LADY Mary was daughter to the Earl of Brumpton by his second wife, who survived the birth of her child but a few hours. The earl died when his daughter was about ten years old, and having before his second marriage mortgaged to its full value all of his estate which was not settled on a son born of his first lady, his daughter was left entirely destitute of provision. But as she was too young to be much affected with this circumstance, so she had little reason to regret it, when an increase of years might have awakened a sensibility to that particular. Immediately on her father's death she was taken by her aunt Lady Sheerness, who declared she should look upon her as her own child, and indeed her indulgence verified the truth of her declaration.

[handwritten marginalia: Lady Sheerness]

Lady Sheerness was a widow; her jointure considerable; and her lord at his decease left her some thousand pounds in ready money. When he died she was about twenty five years old, with a good person, and infinite vivacity. An unbridled imagination, ungovernable spirits, with a lively arch countenance, and a certain quaintness of expression, gained her the reputation of being possessed of a great deal of wit. Her lord, in the decline of life, had been captivated by her youthful charms, when she was but sixteen years old. His extreme fondness for her, led him to indulge her vivacity in all its sallies; and frequently while he was laid up at home in the gout, her ladyship was the finest and gayest woman at every place of public resort. Often, when the acuteness of his pains obliged him to seek relief from the soporific influence of opium, she collected half the town, and though his rest was disturbed every moment by a succession of impetuous raps at the door, he was never offended; on the contrary, he thought himself obliged to her for staying at home, which she had assured him was, 'because she could not bear to go abroad when he was so ill.' This, as the greatest mark of her tenderness he ever received, he failed not to acknowledge with gratitude. She scarcely took more pleasure in having a train of admirers, than his lordship felt from it; his vanity was flattered in seeing his wife the object of admiration, and fancied himself much envied, for so valuable a possession. Her coquettry charmed him, as the sallies of that vi-

another example of a flawed education

vacity of which he was so fond. He had no tincture of jealousy in his whole composition; and acknowledged, as favors conferred on himself, the attentions paid to his wife.

Though Lord Sheerness's conduct may appear rather uncommon, yet it seemed the result of some discernment, or at least his lady's disposition was such as justifies this opinion; she had received a genteel education; no external accomplishments had been neglected; but her understanding and principles were left to the imperfection of nature corrupted by custom. Religion was thought too serious a thing for so young a person. The opinion of the world was always represented to her as the true criterion by which to judge of every thing, and fashion supplied the place of every more material consideration. With a mind thus formed, she entered the world at sixteen, surrounded with pomp and splendor, with every gratification at her command, that an affluent fortune, and an indulgent husband could bestow: by nature inclined to no vice, free from all dangerous passions, the charm of innocence accompanied her vivacity; undesigning and artless, her follies were originally the consequences of her situation, not constitutional, though habit engrafted them so strongly, that at length they appeared natural to her. Surrounded with every snare that can entrap a youthful mind, she became a victim to dissipation, and the love of fashionable pleasures; destitute of any stable principles, she was carried full sail down the stream of folly. In the love of coquetry and gaming, few equalled her; no one could exceed her in the pursuit of every trifling amusement; she had neither leisure nor inclination to think, her life passed in an uninterrupted succession of engagements, without reflexion on the past, or consideration on the future consequences.

the reflicon coquette

The lightness of her conduct exposed her to the addresses of many gay[1] men during the life of her lord; but an attachment was too serious a thing for her; and while her giddiness and perpetual dissipation exposed her to suspicion, they preserved her from the vice of which she was suspected: she daily passed through the ordeal trial; every step she took was dangerous, but she came off unhurt. Her reputation was indeed doubt-

---

1   gay] light-hearted and exuberant, here with an implication of insincerity or impertinence; the word did not come to mean homosexual until almost two centuries later

ful, but her rank and fortune, and the continual amusements which her house yielded to her acquaintance, rendered her generally carressed.

Her lord's death made no alteration in her way of life; and as her mind was never fixed an hour on any subject, she thought not long enough of marriage, to prepare for that state, and therefore continued a widow. She was upwards of forty years old, unchanged in any thing but her person, when she took lady Mary Jones, I will not say into her care, for that word never entered into her vocabulary, but into her house. Lady Mary had naturally a very good understanding, and much vivacity, the latter met with every thing that could assist in its increase in the company of Lady Sheerness, the other was never thought of: she was initiated into every diversion at an age, when other girls are confined to their nursery. Her aunt was fond of her, and therefore inclined to indulgence, besides she thought the knowledge of the world, which in her opinion was the most essential qualification for a woman of fashion, was no way to be learnt, but by an early acquaintance with it.

Lady Mary's age and vivacity rendered this doctrine extremely agreeable; she was pretty, and very lively and entertaining in her conversation, therefore at fifteen years of age she became the most carressed person in every company. She entered into all the fashionable tastes, was coquettish and extravagant; for Lady Sheerness very liberally furnished her with money, and felt a sort of pride in having a niece distinguished by the fineness of her dress, and her profusion in every expence, as it was well known to have no other source, but in her Ladyship's generosity. Though Lady Mary received much adulation, and was the object of general courtship, yet she had no serious love made to her,[1] till she was between sixteen and seventeen, when she accompanied her aunt to Scarborough: she was there very assiduously followed by a gentleman, reputed of a large fortune in Wales. He was gay and well-bred, his person moderately agreeable, his understanding specious, and his manner insinuating. There was nothing very engaging in the man, except the appearance of a very tender attachment. She had before found great pleasure in being admired; but her vanity was still more flattered in being loved: she knew herself capable of amusing; but

---

1   had no serious love made to her] had not been courted

till now had never been able to give either pleasure or pain, according to her sovereign decree. She grew partial to Mr. Lenman (that was the name of her lover) because he raised her consequence in her own eyes: she played off a thousand airs of coquettry, which she had never yet had an opportunity to exercise for want of a real lover. Sometimes she would elate him by encouragement; at others, freeze him into despair by her affected coldness: she was never two hours the same, because she delighted in seeing the variety of passions she could excite.

coquettes

Mr. Lenman was certainly sufficiently tormented; but so great a proficiency in coquettry, at so early an age, was no discouragement to his hopes. There are no people so often the dupe of their own arts as coquets; especially when they become so very early in life; therefore, instead of being damped in his pursuit, he adapted his behaviour to her foible, vanity, and by assuming an air of indifference, could, when he pleased, put an end to her affected reserve; though he was not so unpolite a lover, as quite to deny her the gratification she expected from her little arts. He found means, however, to command her attention, by the very serious proposal of matrimony. She had no great inclination for the state, but the novelty pleased her. The pleasure she received from his addresses she mistook for love, and imagined herself deeply enamoured, when she was in reality only extremely fluttered; the common error of her age. In the company she had kept matrimony appeared in no very formidable light; she did not see that it abridged a woman of any of the liberties she already enjoyed; it only afforded her an opportunity of chusing her own diversions; whereas her taste in those points, sometimes differed from her aunt's; to whom, however, she was obliged to submit. Thus prepossessed, both in favour of her lover and his proposal, she listened to him with more attention than she chose he should perceive; but he was too well acquainted with the pretty arts of coquettry, not to see through them. He therefore took courage to insinuate his desire of a private marriage, and ventured to persuade her to take a trip with him to the northern side of Berwick upon Tweed.[1]

an elopement

---

1   northern side of Berwick upon Tweed] English couples wishing to marry despite parental objections would often go to Scotland, which was to the north of Berwick, in order to do so, since conditions for being married were less stringent there

Lady Mary could not see as Mr. Lenman's[1] fortune was considerable, and her's entirely precarious, why he was so apprehensive of not being accepted by her aunt, but there was something spirited in those northern journies, that had always been the objects of her envy. An adventure was the supreme pleasure of life, and these pretty flights gave marriage all the charms of romance. To be forced to fly into another kingdom to be married, gave her an air of consequence; vulgar people might tie the knot at every parish-church, but people of distinction should do every thing with an eclat. She imagined it very probable, that her aunt would consent to her union with Mr. Lenman; for, though he was not equal to her in birth, yet he was her superior in fortune; but yet she looked upon his fears of a refusal as meritorious, since he assured her they arose from his extreme affection, which filled him with terrors, on the least prospect of losing her. 'Should Lady Sheerness, he urged, reject his proposal, she might then be extremely offended with their marrying, after they knew her disapprobation; but if they did it without her knowlege, she would not have room to complain of downright disobedience, and if it was displeasing to her, yet being done, and past remedy, she would be inclined to make the best of what was unavoidable, and forgive what she could not prevent.'

These arguments were sufficiently solid for a girl of sixteen, who never thought before, and could scarcely be said to do so then. Lady Mary complied with his plan, and the day was fixed when they were to take this lively step; their several stages settled, and many more arts and contrivances to avoid discovery concerted, than they were likely to have any occasion for; but in that variety of little schemes, and romantic expedients, her chief pleasure in this intended marriage consisted.

The day before that on which Lady Mary and her lover were to set out for Scotland, she was airing with Lady Sheerness, when one of the horses taking fright, they were overturned down a very steep declivity. Lady Sheerness was but very little hurt, but Lady Mary was extremely bruised; one side of her face received a blow, which swelled it so violently, that her eye was quite closed, and her body was all over contusions. She was taken up senseless, entirely stunned by the shock. As

---

1   Lenman's] Linman's in first edition

soon as she was carried home, she was put to bed; a fever ensued, and she lay a fortnight in a deplorable condition, though her life was not thought to be in danger. Her pain, for the greatest part of that time, was too acute to suffer her to reflect much on the different manner in which she had intended to employ that period; and when her mind became more at liberty, her disappointment did not sit heavy on her spirits; for as her heart was not really touched, she considered the delay which this ill-timed accident had occasioned without any great concern, and rather pleased herself with thinking, that she should give an uncommon proof of spirit, in undertaking a long journey, so soon after she was recovered, from a very evident proof, that travelling is not free from danger. As she had during this confinement, more time to think than all her life had yet afforded her, a doubt would sometimes occur, whether she did right in entering into such an engagement without the consent of her aunt, to whom she was much obliged. But these scruples soon vanished, and she wondered how such odd notions came into her head, never having heard the word duty used, but to ridicule somebody who made it the rule of their conduct. By all she had been able to observe, pleasure was the only aim of persons of genius,[1] whose thoughts never wandered but from one amusement to another, and, 'why should not she be guided by inclination as well as other people?' That one question decided the point, and all doubts were banished.

Before the blackness which succeeded the swelling was worn off her face, and consequently before she could appear abroad, a young Lady of her acquaintance, who, out of *charity*, relinquished the diversions of the place, to sit an afternoon with Lady Mary, told her, as a whimsical piece of news she had just heard (and to tell which was the real motive for her kind visit, having long felt a secret envy of Lady Mary) that, 'her lover, Mr. Lenman, had been married some years, to a young lady of small fortune, whom he treated on that account with so little ceremony, that for a considerable time he did not own his marriage, and since he acknowleged it, had kept her constantly at his house in Wales.'

This was indeed news of consequence to Lady Mary, but she was little inclined to believe it, and enquired what proof there was of this

---

1   genius] superiority through distinctive individuality

fact. The young lady replied, that 'she had it from a relation of her's lately arrived at Scarborough,[1] who having been often in Mr. Lenman's neighbourhood, was well acquainted both with him and his wife, and had in a pretty large company, where she was present, asked him after Mrs. Lenman's health, to which he made as short an answer as he could, but such as shewed there was such a person, and his confusion on this question made her relation enquire what could be the meaning of it, which all the company could easily explain.'

Lady Mary was prodigiously disconcerted with this intelligence; her informer imagined the visible agitation of her spirits proceeded from her attachment to Mr. Lenman, but in reality it was the effect of terror. She was frighted to think how near she was becoming the object of general ridicule and disgrace, wedded to a married man, and duped by his cunning; for she immediately perceived why her aunt was not to be let into the secret. How contemptible a figure must she afterwards have made in the world! There was something in this action of Mr. Lenman's very uncommon, fashionable vices and follies had in her opinion received a sanction from custom, but this was of a different and a deeper dye; and little as she had been used to reflect on good and evil, in any other light than as pleasant and unpleasant, she conceived an horror at this action.

After her visitor departed, she began to reflect on the luckiness of the overturn, which had obstructed her rash design, and admiring her good fortune, would certainly have offered rich sacrifices on the shrine of Chance, had there been a temple there erected to that deity.

While her mind was filled with these impressions, the nurse, who had attended her in her sickness, and was not yet dismissed, entered the room, crying with joy, and told her, that 'she had just received the news of the ship's being lost wherein her son was to have embarked, had he not been seized with a fit of sickness two days before it set sail, which made it impossible for him to go on board.' The poor woman was profuse in her acknowledgements for God's great mercy, who had by this means prevented the destruction of her dear child; 'to be sure,

---

1   Scarborough] town on the coast of Yorkshire frequented as a holiday and health resort because of its mineral springs and bracing air

added she, I shall never again repine at any thing that happens to me. How vexed I was at this disappointment, and thought myself the most unfortunate creature in the world, because my son missed of such a good post as he was to have had in this ship; I was continually fretting about it, and fancied that so bad a setting out was a sign the poor boy would be unlucky all his life. How different things turn out from what we expect! Had not this misfortune, as I thought it, happened, he would now have been at the bottom of the sea, and my poor heart would have been broken. Well, to be sure, God is very kind! I hope my boy will always be thankful for this providence, and love the Lord who has thus preserved him.'

This poor woman spoke a new language to Lady Mary. She knew, indeed, that God had made the world, and had sent her into it, but she had never thought of his taking any farther care about her. She had heard, that he had forbidden murder, and stealing, and adultery, and that, after death, he would judge people for those crimes, and these she supposed was the utmost extent of his attention. But the joy she felt for her own deliverance, from a misfortune into which she was so near involving herself, and the resemblance there was in the means of her preservation, to that for which her nurse was so thankful, communicated to her some of the same sensations, and she felt a gratitude to him who, she imagined, might possibly be more careful over his creatures than she had ever yet supposed.

These impressions, though pretty strong at the time, wore off after she got abroad. A renewal of the same dissipation scattered them with every other serious thought; and she again entered into the hurry of every trifling amusement. Mr. Lenman, as soon as he found that his marriage was become public, despairing of the success of his scheme, left the place before Lady Mary was out of her confinement, afraid of meeting the reproachful glances of a woman, whom he designed to injure; and whose innocence, notwithstanding her levity, gave her dignity in the eyes of a man, who had really conceived an ardent passion for her.

Lady Sheerness and her niece staid but a short time at Scarborough after the latter was perfectly recovered, the season being over. They returned to London, and all the gaiety it affords; and though the town was at that time not full, yet they had so general an acquaintance, and Lady Sheerness rendered her house so agreeable, that she never wanted company. Every season has its different amusements, and these ladies had an equal taste for every thing that bore the name of diversion. It is true, they were not always entertained; but they always expected to be so, and promised themselves amends the following day, for the disappointment of the present. If they failed of pleasure, they had dissipation, and were in too continual a hurry to have time to ask themselves whether they were amused; if they saw others were so, they imagined themselves must be equally entertained; or if the dullness of the place was too great to be overlooked, they charged it on their own want of spirits, and complained of a languor, which rendered them incapable of receiving pleasure.

Lady Mary fortunately had had no confidant in her design of running away with Mr. Lenman, and the part he had acted was so dishonourable, he could not wish to publish it; her imprudence was therefore known only to herself; and the fear of disobliging her aunt, by letting her intended disobedience reach her ears, induced her to conceal it; otherwise, most probably, in some unguarded hour, she would have amused her acquaintance with the relation, embellished with whatever circumstances would have rendered it amusing; for the love of being entertaining, and the vanity of being listened to with eagerness, will lead people of ungoverned vivacity to expose their greatest failings.

Lady Mary's levity encouraged her admirers to conceive hopes, which her real innocence should have repressed. Among this number was Lord Robert St. George. He was both in person and manner extremely pleasing; but what was a stronger charm to a young woman of Lady Mary's turn of mind, he was a very fashionable man, much caressed[1] by the ladies, and supposed to have been successful in his addresses to many. This is always a great recommendation to the gay and giddy; and a circumstance which should make a man shunned[2] by every woman of virtue, secures him a favourable reception from the most fashionable part of our sex.

Lady Mary would have accused herself of want of taste, had she not liked a man, whom so many others had loved: She saw his attachment to her in the light of a triumph over several of her acquaintance; and when a man raises a woman in her own esteem, it is seldom long before he gains a considerable share of it for himself. Vanity represented Lord Robert as a conquest of importance, and his qualifications rendered him a very pleasing dangler. Lady Mary liked him as well as her little leisure to attend to one person would permit: She felt that pleasure on his approach, that pain at his departure, that sollicitude for his presence, and that jealousy at the civilities he paid any other woman, which girls look upon as the symptoms of a violent passion, whereas if they were to examine their hearts very nicely they would find, that only a small part of it proceeded from love.

Lord Robert was too well skilled in these matters, to remain ignorant of the impression he had made; and if he had been less quick-sighted, the frequent intelligence he received of it, would not have suffered him long to remain in ignorance. Lady Mary, vain of her conquest, and proud of being in love, as is usual at her age, let every intimate into her confidence, and by mutual communication they talked a moderate liking into a passion. Each of these young Ladies were as ready to tell their friend's secrets as their own, till the circle of that confidence included all their acquaintance. From many of these Lord Robert heard of Lady Mary's great attachment to him, which served not a little to flatter his hopes. He imagined he should meet with an easy conquest of a giddy, thoughtless girl, entirely void of all fixed principles, and violently in love with him; for his vanity exaggerated her passion. In this persuasion he supposed nothing was wanting to his success but opportunity, for which he took care not to wait long.

He was intimately acquainted with an old lady, whom he often met at Lady Sheerness's, whose disposition he knew well suited to his purpose; she had before proved convenient to him and others; not indeed by unrewarded assistance; for as her fortune was too small to supply the expences of the genteel way of life she aimed at, she was glad to have that deficiency made up by presents, which she was therefore very assiduous to deserve. This lady, as she was a woman of fashion, and lived in figure, was politely received in all gay companies, who were not disposed to take the trouble of examining scrupulously into her character. She had one material recommendation; she played high[1] at cards, and omitted

---

1   played high] bet for large stakes

nothing to make her house agreeable; and few were more crouded.

This Lady had often been visited by Lady Sheerness and her niece, though generally at the same time with the multitude; but one day, when she knew the former was confined at home by indisposition, she invited Lady Mary, whose aunt's complaisance would not suffer her to refuse the invitation on her account.

Lord Robert was there, and as it was only a private party, there was no card-tables but in the outward room. The mistress of the house drew Lady Mary into the inner, on pretence of having something particular to say to her; Lord Robert soon followed. The conversation grew lively between him and Lady Mary; and when the convenient gentlewoman saw them thoroughly engaged and animated in discourse, she quietly withdrew, returning to the company, whose attention was too much fixed on the cards, to perceive that any one was missing; and to keep their thoughts more entirely engrossed, she betted with great spirit at every table.

Lady Mary did not perceive she was left alone with Lord Robert, till the growing freedom of his address made her observe it; but as prudence was not one of her virtues, she was not at all disconcerted with this *tête à tête*; nor did it lessen her vivacity. Lord Robert, encouraged by her easiness on the occasion, declared himself so plainly, that she was no longer able to blind herself to his views, and with surprize found seduction was his aim, if that word may be used for a man's designs against the honour of a woman who seems so careless of it. Her heart was entirely innocent of vice, and she could not imagine how his lordship could conceive it possible to succeed with her in intensions of that sort. She had always thought such imprudence in a woman a very great folly, for in a graver light she had never beheld it, and shewed herself offended at his supposing her capable of such a weakness; but without that honest indignation which a woman would have felt, who had acted on better principles.

Lord Robert was not much discouraged; a woman is under great disadvantage, when her lover knows himself to be so much beloved, that she dare not let her anger continue long, for fear of losing him for ever. He was well convinced, that meer worldly prudence could not make a lasting resistance against a strong passion, and such he flattered himself her's was. He therefore ventured to resume the subject; but his *she refuses, but for the wrong reasons*

perseverance increased Lady Mary's surprize, and she began to think herself affronted. Her partiality pleaded in his favour some time; but at length she thought it necessary to retire, notwithstanding his utmost endeavours to detain her. As she left him, she desired him to learn to believe better of her understanding: she perceived it no otherwise an insult; her education had deprived her of that delicacy, which should have made her feel a severe mortification at the little share she had of the good opinion of a man she loved; on the contrary, she esteemed the affront she had received a proof of his affection. She had often indeed heard the name of virtue, but by the use she had known made of the word, it appeared to her to have no other signification than prudence. She was not at all shocked with Lord Robert's conduct; but resolved not to concur in his views, because she had no inclination to do so, that overbalanced her very moderate degree of prudence. On this account she determined to avoid being again alone with him.

Lady Mary's natural sense gave rise to some doubts, whether the very open professions of gallantry, which Lord Robert had made to her were common; she had been frequently addressed with freedom, but his behaviour seemed more than commonly presuming. In order to find what others would think of it; she often turned the conversation to those sort of subjects, and was a good deal startled one day by a lively, but amiable and modest young lady, who said, she believed no man that was not an absolute fool, or at the time intoxicated, ever insulted a woman with improper behaviour or discourse; if he had not from some impropriety in her conduct seen reason to imagine it would not be ill received; and I am sure, added she, 'if such a thing was ever to befal me, it would convert me into a starched prude, for fear that hereafter innocent vivacity might be mistaken for vicious levity: I should take myself very severely to task, convinced the offence was grounded on my conduct; for I am well persuaded there is something so respectable in virtue, that no man will dare to insult it, except when a great disparity in circumstances encourages an abandoned wretch to take advantage of the necessity of the indigent.'

Lady Mary was greatly affected by this sentiment: she began to reflect on her own behaviour; and could not but see, that Lord Robert might, without any great danger of offending, hazard the behaviour he had been guilty of; since in effect she had not conceived much anger

more lessons
the fault lies with the women

against him, and though she had hitherto avoided being again alone with him, yet she had not shewn any very great marks of displeasure. She now watched with attention the conduct of other young ladies; many of them seemed to act on the same principles as herself; but she observed that she who had by her declaration, first raised in her suspicions about her own behaviour, had a very different manner from her's. She was indeed gay and lively; but her vivacity seemed under the direction of modesty. In her greatest flow of spirits, she hazarded no improper expression, nor suffered others to do so without a manifest disgust: she saw that the gentlemen who conversed with her, preserved an air of respect and deference, which they laid aside when they addressed women, whose vivacity degenerated into levity. She now began to perceive some impropriety in her own behaviour, and endeavoured to correct it; but nothing is more difficult than to recover a dignity once lost. When she attempted to restrain her gaiety within proper bounds, she was laughed at for her affectation: if, when the conversation was improper, she assumed an air of gravity, she was accused of the vapours, or received hints that she was out of humour.

These were great discouragements in her endeavours to correct the errors of her conduct, but gave her less pain than the difficulties she was under about Lord Robert St. George. He still continued to address her with a freedom of manners which she now perceived was insulting; she wanted to discourage his insolence, but feared giving a total offence to a man who had too great a share of her affections; she was apprehensive, that if she quite deprived him of his hopes, she should entirely lose him, and he would attach himself to some other woman. This situation was dangerous, and Lord Robert knew the power he had over her. The dilemma she was in really abated the vivacity she wished to restrain, but it was immediately attributed to the anxiety of a love-sick mind, and she was exposed to continual raillery on that subject. Her lover secretly triumphed, flattering himself, that her passion was now combating on his side.

In this situation she was unable to determine what part to act, and all her intimates were too much like herself, to be capable of advising her. Thus distressed, she resolved to cultivate the acquaintance of the young lady who had opened her eyes to her own conduct, and try what relief she could obtain from her advice. This was easily effected;

Lady Mary was too amiable, not to have any advances she made answered with pleasure. An intimacy soon ensued.

Lady Mary communicated to her new friend all the difficulties of her situation, and confessed to her the true state of her heart. That young lady was not void of compassion for her uneasiness; but told her, that, 'while she was encouraging Lord Robert's passion, she was losing his esteem, which alone was worth preserving. I allow, said she, that by depriving him of his hopes, you may put an end to his addresses; but consider, my dear Lady Mary, what satisfaction they can afford you, if they are only the result of a fondness for your person, which would lose all its charms for him, as soon as it became familiarized by possession. You would then at once find yourself both neglected and despised by the man, for whose sake you had rendered yourself truly despicable. I know you are incapable of an action that would at the same time rid you of his esteem, and of the more valuable consciousness of knowing yourself to be truly estimable. I am not of the opinion of those, who think chastity the only virtue of consequence to our sex; but it is certainly so very essential to us, that she who violates it, seldom preserves any other. And how should she? for if there are others as great, greater there cannot be, there is none so necessary. But herein I know you are of my opinion; I only therefore intreat you to shew Lord Robert that you are so; do not let him mistake your real sentiments; nor in order to preserve his love, if custom will oblige me to call his passion by that name, leave him reason to flatter himself that you will fall a victim to his arts, and your own weakness.

'Consider with yourself, continued she, which is most desirable, his esteem or his courtship? if you really love him, you can make no comparison between them; for surely there cannot be a greater suffering than to stand low in the opinon of any person who has a great share of our affections. If he neglects you, on finding that his criminal designs cannot succeed, he certainly does not deserve your love, and the consciousness of having raised yourself in his opinion, and forced him to esteem you, together with the pleasure of reflecting that you have acted as you ought, will afford you consolation.'

These arguments had due weight with Lady Mary; she determined to follow her friends advice, and submit to the consequences. Lady Sheerness had company that evening, and among the rest Lord Robert.

He was, as usual, assiduous in his addresses to Lady Mary, who withdrawing to a little distance from the company, told him, that, 'she had too long suffered his lordship to continue a courtship, which he had plainly acknowledged was made with such views, as gave her great reason to blame herself, for ever having listened to it. She acknowledged, that the levity of her conduct had been such, as lessened her right to reproach him. Encouraged by her errors, and presuming perhaps on a supposition, that he was not unpleasing to her, he had ventured to insult her in a flagrant manner; but without complaining of what was past, she thought herself obliged to tell him his pursuit was in vain; that the errors in her conduct were the fault of education; nor might she so soon have been convinced of them, if his behaviour had not awakened her to a sense of some impropriety in her own conduct, which, conscious of the innocence of her intentions, she had never suspected: she then told him, that if he did not entirely desist from all addresses to her, she should be obliged to acquaint her aunt with his behaviour, who could not suffer such an insult on her neice to pass unresented.'

As soon as she had thus explained herself to Lord Robert, she mingled with the croud, though with a mind little inclined to join in their conversation; but her young friend was there, and endeavoured to support her spirits, which were overcome by the effort she had made. This young lady soon after went into the country, and returned no more to London.

Lord Robert was so disconcerted, that he left the room as soon as Lady Mary had thus given him his dismission. As their acquaintance lay much in the same set, they frequently saw each other. Lord Robert endeavoured to conquer Lady Mary's resolution, by sometimes exciting her jealousy, and at others making her the object of his addresses; but she continued steady in her conduct, though with many secret pangs. He began at last to converse with her with greater ease to himself, as his passion abated when no longer nourished by hope; and notwithstanding a remainder of pique, he could not forbear treating her with a respect which her conduct deserved; for he plainly saw she had acted in contradiction to her own heart. This alteration in his behaviour afforded her great satisfaction; and though her love was not extinguished, it ceased to be very painful, when she was persuaded she had obtained some share of his esteem.

When Lady Mary was in her twentieth year, Lady Sheerness was seized with a lingering, but incurable disorder. It made little alteration in her mind. In this melancholy situation she applied to cards and company to keep up her spirits, as assiduously as she had done during her better health. She was incapable indeed of going so much abroad, but her acquaintance, who still found her house agreeable, applauded their charity in attending her at home. Cards even employed the morning, for fear any intermission of visitors should leave her a moment's time for reflection. In this manner she passed the short remainder of her life, without one thought of that which was to come. Her acquaintance, for I cannot call them as they did themselves, friends, were particularly careful to avoid every subject that might remind her of death. At night she procured sleep by laudanum; and from the time she rose, she took care not to have leisure to think; even at meals she constantly engaged company, lest her niece's conversation should not prove sufficient to dissipate her thoughts. Every quack who proposed curing what was incurable was applied to, and she was buoyed up with successive hopes of approaching relief.

She grew at last so weak, that unable even to perform her part at the card-table, Lady Mary was obliged to deal, hold her cards, and sort them for her, while she could just take them out one by one, and drop them on the table. Whist and quadrille became too laborious to her weakened intellects, but loo[1] supplied their places, and continued her amusement to the last, as reason or memory were not necessary qualifications to play at it.

Her acquaintance she found at length begin to absent themselves, but she re-animated their charity, by making frequent entertainments for them, and was reduced to order genteel suppers to enliven the evening, when she herself was obliged to retire to her bed. Though it was for a considerable time doubtful whether she should live till morning, it was no damp to the spirits of any of the company from which she

---

1   whist] a card-game usually played by four people in two pairs, similar to present-day bridge; quadrille] a card-game played by four people with a pack of forty cards, the eights, nines, and tens of the ordinary pack being discarded; it was fashionable from the 1720s, and was replaced in popularity by whist; loo] a card-game played by varying numbers of players, in which a player who fails to take a trick or infringes the rules must pay a forfeit or "loo" to the pool

had withdrawn, except to Lady Mary, who, with an aching heart, was obliged to preside every evening at the table, and to share their unfeeling mirth, till two or three o'clock in the morning.

She was greatly afflicted with the thought of her aunt's approaching death, whose indulgence to her, however blameable, had made a deep impression on her heart; as this gave a more serious turn to her mind, she could not see Lady Sheerness's great insensibility to what must happen after death without much concern. The great care that was taken to rob her of leisure to reflect on matters of such high importance shocked her extremely; and she was disgusted with the behaviour of those she called her friends, who she plainly perceived would have fallen into a total neglect of her, had she not found means to render her house more amusing to them, than any into which they could enter. She now saw that friendship existed not without esteem; and that pleasurable connections would break at the time they were most wanted.

This course of life continued, till one evening Lady Sheerness was seized with a fainting fit at the card-table; and being carried to her bed, in half an hour departed to a world of which she had never thought, and for which she was totally unprepared.

As Lady Mary was not able to return to the company, they in decency, not in affliction, retired.

Having long expected this event, her grief was greater than her surprize. She sent for the gentleman who she knew was her aunt's executor, that her will might be opened, and necessary directions given for the funeral. Lady Mary had no doubt of succeeding to an easy fortune, and when the will was read it confirmed her in that supposition, by appointing her sole heiress. But the executor told her he feared she would find no inheritance. The will was made on her first coming to Lady Sheerness, when there was some remains of the money her lord had left her; but he was well convinced, it had since been not only entirely expended, but considerable debts incurred.

This account was soon proved true, by the demands of numerous creditors. Lady Mary gave up all her aunt's effects, which fell short of the debts, and remained herself in the same destitute condition from which Lady Sheerness had rescued her. This was a very severe shock; she had seen sufficient proof of the little real friendship to be found in such fashionable connexions as she had been engaged in, to know that she had nothing to hope from any of her acquaintance. Her father had been at varience with most of his relations, and Lady Sheerness had kept up the quarrel. She had therefore little expectation of assistance from them, in the only wish she could form, which was to obtain a pension from the government, whereto her rank seemed to entitle her. She saw no resource but in the pride of some insolent woman, who would like to have a person of her quality dependant on her; a prospect far worse than death. Or possibly, good-nature might procure her a reception among some of her acquaintance; but as she had nothing even to answer her personal expences, how soon would they grow weary of so chargeable a visitor?

her *clism..l* *prospect*

While she was oppressed with these reflexions, and had nothing before her eyes but the gloomy prospect of extreme distress, she received a message from Lady Brumpton, who waited in her equipage at the door, desiring to be admitted to see her, for Lady Mary had given a general order to be denied, being unfit to see company, and unwilling to be exposed to the insulting condolence of many, whose envy at the splendor in which she had lived, and the more than common regard that had usually been shewn her, would have come merely to enjoy the triumph they felt on her present humiliation.

Lady Brumpton

Lady Brumpton was widow to Lady Mary's half brother. She had been a private gentlewoman of good family, but small fortune; by marrying whom, her lord had given such offence to his father, that he would never after admit him to his presence. Lady Sheerness had shewn the same resentment, and there no longer subsisted any communication between the families. Lord Brumpton had been dead about three years, and left no children.

His widow was still a fine woman. She was by nature generous and humane, her temper perfectly good; her understanding admirable. She had been educated with great care, was very accomplished, had read a great deal, and with excellent taste; she had great quickness of parts, and a very uncommon share of wit. Her beauty first gained her much admiration; but when she was better known, the charms of her understanding seemed to eclipse those of her person. Her conversation was generally courted, her wit and learning were the perpetual subjects of panegyric in verse and prose, which unhappily served to increase her onily failing, vanity. She sought to be admired for various merits. To recommend her person she studied dress, and went to a considerable expence in ornaments. To shew her taste, she distinguished herself by the elegance of her house, furniture, and equipage. To prove her fondness for literature,[1] she collected a considerable library; and to shew that all her esteem was not engrossed by the learned dead, she caressed all living geniuses;[2] all were welcome to her house, from the ragged philosopher, to the rhiming peer; but while she only exchanged adulation with the latter, she generously relieved the necessities of the former. She aimed at making her house a little academy; all the arts and sciences were there discussed; and none dared to enter who did not think themselves qualified to shine, and partake of the lustre which was diffused round this assembly.

Though encircled by science and flattery, Lady Mary's distress reached Lady Brumpton's ears, and brought her to that young lady's door, who was surprized at the unexpected visit, but could not refuse her admittance. Lady Brumpton began by apologizing for her intrusion, but excused herself on the great desire she had of being acquainted with so near a relation of her lord's, who, as she was too young to have any share in the unhappy divisions in the family, she was persuaded was free from those ill-grounded resentments, which the malice and impertinence of tale-bearers are always watchful to improve; and when she considered herself as the first occasion of the quarrel, she thought it her duty, in regard to her deceased lord's memory, to offer that protection his sister might justly demand from her, and which her youth rendered necessary.

Lady Mary was charmed with the politeness of Lady Brumpton's address, but still more with the generosity of her behaviour in seeking her out, at a time when so many were diligent to avoid her. The acknowledgments she made for the favour done her, spoke as much in her recommendation as her person. Lady Brumpton after some conversation told her she had a request to make, to which she could not

---

1   literature] polite learning, especially in the humanities, rather than the later sense of serious writings with artistic merit

2   geniuses] genius's in first edition

well suffer a denial; this was no other than that, 'she would leave that melancholy house, and make her's the place of her fixed abode; for as, by Lord Brumpton's will, he had bequeathed her his whole fortune, she should not enjoy it with peace of mind, if his sister did not share in the possession.'

This very agreeable invitation filled Lady Mary with joy and surprize. She made a proper return to Lady Brumpton for her generosity, and they agreed, that Lady Mary should remove to her house the next day.

When Lady Mary was left alone to reflect on this unexpected piece of good fortune, and considered the distress she had been in but two hours before, and from which she was now so happily delivered; when she reflected on the many calamities wherewith from her childhood she had been threatened, and by what various means she had been saved so often from ruin, she could not forbear thinking that she was indeed the care of that Being, who had hitherto employed so little of her thoughts. Such frequent mercies as she had received, sometimes in being preserved from the fatal consequences of her own follies, at others from the unavoidable distresses to which she had been exposed, awakened in her mind a lively gratitude to the supreme Disposer of all human events. The poor consolations to which her aunt had been reduced in the melancholy conclusion of her life, shewed her, that happiness did not consist in dissipation, nor in tumultuous pleasures, and could alone be found in something which every age and every condition might enjoy. Reason seemed this source of perpetual content, and she fancied that alone would afford a satisfaction suitable to every state of mind and body. Some degree of religion she imagined necessary, and that to perform the duties it required was requisite to our peace. But the extent of true religion she had never considered, though her great good fortune told her, that she ought to be thankful for the blessings conferred, and not distrust the care of providence, of which she had received such signal proofs.

She had often heard Lady Brumpton ridiculed under the appellation of a genius, and a learned lady; but when she recollected who those persons were, no other than the open professors of folly, it did not prejudice that lady in her opinion, but rather raised her expectation of being introduced into a superior race of beings, for whose conversation she knew herself unqualified, but from whom she hoped for some improvement to her understanding, too long neglected.

In this disposition of mind Lady Brumpton found her at the hour that she had appointed to fetch her. They went directly into Lady Brumpton's dressing room, who presented Lady Mary with a settlement she had prepared of a hundred pounds a year, which she begged her to accept for her cloaths; and desired, that whenever she found it insufficient, she would draw on her for more: she at the same time, made her the first payment.

Lady Mary now entered into a new set of company, frequently found herself entirely at a loss; for she was so totally unacquainted with the subjects of their discourse, that she understood them almost as little as if they had talked another language; she told Lady Brumpton how much she was concerned at her own ignorance, and begged she would give her some directions what she should read. That Lady, whose chief aim was to shine, recommended to her the things most likely to fall into conversation, that she might be qualified to bear her part in it. Lady Mary took her advice, and read some moral essays, just published; then a new play; after that the history of one short period; and ended with a volume of sermons then much in fashion. When she began to examine what she had acquired by her studies, she found such a confusion in her memory, where an historical anecdote was crouded by a moral sentiment; and a scrap of a play interwoven into a sermon, that she determined to discontinue that miscellaneous reading, and begin a regular and improving course, leaving to others the privilege of setting[1] in judgment on every new production.

In this situation Lady Mary continued some years, without any mortification, except what she felt from seeing the consequences of Lady Brumptons too great vanity. It led her into expences, which though they did not considerably impair her fortune, yet so far straightened it, that she frequently had not power to indulge the generosity of her mind, where it would have done her honour, and have yielded her solid satisfaction. The adulation which she received with too much visible complacency, inspired her with such an opinion of

---

[1] setting] altered to sitting in later editions; sit and set had long been used interchangeably

[handwritten margin notes: "blaws in Lady B — vanity", "a too-open Salon", "how 'conversa'n can fail —"]

herself, as led her to dispise[1] those of less shining qualities, and not to treat any with proper civility, whom she had not some particular desire to please, which often gave severe pangs to bashful merit, and called her real superiority in question; for those who observed so great a weakness, were tempted to believe her understanding rather glittering than solid. The desire of attracting to her house every person who had gained a reputation for genius, occasioned many to be admitted, whose acquaintance were a disgrace to her, and who artfully taking advantage of her weakness, by excess of flattery, found means of imposing on her to any degree they pleased.

The turn of conversation at her house was ridiculed in every other company, by people who appeared most desirous of being in her parties. And indeed it was capable of being so; the extreme endeavour to shine, took off from that ease in conversation which is its greatest charm. Every person was like a bent bow, ready to shoot forth an arrow; which had no sooner darted to the other side of the room, than it fell to the ground, and the next person picked it up, and made a new shot with it. Like the brisk lightning in the Rehearsal,[2] they gave flash for flash; and they were continually striving whose wit should go off with the greatest report. Lady Mary, who has naturally a great deal of vivacity, and a sufficient share of wit, made no bad figure in the brilliant assembly; for though she perceived an absurdity in these mock skirmishes of genius, yet she thought proper to conform to her company; but saw plainly that a sprightly look, and lively elocution, made the chief merit of the best *bons mots*[3] that were uttered among them.

After she had spent about five years with Lady Brumpton, this lady was seized with a nervous fever, which all the art of her physicians could not entirely conquer. Her spirits were extremely affected, and her friends decreased in their attentions, as her vivacity decayed. She had indeed always been superior to her company, in every requisite to please and entertain, therefore when she could not bear her part the conversation flagged; they dwindled from something like wit into

---

1   dispise] often used for despise in the eighteenth century; altered to despise in later editions
2   Rehearsal] *The Rehearsal* (1671), a play burlesquing the heroic tragic drama of its time
3   *bons mots*] clever or witty sayings; a French phrase widely used in English from the second third of the eighteenth century

oddity, and then sunk into dullness. She was no longer equally qualified to please or to be pleased; her mind was not at unison with shallow
jesters, and therefore they could make no harmony.

Her disorder wore her extremely, and turned to an atrophy. In that
gradual decay she often told Lady Mary, 'she was awakened from a
dream of vanity; she saw how much a desire to gain the applause of a
few people, had made her forget the more necessary aim of obtaining
the approbation of her Creator. She had indeed no criminal actions to
lay to her charge; but how should she? vanity preserved her from doing
any thing which she imagined would expose her to censure. She had
done some things commendable, but she feared the desire of being
commended was part of her motive. The humility and calmness of a
true christian disposition had appeared to her meanness of spirit or
affectation, and a religious life as the extremest dullness; but now too
late she saw her error, and was sensible she had never been in the path
of happiness. She had not erred from want of knowledge, but from the
strong impulse of vanity, which led her to neglect it; but sickness, by
lowering her spirits, had taken away the false glare which dazled[1] her
eyes, and restored her to her sight.'

Lady Brumpton was sensible of her approaching death some weeks
before she expired, and was perfectly resigned. Lady Mary had a second time the melancholy office of closing the eyes of a benefactress and
relation whom she sincerely loved. Lady Brumpton, to remove from
her any anxiety on her own account, acquainted her, as soon as her dis-
ease became desperate, that she had bequeathed her ten thousand
pounds, and all her plate[2] and jewels.

Lady Mary found this information true, and received the sum. She
was tenderly concerned for the loss of so good a friend; and by the various circumstances of her life, and the many blessings bestowed on her,
had a heart so touched with the greatness of divine mercy, that her
mind took a more serious turn than common; and tired of the multitude in which she had so long lived, she was seeking for a retirement,
when she met Mrs. Morgan and Mrs. Mancel at Tunbridge; and as I

---

1   dazled] a common variant of dazzled in the eighteenth century
2   plate] tableware and utensils, supposedly made of silver or gold

have already told you, came hither with them.

Mrs. Maynard was not a little wearied with so long a narrat. therefore did not continue much longer with us; but Lamont an mained in the park till dinner.

In the afternoon the Ladies proposed we should go upon the w ...r, a scheme very agreeable to us all; some of the inhabitants of the other community were of the party. We got into a very neat boat, of a size sufficient to contain a large company, and which was rowed by the servants of the family. We went about three miles up the river, with great pleasure, and landed just by a neat house, where we understood we were to drink tea. The mistress of it received us with great joy, and told the ladies she had longed to see them, their young folks having quite finished her house, which she begged leave to shew us. Its extreme neatness rendered it an object worthy observation; and I was particularly attentive, as its size suiting my plan of life, I determined to copy it.

The rooms were neither large nor numerous, but most of them hung with paper, and prettily adorned. There were several very good drawings framed with shells,[1] elegantly put together; and a couple of cabinets designed for use, but they became ornamental by being painted, and sea-weeds stuck thereon, which by their variety, and the happy disposition of them, rendered the doors, and each of the drawers, a distinct landscape. Many other little pieces of furniture were by the same art made very pretty and curious. I learnt in a whisper from Mrs. Maynard, that this gentlewoman was widow to the late minister of the parish, and was left at his death with five small children, in very bad circumstances. The ladies of Millenium Hall immediately raised her drooping spirits, settled an income upon her, took this house, furnished it, and lent her some of their girls to assist in making up the furniture, and decorating it, according to the good woman's taste. She carried us into her little garden, that was neat to an excess, and filled with flowers, which we found some of her children tying up, and putting in order, while the younger were playing about, all dressed with the same exact neatness as herself.

---

1   framed with shells] framing pictures and making other domestic ornaments of shellwork were
     pastimes of Sarah Scott's companion, Lady Barbara Montagu

When we had performed this little progress we found tea ready, and spent the afternoon with greater pleasure, for observing the high gratification which this visit seemed to afford the mistress of the house. In the room where we sat was a book-case well stocked; my curiosity was great to see what it contained, and one of the ladies, to whom I mentioned it, indulged me by opening it herself, and looking at some of the books, I found they consisted of some excellent treatises of divinity, several little things published for the use of children, and calculated to instill piety and knowledge into their infant minds, with a collection of our best periodical papers,[1] for the amusement of lighter hours. Most of these books, I found, were Mrs. Mancel's present.

The fineness of the evening made our return very delightful, and we had time for a little concert before supper.

The next morning I called up Lamont very early, and reminded the house-keeper of her promise of shewing us the schools; which she readily performing, conducted us first to a very large cottage, or rather five or six cottages laid together. Here we found about fifty girls, clad in a very neat uniform, and perfectly clean, already seated at their respective businesses. Some writing, others casting accounts, some learning lessons by heart, several employed in various sorts of needle-work, a few spinning, and others knitting, with two school-mistresses to inspect them. The school-room was very large, and perfectly clean, the forms and chairs they sat on were of wood, as white as possible; on shelves were wooden bowls and trenchers equally white, and shining pewter and brass seemed the ornaments of one side of the room; while pieces of the children's work of various kinds decorated the other; little samples of their performances being thus exhibited as encouragement to their ingenuity.

I asked many questions as to their education, and learnt, that they

---

1 treatises of divinity published for the use of children; periodical papers] exploiting their supposedly "natural" understanding of children, many women began to publish books "for the use of children"; periodical papers, such as *The Spectator* and *The Tatler* were often recommended as moral reading suitable for women because they were in entertaining desultory form and would not tax women's supposedly delicate minds as much as philosophy; in contrast, and following the same line of argument, women were always warned against reading "treatises of divinity"

are bred up in the strictest piety; the ladies by various schemes, and many little compositions of their own, endeavour to inculcate the purest principles in their tender minds. They all by turns exercise themselves in the several employments which we saw going forward, that they may have various means of gaining their subsistence, in case any accident should deprive them of the power of pursuing any particular part of their business. The ladies watch their geniuses[1] with great care; and breed them up to those things, which seem most suitable to the turn of their minds. When any are designed for service, they are taught the business of the place they are best fitted for, by coming down to the hall, and performing the necessary offices under the direction of the excellent servants there.

A very large kitchen garden belongs to the house, which is divided into as many parts as there are scholars; to weed, and keep this in order, is made their principal recreation; and by the notice taken of it, they are taught to vye with each other which shall best acquit themselves, so that perhaps never was a garden so neat. They likewise have no small share in keeping those at the hall in order; and the grotto and seats are chiefly their workmanship.

I gave them due praise upon their performances at the clergyman's widow's, and delighted two of them very much by my admiration of a little arbour, which they had there planted with woodbines and other sweet shrubs. In their own garden they are allowed the indulgence of any little whim which takes not up too much room; and it is pretty to see their little seats, their arbours and beds of flowers, according to their several tastes. As soon as school breaks up, they run with as much eagerness and joy to their garden, as other children do to their childish sports; and their highest pleasure is the approbation their patronesses give to their performances. They likewise take it by turns to do the business of the house, and emulation excites them to a cleanliness, which could not by any other means be preserved.

From this school we went to one instituted for boys, which consisted of about half the number, and most of them small, as they are dismissed to labour as soon as they are able to perform any work, except

---

1   geniuses] qualities of mind, or talents; first edition has genius's

incapacitated by ill health. This is instituted on much the same principles as the other, and every boy of five years old has his little spade and
rake, which he is taught to exercise.

We returned from our little tour time enough for prayers, with
minds well prepared for them, by the view of such noble fruits of real
piety. Indeed the steward who reads them, does it with such extreme
propriety, and such humble and sincere devotion, as is alone sufficient
to fix the attention, and warm the hearts of his hearers.

After breakfast was over, we got Mrs. Maynard to accompany us
into the garden, she in complaisance to us, abstaining while we were at
the hall, from her share in the daily visits the ladies pay to their several
institutions, and to the poor and sick in their village. Their employments are great, but their days are proportionable; for they are always
up by five o'clock, and by their example the people in the village rise
equally early; at that hour one sees them all engaged in their several
businesses, with an assiduity, which in other places is not awakened till
much later.

I called on Mrs. Maynard to continue her task, which without any
previous ceremony she did as follows.

THE HISTORY OF
Mrs. SELVYN.

M R. Selvyn, the younger brother of an ancient family, whose fortune was inferior to the rank it held in the country, where it had long been fixed, was placed in trade[1] in London; but his success not answering his hopes, he gave it up before it was too late to secure himself a small subsistence, and retired into the country, when Miss Selvyn was about five years old. His wife had been dead two years; thus his little girl's education devolved entirely on himself.

He bred her up genteely, though his fortune was small, and as he was well qualified for the part, became himself her tutor, and executed that office so well, that at twelve years old she excelled all the young ladies in the neighbourhood of her own age, in French, and writing, either for hand or stile; and in the great propriety and grace with which she read English. She had no small knowledge of accounts; and had made some progress in the study of history. Her person was elegant and pleasing, and her temper and manner perfectly engaging; but yet these charms could not induce the neighbouring families, to forgive her for excelling other girls in her accomplishments.

They censured Mr. Selvyn, 'for giving his daughter an education, to which her fortune was so little suited, and thought he would have done better to have bred her up to housewifery, and qualified her for the wife of an honest tradesman;' for part of what he had was known to be a life income; a small *sine cure* having been procured him by his friends in town, before he retired into the country.

The censures of those who love to shew their own wisdom by blaming others, had little effect on Mr. Selvyn; he continued his diligence in cultivating his little girl's mind; and even taught himself many things, that he might be able to instruct her. If he did not breed her up in a manner to gain a subsistence by the most usual means, he however

---

1   trade] a mercantile occupation, considered in the eighteenth century to disqualify a man from the status of gentleman

qualified her to subsist on little; he taught her true frugality without narrowness of mind; and made her see how few of all the expences the world ran into were necessary to happiness. He deprived her of all temptation to purchase pleasures, by instructing her to seek only in herself for them; and by the various accomplishments he had given her, prevented that vanity of mind, which leads people to seek external amusements. The day was not sufficient for her employments, therefore she could not be reduced to trifle away any part of it, for fear of its lying heavy on her hands.

Thus Miss Selvyn was bred a philosopher from her cradle; but was better instructed in the doctrine of the ancient moralists, than in the principles of christianity. Mr. Selvyn was not absolutely a free-thinker; he had no vices that made him an enemy to christianity; nor that pride which tempts people to contradict a religion generally received; he did not apprehend that disbelief was a proof of wisdom, nor wished to lessen the faith of others, but was in himself sceptical; he doubted of what he could not entirely comprehend, and seemed to think those things at least improbable which were not level to his understanding. He avoided the subject with Miss Selvyn, he could not teach her what he did not believe; but chose to leave her free to form that judgment, which should in time seem most rational to her.

'I could not forbear interrupting Mrs. Maynard, to signify my approbation of Mr. Selvyn's conduct in this particular, as the only instance I had ever met with of a candid mind, in one who had a tendency towards infidelity;[1] for 'I never knew any who were not angry with those that believed more than themselves, and who were not more eager to bring others over to their opinions than most foreign missionaries; yet surely nothing can be more absurd, for these men will not dare to say that the virtues which christianity requires are not indispensible duties; on the contrary, they would have us imagine they are most sincerely attached to them; what advantage then can accrue to any one, from being deprived of the certainty of a reward for his obedience? If we deny revelation, we must acknowledge this point to be very uncertain; it was the subject of dispute and doubt among all the philosophers of an-

---

1   infidelity] unbelief in religious matters

tiquity; and we have but a poor dependance for so great a blessing, if we rest our expectation where they did theirs. Can a man therefore be rendered happier by being deprived of this certainty? Or can we suppose he will be more virtuous, because we have removed all the motives that arise from hope and fear? And yet, what else can excuse an infidel's desire to make converts? Nothing. Nor can any thing occasion it but a secret consciousness that he is in the wrong, which temps[1] him to wish for the countenance of more associates in his error; this likewise can alone give rise to his rancour against those who believe more than himself; he feels them a tacit reproach to him, which to his pride is insupportable.'

'But, said Lamont, do you imagine that a free-thinker may not be certain of a future state?'

'Not positively, answered Mrs. Maynard; if he is certain of that point, he is a believer without owning it; he must have had his certainty from Scripture; all the reason he boasts can only shew it probable, and that probability is loaded with so many difficulties, as will much weaken hope. Where can reason say immortality shall stop? We must allow that Omnipotence may bestow it on such ranks of being as he pleases: But how can reason tell us to whom he has given it? Whether to all creation, or no part of it? Pride, indeed makes man claim it for himself, but deny it to others; and yet the superior intelligence perceivable in some brutes, to what appears in some of his own species, should raise doubts in him who has nothing but the reasonings of his own weak brain to go upon. But to proceed with my subject.'

story resumed

The minister of the parish wherein Mr. Selvyn dwelt, was a gentleman of great learning and strict probity. He had every virtue in the most amiable degree, and a gentleness and humility of mind which is the most agreeable characteristic of his profession. He had a strong sense of the duties of his function, and dedicated his whole time to the performance of them. He did not think his instructions should be confined to the pulpit; but sensible that the ignorant were much more effectually taught in familiar conversation, than by preaching; he visited frequently the very poorest of his parishioners; and by the humility

---

1   temps] altered to tempts in later editions

of his behaviour, as much as by his bounty (for he distributed great part
of his income among the necessitous) he gained the affections of the
people so entirely, that his advice was all-powerful with them.

the local minister

This gentleman's great recreation was visiting Mr. Selvyn, whose
sense and knowledge rendered his conversation extremely entertaining, and Miss Selvyn's company was a great addition to the good minister's pleasure; he took delight in seeing her, as Hamlet says, 'bear her
faculties so meekly.'[1]

She was entirely void of conceit and vanity, and did not seem to
have found out that her knowledge exceeded that of most persons of
her age, at least she looked upon it as a casual advantage, which
reflected no honour to herself, but was entirely owing to Mr. Selvyn.
Her youthful chearfulness enlivened the party, without rendering the
conversation less solid; and her amiable disposition made the good
minister particularly anxious for her welfare.

He soon found out Mr. Selvyn's scepticism, and endeavoured to remove it. He represented to him that, 'his not being able to understand
the most mysterious parts of christianity was no argument against the
truth of them. That there were many things in nature, whose certainty
he by no means doubted, and yet was totally ignorant of the methods
whereby many of them operated, and even of the use of some of them.
Could he say what purpose the fiery comet answers? How is its motion
produced, so regular in its period, so unequal in its motion, and so ex-
centric in its course? Of many other things man is in reality as ignorant,
only being able to form a system, which seems to suit in some particulars, he imagines he has discovered the whole, and will think so till
some new system takes place, and the old one is exploded. He asked
Mr. Selvyn, If they descended to the meanest objects, in what manner
could they account for the polypus's property of supplying that part of
its body which shall be cut away? That insect[2] alone, of all the creation,
does not continue maimed by amputation, but multiplies by it. To
what can we attribute this difference in an insect, which in all particu-

---

1   'bear her faculties so meekly'] Shakespeare, not *Hamlet* but *Macbeth*, act I, scene vii, line 17:
     "This Duncan hath borne his faculties so meek"
2   polypus] cuttle-fish or octopus, polyp; insect] in the eighteenth century commonly used, as
     here, to refer to any small creature

lars beside, resembles so many others? Yet who doubts of the reality of these things? If we cannot comprehend the smallest works of almighty wisdom, can we expect to fathom that wisdom itself? And say, that such things he cannot do, or cannot chuse, because the same effects could be produced by other means? Man no doubt might exert the same functions under another form, why then has he this he now wears? Who will not reply, because his Maker chose it, and chose it as seeing it best. Is not this the proper answer on all occasions, when the decrees of the Almighty are discussed? Facts only are obvious to our reason; we must judge of them by the evidence of their reality; if that is sufficient to establish the facts; why, or how they were produced, is beyond our comprehension. Let us learn that finite minds cannot judge of infinite wisdom, and confine our reason within its proper sphere.' By these, and many other arguments, Mr. Selvyn was brought to believe the possibility of what he did not comprehend; and by this worthy clergyman's care, Miss Selvyn was early taught the truths of christianity, which though the most necessary of all things, was at first the only one neglected.

In this retired situation they continued till Miss Selvyn was near seventeen years old; Mr. Selvyn then determined to remove to London; and taking a small house in Park-street, fixed his abode there. Lady Emilia Reynolds lived next door; and soon after their arrival made them a visit; a compliment she said, she looked upon as due to so near a neighbour. Some other ladies in the same street followed her example, and in a very short time Miss Selvyn was introduced into as large an acquaintance as was agreeable to her, for she was naturally averse to much dissipation.

Lady Emilia Reynolds was a single lady of very large fortune, her age upwards of thirty, her person fine, her manner gentle and pleasing, and an air of dejection did not render her countenance the less engaging. She was grave and sensible, and kept a great deal of good company, without entering into a gay way of life. Miss Selvyn's modesty and good sense seemed to have great charms for her; she cultivated a friendship with her, notwithstanding some disparity in their ages; and neither of them appeared so happy as when they were together.

Mr. Selvyn could not be displeased at an intimacy so desirable; nor could Miss Selvyn be more properly introduced into the world, than by a person of Lady Emilia's respectable character.

At her house Miss Selvyn saw a great deal of good company, and was so generally liked, that many intreated Lady Emilia to bring her to them, whenever her ladyship favoured them with a visit. These invitations were generally complied with, as under such a protectress Miss Selvyn might properly venture to any place. Lady Sheerness was one of this number, whose rank, and some degree of relationship, brought acquainted with Lady Emilia, though the different turn of their minds, and their very opposite taste of life, prevented any intimacy between them. Lady Emilia was not blind to Lady Sheerness's follies, but she esteemed them objects of her compassion, not of her censure; nicely circumspect in her own conduct, she judged with the extremest lenity of the behaviour of others, ready to attempt excusing them to the world, and not even suffering herself to blame what she could not approve; she sincerely pitied Lady Mary Jones, who seemed by fortune sacrificed[1] to folly; and she was in continual fear lest she should fall a victim to that imprudence, which in her case was almost unavoidable.

By this means Miss Selvyn became acquainted with Lady Mary, and was the young woman I before mentioned, as Lady Mary's adviser and conductor, in putting an end to Lord Robert St. George's courtship.

Not long after she had the satisfaction of thus assisting a young lady, whose failings gave her almost as many charms as they robbed her of, she had the misfortune to lose Mr. Selvyn. All that a child could feel for the loss of a tender parent Miss Selvyn suffered. His death was not so sudden, but that it afforded him time to settle his affairs, and to give every direction to Miss Selvyn, which he thought might save her from all embarassment on the approaching event. He recommended to her, as her fortune would be but small, to attach herself as much as possible to Lady Emilia, since she now became still more necessary as a protectress, than she had before been desirable as a friend, and that interest as much as gratitude required her cultivating the affection that Lady had already shewn her.

The latter motive was sufficient to influence Miss Selvyn, whose heart sincerely returned the regard Lady Emilia had for her; but at that

---

1   sacrificed] sacrified in first edition

time she was too much affected with Mr. Selvyn's approaching disso- *[Mr. Selvyn's decease]* lution to think of any thing else. His care for her in his last moments, still more endeared him, who through life had made her happiness his principal study. Her affliction was extreme, nor could Lady Emilia by the tenderest care for some time afford her any consolation.

Miss Selvyn found herself heiress to three thousand pounds, a fortune which exceeded her expectation, though it was not sufficient to suffer her to live in London with convenience. Lady Emilia invited her to her house; and as the spring advanced, her ladyship inclining to pass the fine season in the country, hired a house about a hundred miles from London, which she had formerly been fond of, and was but just become empty. She had been but little out of town for some years, and went to her new habitation with pleasure. Miss Selvyn bid adieu without regret to every thing but Lady Mary Jones, for whom she had conceived a real affection, which first took its rise from compassion, and was strengthened by the great docility with which she followed her advice about Lord Robert, and the resolution with which she conquered her inclination. Lady Mary grieved to lose one whom she esteemed so prudent and faithful a friend, and considered her departure as a real misfortune; but they agreed to keep up a regular correspondence as the best substitute to conversation.

[Lady E & Miss Selvyn — Another mini-commun]

The country was perfectly agreeable to Lady Emilia and her young friend. The life they led was most suitable to their inclinations, and winter brought with it no desires to return to London; whereupon Lady Emilia disposed of her house there, and settled quite in the country. They were both extremely fond of reading, and in this they spent most of their time. Their regular way of life, and the benefits of air and exercise, seemed to abate the dejection before so visible in Lady Emilia; and she never appeared to want any other conversation than that of Miss Selvyn, whom she loved with a tenderness so justly due to her merit.

After they had been settled about two years in the country, Lord Robert St. George, who was colonel of a regiment quartered in a town not far from them, came to examine into the state of his regiment; and having at that time no other engagement, and the lodgings he had taken just out of the town being finely situated, he determined to make some stay there. Here he renewed his slight acquaintance with Lady

Lord Robert reappears + falls for Miss S.

Emilia and Miss Selvyn; and by favour of his vicinity saw them often. Lord Robert's heart was too susceptible of soft impressions, not to feel the influence of Miss Selvyn's charms. He was strongly captivated by her excellent understanding and engaging manner; as for her person, he had known many more beautiful, though none more pleasing; but the uncommon turn of her mind, her gentleness, and sensible modesty, had attractions that were irresistible.

Lord Robert's attachment soon became visible; but Miss Selvyn knew him too well to think his addresses very flattering, and by his behaviour to Lady Mary Jones, feared some insulting declaration; but from these apprehensions he soon delivered her. Real affection conquering that assurance which nature had first given, and success encreased, he had not courage to declare his passion to her, but applied to Lady Emilia, to acquaint her friend with his love, and begged her interest in his behalf, fearing that without it, Miss Selvyn's reserve would not suffer her to listen to his addresses.

Lady Emilia promised to report all he had said, and accordingly gave Miss Selvyn a circumstantial account of the whole conversation, wherein Lord Robert had laid before her the state of his fortune, which was sufficient for a woman of her prudence; and she added, that 'she did not see how Miss Selvyn could expect to be addressed by a man more eligible, whether she considered his birth, his fortune, or his person and accomplishments.'

Miss Selvyn was a little surprized, that so gay a man should take so serious a resolution. She allowed the justness of what Lady Emilia said in his favour, and confessed, that it was impossible Lord Robert could fail of pleasing; but added, that 'it could not be advisable for her to marry; for enjoying perfect content, she had no benefit to expect from change; and happiness was so scarce a commodity in this life, that whoever let it once slip, had little reason to expect to catch it again. For what reason then should she alter her state? The same disposition which would render Lord Robert's fortune sufficient, made her's answer all her wishes, since if she had not the joy of living with her ladyship, it would still afford her every thing she desired.'

Lady Emilia said some things in recommendation of marriage; and seemed to think it improbable Miss Selvyn should not be a little prejudiced in favour of so amiable a lover as Lord Robert, which tempted that young lady to tell her, that 'though she allowed him excessively pleasing, yet by some particulars, which formerly came to her knowledge, she was convinced his principles were such, as would not make her happy in a husband.'

Lady Emilia allowed the force of such an objection, and did not press a marriage, for which she had pleaded only out of an apprehension lest Miss Selvyn's reserve might lead her to act contrary to her inclinations; and therefore she had endeavoured to facilitate her declaration in favour of Lord Robert, if she was in reality inclined to accept his proposals. She acquiesced then readily in her friend's determination; only desired she would herself acquaint Lord Robert with it, as he would not easily be silenced by a refusal which did not proceed from her own lips.

His lordship came in the evening to learn his fate, and Lady Emilia having contrived to be absent, he found Miss Selvyn alone. Though this was what he had wished, yet he was so disconcerted, that Miss Selvyn was reduced to begin the subject herself, and to tell him, that 'Lady Emilia had acquainted her, with the honour he had done her, that she was much obliged to him, for his good opinion, and hoped he would be happy with some woman much more deserving than herself; but she could by no means accept the favour he intended her, being so entirely happy in her present situation, that nothing in the world should induce her to change it.'

This declaration gave rise to a very warm contest; Lord Robert solliciting her to accept his love, with all the tenderness of the strongest passion, and she with equal perseverance persisting in her refusal. He could not be persuaded, that her motive for doing so was really what she alledged, but as she continued to affirm it, he begged however to know, 'if she had not made so strange a resolution in favour of a single life, whether she should have had any particular objection to him?'

Miss Selvyn shewed the uselessness of this question, since the reason of her refusing the honour he intended her, would have made her reject the addresses of every other man in the world. Lord Robert could not believe this possible, and therefore desisted not from urging a question so disagreeable to answer.

When Miss Selvyn found it impossible to avoid satisfying him in this particular, she told him, that 'if he were entirely unexceptionable, she should be fixed in the same determination; but since he insisted on knowing if she had any objection to him, she was obliged to confess, that had she been better inclined to enter into the matrimonial state, his lordship was not the man she should have chosen, not from any dislike to his person or understanding, but from disapprobation of his principles; that, in regard to her sex he had a lightness in his way of thinking, and had been so criminal in his conduct, that of all men she knew, she thought him most improper for an husband.'

Lord Robert was surprised at so new an objection, and told her, that 'he did not apprehend himself more blamable in those respects than most young men. Gallantry was suitable to his age, and he never imagined, that any woman would have reproached him with his regard for her sex, when he gave so strong a proof of an inclination to leave them all for her.'

'I am sorry, replied Miss Selvyn, that your Lordship thinks me mean enough to take pleasure in such a triumph, or so vain as to imagine I can reform a man of dissolute manners,[1] the last thing I should hope or endeavour to succeed in. Such a tincture of corruption will always remain in the mind of what you are pleased to term a gallant man, to whom I should give the less polite appellation of vicious, that I could not be happy in his society. A reformed rake may be sober, but is never virtuous.'

Lord Robert growing very urgent to know what she had particularly to lay to his charge; she told him frankly, that 'his treatment of Lady Mary Jones had disgusted her, as she, and perhaps she only, had been acquainted with the whole.'

Lord Robert endeavoured to excuse himself on the encouragement Lady Mary's levity had given to his hopes; observing, that 'when a woman's behaviour was very light, his sex were not apt to imagine there was any great fund of virtue; nor could it be expected, that any one else should guard that honour, of which she herself was careless.'

'I am sure, replied Miss Selvyn, your lordship's hopes must have

---

1   reform a man of dissolute manners] conduct books for women and novels of manners commonly warned women against trying to reform a rake, or licentious man, by marrying him

been founded on Lady Mary's folly, not her real want of innocence; a folly which arose from the giddiness of youth, and the hurry of dissipation; for by nature Lady Mary's understanding is uncommonly good. By what you say, you imagined her honour was lawful prize, because she appeared careless of it; would this way of arguing be allowed in any other case? If you observed a man who neglected to lock up his money, and seemed totally indifferent what became of it, should you think yourself thereby justified in robbing him? But how much more criminal would you be, were you to deprive him of his wealth, because he was either so thoughtless or so weak, as not to know its value? And yet surely the injury in this case would be much less than what you think so justifiable. If the world has but the least sense of real honour, in this light they must see it; and to that tribunal I imagine you only think yourself answerable; for did you reflect but one moment, on another bar, before which you will be summoned, you would see, there can be no excuse for violating the laws by which you are there to be tried. If you could justify yourself to the world, or to the women of whose folly you take advantage, by the fallacious arguments which you have so ready for that purpose, such cobweb sophistry cannot weaken the force of an express command.'

'I will not pretend, answered Lord Robert, to deny the truth of what you say, but must beg you will consider it is more easy for you to urge these truths, than for those to obey them who are exposed to, and susceptible of temptations. When a woman has no title to our respect, how difficult is it to consider her in the light you require! levity of conduct we are apt to look upon as an invitation, which a man scarcely thinks it consistent with his politeness to neglect.'

'I wish, replied Miss Selvyn, that women were better acquainted with the ways of thinking so common with your sex; for while they are ignorant of them, they act to a great disadvantage. They obtain by that levity which deprives them of your esteem, a degree of notice and pretended liking, which they mistake for approbation; did they but know that you in your hearts despise those most, to whom you are most assiduously and openly attached, it would occasion a great change in their behaviour; nor would they suffer an address, to which they cannot listen without incurring your contempt. How criminally deceitful is this behaviour? And what real virtue can a man truly boast, who acts in this manner? What woman in her senses can enter into an union for life with such a man?'

'Why not, madam? said Lord Robert, my behaviour to you shews, that we yield to merit the homage it deserves; you would lose all your triumph, were we to put you and the lighter part of your sex on an equality in our opinions. We are always ready to esteem a woman who will give us leave to do so; and can you require us to respect those who are not in the least respectable?'

'No, answered Miss Selvyn, I only wish you would cease your endeavours to render those women objects of contempt, who deserve only to be neglected, and particularly not to deprive them of the very small portion of regard they are entitled to, by the fallacious appearance of an attachment of the tenderest kind; which in reality arises from contempt, not love. But, added she, I have said more than I designed on the subject; I only meant to answer the question you put to me with so much importunity; and must now confirm what I have already declared, by telling you, that were I inclined to marry, I would not on any account take an husband of your lordship's principles; but were you endowed with all the virtues that ever man possessed, I would not change my present happy situation for the uncertainties of wedlock.'

When Lord Robert found all his sollicitations unavailing, he left the country, and returned to London, where he hoped, by a series of diversions, to efface from his heart the real passion he had conceived for Miss Selvyn; she forbore informing Lady Mary Jones, though their correspondence was frequent, of Lord Robert's courtship; she did not doubt but her ladyship was sincere, when she assured her, she now beheld him with the indifference he deserved, but thought that to tell her she had received so very different an address from him, would bear too much the air of a triumph, a meanness which her heart abhorred.

Lady Emilia and Miss Selvyn had lived several years in the country with great rational enjoyment, when the former was seized with a fever. All the skill of her physicians proved ineffectual,[1] and her distemper encreased daily. She was sensible of the danger which threatened

---

1   ineffectual] ineffectal in first edition, probably based on the pronunciation common at the time

her life, but insisted on their telling her, if they had any great hopes of her recovery, assuring them, that it was of importance to her, to know their opinions with the utmost frankness. Thus urged, they confessed they had but little hopes. She then returned them thanks for their care, but still more for their sincerity; and with the greatest composure took leave of them, desiring to be left alone with Miss Selvyn, who was in tears at her bed-side. Every one else withdrew, when taking Miss Selvyn in her arms, and shedding a few silent tears, she afterwards thus addressed her.

'At the moment that I must bid you a long farewel, you will know, that you have a mother in her whom you before thought only your friend. Yes, my dearest Harriot, I am your mother, ashamed of my weakness, and shocked at my guilt, while your gentle but virtuous eyes could reproach your unhappy parent, I could not prevail on myself to discover this secret to you, but I cannot carry to my grave, the knowledge of a circumstance which concerns you. Yes, you are my daughter, my child, ever most dear to me, though the evidence and continual remembrancer of my crime.'

Miss Selvyn imagined the distemper had now seized Lady Emilia's brain, which it had hitherto spared; and entreated her 'to compose herself, assuring her, that what so much agitated her decaying frame, was only the phantom of an over-heated imagination; for her parents were well known, neither was there any mystery in her birth.'

'Oh! interrupted Lady Emilia, do not suspect me of delirium; it has pleased the Almighty to spare my senses throughout this severe disorder, with a gracious design of allowing me even the last moments of my life to compleat my repentance. What I tell you is but true, Mr. Selvyn knew it all, and like a man of honour saved me from shame, by concealing the fatal secret; and acted the part of a father to my Harriot, without having any share in my guilt. But I see you do not yet believe me; take this, pulling a paper from under her pillow, herein you will find an account of the whole unfortunate affair, written a year ago; lest at the time of my death I should not be able to relate it; this will prove, by the nice connexion of every circumstance, that the words therein contained are not the suggestions of madness.'

Miss Selvyn accordingly read as follows,

'When I was seventeen years old, Lord Peyton asked me of my fa-

(lady Emilia's story)

o ho!

ther, but not till after he had secured my tenderest affections. His estate was sufficient to content a parent who was not regardless of fortune and splendor; and his proposals were accepted. But while the tediousness of the lawyers made us wait for the finishing of settlements,[1] Lord Peyton, who was in the army, was commanded to repair immediately to his regiment, then stationed in Ireland. He endeavoured to prevail with my father to hasten our marriage, offering every kind of security he could desire, instead of the settlements so long delayed; my wishes concurred with his, rather than suffer him to go without me into a kingdom, which I imagined would not prove very amusing to him. But my father, who was a very exact observer of forms, would not consent to any expedient. No security appeared to him equivalent to settlements; and many trifling circumstances requisite to the splendor of our first appearance were not ready; which to him seemed almost as important, as the execution of the marriage writings.

'When Lord Peyton found my father inexorable, he attempted to persuade me to agree to a private marriage; only desiring, he said, to secure me entirely his before he left the kingdom; and proposed, that after his return, we should be pubickly married, to prevent my father's suspecting that we had anticipated his consent. But this I rejected; disobedience to a parent, and other objections, were sufficient to make me refuse it; and we saw ourselves reduced to separate when we were so near being united. As Lord Peyton was an accepted lover, and our intended marriage was publickly known, and generally approved, he passed great part of his time with me. My father was obliged to go out of town on particular business, the day before that appointed for Lord Peyton's departure. It is natural to suppose we passed it intirely together. The concern we were both under, made us wish to avoid being seen by others, and therefore I was denied to all visitors. Lord Peyton dined and supped with me; and by thus appropriating the day to the ceremony of taking leave, we rendered the approaching separation more afflicting than in reason it ought to have been, and indeed made it a lasting affliction; a grief never to be washed away.

'Lord Peyton left London at the appointed hour, but the next days,

---

1   settlements] legal arrangements and contracts pertaining to marital property and other matters

and almost every succeeding post, brought me the tenderest expressions of regret for this inforced absence, and the strongest assurances of the constancy of his affection. Mine could not with truth be written in a more indifferent strain, my love was the same, but my purpose was much altered; as soon as I had calmness of mind enough to reflect on what had passed, I resolved never to be Lord Peyton's wife. I saw my own misconduct in all its true colours. I despised myself, and could not hope for more partial treatment from my husband. A lover might in the height of his passion excuse my frailty, but when matrimony, and continued possession had restored him to his reason, I was sensible he must think of me as I was conscious I deserved. What confidence, what esteem could I hope from an husband, who so well knew my weakness; or how could I support being hourly exposed to the sight of a man, whose eyes would always seem to reproach me! I could scarcely bear to see myself; and I was determined not to depend on any one who was equally conscious of my guilt.

'I soon acquainted Lord Peyton with this resolution, which he combated with every argument love could dictate. He assured me in the most solemn manner of his entire esteem, insisted that he only was to blame, and that he should never forgive himself for the uneasiness he had already occasioned me; but intreated me not to punish him so severely, as ever again to give the least intimation of a design not to confirm our marriage. As I resisted my own passion, it may be supposed that, although too late, I was able to resist his. I saw that a generous man must act as he did, but no generosity could restore me to the same place in his esteem I before possessed. His behaviour on this occasion, fixed my good opinion of him, but could not restore my opinion of myself. All he could urge therefore was unavailing; the stronger my affection, the more determined I was in my purpose; since the more I valued his esteem, the greater would my suffering be, at knowing that I had forfeited it. I acquainted my father with my resolution, alledging the best excuses I could make. He was at first angry with my inconstancy, charged me with capriciousness, and want of honour; but at last was pacified, by my assuring him I would never marry any man. As he had been sorry to part with me, the thought of my continuing with him as long as he lived, made my peace.

'Lord Peyton's impatience at being detained in Ireland, increased with his desire of persuading me to relinquish a design so very grievous to my own heart, as well as to his; but he could not obtain leave to return into England, before I found, to my inexpressible terror, that the misfortune I so sincerely lamented, would have consequences that I little expected. In the agony of my mind I communicated my distress to Lord Peyton, the only person whom I dared trust with so important a secret.

'Instead of condoling with me on the subject of my affliction, he expressed no small joy in a circumstance, which he said must reduce me to accept the only means of preserving my reputation; and added, that as every delay was now of so much importance, if the next packet did not bring him leave of absence, he should set out without it; and rather run the hazard of being called to account for disobedience, than of exposing me to one painful blush.

'I confess his delicacy charmed me; every letter I received increased my esteem and affection for him, but nothing could alter my purpose. I looked upon the execution of it as the only means of re-instating myself in *his* good opinion, or my *own*, in comparison of which even reputation seemed to lose its value. But severe was the trial I had to undergo upon his return into England, which was in a few days after his assurance of coming at any hazard. He used every means that the tenderest affection and the nicest honour could suggest, to persuade me to marry him; and the conflict in my own heart very near reduced me to my grave; till at length pitying the condition into which I was reduced, without the least approach to a change of purpose, he promised to spare me any farther sollicitation, and to bury his affliction in silence; after obtaining a promise from me, that I would suffer him to contrive the means for concealing an event, which must soon happen; as my unintriguing[1] spirit made me very incapable of managing it with tolerable art and secrecy.

'Lord Peyton had maintained his former friendship with my father, who thought himself obliged to him, for not resenting my behaviour in the manner he imagined it deserved. When the melancholy and much dreaded time approached, Lord Peyton gave me secret informa-

---

1   unintriguing] unable to carry on a clandestine plot or affair

tion that he would invite my father into the country, on pretence of as-sisting him by his advice in some alterations he was going to make there; and assured me of careful attendance, and the most secret reception, from a very worthy couple, to whose house he gave me a direction, if I could contrive, under colour of some intended visit, to leave my own.

'All was executed as he had planned it; and when my servants thought I was gone to visit a relation some miles distant from London, I went as directed, and was received with the greatest humanity imaginable by Mr. and Mrs. Selvyn; not at their own house, but at one taken for that purpose, where the affair might be more secretly managed. Lord Peyton had concealed my name even from them; and secured their care of me under a borrowed appellation.

'The day after I got to them I was delivered of you, my dearest child, whom I beheld with sorrow as well as affliction; considering you as the melancholy memorial and partner in my shame.

'Mr and Mrs. Selvyn attended me with the greatest care, and were never both absent at a time; they acquainted Lord Peyton with the state of my health by every post; and I was enabled, by the necessity of the case, to write to my father as frequently as I usually did, when absent from him. Within the fortnight from the time of my departure from my own house I returned to it again, after delivering my dear Harriot into the care of these good people, who promised to treat her as their own child. Under pretence of a cold I confined myself till I was perfectly recovered.

'Lord Peyton detained my father till he heard I was entirely well; and then went with impatience to see his little daughter, over whom he shed many tears, as Mr. Selvyn afterwards informed me; telling it that it was a constant memorial of the greatest misfortune of his life, and could never afford him a pleasure that was not mingled with the deepest affliction.

'Mrs. Selvyn had lain in about six weeks before I went to her, the child she brought into the world lived but a few months; upon its death, at Lord Peyton's desire, they took you from nurse, and pretending you their own, privately buried their child, who was likewise nursed abroad. Mr. Selvyn was a merchant, but had never been successful, his wife died when you were about three years old. Having no children to provide for, and not being fond of trade, he was desirous of retiring into the country. Lord Peyton to facilitate the gratification of his wish, procured him a small *sine cure*; gave into his possession three thousand pounds, which he secured to you; and allowed him an hundred a year for the trouble of your education; with an unlimited commission to call on him for any sums he should want.

'The constant sense of my guilt, the continual regret at having by my own ill conduct forfeited the happiness, which every action of Lord Peyton's proved that his wife might reasonably expect, fixed a degree of melancholy on my mind, which no time has been able to conquer. I lived with my father till his death, which happened not many years ago; at his decease, I found myself mistress of a large fortune, which enabled me to support the rank I had always enjoyed. Though Lord Peyton had provided sufficiently for Mr. Selvyn's and our convenience, yet I constantly sent him a yearly present; till no longer able to deny myself the pleasure of seeing my dear child, I prevailed on him to remove to London, and to fix in the same street with me, taking care to supply all that was requisite to enable him to appear there genteelly. You know with what appearance of accident I first cultivated a friendship with you, but you cannot imagine, with how much difficulty I concealed the tenderness of a mother under the ceremonies of an acquaintance.

'Of late I have enjoyed a more easy state of mind: I have sometimes been inclined to flatter myself, that your uncommon merit, and the great comfort I have received in your society, are signs that Heaven has forgiven my offence, and accepted my penitence, which has been sincere and long, as an atonement for my crime; in which blessed hope I shall, I trust, meet death without terror, and submit, my dear daughter, whenever I am called hence, in full confidence to that Power, whose mercy is over all his works. I ought to add a few words about your dear father, who seemed to think my extreme regular conduct, and the punishment I had inflicted on myself, such an extenuation of my weakness, that he ever behaved to me with the tenderest respect, I might almost say reverence, and till his death gave me every proof of the purest and the strongest friendship. By consent we avoided each others presence for three years, by which time we hoped the violence of our mutual passion would be abated. He spent the greatest part of it abroad; and at the end of that period we met with the sincerer joy, from finding we were not deceived in our hopes. Our attachment was settled into the tenderest friendship; we forbore even the mention of your name, as it must have reminded us of our crime; and if Lord Peyton wanted to communicate any thing concerning you, he did it by letter; avoiding with the extremest delicacy ever to take notice, that any such letters had passed between us; and even in them he consulted about his child, in the stile of a man who was writing to a person that had no other connexion with it than what her friendship for him must naturally occasion, in a point where he was interested by the tenderest ties of the most extreme paternal love.

'I have often with pleasure heard you mention his great fondness for you in your childhood, when he visited at your father's; your growing years encreased it, though it obliged him to suppress the appearance of an affection which you would have thought improper. I need not tell you, that I had the misfortune to lose this worthiest of friends, about half a year before you came to London, which determined me to send for you, that I might receive all the consolation the world could give me, and see the inheritor of her dear father's virtues. While he lived I dared not have taken the same step; your presence would have been too painful a testimony against me, and continually reminded my lord of a weakness, which I hope time had almost effaced from his remembrance.'

Miss Selvyn was extremely affected with the perusal of this paper; she was frequently interrupted by her tears; grieved to the heart to think of how much uneasiness she had been the cause. As soon as she had concluded it, she threw herself on her knees at Lady Emilia's bedside, and taking one of her hands, which she bathed with her tears, 'Is it possible then, said she, that I have thus long been ignorant of the best of parents? And must I lose you when so lately found? Oh! my dear mother, how much pleasure have I lost by not knowing that I might call you by that endearing name! What an example of virtue have you set me! How noble your resolution! How uniform and constant your penitence! Blest you must be supremely by him who loveth the contrite heart; and you and my father I doubt not will enjoy eternal felicity together, united never more to part. Oh! may your afflicted daughter be received into the same place, and partake of your happiness; may she behold your piety rewarded, and admire in you the blessed fruits of

[margin handwritten note: and Miss S. blames herself?]

timely repentance; a repentance so immediately succeeding the offence, that your soul could not have received the black impression!'

'Can you, who have never erred, said Lady Emilia, see my offence in so fair a light? What may I not then hope from infinite mercy? I do hope; it would be criminal to doubt, when such consolatory promises appear in almost every page of holy writ. With pleasure I go where I am called, for I leave my child safe in the Divine Protection, and her own virtue; I leave her, I hope, to a happy life, and a far more happy death; when joys immortal will bless her through all eternity. I have now my love discharged the burden from my mind; not many hours of life remain, let me not pass them in caressing my dear daughter, which, though most pleasing to my fond heart, can end only in making me regret the loss of a world which will soon pass from my sight. Let me spend this hour, as I hope to do those that will succeed it through all eternity. Join with me in prayers to, and praises of him, in whom consists all our lasting happiness.'

Miss Selvyn sent for the Minister of the parish, at Lady Emilia's[1] desire, and the remainder of her life passed in religious exercises. She expired without a groan, in the midst of a fervent prayer, as if her soul was impatient to take its flight into the presence of him, whom she was addressing with so much ardour.

Miss Selvyn's affliction was at first extreme, but when she reflected on her mother's well-spent life, and most happy death, it much abated the excess of her grief. By that lady's will, she found herself heir to twelve thousand pounds, and all her personal estate. She had been charmed with the account Lady Mary Jones had sent her of this society, and wished to increase her acquaintance with that lady, and therefore offered, if proper, to make her a short visit, as soon as her necessary affairs were settled. This met with the most welcome reception, and she came hither as a visitor. Her stay was gradually prolonged for near two months; when having reason, from the great regard shewn her, to think she should be no disagreeable addition, she asked leave to join her fortune to the common stock,[2] and to fix intirely with them.

---

1   Emilia] spelled Emelia in first edition
2   common stock] the fund held by all, but the phrase also suggests the commercial institution of particular funds of capital used for investment

Nothing could be more agreeable to the other three ladies than this offer, and with extream satisfaction she settled here.

Upon this increase of income it was that my friends established the community of indigent gentlewomen, which gave you so much pleasure.

the lesson

Lamont was much struck with the conduct of Lady Emilia; she had shewn, he said, a degree of delicacy and prudence, which exceeded what he had a notion of; he never met with a woman who foresaw the little chance she had for happiness, in marrying a man who could have no inducement to make her his wife, but a nice, often a too nice, sense of honour; and who certainly could have no great opinion of her virtue. The folly of both men and women in these late unions was the subject of our conversation till we separated.

In the afternoon the ladies asked us to accompany them to the house they had just taken for the new community, to which they were obliged to go that day, as they had set several persons to work there. They keep a post-coach and post-chaise,[1] which with the help of our's, were sufficient to accommodate us all. A short time brought us to the house, a very old, and formerly a very fine mansion, but now much fallen to decay. The outside is greatly out of repair, but the building seems strong. The inside is in a manner totally unfurnished; for though it is not empty, yet the rats and mice have made such considerable depredations on what time had before reduced to a very tattered condition, that the melancholy remains can be reckoned little better than lumber.

The last inhabitant of this house we were informed was an old miser, whose passion for accumulating wealth, reduced him into almost as unfortunate a state as Midas, who, according to the fable, having obtained the long desired power of turning every thing he touched to gold, was starved by the immediate transmutation of all food into that metal, the instant it touched his lips. The late possessor of the house I am speaking of, when he was about fifty years old, turned away every servant but an old woman, who if she was not honest, was at least too

the story of the new house

---

1   post-coach] a stage-coach for carrying the mail, along with passengers; post-chaise] a travelling carriage hired from stage to stage of a journey

weak to be able to put any dishonesty in practise. When he was about threescore, she died, and he never could venture to let any one supply her place. He fortified every door and window with such bars of iron, that his house might have resisted the forcible attack of a whole army. Night and day growled before his inhospitable door a furious Dutch mastiff,[1] whose natural ferocity was so increased by continual hunger, for his master fed him most sparingly, that no stranger could have entered the yard with impunity.

Every time this churlish beast barked, the old gentleman, with terror and dismay in his countenance, and quaking limbs, ran to the only window he ever ventured to unbar, to see what danger threatened him; nor could the sight of a barefoot child, or a decrepid[2] old woman, immediately dispel his fears. As timorous as Falstaff,[3] his imagination first multiplied, and then cloathed them in buckram; and his panic ceased not till they were out of view.

This wretched man upon the death of his only servant, agreed with an old woman to buy food for him, and bring it to the well defended door of his yard; where informing him of her arrival, by a signal agreed upon between them, he ventured out of his house to receive it from her; and dressed it himself; till worn out by anxiety of mind he grew too weak to perform that office, and ordered the woman to bring it ready prepared; this continued for a little time, till at last he appeared no more at his gate. After the old woman had knocked three days in vain, the neighbourhood began to think it necessary to take some measures thereupon; but not chusing to run the hazard of breaking open the house, they sent to the old gentleman's nephew, whose father had been suffered to languish in extreme poverty many years before his death; nor was the son in much better condition; but he had acquainted some of the neighbours with the place of his abode, in hopes of the event which now induced them to send for him.

As soon as he arrived, he prepared to force his way into the house, but it was found so impracticable, that at length they were obliged to

---

1 Dutch mastiff] a particular breed of the large watch-dog, supposedly originating in Holland
2 decrepid] at that time a common variant of decrepit
3 Falstaff] the scapegrace comic character in Shakespeare's *Henry IV* and *The Merry Wives of Windsor*; in *Henry IV*, part 1, he lies about chasing off some attackers and progressively exaggerates their number (Act 2, Scene 4, lines 181 and following)

wealthy miser, spendthrift son

untile part of the roof, from whence a person descended, and opened the door to those who did not chuse so dangerous an entrance, as that through which he had passed.

They found the old man dead on a great chest which contained his money, as if he had been desirous to take possession even in death.

His nephew was just of age, and having till then been exposed to all the evils of poverty, was almost distracted with joy at the sudden acquisition of a large fortune. He scarcely could be prevailed with to stay long enough in this house to pay the last duties to an uncle, who had no right to any thing more from him than just the decent ceremonies; and without giving himself time to look over his estate, hastened to London.

He hired a magnificent house in Grosvenor-Square;[1] bespoke the most elegant equipages; bought the finest set of horses he could hear of, at double their real value; and launched into every expence the town afforded him. He soon became one of the most constant frequenters of Whites;[2] kept several running horses; distinguished himself at Newmarket,[3] and had the honour of playing deeper, and betting with more spirit, than any other young man of his age. There was not an occurrence in his life about which he had not some wager depending. The wind could not change, or a shower fall without his either losing or gaining by it. He had not a dog or cat in his house on whose life he had not bought or sold an annuity. By these ingenious methods in one year was circulated through the kingdom, the ready money which his uncle had been half his life starving himself and family to accumulate. The second year obliged him to mortgage great part of his land, and the third saw him reduced to sell a considerable portion of his estate, of which this house, and the land belonging to it made a part.

I could not help observing the various fate of this mansion, originally the seat of ancient hospitality; then falling into the hands of a miser, who had not spirit to enjoy it, nor sense enough to see, that he was

and the lesson.

---

1 Grosvenor-Square] a neighbourhood in the fashionable district of Mayfair in London
2 Whites] originally a chocolate-house in the fashionable west end of London, it became by the mid-eighteenth century a men's club known for gambling
3 Newmarket] a town on the border of Cambridgeshire and Suffolk, well known as a site for horse-racing and betting since the seventeenth century

impairing so valuable a part of his possessions, by grudging the necessary expences of repairs; from him devolving to a young coxcomb,
who by neglect let it sink into ruin, and was spending in extravagance,
what he inherited from avarice; as if one vice was to pay the debt to society which the other had incurred; and now it was purchased to be the
seat of charity and benevolence. How directly were we led to admire
the superior sense, as well as transcendent virtue of these ladies, when
we compared the use they made of money, with that to which the two
late possessors had appropriated it! While we were in doubt which
most to blame, he who had heaped it up without comfort, in sordid in-
humanity; or he who squandered it in the gratification of gayer vices.
Equally strangers to beneficence, self-indulgence was their sole view;
alike criminal, though not equally unfashionable, one endeavoured to
starve, the other to corrupt mankind; while the new owners of this
house had no other view, than to convenience, and to reform all who
came within their influence, themselves enjoying in a supreme degree,
the happiness they dispersed around them.

It was pleasing to see numbers at work to repair the building, and
cultivate the garden, and to observe, that at length from this inhospitable mansion 'Health to himself, and to his children bread, the labourer
bears.'[1] Within it were all the biggest school girls, with one of their
mistresses to direct them in mending such furniture as were not quite
destroyed; and I was pleased to see with how much art they repaired
the decays of time, in things which well deserved better care, having
once been the richest part of the furniture belonging to the opulent
possessors.

In our way home we called at a clergyman's house, which was
placed in the finest situation imaginable, and where we beheld that
profusion of comforts, which sense and œconomy will enable the possessors of narrow fortunes to enjoy. This gentleman and his wife have
but a small living, and still less paternal estate; but the neatness, pretti-
ness, and convenience of their habitation, were enough to put one out

---

1   'health to himself, and to his children bread, the labourer bears'] Alexander Pope, *Moral
Essays IV: To Burlington*, lines 170-71: "Health to himself, and to his Infants bread/The
Lab'rer bears"

of humour with riches, and I should certainly have breathed forth Agar's prayer[1] with great ardour, if I had not been stopped in the beginning, by considering how great a blessing wealth may be when properly employed, of which I had then such hourly proof.

At our return to Millenium-Hall we found some of the neighbouring society, who were come to share the evening's concert, and sup with us. But at ten o'clock they departed; which I understood was somewhat later than usual, but they conformed to the alteration of hours our arrival had occasioned.

The next day being very hot, we were asked to breakfast in a delightful arbour in the Flower garden. The morning dew, which still refreshed the flowers, increased their fragrance to as great an excess of sweetness as the senses could support. Till I went to this house, I knew not half the charms of the country. Few people have the art of making the most of nature's bounty; these ladies are epicures in rural pleasures, and enjoy them in the utmost excess to which they can be carried. All that romance ever represented in the plains of Arcadia,[2] are much inferior to the charms of Millenium-Hall, except the want of shepherds be judged a deficiency, that nothing else can compensate; there indeed they fall short of what romantic writers represent, and have formed a female Arcadia.

After breakfast all the ladies left us except Mrs. Maynard. We were so charmed with the spot we were in, that we agreed to remain there, and I called on my cousin to continue the task she had undertaken; which she did in the following manner.

---

1   Agar's prayer] in the book of Genesis in the Bible, Hagar is sent away by Abraham, her master and father of her son Ishmael, at the behest of Abraham's wife, Sarah; without water in the desert, Hagar prayed not to have to witness the death of her son, whereupon God caused a well to appear and told Hagar that her son would found a great nation

2   Arcadia] a mountainous region in Greece, in mythology supposedly presided over by the god Pan and characterized by rustic happiness and simple pastoral life; literary representations of Arcadia as a retreat from oppressive modern society were popular amongst the upper classes during the Renaissance and after

THE HISTORY OF
Mrs. TRENTHAM.

MRS. Trentham never knew the blessing of a mother's care, her's died the same month which gave her daughter birth; and Mr. Trentham survived his wife but eight years. He left his little girl eleven thousand pounds, recommending both her person and fortune to his Mother Mrs. Alworth.

Mrs. Alworth was an old lady of good sense and merit. She had felt the most melancholy, but not unusual effect of long life, having outlived all her children. This misfortune she alleviated in the best manner she was able, by receiving her grand-children into her family. Her son by her second husband left behind him a boy and girl, the former at the time I speak of, about eleven years old, the latter ten. Her daughter had married Mr. Denham, and at her death left two girls. Mr. Denham entering into wedlock a second time, very willingly complied with Mrs. Alworth's desire of having his two daughters. The eldest of these was twelve years old, the youngest eleven.

These children had lived with the old lady some years, when she took home Harriot Trentham. As their grand-mother was rich, there had been a strong contention among them for her favour, and they could not without great disgust see another rival brought to the house. Harriot was extremely handsome and engaging. The natural sweetness of her temper rendered her complying and observant; but having been bred under the care of a sensible and indulgent father, she had never been taught the little arts of behaviour, which mothers too commonly inculcate with so much care, that children are as void of simplicity at eight, as at eight and twenty years old. The first thing a girl is taught is to hide her sentiments, to contradict the thoughts of her heart, and tell all the civil lies which custom has sanctified, with as much affectation and conceit as her mother; and when she has acquired all the folly and impertinence of a riper age, and apes the woman more ungracefully than a monkey does a fine gentleman, the parents congratulate themselves with the extremest complacency, on the charming education they have given their daughter.

Harriot had been taught no such lessons. Her Father had a strong dislike to prematurity, and feared that communication with the world would too soon teach her art and disguise, the last things he would have chosen to anticipate.

By teaching her humanity, he initiated her into civility of manners. She had learnt, that to give pain was immoral; and could no more have borne to have shocked any person's mind, than to have racked his body. Any thought therefore that could hurt she suppressed as an indispensable duty, and to please by her actions, and not offend by her words, was an essential part of the religion in which she was educated: but in every thing whereby no one could suffer, she was innocence and simplicity itself; and in her nature shone pure and uncorrupted, either by natural or acquired vices.

Mrs. Alworth, though fond of all her grand-children, could not conquer a degree of partiality for Harriot, whose attractions, both personal and mental, were very superior to those of her cousins. Her beauty secured her the particular attention of all strangers, she gained their favour at first sight, and secured it by her amiable disposition when they became more acquainted with her.

Envy is one of the first passions that appears in the human mind. Had Miss Alworth and Miss Denham[1] been much younger, Harriot would not have passed unenvied. Every day increased their dislike to her, as she grew daily more beloved by others, and they let no opportunity escape of making her feel the effects of their little malice. Their hatred to her produced an union among themselves; for the first time they found something in which they all agreed. They were continually laying little plots to lessen her in their grand-mother's opinion; frequent were the accusations against her, but her innocence always triumphed, though it never discouraged them from repeating the same unsuccessful attempts. Mrs. Alworth was extremely fond of them all, but yet she saw through their malice, and their behaviour only served to endear Harriot the more, who defended herself without anger, and retained no rancour in her mind. Free from resentment or suspicion she was ever open to their arts, and experience did not teach her to be

---

1   Denham] Denhams in first edition

on her guard against them, which often occasioned their having appearances on their side, and might have raised prejudices against her in Mrs. Alworth's mind, had she not found a defender in Master Alworth, who alone of all her cousins was free from envy. He was naturally of an honest and sweet disposition, and being fond of Harriot, for beauty has charms for all ages, felt great indignation at the treatment she received, and would often express a resentment from which she was wholly free.

Mrs. Alworth's great fondness for her grandson, and strong prejudices against schools, from a belief that boys acquire there more vice than learning, had determined on a private education. She therefore provided a tutor for him before he was seven years old; a man of learning and sense, with a great deal of religion and good humour; and who was very attentive to the employment for which he had been chosen.

Master Alworth, by being thus kept at home, had frequent opportunities of observing the malice of his sister and Miss Denham against Harriot, and never failed exposing their practices to his grand-mother; who from thence learnt to suspect their reports about things which passed in his absence, and consequently could not be cleared up by him. His fondness for Harriot soon made him beloved by her, and as she found little pleasure in the society of her other cousins, she sought his company, but as he was much engaged by his studies, she seldom found him at leisure to play. The tutor greatly delighted with her, tried to awaken in her mind a desire of improvement, and found it an easy task; she was inclined to learn, and capable of doing it with great quickness. Mrs. Alworth readily entered into the good man's views, and was pleased with the eagerness of Harriot's application. Master Alworth was far enough advanced in learning to assist his favourite, and from him she received instruction with double pleasure, and more easily comprehended his explanations than those of their tutor, who found it difficult to divest himself sufficiently of scientific terms, which greatly retard the increase of knowlege in a youthful mind.

Thus beloved by her grand-mother and Mr. Alworth, and hated and traduced by her female cousins, Harriot lived till she was sixteen. Years had still improved her person, and she had made considerable progress in learning, when Mrs. Alworth judged it proper that her grandson should go abroad, to compleat an education which she flattered herself was hitherto faultless. He had no objection to the scheme but what arose from his unwillingness to leave Harriot, who saw his departure approach with great concern. She loved and respected her grand-mother, but Mr. Alworth was the only person whom she could look upon in the tender and equal light of a friend. To be deprived of his society was losing the chief pleasure of her life, and her best guardian against her enemies.

Mrs. Alworth was pleased with the affection which so evidently appeared between these two young people, she hoped to see an happy union arise from it. Their fortunes and ages were properly suited, and a love which had taken root in childhood, and grown with their encreasing years, seemed to promise a lasting harmony, of which the sweetness of their dispositions would be no bad security. These pleasing ideas amused this worthy woman, but the two friends themselves had not extended their views so far. Bred up like brother and sister, a tenderer degree of relation had not entered their thoughts, nor did any thing more appear necessary to their happiness, than a constant enjoyment of each others friendship.

In this disposition they parted when Mr. Alworth went abroad. His tutor thinking himself not properly qualified to conduct him in his travels, recommended another gentleman, and Mr. Alworth, at Harriot's request, prevailed with their grandmother to detain his old tutor till Harriot's education was compleated.

Mr. Alworth continued abroad two years, during which time Harriot had applied with such unwearied diligence, that she was perfect mistress of the living languages, and no less acquainted with Greek and Latin. She was well instructed in the ancient and modern philosophy, and in almost every branch of learning.

Mr. Alworth found his cousin not alone improved in understanding, her beauty was just then in its perfection, and it was scarcely possible to conceive any thing handsomer. She had great elegance of manner, a point wherein her grand-mother excelled, and was as far removed from conceit as from ignorance. Her situation was much mended by the marriage of the eldest Miss Denham; and Miss Alworth waited only for her brother's arrival and approbation, to enter into the same state. The gentleman to whom she was going to be married had first made his addresses to Harriot; but, as well as several others, was refused by her. She was not inclined to change her situation, or this gentleman's fortune, person, and character were unexceptionable; however one circumstance without any other objection would have been sufficient to have rendered his suit unsuccessful; she perceived that Miss Alworth was in love with him, and though she had little reason to have much regard for her, yet good nature made her anxious for the success of a passion which she saw was deeply rooted.

She therefore, while she discouraged his addresses, took every means of recommending Miss Alworth, whose treatment of her she believed rather proceeded from compliance with Miss Denham's than from ill temper.

This gave her hopes that she might make a good wife to Mr. Parnel, the object of her affections. He soon perceived, that Miss Alworth did not behold him with indifference; but as he was much captivated by Harriot's charms, it at first had no other effect, than leading him to indulge in complaints of her cruelty to Miss Alworth, who listened with compassion. Harriot often represented to him how little he ought to wish for her consent to marry him, which he so strongly sollicited; for should she grant it, he would be miserable with a wife who did not love him. She told him, that 'were he indifferent, her being so might do very well, and they live on together in that eternal *ennui*, which must ever subsist between a married couple who have no affection for each other, and while natural good temper and prudence enabled them to dream away a dull life in peace and dead insensibility, the world might call them happy; but that if he really loved her, her indifference would render him more wretched than the most blameable conduct.' She would then represent the advantages of marrying a woman whose sole affections he possessed, though at first he felt for her only esteem and gratitude; and advised him by all means to seek for one whose heart was in that situation, which he was well qualified to find.

Though Harriot forbore to mention Miss Alworth's name, Mr. Parnel well understood to whom she alluded, but found it difficult to take her advice. At length however, deprived of all hope of obtaining the woman he loved, and moved to compassion by the visible unhappiness of one who loved him, he began to listen to it, and frankly told Harriot, that he understood the aim of what she had said. She was not sorry to throw off all restraint, as it gave her the power of speaking more to the purpose; and at length brought him to say, that he should not be unwilling to marry her. Harriot feared lest the belief of Mr. Parnel's still retaining an affection for her, might render Miss Alworth uneasy, and therefore advised him gradually to slacken his addresses to her, and at the same time to increase in proportion his attentions for Miss Alworth, that he might appear to prefer her, since a symptom of inconstancy she knew would not so much affect her as any sign of indifference, and Harriot's generosity so far exceeded her vanity, that she very sincerely desired to be thought neglected, rather than give any alloy to the happiness of her cousin.

There was the more colour for this supposition, as Mr. Parnel had never been publicly discarded by her, since for the completion of her views she had found it necessary to preserve his acquaintance.

Miss Alworth was happy beyond expression when she found herself the object of Mr. Parnel's addresses. Her wishes so far blinded her, that she really believed Harriot was neglected for her; but yet knew she had long been endeavouring to serve her, and was obliged to her for some instructions how to behave so to Mr. Parnel as to secure his esteem and confidence, the best foundation for love. As her brother was then soon expected over, Mrs. Alworth thought that to wait for his approbation was but a proper compliment.

Mr. Alworth was not at all inclined to object to so good a match, especially as it was much desired by his sister, and the marriage was celebrated soon after his return. This ceremony did not so engage his attention, as to render him less sensible of the pleasure of renewing his friendship with Harriot, who received him with the sincerest joy. He found her greatly improved, and every hour passed agreeably that was spent in her company. They were continually together, and never happy but when they were so. Every one talked of their mutual passion; and they were so often told of it that they began to fancy it was true, but were surprized to find that name should be given to an affection calm and rational as theirs, totally free from that turbulency and wildness, which had always appeared to them the true characteristics of love. They were sensible however, that nothing was so dear to them as each other, they were always sorry to part, uneasy asunder, and rejoiced to meet; a walk was doubly pleasing when they both shared it; a book became more entertaining if they read together; every thing was insipid that they did not mutually enjoy. When they considered these symptoms, they were inclined to think the general opinion was just, and that their affection, being free from passion, proceeded from some peculiarity of temper.

Mrs. Alworth thought she should give them great satisfaction in proposing a speedy marriage; and rejoiced to see the first wish of her heart, which had been for their union, so nearly compleated. The old lady's proposal made them a little thoughtful; they saw no very good reason for their marrying; they enjoyed each others society already, and did not wish for any more intimate tie. But neither knew how to refuse, since the other might take it for an affront, and they would not for the world have had the sincerity and tenderness of their affection brought into doubt. Besides they began to think, that as their love was so generally looked upon as certain, it might become difficult to continue the same degree of intimacy without exposing themselves to censure. This thought was sufficient to determine them to marry; and their entire affection for, and confidence in each other, convinced them they ran no hazard in this step; and that they could not fail of being happy as man and wife, who had so long enjoyed great felicity in the most intimate friendship.

In consequence of this resolution, lawyers were employed to draw up settlements, and every thing requisite for a proper appearance on their marriage was ordered; but they were so very patient on the subject, that the preparations went on slowly. Some who hoped to have their diligence quickened, in a manner usual on such occasions, affected delays, but were surprized to find that no complaint ensued. They grew still more dilatory, but the only consequence that arose from it was a decent solicitation to dispatch, without any of those more effectual means being used, which impatient love or greedy avarice suggest.

These young people were perfectly happy and contented, and therefore waited with composure for the conclusion of preparations, which however slowly did however proceed. The old lady indeed was less patient, but a grandmother's sollicitations have no very powerful effect on lawyers; therefore her's availed little.

During these delays Mrs. Tonston, formerly the eldest Miss Denham, having been extremely ill, was sent to Buxton[1] for the recovery

---

1   Buxton] a town in Derbyshire that became a place of fashionable resort in the eighteenth
     century, for its supposedly healthful natural spring water

of her health. As this place was but a day's journey from Mrs. Alworth's house, she expressed a desire to see her grand-daughter, and Mr. Alworth and Harriot, as well as Miss Denham, very readily accompanied her thither.

The accommodations at Buxton allow very little seclusion; and as Mrs. Tonston was sufficiently recovered to conform to the customs of the place, they joined in the general society. The first day at dinner Mr. Alworth's attention was much engrossed by Miss Melman, a very pretty woman. She was far from a perfect beauty, but her countenance expressed an engaging vivacity, and great good humour, though a wandering unfixed look, indicated a light and unsteady mind. Her person was little but elegant; there was a sprightliness in her whole figure which was very attractive: her conversation was suitable to it, she had great life and spirit, all the common *routine*[1] of discourse, and a fashionable readiness to skim lightly over all subjects. Her understanding was sufficiently circumscribed; but what she wanted in real sense, she made up in vivacity, no unsuccessful substitute in general estimation.

This young lady was almost a new character to Mr. Alworth. He had lived constantly at his grand-mother's till he went abroad, and as soon as he returned into the kingdom he went thither; from which, as it was the middle of summer, and consequently London had no temptations, he had never stirred. He therefore had been little used to any woman but his sober and sensible grand-mother's two cousins who were pretty enough, but had no great charms of understanding; a sister rather silly, and the incomparable Harriot, whose wit was as sound as her judgment solid and sterling, free from affectation, and all little effeminate arts and airs. Reason governed her thoughts and actions, nor could the greatest flow of spirits make her for a moment forget propriety. Every thing in her was natural grace, she was always consistent and uniform, and a stranger to caprice.

Miss Melman[2] was a compleat coquet, capricious and fantastical.[3] As Mr. Alworth was the prettiest man at the place, and known to have a

---

1   *routine*] *rontine* in first edition
2   Melman] Milman in first edition
3   fantastical] fanciful, impulsive

good fortune, she soon singled him out as a conquest worthy of her, and successfully played off all her arts. By appearing to like him, she inticed him to address her; and by a well managed capriciousness of behaviour kept up the spirit of a pursuit. She frequently gave him reason to believe her favourably disposed towards him, and as often, by obliging him to doubt of it, encreased his desire to be certain it was true. She kept him in a state of constant anxiety, and made him know her consequence by the continual transition from pleasure to pain in which he lived.

He had not been much more than a fortnight at Buxton, when his attachment to Miss Melman became very apparent. Harriot saw an assiduity in his behaviour very different from what he had ever shewn to her. He felt that in the circumstances wherein he and Harriot then were, his conduct must appear injurious, and shame and the secret reproaches of his conscience made him take all possible opportunities of avoiding her presence: if he was obliged to converse with her, it was with an air so restrained and inattentive, as made her fear his regard for her was entirely vanished. The sincere affection she had for him rendered this apprehension extremely painful. She would have been contented to have seen another woman his wife, but could not bear the thought of losing his friendship. At first she passed over this change in silence, and appeared even not to observe it; but when they received an account that the marriage writings were finished, she thought an affected blindness highly unseasonable, and told him, in the most friendly and generous manner, that, 'nothing remained to be done but to cancel them, that, she plainly perceived another had obtained the heart she never possessed; that, the measures taken for their marriage were of no sort of consequence, and she flattered herself she might retain his friendship, though he gave his hand to another.'

Mr. Alworth at first appeared confounded, but recovering himself, confessed to her frankly, 'he never knew the weakness and folly of the human heart, till his own convinced him of it; that, he had always felt for her the most perfect esteem, joined with the tenderest affection; but his passions had had no share in his attachment. On the contrary, he found them strongly engaged on the side of Miss Melman, and felt an ardour for her which he had never before experienced. That, he could not think of being her husband without rapture, though he saw plainly she was inferior to his Harriot both in beauty and understanding; and as for her principles, he was totally ignorant of them. He now, he said, perceived the difference between friendship and love, and was convinced, that esteem and passion were totally independant, since she entirely possessed the one, while Miss Melman totally engrossed the other.'

Harriot was pleased with the frankness of Mr. Alworth's confession, and wished only to be secure of his esteem, but she saw him so wholly taken up with Miss Melman, that she was convinced passion had greater power over his sex than esteem, and that while his mind was under the tumultuous influence of love, she must expect very little satisfaction from his friendship.

She took upon herself the task of breaking off their treaty of marriage, and acquainted her grand-mother with her resolution, who saw too plainly the reason for her doing so to blame her conduct, though she grieved at the necessity for it, and could not sincerely forgive her grandson's levity and want of judgment, in preferring a wild fantastic girl, to the extreme beauty, and solid well-known merit of Harriot, an error for which she prophetically saw he would in time be severely punished.

Harriot, from the intended bride, now became the confidant of Mr. Alworth, though with an aching heart; for she feared that after experiencing the more active sensations of a strong passion, friendship would appear too insipid to have any charms for him. She accompanied Mrs. Alworth home before the lovers chose to leave Buxton, but not till she had prevailed with her grandmother to consent to the marriage between Miss Melman and Mr. Alworth should be celebrated at her house.

When every thing requisite for the ceremony was ready, they came to Mrs. Alworth's, where the indissoluble knot was tied, and in the bride-groom's opinion the most perfect happiness secured to his future years. They staid but a few days after the marriage, and then went to her father's house, till the approaching winter called them to London.

Harriot found a great loss of a friend she so sincerely loved, but she hoped he would be as happy as he expected, and had the satisfaction of believing he retained a tender regard for her. They corresponded frequently; and his letters assured her of his felicity. After he had been some time fixed in London, he grew indeed less eloquent on the subject, which did not surprize her, as the variety of his engagements shortened his letters, and denied him leisure to expatiate on the most pleasing topics.

Miss Denham had accompanied her sister home, and in the winter Mrs. Alworth was informed by Mrs. Tonston, that Miss Denham had received a proposal from a gentleman of a good estate, but he insisted on a fortune of nine thousand pounds, which was two more than she was possessed of; and as they wished the old lady to make that addition, Mrs. Tonston as an inducement added, that the gentleman was extremely agreeable to her sister.

Mrs. Alworth was not inclined to comply with their views, and made no other answer to all Harriot urged to prevail with her to give the requisite sum, than that it was more than perhaps would at her death fall to Miss Denham's share, and she saw no temptation to purchase so mercenary a man. When Harriot found that all she could say was unavailing, she told Mrs. Alworth, that, 'if she would give her leave, she was determined to make the required addition out of her fortune; for she could not bear her cousin should be disappointed in a particular she thought essential to her happiness, by the want of a sum of money which she could very well spare; adding, that the treatment she had received from her cousins, she attributed to childishness and folly, and should be far worse than they were, if she could remember it with resentment.'

Mrs. Alworth was greatly touched with this instance of Harriot's generosity, and finding that nothing but the exertion of her authority, which her grand-daughter acknowleged absolute, and always obeyed implicitly, could prevent her from performing her purpose; she determined to take the most effectual means of hindering it, by advancing the money herself, and invited Miss Denham and her lover to her house; where the marriage was performed, and they departed.

Mrs. Alworth began to feel the infirmities of age, and now that she and Harriot were left to continual *tête à tête*, absolute quiet might have degenerated into something like dullness; but the disturbance they found not at home, reached them from abroad. Mr. Parnel was wearied with his wife's fondness,[1] who not considering that he had married her more out of gratitude than affection, had disgusted him with the

---

1   fondness] showing excessive affection

continual professions of a love, to which his heart would not make an equal return. This fondness teazed a temper, naturally good, into peevishness, and was near converting indifference into dislike. Mrs. Parnel distressed beyond measure at an effect so contrary to what she intended, reproached him with ingratitude, and tormented him with tears and complaints.

Harriot, who considered this match as in a great measure her own work, was particularly desirous of redressing these grievances, and took great pains to persuade Mrs. Parnel to restrain her fondness, and suppress her complaints, while she endeavoured to make her husband sensible, that he ought, in consideration for the cause, to pardon the troublesome effects, and not to suffer himself to be disgusted by that affection in his wife, which to most husbands would appear a merit. Mrs. Alworth joined to Harriot's persuasion, the influence her age and respectable character gave her, and though not without great difficulty, they at last saw Mr. and Mrs. Parnel live in peace and amity, without any of the pleasures arising from strong and delicate affections, or the sufferings occasioned by ill humour and hatred; and whatever void they might find in their hearts, they were so happy as to have well filled by two very fine children, which Mrs. Parnel brought her husband; who always treated her with great indulgence, in hopes of fixing Harriot's good opinion; for though despair had damped his passion, yet he still loved her with the tenderest respect and reverence.

Towards the latter end of the second year of Mr. Alworth's marriage, his grand-mother died, much regretted by Harriot, whom she left mistress of her own fortune, with the addition of four thousand pounds, part of it the accumulated interest of her paternal inheritance, the rest Mrs. Alworth's legacy. Her grandson succeeded to her house, and intreated Harriot, that he might find her there when he came to take possession.

Their correspondence had been regular, but they had never met since his marriage.[1] Mrs. Alworth was not fond of the conversation of an old lady; and from seeing herself not very agreeable to her grandmother, felt an uncommon awe in her presence. Harriot had received

---

1   marriage] mariage in first edition

repeated invitations from them, but could not be prevailed with to leave old Mrs. Alworth, who had no other companion.

The only relief she found in her affliction for the loss of so worthy a parent, was putting the house, and all belonging to it, in order, for the reception of her first friend, in whose society she expected to renew the happiness she had so long enjoyed from it. Nor was she disappointed in her hopes of finding him still her friend; they met with mutual joy, and Mrs. Alworth seemed at first as much pleased with her new possession, as they were with each other. But Harriot soon found her happiness considerably damped. Mr. Alworth, unwilling to let his grandmother know the ill success of an union which he was sensible she disapproved, had been silent on that subject in his letters, but he was too well acquainted with the generosity of Harriot's temper, to fear she would triumph at the natural consequence of his ill-grounded passion, and therefore concealed not from her any part of the uneasiness which his wife's disposition gave him. He too late saw the difference between sensible vivacity and animal spirits, and found Mrs. Alworth a giddy coquet, too volatile to think, too vain to love; pleased with admiration, insensible to affection, fond of flattery, but indifferent to true praise; imprudently vivacious in mixed companies, lifeless when alone with him; and desirous of charming all mankind except her husband, who of his whole sex seemed the only person of no consequence to her. As her view was to captivate in public, she covered a very pretty complexion with pearl-powder[1] and rouge, because they made her more resplendent by candle-light, and in public places. Mr. Alworth had in strong terms expressed his abhorence of that practice; but, 'she was surprized he should intermeddle in an affair that was no business of his, surely she might wear what complexion she pleased.' The natural turn of his temper inclined him to rational society, but in that his wife could bear no part. The little time she was at home was employed in dressing, and a multitude of coxcombs[2] attended her toilet.[3] Mr. Alworth's extreme fondness for her made him at first very

---

1   pearl-powder] a cosmetic giving unusual whiteness to the skin
2   coxcombs] conceited and showy men
3   toilet] in the eighteenth century, the process of dressing and grooming oneself, during which
     it became fashionable, especially for ladies, to converse with visitors of either sex

wretched; he soon found himself the most disregarded of all mankind, and every man appeared his rival; but on nearer observation he perceived his jealousy was groundless, and that she was too giddy to love any thing. This made his pride easy, but his tenderness still had much to endure, till at length contempt produced some degree of indifference, and his sufferings became less acute, though he lived in continual grief, at finding himself disappointed of all his airy hopes of happiness.

Harriot was scarcely less afflicted than himself, she endeavoured to render him more contented with his situation, and attempted to teach Mrs. Alworth to think, but in both was equally unsuccessful. However this was not all she had to endure. When Mr. Alworth began with unprejudiced eyes to compare her he had lost, with the woman for whom he relinquished her; when he saw how greatly Harriot's natural beauty eclipsed Mrs. Alworth's, notwithstanding the addition of all her borrowed charms, he wondered what magic had blinded him to her superiority. But when he drew a comparison between the admirable understanding of the one, her great fund of knowlege, the inexhaustible variety in her conversation, with the insipid dulness, or unmeaning vivacity of the other, he was still more astonished, and could not forgive his strange infatuation. This train of thought perhaps had no small share in giving rise to a passion for Harriot, which he had never felt, while it might have been the source of much happiness to them both. In short, he became violently in love with her, and fell a prey to the most cruel regret and despair; sensible that all he suffered was the consequence of his own folly.

Respect for Harriot made Mr. Alworth endeavour to conceal his passion, but could not prevent its daily increase. At this time I became acquainted with her, during a visit I made in the neighbourhood; and as the natural openness both of her disposition and mine, inclined us to converse with much freedom, I one day took the liberty to tell her how much Mr. Alworth was in love with her. She had not the least suspicion of it, the entire affection which had always subsisted between them, she imagined sufficient to lead me into that error, but told me the thing was impossible; and to prove it, related all the circumstances of their intended union. Appearances were too strong to suffer me to be persuaded that I was mistaken; I acknowleged that what she urged seemed to contradict my opinion, but that it was no proof; for the perverseness of human nature was such, that it did not appear to me at all improbable that the easiness of obtaining her, when they had both been, as it were, bred up with that view, might be the sole occasion of his indifference; and the impossibility of ever possessing her now, would only serve to inflame his passion.

Harriot accused me of representing human nature more perverse and absurd than it really was, and continued firm in the persuasion of my being mistaken. Whatever glaring signs of Mr. Alworth's love appeared, she set them all down to the account of friendship; till at length his mind was so torn with grief and despair, that no longer able to conceal the cause of his greatest sufferings, he begged her to teach him how to conquer a passion, which, while it existed, must make him wretched; and with the greatest confusion told her how unaccountably unfortunate he was, both in not loving, and in loving, each equally out of season. Almost distracted with the distressful state of his mind, he was in the utmost horror lest this declaration should offend her; and throwing himself at her feet, with a countenance and manner which shewed him almost frantic with despair, terrified her so much, that she did not feel half the shock this declaration would have given her, had it been made with more calmness.

She strove to silence him; she endeavoured to raise him from her feet, but to no purpose; she could not abate the agonies of his mind, without assuring him she forgave him. Her spirits were in extreme agitation till she saw him a little composed; for she feared his senses were affected; but when her alarm began to abate, the effect of her terrors and her grief appeared in a flood of tears; Mr. Alworth found them infectious, and she was obliged to dry them up in order to comfort him. When he grew more composed, Harriot ventured, after expressing her concern for his having conceived so unfortunate a passion, to intimate that absence was the best remedy, and that there was nothing to be done but for her to leave the house.

Mr. Alworth was not able to support the mention of her going away, and intreated her, at least to give him time to arm himself against the greatest misfortune that could befal him, the loss of her society. She dared not controul him in any thing material, while his mind continued in that desperate situation, and therefore consented to stay some time longer. She found it very difficult to make him think, that there ever was a proper time for her to depart, though his passion was much less tormenting since he had ventured to declare it; and what before arose nearly to distraction, sunk now into a soft melancholy. Mrs. Alworth paid so little attention to her husband, that she had not perceived the conflict in his mind. She was wearied with the country to the greatest degree, and made the *tiresome* days as short as she could, by not rising till noon; from that time till dinner, her toilet found her sufficient employment. As the neighbourhood was large, she very frequently contrived to make a party at cards; but as her company was not used to play high, this afforded her little relief, except she could find somebody to bet with her, which was not very difficult, as she was contented to do it to a disadvantage.

In this way she contrived, just, as she called it, 'to drag on life; and wondered how so fine a woman as Harriot, could have so long buried herself in that place, scarcely more lively than the family vault.'

When Harriot thought she had sufficiently convinced Mr. Alworth of the necessity of her absence, she took her leave with much greater concern than she would suffer to appear, though she did not affect indifference; but the truth was, Mr. Alworth's passionate tenderness for her, had made an impression on her heart, which without it, all his merit could not effect. The melancholy langour which overspread his countenance, gave it charms she had never before discovered in it; the soft accents in which he breathed the most delicate love, penetrated to her very soul, and she no longer found that indifference which had been so remarkable a part of her character. But she carefully concealed these new sensations, in hopes that he would more easily conquer his passion, for not thinking it returned.

Though the winter was scarcely begun, yet having no inducement to go to any other place, she went to London; and as I had prolonged my stay in the country only to gratify my inclination for her company, I went with her to town. Mrs. Alworth did not continue there a month after us; but her husband, whose health was by no means in a good state, went to Bath; and that he might not be quite destitute of pleasure, he carried his little boy with him, though but a year and a quarter old. His wife did not contend with him for this privilege, she would have seen little more of the babe had it been in London.

Harriot Trentham was,[1] at her first arrival, in very low spirits, and every letter she received from Mr. Alworth increased her dejection, as it painted his in very strong colours. As the town filled she began to try if dissipation could dispel her melancholy. Her beauty, the fineness of her person, and her being known to have a large fortune, which Fame even exaggerated, procured her many lovers, and she became the most admired woman in town. This was a new source of pleasure to her. She had lived where she saw not many single men, and though few of these who dared to flatter themselves with hopes, had failed paying their addresses to her, yet these successive courtships were very dull, when compared with all the flutter of general admiration. Her books were now neglected, and to avoid thinking on a subject which constantly afflicted her, she forced herself into public, and was glad to find that the idleness of the men, and her own vanity, could afford her entertainment.

She was not however so totally engrossed by this pleasing dissipation, as to neglect any means of serving the distressed. Mrs. Tonston exerting the genius she had so early shewn for traducing others, set her husband and his family at variance, till at length the falshoods, by which she had effected it, came to be discovered. Her husband and she had never lived well together, and this proof of her bad heart disgusted him so intirely, that he turned her out of his house, allowing her a meer trifle for her support. In this distress she applied to Harriot, who she knew was ever ready to serve even those who had most injured her.

Her application was not unsuccessful. Harriot sent her a considerable present for her immediate convenience, and then went into the country to Mr. Tonston, to whom she represented so effectually his ungenerous treatment, since the fortune his wife brought him gave her a right to a decent maintenance, that he made a proper settlement upon her, and gave the writings into Harriot's hands, who not only saw the money paid regularly, but took so much pains to convince Mrs. Tonston of the malignity of her disposition, that she brought her to a due sense of it, and by applying for his assistance to mend her heart, who

---

1   Trentham was,] Trentham, was in first edition

best knew its defects, she became so altered in temper, that five years after her separation from her husband, Harriot effected a reconciliation, and they now live in great amity together, gratefully acknowledging their obligations to her.

I have anticipated this fact in order to render my narrative less tedious, or I should have stopped at Harriot's procuring a settlement for Mrs. Tonston, and have told you, that by lying in her return at an inn where the small-pox then was, she caught that distemper, and soon after she arrived in London it appeared. I need not say that she had it to a very violent degree. Being then in town I had the good fortune to nurse her, and flatter myself that my care was not useless; for in cases so dangerous, no one who does not feel all the tender sollicitude of a friend, can be a proper nurse.

Mrs. Alworth wrote her husband word of Harriot's illness, who came post[1] to London, filled with the extremest anxiety, and shared the fatigue of nursing with me; she was all the time delirious. When she came to her senses, she at first seemed mortified to think Mr. Alworth had seen her in that disfigured condition; but on reflexion told me, 'she rejoiced in it, as she thought it must totally extinguish his passion; and her greatest sollicitude was for his happiness.' But she afterwards found her expectation was ill grounded.

When she recovered, she perceived that the small-pox had entirely destroyed her beauty. She acknowleged she was not insensible to this mortification; and to avoid the observation of the envious, or even of the idly curious, she retired, as soon as she was able to travel, to a country house which I hired for her.

In a very short time she became perfectly contented with the alteration this cruel distemper had made in her. Her love for reading returned, and she regained the quiet happiness of which flutter and dissipation had deprived her, without substituting any thing so valuable in its place. She has often said, 'she looks on this accident as a reward for the good she had done Mrs. Tonston, and that few benevolent actions receive so immediate a recompence, or we should be less remiss in our duties, though not more meritorious in performing them.' She found retirement better cal-

---

1   post] quickly, using the system of inns or houses with relays of fresh horses and vehicles

culated for overcoming an hopeless passion than noise and flutter. She had indeed by dissipation often chased Mr. Alworth from her thoughts, but at the first moment of leisure his idea returned in as lively colours, as if it had always kept possession of her mind. In the country she had time to reflect on the necessity of conquering this inclination, if she wished to enjoy any tolerable happiness; and therefore took proper measures to combat it. Reason and piety, when united, are extremely prevalent, and with their assistance she restrained her affection once more within its ancient bounds of friendship. Her letters to Mr. Alworth, were filled with remonstrances against the indulgence of his love, and the same means she had found effectual, she recommended to him, and with satisfaction learnt, that though they had not entirely succeeded, yet he had acquired such a command over his heart, that he was as little wretched as a man can be, who is a living monument of the too common folly of being captivated by a sudden glare of person and parts; and of the fatal error of those men who seek in marriage for an amusing trifler, rather than a rational and amiable companion, and too late find that the vivacity which pleases in the mistress, is often a fatal vice in a wife. He lives chiefly in the country, has generally a few friends in the house with him, and takes a great deal of pains in the education of his two sons; while their mother spends almost the whole year in town, immersed in folly and dissipation.

About fourteen years ago Harriot, who I ought to begin to call Mrs. Trentham, came to see a lady in this neighbourhood, and thus was first known to the inhabitants of this mansion. They were much pleased with her acquaintance, and when she had performed her visit, invited her to pass a little time with them. She required no sollicitation, for it was the very thing she wished, and here she has remained ever since. When Mr. Maynard died, leaving me but a small jointure, Mrs. Trentham was indulged in her inclination, of asking me to spend the first part of my widowhood with her and her friends; and I have been fortunate enough to recommend myself so effectually, that they have left me no room to doubt they chuse I should continue with them, and indeed I think I could scarcely support life were I banished from this heavenly society.

Mrs. Trentham and Mr. Alworth keep up a constant correspondence by letters, but avoid meeting. His wife has brought him one daughter, and Mrs. Trentham's happiness has been rendered compleat, by obtaining from her permission to educate this child; a favour, which contrary to what is usual, is esteemed very small by her who granted, and very great by the person that received it. This girl is now ten years old, and the most accomplished of her age of any one, perhaps, in the kingdom. Her person is fine, and her temper extremely engaging. She went about a week ago to her father, whom she visits for about three weeks twice in a year, and never returns unimproved.

As Mrs. Trentham's fortune made a good addition to the income of the society, they on this occasion established in the parish a manufacture of carpets and ruggs,[1] which has succeeded so well, as to enrich all the country round about.

As the morning was not very far advanced, I asked Mrs. Maynard to conduct us to this manufacture, as in my opinion there is no sight so delightful as extensive industry. She readily complied, and led us to a sort of street, the most inhabited part of the village, above half a mile from Millenium-Hall. Here we found several hundreds of people of all ages, from six years old to four-score, employed in the various parts of the manufacture, some spinning, some weaving, others dying the worsted, and in short all busy, singing and whistling, with the appearance of general chearfulness, and their neat dress shewed them in a condition of proper plenty.

The ladies, it seems, at first hired persons to instruct the neighbourhood, which was then burdened with poor, and so over stocked with hands, that only a small part of them could find work. But as they feared an enterprising undertaker[2] might ruin their plan, they themselves undertook to be stewards; they stood the first expence, allowed a considerable profit to the directors, but kept the distribution of the money entirely in their own hands: thus they prevent the poor from being oppressed by their superiors, for they allow them great wages, and by their very diligent inspection hinder any frauds. I never was more charmed, than to see a manufacture so well ordered, that scarcely any one is too young or too old to partake of its emoluments. As the ladies have the direction of the whole, they give more to the children

---

1   ruggs] an early form of rugs
2   undertaker] business entrepreneur

and the aged, in proportion to the work they do, than to those who are more capable, as a proper encouragement, and reward for industry in those seasons of life in which it is so uncommon.

We were so taken up with observing these people, that we got home but just as dinner was carrying in.

In the afternoon we informed the ladies how we had spent the latter part of the morning, and in the course of conversation Lamont told them, that 'they were the first people he ever knew who lived entirely for others, without any regard to their own pleasure; and that were he a Roman Catholic, he should beg of them to confer on him the merit of some of their works of supererrogation.'[1] *as if theyre nuns —*

I do not know where you could find them, replied Mrs. Mancel,' I believe we have not been able to discover any such; on the contrary, we are sensible of great deficiencies in the performance of our duty.'

'Can you imagine, Madam, interrupted Lamont, that all you do here is a duty?'[2]

'Indespensibly so, answered Mrs. Mancel, we are told by him who cannot err, that our time, our money, and our understandings, are entrusted with us as so many talents,[3] for the use of which we must give a strict account. How we ought to use them he has likewise told us; as to our fortunes in the most express terms, when he commands us to feed the hungry, to cloath the naked, to relieve the prisoner, and to take care of the sick. Those who have not an inheritance that enables them to do this are commanded to labour, in order to obtain means to relieve those who are incapable of gaining the necessaries of life. Can we then imagine, that every one is not required to assist others to the utmost of his power, since we are commanded even to work for the means of doing so? God's mercy and bounty is universal, it flows un-

[margin: more lessons for Lamont]

[margin: Duty]

---

1   Roman Catholic ... supererrogation] in Roman Catholic theology acts of supererogation, or good deeds beyond divine commandment, store up merit which the Church may distribute to others who have been deficient in such deeds

2   no quotation mark here in first to third editions

3   talents] the talent was an ancient measure of weight in precious metals; according to Christ's parable of the talents in the Bible, Matthew, ch. 25, verses 14-30, a man going on a journey left different "talents" in varying amounts with his servants and on his return rewarded those who had invested them to profit but punished the servant who had merely buried his talent in the ground, allowing it to lie useless

asked, and unmerited; we are bid to endeavour to imitate him as far as
our nature will enable us to do it. What bounds then ought we to set to
our good offices, but the want of power to extend them farther? Our
faculties and our time should be employed in directing our donations
in a manner the most condusive to the benefit of mankind, the most
for the encouragement of virtue, and the suppression of vice; to assist
in this work is the business of speech, of reason, and of time. These
ought to be employed in seeking out opportunities of doing good, and
in contriving means for regulating it to the best purpose. Shall I allow
much careful thought towards settling the affairs of my houshold with
œconomy, and be careless how I distribute my benefactions to the
poor, to whom I am only a steward, and of whose interests I ought to
be as careful as of my own? By giving them my money I may sacrifice
my covetousness, but by doing it negligently I indulge my indolence,
which I ought to endeavour to conquer as much as every other vice.
Each state has its trials; the poverty of the lower rank of people exercises their industry and patience; the riches of the great are trials of their
temperance, humility, and humanity. Theirs is perhaps the more difficult part, but their present reward is also greater if they acquit themselves well; as for the future, there may probably be no inequality.'[1]

'You observed, Sir, said Mrs. Trentham, that we live for others,
without any regard to our own pleasure, therefore I imagine you think
our way of life inconsistent with it; but give me leave to say you are
mistaken. What is there worth enjoying in this world that we do not
possess? We have all the conveniences of life, nay, all the luxuries that
can be included among them. We might indeed keep a large retinue;
but do you think the sight of a number of useless attendants could
afford us half the real satisfaction, that we feel from seeing the money,
which must be lavished on them, expended in supporting the old and
decrepid, or nourishing the helpless infant? We might dress with so
much expence, that we could scarcely move under the burden of our
apparel; but is that more eligible, than to see the shivering wretch clad
in warm and comfortable attire? Can the greatest luxury of the table
afford so true a pleasure, as the reflection, that instead of its being over-

the pleasures of benevolence

---

1   no quotation mark here in any edition

charged with superfluities, the homely board of the cottager is blessed with plenty? We might spend our time in going from place to place, where none wish to see us except they find a deficiency at the card table, perpetually living among those, whose vacant minds are ever seeking after pleasures foreign to their own tastes, and pursue joys which vanish as soon as possessed; for these would you have us leave the infinite satisfaction of being beheld with gratitude and love, and the successive enjoyments of rational delights, which here fill up every hour? Should we do wisely in quitting a scene, where every object exalts our mind to the great Creator, to mix among all the folly of depraved nature?

'If we take it in a more serious light still, we shall perceive a great difference in the comforts arising from the reflexions on a life spent in an endeavour to obey our Maker, and to correct our own defects, in a constant sense of our offences, and an earnest desire to avoid the commission of them for the future, from a course of hurry and dissipation, which will not afford us leisure to recollect our errors, nor attention to attempt amending them.'

'The difference is indeed striking, said Lamont, and there can be no doubt which is most eligible; but are you not too rigid in your censures of dissipation? You seem to be inclined to forbid all innocent pleasures.'

'By no means, replied Mrs. Trentham, but things are not always innocent because they are trifling. Can any thing be more innocent than picking of straws, or playing at push-pin; but if a man employs himself so continually in either, that he neglects to serve a friend, or to inspect his affairs, does it not cease to be innocent? Should a school-boy be found whipping a top[1] during school hours, would his master forbear correction because it is an innocent amusement? And yet thus we plead for things as trifling, tho' they obstruct the exercise of the greatest duties in life. Whatever renders us forgetful of our Creator, and of the purposes for which he called us into being, or leads us to be inattentive

---

1   picking at straws] a child's game involving picking straws out of a heap one at a time without disturbing others; push-pin] a child's game in which the player pushes a pin with the aim of crossing the other player's; whipping a top] spinning a top by pulling on a string

to his commands, or neglectful in the performance of them, becomes criminal, however innocent in its own nature. While we pursue these things with a moderation which prevents such effects, they are always innocent, and often desireable, the excess only is to be avoided.'

'I have nothing left me to say, answered Lamont, 'than that your doctrine *must* be true, and your lives *are* happy; but may I without impertinence observe, that I should imagine your extensive charities require an immense fortune.'

'Not so much, perhaps, said Mrs. Morgan, as you suppose. We keep a very regular account, and at an average, for every year will not be exactly the same, the total stands thus. The girls school four hundred pounds a year, the boys an hundred and fifty, apprenticing some and equipping others for service one hundred. The cloathing of the girls in the house forty. The alms houses two hundred. The maintenance of the monsters[1] an hundred and twenty. Fortunes and furniture, for such young persons as marry in this and the adjoining parishes, two hundred. All this together amounts only to twelve hundred and ten pounds a year, and yet afford all reasonable comforts. The expences of ourselves and household, in our advantageous situation, come within eight hundred a year. Finding so great a balance in our favour, we agreed to appropriate a thousand a year for the society of gentlewomen with small or no fortunes; but it has turned out in such a manner that they cost us a trifle. We then dedicated that sum to the establishment of a manufacture, but since the fourth year it has much more than paid its expences, though in many respects we do not act, with the œconomy usual in such cases, but give very high wages, for our design being to serve a multitude of poor destitute of work, we have no nice regard to profit. As we did not mean to drive a trade, we have been at a loss what to do with the profits. We have out of it made a fund for the sick and disabled, from which they may receive a comfortable support, and intend to secure it to them to perpetuity in the best manner we can.'

'How few people of fortune are there, said Lamont, who could not afford 1200 *l.* a year, with only retrenching superfluous and burden-

---

1   monsters] persons deviating from the physical norm through some congenital malformation; here not used in a pejorative sense

some expences? But if they would only imitate you in any one branch, how much greater pleasure would they then receive from their fortunes than they now enjoy?'

While he was engaged in discourse with the ladies, I observed to Mrs. Maynard, that by the account she had given me of their income, their expences fell far short of it. She whispered me, that 'their accidental[1] charities were innumerable, all the rest being employed in that way. Their acquaintance know they cannot so much oblige, as by giving them an opportunity of relieving distress. They receive continual applications, and though they give to none indiscriminately, yet they never refuse any who really want. Their donations sometimes are in great sums, where the case requires such extraordinary assistance. If they hear of any gentleman's family oppressed by too many children, or impoverished by sickness, they contrive to convey an adequate present privately, or will sometimes ask permission to put some of their children into business, or buy them places or commissions.'

We acquainted the ladies that we should trouble them no longer than that night, and with regret saw it so soon ended. The next morning, upon going into Lamont's room, I found him reading the New Testament; I could not forbear expressing some pleasure and surprize, at seeing him thus uncommonly employed.

He told me, 'he was convinced by the conduct of the ladies of this house, that their religion must be the true one. When he had before considered the lives of christians, their doctrine seemed to have so little influence on their actions, that he imagined there was no sufficient effect produced by christianity, to warrant a belief, that it was established by a means so very extraordinary; but he now saw what that religion in reality was, and by the purity of its precepts, was convinced its original must be divine. It now appeared evidently to be worthy of its miraculous institution. He was resolved to examine, whether the moral evidences concurred with that divine stamp, which was so strongly impressed upon it, and he had risen at day break to get a Bible out of the parlour, that he might study precepts, which could thus exalt human nature almost to divine.'

---

1   accidental] coming by chance, or on a chance occasion; casual, occasional

It was with great joy I found him so seriously affected; and when we went to breakfast, could not forbear communicating my satisfaction to my cousin, who sincerely shared in it. As soon as breakfast was over we took leave of the ladies, though not till they had made us promise a second visit, to which we very gladly agreed, for could we with decency have prolonged this, I know not when we should have departed.

You, perhaps, wish we had done it sooner, and may think I have been too prolix in my account of this society; but the pleasure I find in recollection is such, that I could not restrain my pen within moderate bounds. If what I have described, may tempt any one to go and do likewise, I shall think myself fortunate in communicating it. For my part, my thoughts are all engaged in a scheme to imitate them on a smaller scale.

I am, Sir.

FINIS.

— transparent
Christian
subjects —
word + deed are one?

Appendix: From *The History of Sir George Ellison* (1766):

(a) Sir George Ellison's plan for relieving the poor and distressed:

He well knew the only way to obtain a general concurrence, was to gain people by their private interest; and therefore offered to take upon himself the care of the poor of each parish, if the principal parishioners would consent to give him half the sum hitherto paid for the poors rate. So favourable an offer was not likely to meet with much opposition; Sir William Ellison was the only person who scrupled it; which he did from an unwillingness to suffer his cousin to undergo the expence he feared he was bringing upon himself, well persuaded the money he required could not by any means suffice, especially for some years. But Mr. Ellison desired he would not make that an objection, as it was what he himself had foreseen, but chose to incur it rather than suffer the poor to be so improperly provided for; and he believed it possible to put the affair under such regulation, that in a few years the sum contributed might prove sufficient. Sir William, however, generously refused to withdraw his opposition, except Mr. Ellison would suffer him to contribute a large share of the expence; to which the other could have no objection.

These preliminaries being settled, Mr. Ellison hired a row of contiguous cottages, repaired and furnished them comfortably, and then removed the poor into them. His house-keeper undertook to find him a man and woman proper for overseers, who should honestly, and even indulgently, take care to provide them plentifully with all necessaries, and even comforts, carefully watch over their conduct, and see them execute such employments as he should assign them. When we consider where she had been bred, we shall not think this was a difficult task for her to perform; and indeed, she with ease found persons well qualified for this office; who were glad, for the good salary Mr. Ellison allowed them, to leave their former abode and friends. There were few of these poor men so old, as to be incapable of cultivating their little gardens, which yielded good part of their subsistence; he required each likewise to keep his own room very clean and neat, and not to expect that service from the women, for whom it was more easy to find out profitable employment; as they could nurse the children thrown upon the parish, attend the sick, do plain work, and spin and knit sufficient cloathing for themselves, and all the rest of the poor, both male and female. Some of the men could assist in the two last employments, and those who could not already do it, were made to learn; rather to take from them the temptation of pretending ignorance in order to be idle, than from any advantage to be expected from them, as they were by age and disuse rendered so awkward, that they could scarcely gain enough to pay for the waste they made, and the wool they spoiled.

Amongst the number of each sex these houses contained, Mr. Ellison found some qualified to teach the children whatever might be useful to persons in their condition, and therefore made it their chief employment, appropriating rooms for that purpose; and he seldom failed a daily inspection of his work-house, examining minutely into every particular. As he killed his own meat, he provided them with food at a less expence than if bought at market, and took care it was of the most wholesome kind. He allowed no punishments, as he thought none could properly be inflicted on the sick or aged; but endeavoured by encouragement and indulgences to make them act as he wished; and promoted social comfort, and friendly intercourse among them; omiting nothing that might conduce to their happiness, and the relief of their infirmities.

By observation Mr. Ellison found that great distress was sometimes suffered by persons, who either by the law had no right to demand assistance of the parish, without giving up some little tenement they had inherited, and wished to leave to their children; or who from an unuseful, and no blamable pride, were unwilling to be ranked among the parish poor; these people were mostly labourers, who in health could gain a subsistence for their families, but by long sickness were sometimes reduced to extreme distress. For the removal of this evil, he set on foot two subscriptions, one among the men, the other among the women; according to which, by paying a trifle weekly, so little as could not be felt in the poorest family, a fund was raised sufficient to afford each subscriber, in times of sickness, an allowance somewhat exceeding what in health they gained by their labour. This he knew was practised in many places; and the only inconvenience that ever attended it arose from the bad choice of a treasurer, the sum proving sometimes a temptation too great for the honesty of the man they trusted;

who frequently was as poor as themselves, and embezzled or went off with the money. To secure the people in his neighbourhood from this danger, Mr. Ellison undertook to be their treasurer, keeping a very regular account of the receipts and disbursements; and as a sufficient fund could not be immediately raised to answer any great calls, he, out of the money he had assigned for the parish poor, subscribed eight guineas to each fund, which made them equal to all immediate necessities. (vol. 1, pp. 180–5)

(b) The Ellisons' formula for a successful marriage; separate but connected spheres in social control:

Nothing is more conducive towards preserving affection than what prevents a married pair from continuing in each other's company after they are weary of it. Conversation will sometimes flag among the most ingenious and most affectionate; but if it happens frequently, the dulness it occasions is apt to be tacitly charged on each other; and an apprehension that the next day may be deadened by the same weariness goes a great way towards producing it, as the fear damps the spirits of both: thus what would be almost unavoidable in the same connection with any other persons, grows to be considered as some particular deficiency in each other. From this evil Sir George and his lady were secured by the very frequent calls of benevolence, and the various interruptions occasioned by the business in which humanity engaged them: as therefore they were strangers to satiety, they continued to feel the impatience of lovers, and were ingeniously inventive to procure little snatches of each other's conversation, to enliven the long interruptions they could not, consistent with duty (or at least with their notion of it) avoid; for lady Ellison would have been sorry to have fallen short of Sir George in humanity, a virtue which she possessed in a great degree, and found the source of inexpressible pleasure, not only from the benevolence of her heart, but from perceiving how much it endeared her to him.

Her sphere, indeed, was different and more minute; but if her charities were less considerable in expence and in their various consequences, they were however very important, as they administered to the happiness, or at least comfort of many. Her attention was more particularly directed to her own sex. From her every poor woman was sure, during her lying-in, to receive all the assistance and conveniencies that could administer comfort in her state: she supplied her with cloathing for her child; and pitying the sufferings of such poor babes, through the intolerable custom of lacing them up almost as soon as born in stiff stays, a practice, though discontinued among persons of higher rank, still prevalent with the poor, who make the little wretches yet more miserable, out of cruel œconomy, allowing in the height of their stays for two or three years growth; I say, pitying the little sufferers, she prevailed with the parents to permit her to substitute waist-coats, and continued to supply them with such till they grew near woman's estate, only making them somewhat stiffer as they advanced in size, being as great an enemy to the slatternly appearance of too unconfined a waist, as to the impenetrable boddice worn by the common people in the country. This may seem a trifling circumstance, but was much otherwise in effect, as it proved of great service to their health, and rendered them strong and well-shaped; in this last article the consequence was remarkable, for in fifteen years after she began this practice, there was scarcely a crooked young person to be seen within ten miles of her house: this gift not being confined to the poor; for, though not without difficulty, she prevailed with even the richest farmers to accept it from her, and as an inducement to them to do so, she herself made the waistcoats she gave them, that being her own work might seem to stamp a value upon them. Her attention to chil-dren was still more minute; for to prevent their little bodies from being more full of wounds than the anatomical figure in an almanack, through the aukward hands which dress them, and seem to look upon them rather as pin-cushions than as creatures endued with feeling, she distributed dresses for new born infants that did not require one pin, and even courted people to accept them.

Lady Ellison was as careful of the minds of her young female neighbours as of the bodies of the children; and as assiduously endeavoured to preserve the purity of the one, as the ease of the others. Every girl, who at fifteen was sober, modest, industrious, and cleanly, she formally received under her protection, and gave her on the occasion a scarlet ribbon, which was after-wards worn on Sundays, as a distinguishing mark of lady Ellison's favour. These young women were called in the neighbourhood Lady Ellison's Maidens; and it was well known, that whoever married them with her ap-probation, which was easily obtained by an honest, industrious man, was sure of receiving in dower with his wife furniture for a cottage, a cow, a pig, a male and two females of different sorts of poultry, a decent sober wedding-dinner for themselves and their parents, and to the bride more particularly was given a neat linen gown, with every other part of apparel suitable to it, as her bridal garments. This portion seldom failed of getting these maidens good husbands, and the rather as it was a testimonial of their good qualities; and their protectress's favour was known to be the source of still farther advantages, if after marriage they continued to deserve it. The scarlet ribbon became esteemed as a badge of great honour among them; if any one presumed to wear the colour to whom lady Ellison had not given it, the outcry against her assurance and presumption was so great, that she was reduced to lay it aside, and appeared more discountenanced than the jay stripped of his borrowed feathers. If a young man was inclined to marry, he was directed more by the top-knot than by the face in his choice of a wife, that being the first object of his attention. If youthful levity at any time led one of these girls to be a little too free in her conduct, if she appeared slatternly in her dress, was remiss in her business, or neglected going to church, if a friend asked her what was become of her ribbon, the recollection never failed producing an amendment; nor was lady Ellison ever obliged but once to withdraw this mark of favour, and that not till emulation had excited all the young girls in the neighbourhood to aim at the conduct which procured it. By its becoming general it at length grew no distinction, and thereby lost so much of its influence, that one of these young women behaved with great indiscretion, and lady Ellison thought it necessary, for examples sake, to order her to return the ribbon, that the rest might not be disgraced by a seeming companionship with her. The girl hoped no worse consequences would ensue from the withdrawing of lady Ellison's favour than the loss of the pecuniary advantages attending it, but she soon experienced effects still more mortifying; for she received such frequent marks of contempt, and was so continually reproached by her friends, that not enduring to live in a neighbourhood where she was despised and neglected, she went into a distant county; a lady, at the secret desire of lady Ellison, having promised, by means of a friend who lived there, to procure her a service, and give her the means of regaining her character; which she did so effectually, that marrying near the place where she had lived in service, lady Ellison's bounty reached her, and added comforts to those naturally attending a reformation. The disgrace of this young woman revived the people's sense of the honour of their protectress's favour, and made it as much valued as at first, though by the virtues it had encouraged it was become so general.

"capitalism... and a thorough plan of social control" (40)

Instead of forming schools for girls, Sir George and lady Ellison prevailed with the ladies of Millenium Hall to establish some of the two lower ranks in their neighbourhood, where they boarded the children they took from over-burdened parents, and those to whose orphan-state they chose to supply the want of parental care. The visitation of these schools was one of lady Ellison's constant duties, and a most pleasing employment, as she saw the school-mistresses endeavours succeed equal to her warmest wishes; and anticipated in hope the great benefit the rising generation in that neighbourhood would reap from so useful an institution. (vol. 2, pp. 214-22)

Marriages—
an unequal one – the Melvyns' (83)
a woeful one– Mrs Morgan's – 156ff –
(yet it results in the inheritance of M)
Miss Mancel's almost-marriage (p161)
Marriage for the girls but not for them (163)
lady Sheerness p172ff

The narrator and Lamont as listeners – to what use does Scott put them?

p.111 – true "society"!

p124– Duty – Miss Melvyn's to society
+ p.127 – how she justified her marriage
(p.128) lady Emilia's duty (213)
Duty of "the great" p165

p.166 – They are NOT reformers!
lady Mary's uniqueness – PROVIDENCE? (191)